Written by Brandon Varnell
Illustrated by Kirsten Moody
Edited by Crystal Holdefer

To see Brandon Varnell's other works, or to ask for permission to use his works, visit him at www.varnell-brandon.com, facebook at www.facebook.com/AmericanKitsune, twitter at www.twitter.com/BrandonbVarnell, and instagram at www.instagram.com/brandonbvarnell.

ISBN: 1977610161
ISBN: 978-1977610164

<u>Words you should know:</u>

Chūnibyou: A Japanese slang term which roughly translates to "Middle School 2nd Year Syndrome". People with chuunibyou either act like a know-it-all adult and look down on real ones, or believe they have special powers.

Kanji: One of the three writing systems in Japan. It uses Chinese characters.

Tsundere: A Japanese term for a character development process that describes a person who is initially cold and even hostile toward another person before gradually showing a warmer side over time. Gets easily embarrassed.

Yōkai: A class of supernatural monsters, spirits and demons in Japanese folklore. The word yōkai is made up of the kanji for "bewitching; attractive; calamity;" and "spectre; apparition; mystery; suspicious."

Youki: The energy source used by yōkai

Nue: A legendary Japanese yōkai.

Rumi Takahata: A character from an eroge called Cat Girl Alliance.

Gundam: A science fiction media franchise created by Sunrise that feature giant robots (or "mecha") called "mobile suits," with titular mobile suits that carry the name "Gundam."

Yandere: A word commonly used to refer to a character in anime and manga who, at first glance, appears to be extremely cute and kind, but will later show stalker tendencies and even murder people who get too close to their love interests.

Gyakujutsu: Techniques used in feudal era Japan to combat against yōkai. There are only a few humans alive who can use these techniques now.

Shōnen: The demographic of manga for young boys. Shōnen literally translates to "young boy." Typically, this is referring to teenagers between 13 and 17.

Iaidō: A Japanese martial art that emphasizes being aware and capable of quickly drawing the sword and responding to a sudden attack.

Natsumo Shinobi: A fictional manga inside of the American Kitsune universe. This manga series was inspired by and parodies a real series called Naruto.

Kenjutsu: The umbrella term for all (koryū) schools of Japanese swordsmanship, in particular those that predate the Meiji Restoration.

Yamato Nadeshiko: A Japanese term meaning the "personification of an idealized Japanese woman", or "the epitome of pure, feminine beauty." It is a floral metapho that combines the words Yamato, an ancient name for Japan, and nadeshiko, a delicate frilled pink carnation called Dianthus superbus.

Baka: the Japanese word for idiot.

Kudagitsune: A minor fox spirit that kitsune conjure. They often serve as messengers and spies.

Yuki Rito: The main character to the manga/anime series To LOVE-RU and To LOVE-RU Darkness.

Doujinshi: Self-published manga often created by amateurs. Some amateurs go on to become mangaka, while some mangaka go on to create doujinshi.

CONTENT

Chapter 1

The Last Day of School

Fan Shénshèng stared at her reflection in the mirror. Dark eyes were set within a round face. Her fair skin complemented her golden locks of hair, a trait of her clan, which trailed all the way down her back before branching out into a dolphin's tail. Her cherubic features contrasted with her stature and ninety-two centimeters of bust.

Many of her fellow clan members often told her that she had a young-looking face, and they were right. Despite being 216 years old, she still had a bit of a baby face that didn't quite match her womanly body.

Maybe that's why I'm the one pretending to be a high school student.

Fan scowled at the thought of going to school. Just contemplating returning to that dump of an educational institute for another day, another minute, even another second, was enough to make her stomach curl. Desert Cactus High School was such a bore. There was nothing to do there. The people were boring, the classes were boring, just about the only thing that wasn't boring was watching her target. Even then, she still disliked going to school.

Spying wasn't her thing; it was Zhìlì's.

"Lady Fan? Are you awake yet?" asked a voice from the other side of her door. It was deep, a low baritone that made her bones rumble.

"Of course I'm awake," she called back. "What do you want, Li?"

"If you've finished getting dressed, please come down to the kitchen and have breakfast," Li said. "Today's the day we complete our mission. Guang is already here. We're going to go over the plan before you head to school."

For the first time since arriving in Phoenix, Fan felt a burst of relief. She was more than ready to leave this state. Arizona was a place that she would never wish to live in. The sweltering heat made her skin burst with sweat, the arid atmosphere caused her flesh to dry and crack, and the desert landscape bored her to tears. She had been counting the days before they could leave.

"Really? That's great! I'll be out in just a second!"

"All right, but don't take much longer getting ready."

Li's footsteps receded, growing softer and softer, until they vanished altogether. Fan waited a moment longer to see if they would return. When they didn't, she turned back to the mirror that hung from her closet and studied her attire.

That day she had chosen to wear her newest outfit. Her white Lolita dress had a tight bodice that pushed her chest out, further accentuating her sizable bust. The ruffles accenting her shoulders were longer than normal, and bows decorated the front below her chest. Voluminous sleeves hid her hands from view, and the dress flared out after reaching her hips. Knee high socks went up to her ankles. White slippers adorned her small feet.

She twirled around, allowing her dress to lift and flutter. Completing her spin, she reached down and held the ends of her skirt, curtsying.

"Hmm, I wonder if my dearest little brother would enjoy seeing me in this outfit?" she asked herself, feeling just a hint of bitterness seep into her heart. "Not that he'll be able to enjoy seeing it anymore."

Straightening back up, Fan whirled around and walked out of the room, her mind teeming with dark thoughts.

Lilian Pnéyma, I hope you've enjoyed your life up to this point, because I am going to enjoy taking everything from you... just like you took everything from my little brother.

***

Kevin Swift's lungs burned every time he breathed. Sweat covered his forehead, causing his messy blond hair to stick to his face. It ran

2

down his forehead and dripped into his blue eyes, stinging them something fierce. Even so, he dared not close them. He knew that if he did, he would lose, and losing meant being on the wrong side of a brutal ass kicking.

She came at him more swiftly than Tohru chasing after Miss Kobayashi, attacking his weak points—or what she thought were weak points. Her blonde hair, styled in a bob cut, bounced as she launched several kicks.

None of them hit.

With his breathing ringing harshly in his ears, with sweat caking his shirt to his skin, Kevin avoided the first kick by sidestepping. Then he swerved around the follow-up reverse heel kick that would have broken his solar plexus. He then leapt over the low kick that followed the reverse, tucking his legs into his chest to keep her from hitting his shins.

The style that Kevin used didn't have a name yet. It was a style that he had created specifically for the purpose of fighting against yōkai. By presenting someone with an obvious hole in his guard, he could predict where they would attack.

Of course, he called it predicting, but it was more like he was manipulating them into attacking that opening. Fighters relied on instinct to battle. When a fighter saw an opening, they went for it. They didn't have time to think about whether it was a feint or a trap. It was even worse with yōkai, whose animalistic nature made them naturally predisposed toward attacking any opening they saw.

"You're never going to beat me if all you can do is dodge!" Heather shouted. Kevin didn't deign her with a response. He lacked the oxygen necessary to respond.

She came at him again, even faster this time. Kevin bit his lip as he avoided a series of punches and kicks by shuffling along the sparring mat. His movements happened at nearly the same time as hers. He knew that to the average eye, it would have looked like he was moving before she even attacked. Heather probably knew differently, but that didn't stop her from getting frustrated when none of her punches and kicks hit him.

"Dammit! What are you waiting for? An invitation? Hurry up and attack me!"

Kevin didn't let himself be goaded by her taunts. If he attacked now, if he acted on impulse, then he would lose. He only had one advantage over her, and that was his fighting style, which he had been working on ever since the disastrous spring break vacation to California.

Two months ago, Kevin and Lilian, along with his friends and family, had gone to California to enjoy the beach and the San Diego Comic-Con. However, Lilian and he were nearly killed during their beach trip—an assassin attacked Lilian, and they were caught in a battle between a kitsune clan and an anti-yōkai terrorist group at the Comic-Com. While Kevin had been in several dangerous situations before that, it was the trip to California that really hammered this fact home: The yōkai world was a dangerous place.

While there had been some issues upon their return to Arizona, Kevin had eventually come around and accepted what had happened. All he could do now was press forward. That was why he was working on perfecting this fighting style.

That was also why Kevin didn't fall for Heather's taunts and waited for her to make the first move. Heather's fists blurred by him on either side, ruffling his hair, practically shaving off layers of skin with their speed and power, but still he waited. His chest was beginning to ache, but he kept waiting.

Heather launched another attack at the opening that he gave her. It was a straight jab at his left flank, an easy attack that even a beginner could replicate with ease. It should have been easy for her to do; however, due to her irritation at his continued defense and her inability to hit him, she overextended herself and stumbled forward.

Now!

To an onlooker, it would have looked like Kevin moved before the attack was made. His left foot came forward into Heather's instep, keeping her from proceeding further. He moved his left hand up and redirected her jab to the side. He felt a surge of triumph as he launched his first attack, a short jab to the kidneys. This battle was as good as his —

"YEOWCH!"

… Or not.

Pain exploded in Kevin's chest as something hard and sharp stung him worse than a hundred bee stings. He could feel something gooey sticking to his skin, having gone straight through his T-shirt. As he hit the ground, his hands came up to clutch at where he had been hit, a hiss of pain escaping his clenched teeth.

"Shishishi." Heather chuckled as she twirled her paintball gun around her finger like a cowboy. The weapon, a black gun designed to look like a Millennium G2 9mm compact pistol, seemed to taunt him as it spun with an almost lazy arrogance. "Did you really think it would be that easy to beat me? Come on, Kev, I've been trained to fight against all manner of opponents. I'll admit that style you're trying to create is frightening, but it only works if you don't know how your opponent thinks."

"G-gu." Kevin covered his face with a hand as though hoping to hide his blush. "So you're saying that all those angry remarks and that last overextension on your punch was done to lull me into a false sense of security so I would attack and you could shoot me?"

"Pretty much."

Kevin only had one thing to say to that.

"… All my hate."

Heather's loud laughter rang out through the sparring center. Kevin grimaced as he rubbed his chest, wiping the paint off. He could feel the mark the paintball had left on his skin. It felt like a tiny crater dotting the canyon between his pectorals. And it stung. By Inari's hairy left testicle, did it sting.

"Ha… don't feel too bad about losing… again." Heather chuckled when Kevin growled at her. "You did really well this time. Your stamina has increased a lot too. Give yourself another year or two and you might even get better than me. Of course, that's only if you can remember to start using your guns. Kiara bought those for a reason, you know?"

Heather held out her hand, which Kevin accepted, allowing her to help him up. He winced a bit when cool air hit his chest, but that was his only reaction to the ugly red crater marring his flesh.

"I would if I could, but it's hard for me to unholster them at the drop of a hat like you can." He patted the two holsters hiding underneath his armpits and sighed. "I've been practicing, but my fastest time is three seconds. The placement of my holsters doesn't help. It's hard to pull them out from underneath my armpits."

Lilian had been recording his gun drawing speed. It had been pretty bad at first, ten seconds just to get them out of his holsters and another five to aim them. Now it only took three to four seconds for the whole process. It was better, but it still wasn't good enough.

"Yeah, that kind of speed won't do much against someone like me." Heather crossed her arms and nodded. "I'd shoot you before you could put a hand on them. Still, I think three seconds is enough time for you to get the drop on any yōkai who's not trained in combat."

"It wouldn't work on yōkai with a predisposition for combat, though," another voice spoke up.

Kevin and Heather turned to Kiara, who had been watching them spar. She pushed off the wall that she had been leaning against and walked up to them. Her dark brown hair looked as feral as always, jagged and spiky like a dog gone Super Saiyan 3. She had grown it out a bit more, and it now hung past her shoulders, making her whole Amazonian appearance seem even more, well, *Amazonian,* he guessed.

She wasn't wearing her standard business suit that day. A white sleeveless shirt showed off her lean arm, which had several scars and incredible muscle definition. Her thin waist made a sharp contrast with her modest bust. Black shorts adorned her waist. They were booty shorts, so it pretty much looked like she was wearing a second skin, which meant he saw the ridiculous muscles her thighs were sporting.

I feel emasculated every time I see this woman wearing clothing like this. She cuts such an imposing image, even with the missing arm.

Kevin glanced briefly at the stump where Kiara's arm had been. The skin around her arm had healed, though the pink flesh still had scars from being cauterized. He found it odd, but her missing an arm made Kiara look even tougher than if she still had the appendage.

She had lost that arm the previous year, during a rescue operation when Lilian had been kidnapped by a two-tailed brat of a kitsune named Jiāoào Shénshèng. The arm had been hit by a kitsune's void fire. The all-consuming flame was something that couldn't be extinguished. It was a terrifying power that erased the very concept of that which it consumed. To keep herself from being taken by oblivion, she had torn her own arm off.

Kevin used to feel guilty. He was kind of the reason she had lost it, but Kiara had never expressed dissatisfaction with her missing limb, and in fact, she seemed to take pride in it. She displayed her stump of an arm like a badge of honor.

"Done checking me out, boya?" asked Kiara, a feral grin peeling her lips back and revealing her sharp canines.

Kevin's right eye twitched. "I wasn't checking you out. I was looking at your scars."

"So, you're admiring my battle wounds?"

Kevin tried not blush. He liked to think he did an admirable job, especially considering how, nine months ago, a comment like that would have made him blush like a schoolboy in front of his crush.

A Fox's Revenge

"Something like that."

Kiara's grin spoke of her amusement better than words could. "I'll tell you how I got some of these sometime. Maybe when you finally beat Heather."

"Trying to motivate me with a story?" Kevin crossed his arms and pouted. "I'm not that easy to please, you know? And besides, I'm trying my hardest."

"And you've gotten pretty good," Heather informed him as she stretched. Kevin tried not to look at her breasts as the fabric of her hot pink shirt stretched across them. She wasn't wearing a bra. "You've come a long way from the boy who got kidnapped like a damsel in distress and had to be rescued."

Kevin felt an acute pain in his chest at her words, which were about as emasculating to him as Kiara's ripped body. "That was a low blow."

Heather's pleased grin reminded him of a Cheshire cat. "And no less true."

"Anyway," Kiara interrupted Kevin before he could retort, "you should probably head home now. You'll want to have your mate heal that paintball wound before it scars."

Kevin grimaced at the reminder of his wound. "... Right."

The life of a teenage punching bag was a never-ending battle.

***

Kiara watched as Kevin left the sparring room. If he followed his normal habits, he'd hop in the shower, get changed, and then head home. Then again, he might just head home to get that nasty wound on his chest healed.

"He really is getting better, isn't he?" asked Heather.

She turned to Heather, who had her eyes on the door that the young man had disappeared through. The woman's face was flushed with exertion, and her shoulders and chest heaved with every breath. It wasn't the deep, gasping breaths of someone who had pushed themselves beyond their physical limitations, but it told Kiara that Heather had been forced to exert herself more than usual.

"He's definitely improved a lot." She stroked her jaw with her only remaining hand. "His skills in hand-to-hand combat have improved greatly, and he's an even better shot... when he's standing still. He still has trouble aiming when moving, and he can't pull his guns out in mid-combat, which is a problem we'll have to rectify. That's something I

7

think we need to have him start working on."

"Agreed."

A moment of silence passed between them. Kiara gazed at the sparring room. It was her own personal sparring room, which she let Kevin and Heather use when they were training. The entire floor was composed of a large blue mat. The walls were white and bare of decorations. She preferred it that way. In this room, there were no distractions getting in the way, and she could train to her hearts content.

"… Do you think he'll be ready for the threats he's likely to face in the future?"

Kiara frowned at the question. It was a lot more loaded than it would have been if they were talking about someone else, but they were talking about Kevin. That kid was a magnet for trouble. His track record for getting knee deep into vexing situations was only matched by his mate's capacity to do the same.

"I don't know. There are plenty of threats that a human involved with a yōkai is likely to face. The kid's already been through a lot, so I would say that he is, but then he's also involved with several members of one of the Thirteen Great Kitsune Clans." Kiara rubbed the back of her neck. "Kid's already run into some of the problems that come from being involved with a group of yōkai like that."

"You're talking about that young kitsune and his group that you guys fought in October of last year, right?" Heather asked, getting a nod in return. "But that was an awfully long time ago. We haven't even heard a peep about those, uh… um…"

"The Shénshèng Clan."

"Right! Them!" Heather snapped her fingers. "Anyway, we haven't heard from those people since then. What makes you think they'll try something eight months after the fact?"

Kiara stared at Heather, her face slowly deadpanning, and then she snorted and turned away.

"You clearly don't know a thing about kitsune, girl. They're not the sort of yōkai who would let a transgression against them go, especially not one like this." Turning around, Kiara began walking toward to exit. "Trust me, they'll come seeking revenge sooner or later, and they'll probably do it when we least expect them to."

The sound of footsteps preluded Heather catching up to her. The former Sons and Daughters of Humanity secret operative didn't seem all that bothered by her words.

A Fox's Revenge

"I'm sure it'll be fine. He's got us around to help, after all." Heather paused, her face suddenly shifting into a bit of a pout. "Although I will admit that helping him out is a pain. Do you know how long it's been since I've been able to sit down and play one of my eroge? Months! I started my conquest of Rumi Takahata three months ago, and I've only had enough time to raise two of her flags!"

Kiara chuckled. She had never met another person who was so obsessed with what amounted to Japanese video game porn as Heather was.

"I guess that's true. And I'm rather fond of the kid, so it's not like I can let him face whatever danger comes his way alone. He also has Kotohime and her sister to depend on, not to mention that mate of his and the mate's twin. I'm sure he'll be fine." She paused. "And isn't the reason you never have time for those porn games because you're still teaching at Desert Cactus High School?"

"It isn't porn!"

"Speaking of which, shouldn't you be getting ready to leave?"

Heather blinked at what seemed like a random question.

"What do you... oh, shit!" Heather swore when she looked at her watch and saw the time. "Dammit! I was supposed to attend a meeting before school since today's the last day!"

Rushing ahead of Kiara, the former spandex-wearing secret agent ran out of the room, likely heading for the lockers. The door slammed shut behind the woman. Kiara heard Heather's hurried footsteps quickly receding. After several more seconds of just standing there, she chuckled and continued on her way.

"Life has gotten a whole lot more interesting since I met these people," she mused to herself.

***

"Let's see now... I need one and one-third cups of all-purpose flour, two tablespoons of sugar, one teaspoon of baking powder, half a teaspoon of baking soda..."

Lilian stared hard at the cookbook situated on the marble countertop, her eyes flickering back and forth, scanning the page. She had decided to make blueberry pancakes. Kevin would be coming home soon, and she wanted to have breakfast ready by then.

It would normally be Kotohime who did the cooking. She was their maid, after all. However, Lilian wanted to make something for Kevin,

9

and so she had adamantly told her maid that she was going to cook instead. Kotohime had given Lilian her traditional *"ufufufu"* laugh and left her to it.

"Okay!" Pumping her fist, Lilian psyched herself up. "Time to do this!"

Wanting to get started with a bang, Lilian became a whirlwind of activity. Her two tails shot out from underneath her miniskirt, extending to at least three meters in length. One of them made a beeline for the pantry, while the other began pulling pans, bowls, and mixers from the bottom cupboard.

While her tails got to work, Lilian waltzed up to the fridge and began grabbing ingredients: eggs, milk, butter, sour cream, blueberries, everything she needed. She grabbed them all and put them onto the counter next to the stove. At the same time, her tails retracted and put the items they had grabbed onto the counter with them.

"Okay!" Grinning fiercely, Lilian pumped a fist into the air. "Blueberry pancakes, get ready to be baked!"

It didn't take her long to mix all the ingredients. With her tails helping add them into the bowl, it was almost as if she had four arms. That stupid Goro didn't have squat on her. She mixed and stirred and had all of the ingredients blended together perfectly in a matter of seconds. After that, it was just a matter of heating up the skillet, pouring the batter, and working her magic.

As she poured the batter onto the skillet, the sound of the door opening and closing alerted her to Kevin's arrival seconds before he called out, "I'm home!"

"Welcome home!" Lilian spun around to greet Kevin as he walked past the kitchen "You're earlier than I expected you to be, Bel—Kya! What happened to your chest?!"

"Ah-ahahaha!" Kevin's nervous laughter filled the air as Lilian rushed over to him. "I, uh, well, Heather kinda shot me point blank with a paintball gun, so…"

"She what?!"

Kevin winced at her shout, but Lilian didn't pay attention. She was too busy looking at the ugly black and purple pockmark that looked like the Ptolemaeus Crater between his pectorals. It was a hideous wound.

"Uh, yeah, Kiara and Heather said it's time I start learning how to wield guns while fighting at close range, so Heather's taken to pulling them out when we spar."

"You mean she's been shooting you when you spar?!" Lilian growled at the thought of her mate getting shot during training. It was supposed to be a simple spar! They weren't supposed to injure her mate like this! "I'm gonna kill them!"

"I… don't think that would be a good idea," Kevin said. "Remember what happened the last time you fought Kiara?"

"That was months ago," Lilian said dismissively, still staring at his wound. "I've leveled up plenty since then with my super special shōnen-style training from hell. Besides, Kiara only has one arm now. I can take her."

"If you say so…"

"I do say so. Now hold still and let me heal that for you."

Lilian didn't give Kevin a chance to respond before she leaned down and began licking his wound. She channeled youki through her mouth and into her tongue, more specifically her saliva. His skin tasted like a mixture of copper and salt. The rough edge of his injury scratched her tongue, but she didn't stop, and not just because she needed to heal him.

"L-Lilian… not here…"

If her tongue wasn't so busy, she would have grinned. **Kitsune Art: Divine Tongue** was a technique that she had created for just this purpose. It essentially healed people using her saliva, which she infused with her celestial youki. It was the most amazing technique she had ever conceived. Her pride and joy.

"Why not here?" she asked in between her job of coating his chest with saliva. Kevin shuddered under her ministrations. The sweat clinging to his skin had become partially dried. He must have been working really hard.

Muu, I wish I could have seen him work up a sweat.

"B-Because… if Kotohime or one of the others sees us…"

"Kotohime's hanging up the laundry and the others are still asleep."

"She still does that?"

"Mmhmm."

Lilian giggled when she heard Kevin mutter about there being a reason they had a dryer, though she didn't comment. Kotohime was an old-fashioned kitsune. She preferred hanging their laundry up to dry, washing clothes using a bucket and soap, and cleaning with an old-fashioned duster. No matter how many times Kevin asked her to change her ways, Kotohime refused, stating that it *"wasn't proper maid etiquette."*

Kevin's wound healed quickly thanks to her saliva; however, the act of licking her mate's muscular chest made Lilian grow rather hot and bothered. A sensation not unlike burning blossomed in her bosoms. A passionate desire overflowed from her like *Kirche the Ardent*, a character from *Zero no Tsukaima,* or *The Familiar of Zero*, an anime she was watching.

She decided not to stop with just healing his wound, and instead began licking her way up his chest.

"G-gu… L-Lilian."

She smiled when a pair of hands grabbed her butt. She moaned when those same hands began to fondle, caress, and squeeze her plentiful derriere. Pleasant jolts raced up her tailbone. Her tails curled in on themselves. The pleasurable sensations became more prominent when Kevin reached around her front and unbuttoned her skirt, letting it fall to the floor, and then slipped his hands into the waistband of her panties to feel her up directly.

"Beloved, you know that the only time I like tasting your sweat is when I'm the cause for its creation, don't you?"

"U-ugh… that's something I would expect to hear from Iris, not you."

"Is it really?"

Lilian pulled her head back from where she had been licking his neck to stare up at him. His eyes, the brightest azure blue she had ever seen, were dark and hooded with lust. Just seeing the way he stared down at her made a wet trail run down her thighs.

Kevin didn't respond to her question with words. He moved down swifter than she could have anticipated, almost surprising her when he captured her lips in a searing kiss.

Lilian's moan was muffled by the tongue invading her mouth. She fought back as best she could, pushing against the intrusion as her mouth filled with saliva, but it seemed that she had pushed Kevin a little too hard with her actions. This wasn't a dance. He was utterly dominating her.

Her arms quickly found themselves wrapped around Kevin's neck. It was necessary. Her legs were so weak they would no longer support her. They shook and shuddered as Kevin's hands, still trapped inside of her panties, squeezed her ass, generating another loud moan as he pulled her flush against his body, until there was no room left between them.

Kevin had gained a lot of muscle over the past several months. While he had always been fit, these days he had the makings of a regular Adonis. His six-pack abs brushed against her skin, his defined pectorals pushed into her breasts. Broad shoulders. Well-defined arms. Lilian imagined that Kevin would look delectable wearing the Spartan armor from the movie *300*.

A surprised squeal escaped her when, without warning, Lilian felt her feet leave the ground. She quickly locked her legs around Kevin's waist to keep herself from falling. She could feel her panties, already damp from her mate's presence and actions, become stained even more when she met his erection.

"Hnnn!"

Lilian moaned when she felt her breasts mash against his chest as he set her on the table. His hands seared her body when they roamed over her naked back, covered only by her signature green shirt. When those same hands moved to her front, cupping her breasts, she thought her body might explode from overstimulation.

Her breasts were very sensitive.

Their lips parted, but only because they ran out of breath. Lilian felt their mixed saliva dripping down her chin when they broke contact. She almost whined when he didn't start kissing her again, but that soon changed when Kevin bent down and began sucking on her neck.

"B-Beloved…"

Her fingers clenched the back of his shirt when he began licking her. He had discovered several months ago through experimentation that she loved being licked. She didn't know why this was, but having her mate's tongue blaze a wet trail across her skin drove her absolutely nuts. It felt like his tongue was branding her.

"Lilian…"

"Hn!"

Lilian surprised herself by almost orgasming when he said her name. He didn't speak. He growled. It was one of the sexiest things she'd ever heard.

Inari-blessed! I want him inside of me so badly right now!

It was almost a shame that they hadn't done the deed yet. Kevin still wanted to wait before they had sex, claiming that at fifteen years old, he was too young. She didn't really get it. They had been dating for eight months, and in those eight months, they had done plenty of *ecchi* things together.

13

Still, Lilian couldn't find it within herself to complain. Yes, they hadn't had sex yet, but Kevin was still more than capable of pleasing her need for intimacy, and he wasn't afraid of experimenting. And honestly, she was just glad that he no longer hesitated when it came to giving her affection.

To think, nine months ago, Beloved couldn't even talk to me without passing out.

He'd been so cute back then, but she had to admit that she liked this more confident Kevin much better.

Lilian's thoughts were shattered by another moan when Kevin cupped her crotch and began stimulating her over her panties. A jolt traveled from the point of contact, rushing straight to her brain like Pikachu's Thunderbolt. Kevin used his other hand to push her down on the table, even as his lips claimed hers again.

Just as Lilian felt like she might explode, Kevin's hand slipped inside of her panties and began caressing her directly. Her hips bucked as his fingers teased her entrance. One finger slipped inside of her. Then a second was added. Meanwhile, Kevin's thumb went in for the kill.

Lances of ecstasy shot through her. It was electric. She could feel something coiling inside of her, like a knot that was coming undone. Her muscles tightened and her thighs quivered. Her stomach involuntarily clenched, and the heat gathering just below her stomach became almost overbearing. It felt like Mount Fuji was about to erupt inside of her. Her toes curled and her hips jerked as if undergoing muscle spasms.

And then, all at once, she felt it. Waves of what she could only call rapture spread throughout her entire body. She didn't even care that the table underneath her bum was getting soaked with a combination of her own sweat and love nectar, or that she was going to need a new change of panties. All that mattered was the white-hot rapture that cascaded over her, sending her mind crashing over the edge of bliss. It felt like she was having an out-of-body experience.

Once she had calmed down, exhaustion hit Lilian like a *Vacuum Butt Cannon*. Her entire body felt like it was shutting down. Even though the table was cold and hard and wet, she didn't want to move from that spot. She wanted to pull Kevin to her and cuddle beside him until they both fell asleep.

"B... Beloved..."

"Hmm?"

"I love you... so much..." She sighed in bliss.

A Fox's Revenge

Kevin removed his hand from her panties and grinned. "I love you, too." He then stuck his fingers into his mouth and sucked them clean. "I especially love how you taste."

As they stared at each other, Lilian felt her desire for him rise again. She wanted him so badly. She wanted to mate with him, but she didn't. Lilian held back. Kevin was already compromising his own morals for her sake, so the least she could do was keep her own desires in check. Wasn't this also the reason she hadn't let Iris in on their fun?

"I can't believe you two!" a loud voice snarled.

While Kevin jerked back in surprise, Lilian only turned her head to stare. Iris stood in the entryway to the kitchen, wearing a pair of panties and nothing else. Her hair was messy and sticking up everywhere, and her eyes had dark circles under them, yet she still somehow managed to look alluring, like she had just finished having a night of wild and raunchy sex.

She was glaring at them. "I can't believe you two would get all frisky while I'm still asleep! How am I supposed to masturbate to you two if you're going at it when I'm not even awake?!"

"Don't tell us that you plan on masturbating while you watch us!" Kevin snapped. "That just makes me not want to do anything while you're awake!"

"So you would deny me even this?" Iris asked, her tone laced with an angry growl. "What kind of sick pervert are you?"

"I don't want to be called a pervert by someone who masturbates while watching her sister during foreplay!"

Lilian gazed at Kevin with tired eyes as he argued with Iris. Despite his words, he was refusing to so much as look in her twin's direction. What's more, his cheeks were stained with a redness that was reminiscent of a fire truck.

Were she not so tired, she would have giggled. Kevin had grown more confident in the past eight months, and he could even please her need for intimacy, but he was still the same Kevin. Even now he became shy and embarrassed over situations like this.

"Maybe that's why we decided to start doing it right now?" Lilian cut into their argument as she stretched her arms above her head. By the great Lord Inari did she feel satisfied. "Maybe we didn't want to have sexy-times together while you watched us and fingered yourself. Did you ever think of that?"

Kevin facepalmed, and with the hand that he had used to please her

A Fox's Revenge

with to boot. She almost giggled at the sound of his wet hand slapping against his face.

"Do you two really have to talk about sexy-times and masturbation first thing in the morning? Can we just for once curtail any kind of dirty talk?"

"Sorry, Beloved, but it's all written right here in the script."

"The what?"

Iris gave Kevin a heated glare. "Maybe I wouldn't talk about sex if you hadn't fingered my beloved Lily-pad on the kitchen table!"

Kevin's face turned the most interesting shade of crimson as he began sputtering. "T-that's only because she started licking me!"

"I don't care what your reasons are!" Iris scowled and somehow managed to make it look terrifyingly sexy. Lilian didn't know how her sister did it, and she dared not ask for fear of what Iris would ask her to do in exchange for that information. Just thinking about it made her hot and bothered again. "I want my sexy-times, too, dammit! If you two are gonna get all frisky on the kitchen table, then you should invite me to join in!"

Kevin's stare went flat. "Um, no."

Iris huffed and crossed her arms under her breasts, pushing them together in a most enticing manner. Maybe it was because of what she and Kevin had finished doing, but Lilian found herself staring at her sister's tits as they bunched together like a pair of water balloons. The void vixen's light pink nipples were hardened into soft points. Lilian hated herself for it, but seeing Iris's hard nipples made the temptation to take them into her mouth and suckle on them strong.

She closed her eyes and took a slow, deep breath. *Don't think about that. You're with Kevin. Incest isn't accepted in the human world. You don't want Kevin to hate you.*

"Why not?" Iris asked with a plaintive whine.

"Because I don't wanna," was Kevin's childish response.

Lilian knew the moment Kevin said those words that they were the wrong words to say.

Iris's expression became challenging. "Are you saying I'm not good enough for you?"

"Uh…"

Iris smirked at them, and Lilian suddenly felt like she had grabbed a live wire. That look on her sister's face was downright sinful. It brought to mind images of when she had washed her sister's naked body several

17

days after returning from California. Even now, that particular moment had haunted more than a few of her wet dreams. They were often mixed in with her dreams of Kevin, which usually ended with them having a threesome.

I'm so not telling my sister that I've dreamt of having a threesome with her and Beloved. That's definitely not happening.

Iris stalked up to them like a predator stalking her prey. She and Kevin could do nothing as the raven-haired succubus moved, her hips swaying with an alluring sensuality, her bare breasts bouncing as she slinked over to them. Lilian told herself that the reason she was beginning to feel hot had nothing to do with her sister's beautiful and half-naked body. Nothing at all.

"Since you seem so confident that I'm not good enough, why don't we test that out?" Iris suggested, licking her pink lips.

"I-I didn't say that…" Kevin mumbled, unable to tear his gaze away.

"Hmm… is that so? It certainly sounded like that's what you were saying." Iris's grin was terrifying. "Not that it matters. I'm in the mood thanks to you two, and I always get what I want."

Just before Iris could pounce on them, which Lilian knew she would do, their mother stumbled into the kitchen. Camellia's pure white toga was ruffled and falling off her curvaceous figure, revealing slender shoulders and a bust that was nearly two times bigger than Lilian's. Five tails the same black color as her hair hung limply behind her.

I'm surprised she's wearing clothes.

The woman's eyes were half closed. She yawned widely as she rubbed the sleep out of them. She also took several whiffs of the air, as if smelling something strange.

"Hawa? Why does it smell like something is burning?" she asked.

Lilian and Kevin froze. It was only now that her mom mentioned something burning that she could smell it as well. It was the acrid smell of something, well, burning.

"Oh, no! The food!"

"Crap! Quick, Lilian! Get the skillet into the sink! The sink!"

"Don't worry, you guys. I got this."

"Don't use your void powers in here! You'll destroy the whole apartment complex!"

"Then what do you want me to do?"

"I want you to do nothing! Just sit there and look pretty!"

18

A Fox's Revenge

"Heh, so you think I'm pretty, do you, Stud?"

"Oh, shut up!"

"Beloved! Turn on the water! Hurry!"

"I'm hurrying! I'm hurrying!"

Standing on the sidelines, Camellia remained silent as Lilian and Kevin tried to put out the fire that had once been blueberry pancakes. Meanwhile, Iris did what she did best. She sat on the table, crossed one lean leg over the other, and looked devilishly pretty.

Lilian would have asked her mom to help, but honestly, she knew that her mom would probably end up making the situation worse. Camellia was, after all, the clumsiest woman on the face of the planet. The woman could trip over air.

In the end, she and Kevin couldn't save her pancakes.

Or the skillet.

＊

Kotohime eyed the skillet that still sat in the kitchen sink with a flat look. The once shiny metal was black and burnt. There was also a giant hole in the center of it, the edges curled from having been melted. She didn't even know how that was possible. Cookware like this was more than capable of withstanding high temperatures.

"I can't believe we're eating cereal for breakfast," Iris complained as she stuck her spoon into her bowl of Fruit Loops.

"I can't believe we even have cereal," Kevin commented before idly chewing on his Wheaties. "I haven't gone shopping for cereal in years. There was never any point, since I stopped eating cereal once Mom started traveling and leaving me at home."

"I bought the cereal," Kotohime confessed, turning away from the burnt skillet to look at Kevin. "It was something I bought in case of emergencies. For example, if you, Lilian-sama, and Iris-sama failed to wake on time and needed to rush out of the house… or if Kevin-sama and Lilian-sama started sharing intimate relations on the kitchen table and Lilian-sama forgets that she's cooking breakfast…"

Kevin and Lilian both blushed bright red. It amused Kotohime, the way Kevin attempted to hide in his shirt and how Lilian turned her head to keep people from noticing the bright red flush of her cheeks. She doubted that Lilian was embarrassed by what they had done. She was a kitsune. But the twin-tailed redhead most certainly felt mortified about burning breakfast.

19

A Fox's Revenge

The family of kitsune, plus one human and two maids, were gathered around the kitchen table, which Kotohime had cleaned while her charge changed into a new miniskirt and panties. Kevin and Lilian sat on one side, while Iris sat with Camellia on the other. Kotohime and her sister, Kirihime, stood next to their respective charges like any good maid.

She and her sister were a study in contrast. Their faces held the same general shape and features. Porcelain skin. Soft cheeks. A small nose. Full red lips. However, their outfits couldn't have been more different.

Kotohime always wore long, flowing kimonos. She had a strong preference for furisode, which had voluminous sleeves that hid her hands from view. Those sleeves served as excellent distractions during battle. Her enemies were sometimes so drawn to the sleeves that they never noticed the katana until their heads were already falling from their bodies.

On the other hand, Kirihime wore a traditional French maid outfit. The black dress was decked with frills along the hem and had slightly puffy shoulders. A white apron covered her front. More ruffles ran along the outside of the apron, as though accentuating the firmness of her modest bust and thin waist. A pair of gloves adorned her hands. The white choker that she wore had a single black cord running through its center, and the white stockings cladding her legs were held up by black elastic bands. Black slippers and a white bonnet finished her outfit. Three furry black tails with white tips jutted from underneath Kirihime's outfit. They looked a lot like Kotohime's own five tails, which she kept hidden underneath her kimono.

"D-don't blame what happened on me," Kevin muttered. "I-I just arrived home when Lilian pounced on me."

Lilian's cheeks swelled like a balloon as she pouted at her mate. "Are you saying this is my fault?"

"Ah." Kevin scratched his cheek with an index finger and looked anywhere but at Lilian. "W-well, not precisely. It's just that… well… you know, you're kinda the one who started it… and stuff…"

Lilian had to concede Kevin's point, even if Kotohime knew she didn't like it. However, she knew her charge, and so she also knew that the redhead wouldn't take those words without returning fire.

"Well, yeah, but it was also your fault for getting injured during your spar with Heather. If I didn't have to heal that wound on your chest, none of this would have happened."

"U-ugh."

Kotohime hid a smile behind the sleeve of her kimono as Kevin doubled over like he'd been shot in the back with an arrow. She could see the metaphorical arrow as it came out of nowhere and pierced the boy. Being the good maid that she was, Kotohime discreetly reached out and plucked the arrow from his back.

"I'm just upset that you two had an illicit affair without me." Iris looked awfully put out as she glared at the pair, her crimson succubus eyes staring at the two and making them squirm as though they were children who'd been caught touching each other in inappropriate places. Well, they had just been getting frisky on the kitchen table, so it was an apt description.

"We weren't having an illicit affair," Kevin snapped at her. "The very term implies something that is morally wrong or unacceptable. Lilian and I are mates, so there is nothing wrong about what we were doing. It would have only been an illicit affair if *you* had gotten involved."

"Yeah, I guess you're right," Iris conceded with a half-hearted shrug. Then she grinned at Kevin. "Wanna have an illicit affair?"

"Don't make me smack you with my tails," Lilian threatened her sister, who pouted at being denied. Again. Kotohime wondered how many times that made now.

As someone who had been mated with a human once before, Kotohime understood Lilian's concern. Polygamy and incest were accepted and even practiced in the yōkai world, but they weren't legal in the human world, and that wasn't even going into the issues of morality. Kevin, as a human, would have a hard time accepting a polygamous relationship with Lilian and Iris.

There's also the matter of stamina, Kotohime mused to herself. *A human, no matter how strong, cannot possibly have enough stamina to satisfy two kitsune.*

"Camellia doesn't mind eating cereal every now and then." Camellia seemed to have ignored the last few minutes of conversation. She happily munched on her cereal with a childish smile. "Tee-hee, it's been a really long time since Camellia had Frosted Flakes."

Kirihime, standing behind the five-tailed vixen, frowned. "I do not recall you ever eating human cereal, My Lady."

"Tee-hee, you weren't with me. It was when Camellia went into a human town."

"M-My Lady?!" Kirihime squeaked. "Are you telling me that you snuck out of the manor to visit a human city?"

"Um!"

"W-why would you do that? Don't you know how dangerous that is? You could have been hurt, o-or taken advantage of by some human! It's dangerous!"

Kotohime smiled as her sister tried to scold the older kitsune. She didn't do a very good job. Kirihime was a pushover when it came to Camellia. No matter what happened, or how much she tried to reprimand the woman, in the end, she always let the five-tailed kitsune have her way.

"Hawa, don't worry," Camellia tried to reassure her maid-slash-bodyguard, who didn't look very reassured. "Camellia knew what she was doing."

"K-knew what she…" Kirihime slumped over with an air of depressed resignation. "I really wish you wouldn't go off on your own, My Lady."

"Hawa?"

Camellia did what she did best: tilted her head and looked cute.

***

Kevin sat down at his desk with a weary sigh. His body still ached from his spar with Heather, and then there was the moment between him and Lilian in the kitchen. Just remembering that moment made him feel warm and tingly in a *"I really want to go for another round"* kind of way.

Speaking of stuff that happened in the kitchen…

"Have you two noticed something off about your mom?" Kevin asked Iris and Lilian. The two fox-girls who were leaning against their desks, which were situated in front of and behind him respectively, glanced in his direction.

"What do you mean by off?" Lilian asked, tilting her head. "Is there something wrong with her?"

Kevin scratched at his cheek. "I don't think there's anything wrong with her, per se. It's just that she's been acting kind of different lately."

Iris raised a delicate eyebrow. "Different how?"

"Well, she's not as clumsy for one thing," Kevin pointed out. "I don't know if you've noticed, but she hasn't been randomly falling on

22

top of me lately. She's also taken to wearing clothes before leaving the bedroom. Even as far back as last month, Camellia always ran around the house naked. She sort of reminded me of a more childish version of you, Lilian."

Lilian's pout was one of the most adorable things he had ever seen. It still amazed him how someone so gorgeous could also look so cute. He often said that the sexy/adorable dichotomy she had going for her should be considered illegal.

Her long red hair whipped around her face as Lilian shook her head. Bright green eyes stared at him with a sort of childish petulance. She was wearing her standard off-the-shoulder green shirt, which revealed a healthy portion of her creamy cleavage and flat stomach. Her normal shorts were nowhere to be seen. Instead, she was wearing a skirt that stopped around the middle of her thighs.

"Muu, I don't see how Mom's actions are similar to mine. I was trying to seduce you. Mom just doesn't believe in wearing clothes."

"You really shouldn't mention how you tried to seduce me in public." Kevin felt a bit of heat rising to his cheeks. Several people who also heard the comment looked at their small group, gazing at the trio like hyenas looking at a tasty morsel.

A quick glare from Kevin made them look away.

"But now that you mention it, she has been acting kind of differently." Lilian tapped her lower lip with her index finger. "I wonder if she's starting to grow up."

"Ha!" Iris's barking laughter caused several nearby conversations to stop. "Mom grow up? That's like asking *Rikka Takanashi* to stop being a *Chūnibyou*. It's not happening. Can you imagine Mom growing out of her childish personality and acting like an adult?"

"Well, no," Lilian admitted.

Kevin saw the look on her face and almost winced. He knew that his mate wished Camellia would act more like a mother to her and Iris. She had admitted, if only to him during their version of pillow talk, that she wanted her and Camellia to have the mother-daughter bond that other people had.

"You never know." Kevin placed a hand over Lilian's. "She might eventually get better. Maybe whatever happened when she gave birth to you two is slowly reversing."

Lilian directed an appreciative smile his way. Iris snorted.

"You two can believe that if you want to. I prefer not getting my hopes up."

Kevin decided not to bother arguing with Iris. Unlike Lilian, who remained optimistic pretty much twenty-four seven, Iris was a realist with a severe pessimistic streak. She knew how to look at the bright side of things, but she only did so when it involved having an illicit relationship with her sister.

"Hey, you three!"

A voice called out to them seconds before a grinning Lindsay walked up. Her tomboyish blonde hair, styled in a cute pixie cut, bounced as she strolled to her desk, which was next to Lilian's. Her jean shorts fit snugly on her hips and she wore a baggy white T-shirt that said, *"I love soccer!"* in big, bold print on her chest with a soccer ball below the words.

Lindsay and Kevin had known each other since their elementary school days, back when life had been uncomplicated and not fraught with supernatural peril. Even though they had been friends for a long time, Kevin had, until eight months ago, been incapable of speaking to her without passing out. Of course, the same could have been said for any female his own age.

These days, Lindsay spent more time with Lilian, Iris, and Christine than she did him. That was okay. He was happy that Lilian and Iris had found such a good friend. He was happy for Christine, too.

Lilian gave her friend a million-watt smile. "Hey, Lindsay!"

Iris merely crossed her arms. "Oh, it's the dyke."

"K-ku!"

Kevin and Lilian watched as their friend stumbled into her desk, pressing her palms flat against the surface to keep herself aloft. Even then, the tomboy still slouched over, her expression one of abject despondency. For a moment, Kevin thought he saw an arrow sticking out of her back with the *kanji* for dyke written on the shaft. He shook his head and the arrow disappeared.

Must be my imagination.

"Why is she always calling me a dyke? So what if I happen to think girls are attractive. That's not a bad thing. All girls do it... I think..."

"There, there." Lilian pushed off her desk, walked behind the tomboy, and rubbed Lindsay's back. "Don't worry. I don't care what your sexual preferences are. Even if you are a dyke, you're still my friend."

Lindsay turned her head to give Lilian an exasperated look. "You

24

know, when you say things like that, I can't help but think you're being condescending." When Lilian just looked at the girl in genuine confusion, Lindsay sighed and gave her friend a smile. "Still, thank you, I guess. I'm glad you think of me as a friend."

"Of course." Lilian's bright smile was like the sun, blinding if you looked at it directly. "We'll always be best friends."

"Hehe, right."

Before Iris could comment—and Kevin knew that she would if given the chance—the doors to the classroom opened and their teacher walked in.

"All right, class, in your seats. It's time to start our lesson."

While most of the class groaned, Kevin studied their teacher. He was a middle-aged man with bland features. He had the kind of face that was so plain that he would be indistinguishable within a crowd. Even his outfit, a standard gray business suit with a casual cut, seemed designed to blend in with his surroundings. Dull. That's the word Kevin would have used to describe their teacher.

Dr. Allan Spencer had replaced Ms. Vis as their math teacher after Seth Naraka had possessed her. Kevin had heard from Heather that Ms. Vis's brain had been rendered inert. It had basically shut down, turning her into a vegetable. She was still in the hospital, her body alive, but her mind incapable of computing even basic sensory information.

He felt guilty over what had happened to her. If it weren't for him, Lilian, and Iris, she wouldn't have turned out that way.

Dr. Spencer walked up to the front of the class and gazed upon the students. "Today we'll be taking our finals." A chorus of groans erupted from the students. Kevin heard Iris slam her face on the desk behind him, and even Lilian's shoulders slumped at the mention of the dreaded f-word. "I'll be passing out the papers now, so get out your pencils and some paper. And remember, anyone caught cheating will automatically fail and be summarily kicked out of class."

***

"I really hate school," Iris groaned as she stretched her arms above her head. "Why did I ever agree to join you guys?"

Kevin turned away from her, knowing that if he looked, it would be to the sight of her breasts stretching taut against her shirt. Since she didn't wear a bra, he also knew that he'd be greeted to the unadulterated view of her nipples poking through the fabric. He wanted to keep his blood where it belonged: inside of him and not spraying out of his nose like the tail end of a comet, thank you very much.

The first half of the day had ended. He, Lilian, and Iris were walking to their usual lunch spot. It was nearing the end of June. The summer sun blazed away, showering them with ultraviolet rays that caused objects and people in the distance to appear hazy. Kevin felt sweat cling to his brow. He wiped it away with the back of his hand.

"Didn't you join the school so you could spend more time with your sister?" he replied absently.

"Oh, yeah. I did, didn't I?" Iris grinned as she came up behind Lilian and slipped her arms around the redhead's middle.

"The heck are you doing?!"

"Hehehe, come on, my darling Lily-pad. Let me give you some love."

"I don't want your love! Beloved gives me all the love I need!"

"Now don't be like that." Iris pressed her breasts against her sister's back. Lilian's face turned redder than her hair. "There's nothing wrong with sharing a little love with your beloved sister, is there? I don't mind sharing you with the stud."

"T-that's not…"

"Heck, I wouldn't mind if you, the stud, and I had ourselves a good old-fashioned threesome." Iris leaned up and started nibbling on her sister's ear. Lilian went deathly stiff as though rigor mortis—or mortification—had set in. "Just think about it: You, me, and the stud, all naked in bed, our bodies sweaty and flushed from a night of raunchy sex. Imagine it, the stud staring at our nubile flesh, his Excalibur growing hard at the sight of our hot bodies. You and I would push our breasts together with his long, hard cock between us, pleasing him until he shot his sticky spunk all over our tits."

Kevin quickly slapped a hand over his nose and pinched hard. Even so, blood still leaked out from between his fingers. Lilian was even worse. Her eyes had glazed over, her mouth had become slack-jawed, and it looked like she might start slobbering all over her shirt. He would have wondered what she was thinking about, but he had his own problems to deal with.

Guilt. Much as he abhorred the idea, there was some part of him, however small, that thought a threesome with Lilian and Iris would be hot. The other part paled at the thought. Lilian was insatiable and required a lot of effort to please, physically speaking, especially because he still refused to have sex with her. Iris was four times the sex fiend that her sister was. He didn't know if he would be able to keep up with them both at the same time.

They'd drain me dry before we even got past the foreplay!

"Wouldn't that be fun?" Iris continued to whisper in her sister's ear. Kevin noticed the grin on her face and shuddered. Iris's grins were terrifying in how sexy they were. Erotic didn't begin to adequately describe them. "Wouldn't you like that? You and me double-teaming your mate? Sharing his monstrous man meat between us, licking his spunk off each other's hot, sweaty bodies. You know that you—OOF!"

Kevin blinked when Iris's eyes rolled up into the back of her head. She tumbled away from Lilian and crumbled to the floor in a heap of splayed limbs. He stared at the unconscious girl. Then he looked at the person who had knocked said girl unconscious.

Christine looked the same as she always did. Her short stature meant that she barely came up to his chest. Her skin, pale as though she never saw the sun, glistened under the summer heat. Even though she must have been sweltering, she refused to change out of her black gothic lolita outfit. Then again, maybe she was perfectly fine, considering she was half bakeneko.

"Stupid... perverted... fox!"

The yuki-onna glared down at the unconscious fox-girl, her face bright blue as she huffed and panted like she had just finished running a marathon. Steam shot from her ears, billowing like a white cloud, which Kevin knew from experience meant her embarrassment had reached critical mass.

"Christine," he greeted the girl, whose angry eyes turned on him.

"Kevin." The blush left Christine's face, though the frown remained. "Why didn't you stop her? Isn't it your job as Lilian's mate to keep Iris from doing... doing things, like, you know, g-getting all p-p-perverted and stuff...?"

"Uh..."

Kevin wasn't exactly sure how to answer that. He couldn't very well tell Christine that the reason he hadn't stopped Iris was because the vixen's words had invoked erotic images within his mind that caused him to nosebleed. That would just lead to all sorts of trouble.

"N-not that I care or anything," Christine added, crossing her arms and huffing. "I-it's not like I was worried about you and Lilian being taken advantage of by this stupid skank! I'm not! I just... it's not something she should be saying in public! That's the only reason I stopped her! Hmph!"

"Um, right." Kevin ignored the girl's *tsundere-ness*. "Sorry. You're right. I should have stopped Iris."

Christine's decisive nod was that of someone who felt pleased at her advice being taken under serious consideration. "I'm glad you understand that."

"By the way, where's Lindsay? Don't you and she share home ec together?"

"Lindsay went to buy her lunch," Christine told him. "Since I make my lunches, I decided to wait for her at our usual spot. I was heading there right now before I ran into you three."

"Ah." Kevin nodded. "That makes sense."

Lindsay and Christine spent a lot of time together. When they weren't with him—or with Lilian and Iris—the two were often with each other. Lindsay, in particular, seemed to give Christine more attention than anyone else, though Christine didn't seem to notice.

"By the way…" Christine frowned as her eyes flickered toward Lilian. "What's up with Lilian? She hasn't said a word since I knocked out her sister."

Kevin locked onto his mate when he realized that Christine was right. Lilian was still stiffer than a bad case of morning wood. Her eyes were still glazed over and staring into the distance, their gaze unseeing and blank.

"Lilian?" Kevin placed a hand on Lilian's shoulder to try and rouse her from whatever spell she was under. "Lilian, are you—"

He didn't get a chance to finish.

Mere seconds after he touched her, Lilian was blasted off her feet as her nose became a literal geyser. Crimson ichor sprayed from her nostrils like the eruption of Mount Saint Helens. He and Christine gawked as she flew backwards for several feet, crashed into the ground, rolled, and came to an abrupt stop.

"Well," Kevin began as a crowd of people drew around them to take snapshots of the scene, "that just happened."

Christine could do nothing but nod.

***

"My Lord! I am happy to see that you have arrived safely! Please, sit down! I have been keeping your seat warm for you!"

28

"My Lord, My Lord. How are you doing today?"

"My Lord, My Lord. Do you need me to fan you?"

Kevin stared at Alex, Andrew, and Eric with a blank look in his eyes as they knelt before him. They were bowing to him like he was some kind of liege lord, or perhaps a warlord from feudal Japan. This was nothing new. They had been doing this for months. It used to bug the crap out of him. Now...

"Ha... whatever." He sighed and sat down without complaint.

I feel like some small, very beloved part of me has died.

"Would you like me to get you a cool drink, My Lord?" Eric asked as he sat beside Kevin.

"No... I'm fine..."

"Are you sure? It's awfully hot outside. One of us would not mind getting you something to drink."

Alex and Andrew both nodded like a pair of evil twin lackies. While a part of Kevin felt like strangling those two for going along with Eric's whims, another part felt like slamming his face against the table.

"No, I've already got a cold drink." Kevin opened the first tier of his bento box and pulled out his chopsticks.

What I wouldn't give for a fork. Why did Kotohime have to replace all our utensils with chopsticks? Does she think I'm an anime character?

"Really?" asked Eric.

Kevin resisted the urge to facepalm. "Yes, really."

"Really, really?"

"Would you shut up already?!"

"Looks like Kevin's having a hard time," Lindsay said. She was sitting next to Christine and eating her school bought chicken sandwich. Because she sat at the edge of the table, there was no one on her left. "Do you think this is better or worse than the jealousy they used to display?"

"Definitely worse." Christine wrinkled her nose as she punched a straw through her juice box. "Their fawning is absolutely disgusting."

"Why did they start treating him like he was God's gift to man anyway?"

"Because he's living with five hot women, of course." Iris smirked. She sat next to her sister, while Lilian sat between her and Christine. "Didn't you know that the stud has his very own harem?"

"I DO NOT HAVE A HAREM!"

"All hail the Harem Lord!" Alex, Andrew, and Eric all said at the same time.

"SHUT UP!"

Iris chuckled under her breath. Kevin twitched at the sound. Unlike the others who sat facing the table, she was facing the opposite direction as she leaned her back against the table. She stretched out languidly, allowing all those who passed their table to admire her breasts and long legs. Numerous people stared at her. Iris seemed to revel in those stares, the lust barely hidden within their eyes. Even other girls were not immune to her looks.

Kevin shook his head. *You'd think people would be used to her by now...*

As Kevin tried to ignore his friends, he watched Iris as she surveyed the courtyard with a lazy glance. There weren't many people outside. It was simply too hot. Even sitting in the shade like they were, it was still unbearably scorching. Aside from themselves, Kevin only counted about thirty people wandering around. In a school with over 1,000 students, thirty wasn't a lot.

"Hey, Lily-pad, check it out." Iris grabbed her sister's attention by pointing. "It's that other loli chick."

Kevin, Lilian, Lindsay, and Christine all turned to look at the girl as she walked past their table. Her outfit presented a stark contrast to Christine's. Where the yuki-onna's lolita clothing was pure black, hers was whiter than snow. It also featured a much shorter skirt and a dip in the neckline that revealed her cleavage. That was something Christine, who was a B-cup, didn't have.

"Isn't that the girl who transferred here two months ago?" Lindsay asked. "I think her name is Fan Shenlong... something like that."

"You know who that is?" Lilian asked Lindsay.

"Christine would know more about her than I do," Lindsay confessed. "She has several classes with her."

Christine growled as if the mere mention of Fan was enough to piss her off. "How dare that... that scarlet woman tarnish the Lolita name by wearing such a scandalous outfit!"

"I take it you two don't get along?" Iris observed, idly watching the female stride by their table. Her eyes narrowed when Fan's head turned and penetrated her with a stare. It was the kind of look someone gave a person they felt was beneath their notice.

Kevin winced when Iris's expression darkened. He almost felt sorry

30

for that Fan girl. Almost.

"I hate her even more than I hate you," Christine said.

"Aw, you don't hate me." Iris gave the other girl a lazy grin that oozed arrogance. "We both know you love me."

"Tch!"

Iris chuckled when Christine turned her head, her face the same color as a tundra.

"So, you guys are coming to my game tonight, right?" Lindsay asked.

"Do I have a choice?" When Lindsay gave Christine a look, the girl sighed and waved a hand as though warding off a bug. "Fine, fine. Yes, I'm coming to your game."

"You know Beloved and I are coming to your game," Lilian added with a sunny smile. "We wouldn't miss our friend's championship game for the world."

Over where he was sitting, Kevin gave Lindsay a thumbs up. He was listening to their conversation. It was a nice distraction from his male friends' flagrant ass kissing.

"If the stud and Lily-pad are going, I guess I can tag along," Iris said. Lindsay smiled at the group, clearly pleased to know that they would be showing up to cheer her on.

"By the way, My Lord," Eric started. "Do you plan on adding that other lolita hottie to your harem?"

"For the last time, I don't have a harem!"

Deciding to tease Kevin some more, a grinning Iris said, "Everyone who thinks Kevin has a harem, please raise your hand."

She, Alex, Andrew, and Eric all raised their hands. Kevin shot Lindsay and Christine a betrayed look when they also raised their hands.

"How could you two agree with her?"

"D-don't look at me like that." Christine scowled at him with an icy blue face. "How can I not think that when you've got all those women living with you? It doesn't paint you in the best light, you know."

"You have to admit," Lindsay added, "it really does seem like you have your own harem back home. I mean, seriously, have you seen the women living in your apartment? All of them are gorgeous."

"The dyke makes a good point," Iris said, nodding. "We are gorgeous."

"U-urk!"

Iris ignored the sound Lindsay made as the tomboy was speared by arrows that randomly appeared out of thin air. As her friend slumped over the table, Lilian decided to be a good buddy and pulled the metaphorical arrows out of Lindsay's back.

"And everyone knows that when one guy is living with a bunch of sexy women like us, it's because he's a Harem King," Iris continued adding fuel to the fire.

"That's not how that works at all!" Kevin glared at everyone present before turning pleading eyes on Lilian. "Everyone's being mean to me again, Lilian. You don't think I have a harem, do you?"

"Of course not." Lilian smiled at him. "Don't worry, Beloved. I won't let any woman I don't approve of join your harem."

"What?"

"I said I won't let you have a harem."

"Kay." Kevin sniffled. "Thank you, Lilian."

Lilian's eyes were two warm pools of emerald love as she stared at her mate. "You're welcome, Kevin."

"Lilian."

"Kevin."

"Lilian!"

"Kev—"

"I swear to all eight million Shinto gods that if you two start hugging, I'll murder you dead," Christine threatened. Kevin and Lilian pouted at her, but their attention was diverted from Christine by a loud shout.

"There he is, girls! Get him!"

It was a familiar shout. Kevin had heard it many times in the past. It was the angry screaming of women who'd had their purity tarnished and were out for revenge.

The Horde had arrived.

Everyone turned as several dozen angry teenage girls seeking blood rushed their table. Eric squealed like a little girl, leapt to his feet, and bolted as though a shinigami was nipping at his heels. The girls ran past the table and followed the salacious young man. They caught up to him in record time. They surrounded him on all sides, hemming him in.

Then came the screams.

"WHATEVER HAPPENED, I DIDN'T DO IT!"

"DON'T LIE TO US! WE KNOW YOU SNUCK INTO THE GIRLS' LOCKER ROOM AND STOLE OUR PANTIES!"

"NO, I DIDN'T... AT LEAST, NOT THIS TIME!"

"LIAR! WE CAN SEE THEM HANGING OUT OF YOUR POCKET!"

"MY POCKET—WHAT THE HELL?! HOW DID THESE GET IN HERE?!"

"KILL HIM, GIRLS!"

"NO! WAIT! THIS IS ALL A MISUNDERSTANDING, I SWEAR! I—OH, GOD! NOOOOOOooooo…!"

Kevin and the others sat there as The Horde proceeded to physically demolish Eric, whose agonized screams rent the air like nails on a chalkboard. Cries of pain echoed from the mass of bodies. Kevin thought he saw blood arcing through the air, but that could have been his imagination. The screams eventually tapered off into incoherent gurgling. Then they stopped altogether.

"What… what just happened?" Lindsay asked the question that everybody wanted to know.

"Ha…" a sigh came from behind them. "Really, Apprentice, how do you expect to raise your peeping level if you allow yourself to get captured and beaten by girls of this caliber?"

Everyone turned around. Heather stood before them, hands on her hips, an expression that epitomized disappointment plastered all over her face. Her blonde hair remained in its usual bob cut. She was wearing a gym tracksuit with the white and blue school colors. The PE assistant coach shook her head and sighed, right before she noticed that everyone was staring at her.

"Oh. Hello, everyone."

After everyone greeted Heather, Lilian asked the question that was on everybody's mind. "Was all that you're doing?"

"Shishishi, of course." Heather grinned. "It's an important part of my apprentice's ongoing training. To become a Master Peeper, he must learn how to react to a horde of angry women, no matter the situation."

"I see." Lilian paused. "And those panties, did he really steal those?"

"Naw." Heather waved a dismissive hand through the air. "That was my doing. I stole the girls' panties while they were having PE, and then slipped a few into Eric's pocket when he wasn't looking."

In the wake of hearing something so incredibly stupid, Kevin and his friends simply went back to eating their food. It wasn't like Eric getting the crap beaten out of him by a horde of angry women was anything new. Heather doing something dumb and potentially life-threatening to her so-called apprentice in the name of training wasn't anything new either.

As if to shatter the sense of normality, Eric's dad, the Principal of Desert Cactus High School, appeared before them. He rushed toward the horde of teenage girls who were still beating the crap out of his son.

He was wearing nothing but his underwear.

Kevin and everyone else stared in horror as the rotund man raced forward, his flabby gut bouncing in the air like a uniboob, and his bald head gleaming in the light. Oddly enough, while the only article of clothing he was wearing were those ugly white undies, he also had his sunglasses on. He leapt at the girls like a tiger pouncing on its prey—or a really fat and perverted old man pouncing on a horde of young girls.

"Give me some love as well!" he shouted at the group of girls, who all turned their rage on him.

Everyone remained silent as the Principal followed in his son's footsteps. The mob of teenage girls proceeded to unleash unholy hell and massive bodily harm on his person with various locker room implements. The sounds of bat smacking flesh, rake smacking flesh… and claymore smacking flesh rang out across the courtyard.

"This is good too!" was all the Principal shouted as he was pummeled into a mass of bleeding meat.

"Is it just me, or is the Principal even more perverted than usual?" asked Lindsay.

"It's just you," Alex said.

"Totally just you," Andrew agreed. "The Principal was always like this. I think he's just finally become unrestrained."

Christine turned a deadpanned stare on Iris. "I feel like we somehow have you to blame for this."

Iris's unrepentant grin told everyone present that Christine's accusation was right on the money. "Do you really think that I would use an enchantment on our wonderful principal to unleash his normally restrained lecherous tendencies, turning him into a raging idiot of lust and stupidity?"

"Yes," Kevin said while everyone else nodded. "Yes, I do."

Iris gave him an amused glance, her eyes glimmering with an ominous light that spelled nothing good for him. "Huhuhu, it seems you know me too well, Stud."

Kevin had nothing to say to that. However…

"Lilian?" Kevin said in a voice so solemn that everyone paid attention. The curious glance on his mate's face was only matched by his friends leaning in, as though expecting him to share his most embarrassing secret.

"Yes, Beloved?"

"If I won the Holy Grail War, could I ask for a new soul? I think mine's been tainted."

Lilian looked uncertain. "… I don't think so."

"Tch!" Kevin slammed his head on the table. "Figures."

***

The end of school couldn't come fast enough for Fan. She absolutely despised being forced to attend classes. There was nothing duller than sitting behind a desk and listening to some fool lecture her on a subject they didn't know half as much as they thought they did. She hated it even more because she was surrounded by lesser beings, these filthy humans who thought they were at the top of the food chain, even though that couldn't have been further from the truth.

Humans were scum; they were nothing but a group of hairless monkeys. They mistakenly believed that they were the most powerful species on Earth, but the truth was that they were just the most populous. Were it not for their large numbers, humans would have been killed off or enslaved centuries ago.

Everyone stood up from their seats as the bell signaled an end to class, the many students packing their bags and slinging them over their shoulders before rushing out of the classroom quicker than a nekomata being chased by a spray bottle. Her eyes eventually locked onto one particular person in her class, a girl whose childlike body and all-black outfit made her look like the classic definition of a lolita. Their eyes met. She became amused when the girl glared at her before huffing and stalking out of the room.

According to her observations, that girl was Christine, one of her target's friends. She was also a yōkai. Having not seen her powers, Fan couldn't say which type of yōkai for sure, but judging from the cold feel to her youki, she believed that Christine was a creature with control over ice. She was betting on the girl being a yuki-onna. The famed snow women were one of the best-known manipulators of ice in the entire world.

Though just what a yuki-onna is doing here of all places, I'll never understand.

35

She grabbed her own bag, a small sack made from the threaded fibers of an onikuma, slung it over her shoulder, and proceeded outside.

The bright sun hit her eyes as she waded through the crowd of people. The stench of humanity made her nose wrinkle, but she tried to ignore it. A number of boys stared at her as she walked by them, lust obvious in their eyes. These boys were like raging sacks of hormones.

She snorted. *Teenage boys are so easy. You don't even have to show them a little skin before they become drooling sacks of flesh. Honestly, do none of these boys know the meaning of the word restraint?*

Not that she could blame them for lusting after her. A woman as beautiful as her would obviously attract attention. She had a body that was to die for, and when combined with her lolita face, it made for an irresistible combination. She was the best of both worlds, as it were.

She walked past buildings that shielded her eyes from the sun, hideous blocks made of drab colored bricks. There was no sense of aesthetics to these structures. Every building looked exactly the same, with only minor differences in shape and size.

That was another thing she disliked about humans. Their uninspiring architecture. They simply lacked ability to create aesthetically pleasing structures. Everything was too uniform, too plain, too bland.

Hopefully, our mission here will be over soon, and we'll be able to finally go back home.

As she walked into the parking lot, she immediately caught sight of Li. It was hard not to. He towered over everyone there with his nearly seven feet of height. His expression, stern and uncompromising, made for an intimidating sight. Several students looked at him, but they quickly turned their heads when they met his unwavering and serious gaze.

Unlike most members of the Shénshèng Clan, who had blond hair and blue eyes, he had dark brown hair and eyes, which made sense. Unlike the immediate members of the family, Li and Guang were branch members. They served as her bodyguards, though ever since Father had given her this mission, they had acted like a combination of parent and superior—well, Li more than Guang. Her other bodyguard was merely dumb muscle. All brawn and no brain.

"Lady Fan," Li greeted as she walked up to him. "I hope your day at school was eventful."

"Please be serious," she said as Li opened the door to their car, a red

Porsche Boxster. She sat in the front passenger seat, then waited until Li had closed the door and entered through the driver's side before continuing. "You know how I feel about attending this farce of a school. The people are boring, the school is dull, and I'm surrounded by a bunch of filthy humans. Being near this useless species of feces throwing apes is almost more than I can bear."

"You should not be so quick to dismiss humanity," Li warned her in his usual, serious way. "Humans might be frail creatures, but they are also intelligent and crafty. The many technological advancements they've made in the past century, advancements which have forced all yōkai to create laws against revealing our existence to them, proves that the primate race is not to be underestimated."

Fan clicked her tongue, but she didn't argue. Even she knew that human technology posed a threat to their existence. She remembered seeing the aftermath of several nuclear explosions when China had been experimenting with nuclear weaponry. Just recalling the sight of those mushroom shaped clouds, of the intense blast from the detonation, of the fierce winds the explosions had kicked up, sent chills down her spine.

The car's engine thrummed to life as Li pulled out of the parking lot, using his unique talent to avoid people and other cars while continuing to accelerate. It didn't take long before they passed the light blue gates of the school and began traveling down the road.

She watched the wildlife that passed her by in boredom. There wasn't much to see in this state. Its flora and fauna, much like humanity's architecture, was uninspiring and dull. She missed the bamboo forest that surrounded her home, with its beautiful lakes, colorful plants, and various wildlife.

"Do you remember the plan?" Li asked after they had traveled for several miles.

"Of course." Glad to have something that took her attention away from her boredom, Fan turned from the sight of cacti to look at Li. "My job is to take care of Lilian, her human mate, and her sister. They'll be going to a soccer game later today, which means they'll be out of the reach of their bodyguards."

Li nodded approvingly. "Meanwhile, I will take care of Kotohime and Kirihime. I have no doubt that Kotohime will sense any massive youki emissions, especially since none of us specialize in the creation of barriers. They currently pose the greatest threat to our plans and will need to be taken out, or at least kept distracted, until you can complete your mission."

"And while we do that, Guang will take out the *dog*."

Fan wrinkled her nose in disgust. They'd found out early on that the human mate of Lilian was apprenticed to Kiara F. Kuyo, a disgusting inu who was well known in the human world. She didn't understand how that stupid girl could let her mate spend time around a filthy mutt. She didn't want to understand.

"I'm glad to see you know the plan. I'm quite proud of you."

Fan rolled her eyes and went back to staring out the window. Such a boring, dreary landscape.

It'll all be over soon. I'll be coming back home to you. Wait for me... my beloved Jiāoào.

***

Because Lindsay had a soccer game and they had agreed to go see it, Kevin, Lilian, and Iris didn't return home that day. Instead of hopping on the bus and heading back to their apartment, they remained at school with Christine. The idea was to wait around until the game began.

Alex and Andrew had left. They weren't interested in watching a soccer game. Kevin knew that Eric was still around somewhere, but he didn't know where that lecherous jerk was.

"Probably trying to peep on the soccer girls while they're changing," he muttered under his breath.

"Did you say something, Stud?"

"I asked, why are you hanging off me? You're too close."

Iris, her body draped over Kevin's back and her chin resting comfortably on his shoulder, took a moment to seriously ponder the question. She hummed and shifted. Kevin knew she was doing it on purpose. Her nipples were touching his back through their shirts. She was also groping his pecs. Soft hands were slipped underneath his shirt, blatantly trying to play with his nipples in public. Kevin had, for a time, slapped her hands away, but he had stopped several minutes ago.

He didn't know what was worse: the fact that Iris was groping him in public, or the fact that he didn't even care anymore.

"Because I want to," she said at last.

He sighed. "I shouldn't have bothered asking."

"That's right. You shouldn't ask such obvious questions." Kevin could see Iris's sexy smirk out of the corner of his eye. "It's good to see that you're learning, though it's an awfully slow process."

"I almost feel like I should be insulted by your words," Kevin mused.

He and Iris were wandering down one of the many aisles in the library. This aisle was dedicated to manga. He scanned the various titles, most of which he had already read. It was kind of disappointing, but the school library just didn't have a wide manga selection. He thought they were discriminating against manga because it used images instead of words to tell a story.

"You should read this one," Iris suggested, momentarily stopping her groping of his chest to grab a manga from the shelf and present it to him.

Kevin eyed the front cover illustration before shaking his head. The cover had one guy and two girls. One of the girls was a blonde-haired beauty with blue eyes, while the other was a brunette cutie. The title was *Nisekoi*.

"I'm surprised they have this manga, but Lilian and I have already read it."

"Hm, how about this one?"

"Read it."

"That one?"

"Read that too."

"It seems like you've read all the ones here."

"I'm beginning to think I have."

"Too bad they don't have any hentai."

Kevin twitched. "Why would I want to read a hentai?"

"So you can gain some ideas for when you, myself, and my sister start screwing like vixens in heat."

I won't facepalm. I won't facepalm. I won't facepalm.

"Of course, if you wanted to, you could also add Mom, Kirihime, and Kotohime, though the latter two might kill you if you try to sex them up. Maybe we should just add Mom to our orgy, then. That would be hot."

The sound of Kevin's palm smacking against his face echoed throughout the library.

He and Iris soon emerged from the aisle. Kevin had managed to find a manga that he hadn't read. It was the first volume to a series called *The Heroic Legend of Arslan*. The series was actually based on a Japanese fantasy novel. It even had its own anime adaptation, though Kevin had yet to watch it.

A Fox's Revenge

They went over to where Lilian and Christine were sitting. Kevin's mate had a pencil and sketch pad out. She was nibbling on her pencil's eraser as she poured over a book titled *So You Wanna Be a Mangaka?* Christine had a book in her hand as well, the cover of which made him think it must be some kind of romance story. He couldn't see it well, but the cover, with clearly manga-style artwork, was probably a shōjō romance of some kind.

He sat down next to Lilian. Iris looked at him, and then at Christine, who sat on Lilian's other side. She huffed and sat down on the opposite side of the table.

Lilian looked up to greet him.

She paused.

"Why is your face red?"

"Don't ask," Kevin muttered. Iris snickered at him, to which he cast her a withering glare. He then turned back to Lilian. "How are your drawings coming along?"

"A-ah." Lilian blushed as she held her sketch pad to her chest, as though afraid he might try to peek at it. "Th-they're coming along fine… I think… maybe…"

Kevin's lips twitched. Embarrassed Lilian was impossibly cute. No two ways about it. It was too bad she only got like this when it came to her drawings. She was awfully shy about showing them off to others.

Two months ago, Lilian had declared that she would become a manga artist. Kevin had supported her, of course. He even told her that he would be happy to help with her drawings. However, every time he asked if she would let him look at her artwork, she refused. No one, not him, not Iris, not Kotohime, not her mom, no one was allowed to look at her drawings, apparently.

He remembered about one month back when he and Iris had teamed up to see what she was drawing. Not only did Lilian beat them both down, she also refused to speak with him for the rest of the day. While that didn't sound like a very long time to stop talking to someone, it was when your name happened to be Lilian, and the person you stopped speaking to was your mate.

It had been much worse for Iris. Lilian had ignored her for a whole week. She had even locked the other girl out of their room. By the time that week had ended, Iris was a wreck. The girl had been like a vegetable. According to her, she'd been unable to function because she hadn't gotten her *Lily-pad Love Battery* recharged.

40

"You'll show it to me when you're finished, right?" Kevin asked, smiling at the fox-girl. "I really would love to read your manga."

"Ah, um, o-okay," Lilian muttered. "J-just don't make fun of my drawings when you see them, okay?"

"Okay."

"Promise?"

"Pinky promise."

Kevin held out his pinky. She eyed the appendage for a moment before hooking her own pinky through it and shaking.

"You'll show me, too, right?" asked Iris.

"No."

"What?" Iris's eyes widened in appalled shock. "Come on, please? Pretty please?"

"No." Lilian held the sketchpad to her chest. "The only reason I'm even going to let Kevin see them is because he's my mate."

"T-that's so cruel!" Kevin muffled his chuckle behind a hand as Iris looked ready to burst into tears. "You'd show him, but not your lovely sister? How could you, Lily-pad? I thought we shared something special."

"The only thing we share is blood and gender."

"U-ugh!"

Iris dropped to the ground, her arms curling around her knees as she rocked back and forth. Her actions reminded him of a psychotic patient at an insane asylum. She mumbled something to herself, a mantra of some kind, but he couldn't hear it. It likely had something to do with her Lily-pad hating her, or whatever.

He turned his attention to Christine, who'd been silently reading ever since they arrived. "Do you know what time Lindsay's soccer game is?"

Christine didn't even look up from her manga as she answered. "Her game is at six."

Kevin looked at the clock, which told him the time was currently half past four. That meant they had one and a half hours before the game. *Maybe we should have gone home? Ah, well. Too late for that now.*

"Do you all wanna grab a bite to eat before the game? There's a small Mexican restaurant about a mile from here that sells some really good burritos."

Christine and Lilian looked at each other for a moment. Kevin was rather impressed by their silent communication skills, especially when he considered how they'd been bitter rivals seven months ago. It seemed prolonged exposure to each other had helped them get used to the other person's personality.

"I think getting dinner sounds like a good idea," Lilian said. Christine said nothing. She merely put a bookmark on the page that she had been reading and snapped the book shut. Kevin finally got a good look at the cover. *Erotic Fairy Tales: The Little Mermaid.*

I had no idea Christine was into that kind of stuff. That sounds like something Iris would read.

He knew that Christine was into manga, even though she denied it at every opportunity. Kevin had seen her and Lilian exchanging manga when they thought no one was looking. They often made their exchange behind the school lockers between classes.

"Awesome." He stood up. "Then let's go there right now. I'm starving."

"I have noticed that you've been eating a lot more." Lilian also stood up.

"That's because Kiara and Heather have been running me ragged. I probably burn several thousand calories just getting my butt kicked across the sparring mat every morning."

As Christine, Lilian, and Kevin walked out of the library, Iris looked up from where she'd been mumbling in depression and realized that everyone was leaving without her.

She scrambled to her feet and chased after them. "Hey! Wait for me! I'm coming too! Come on! Don't leave me here!"

***

Fan wanted to cover her ears. The sounds of people cheering and jeering assaulted her eardrums, rattling her skull and making her wish she'd been born deaf. The noise was blood curdling. She knew that humans were loud, but she had never realized that they could be this obnoxiously rambunctious.

She sat near the top of the bleachers overlooking a large soccer field. There must have been at least a hundred people with her. The bleachers were filled to bursting. The only reason she didn't have people sitting next to her was because she had cast an illusion over this area that made it look like there were several intimidating individuals sitting beside her.

With her sharp eyes, enhanced by the miniscule amounts of youki she sent to them, Fan had a close-up view of the people playing on the field. There were a total of twenty-two people running across the soccer field. Eleven wore the uniform representing Desert Cactus High School, light blue shorts and a white shirt with blue trim. There was a cactus on the front. The other team wore red and black.

Having never been interested in what humans did in their spare time, she knew little about the sport that was being played before her eyes. She didn't care either. It looked stupid. They were just kicking a ball back and forth.

Why humans put so much effort into the most inane and ridiculous things, I'll never understand.

She tore her gaze from the sight of a bunch of girls kicking a ball. She wasn't there to watch idiots work up a sweat doing something so banal, so instead of staring at the hairless monkeys as they played, she began searching for the person that she was going to kill. Her target was in this crowd somewhere…

"YOU GO, LINDSAY!"

Ah, there she is.

Fan felt the sneer on her face grow as Lilian cheered for her human friend. The girl was standing next to Christine, a raven-haired beauty—Lilian's sister—a blond male, and a boy with a lecherous look in his eyes. Lilian and Christine were holding up a large sign that she couldn't read because it wasn't pointed at her. While Lilian shouted and made a ruckus, Christine retained an expression of supreme embarrassment.

Her face is blue. She's definitely a yuki-onna.

Her eyes then traveled away from Lilian to the red-haired vixen's mate. He stood next to Lilian and Christine, following Lilian's example. His hands were cupped to his mouth as he cheered for their friend. The only one not cheering was the sister, Iris. Unlike everyone else, she sat on the bleachers, one leg crossed over the other. Her expression spoke of boredom.

The perverted one didn't cheer either, but that was merely because he was busy drooling.

Fan had to admit that Kevin was a decent example of the male species. Most females would probably consider him at least mildly handsome. He had a strong build, broad shoulders and chest, and his tousled blond hair gave him a sort of carefree appearance. His eyes weren't the same shade of blue as hers, but they were vibrant nonetheless.

But he's still human. All humans are filthy and disgusting.
She didn't know what Lilian saw in this boy.
She turned my dearest, beloved little brother down for him?
Fan clenched her fists until her knuckles turned white.
Soon, Lilian Pnéyma. Your time is coming soon…

***

Kotohime hummed a gentle tune as she went about taking down the laundry, which she had hung up on the balcony. She was very meticulous in how she worked. Undo the pins, set them in a basket, and then fold up the clothes and put them in the even bigger basket. Kevin often complained about how she hung the laundry up in such an old-fashioned manner, claiming they had a perfectly good dryer that she should use. He just didn't realize that her method was so much better.

As she worked, she thought about the time that she had spent at the Swift residence. It had been a little less than nine months since she had started living with Lilian and her mate. Despite the rocky start she'd had in regards to Kevin, life with him had been rather pleasant.

There had been a few bumps in the road, though. She still grimaced in phantom pain upon remembering her fight with Luna, and of the events that happened during that time. Still, despite what happened, it had all worked out for the best. She had begun training again to sharpen her skills, Lilian had started training with her, and Kevin had become a stronger person because of what happened.

That boy continues to surprise me.

The sound of a door sliding open alerted her to the new presence on the balcony before her sister's voice called out to her. "Sister?"

"Hm?" Kotohime turned around to find her sister. The hem of Kirihime's French maid outfit fluttered in the soft breeze. "Kirihime, is something on your mind? Shouldn't you be looking after Camellia-sama?"

"My Lady is asleep." Kirihime frowned a bit, her brow creasing in worry. "My Lady has been sleeping a lot more lately. I'm getting a little worried about her."

"I have noticed that Camellia-sama has been sleeping quite a bit," Kotohime confessed. "She's also been calmer than normal. I do not think there is anything to worry about, however, so try not to let it trouble you."

"Yes, I suppose I shouldn't worry."

"Good. Now, did you need something?"

Kirihime was about to answer when a large spike in youki alerted them both to imminent danger. Killing intent flooded the area. It was so powerful that were she not a four-tails, she would have been on her knees and struggling to breath, much like Kirihime. Kotohime had less than three-fourths of a second to comprehend what this killing intent meant before their apartment building exploded in a massive shower of light and flames.

***

"One. Two. One-one. Two. Hya!"

Kiara glared at her current opponent, a large punching bag that she'd been pounding away at for the last half an hour. It was a specially designed bag made to her specifications. It was denser than the standard punching bag, made from the hide of an onikuma, and able to withstand the most ferocious of punches and kicks. It wouldn't survive if she punched it at full power, but for the purpose of working up a good sweat, it worked well enough.

The chains attaching the punching bag to the ceiling rattled as she slammed into it with her fist. She shuffled across the mat, moving from side to side as she launched a series of rapid punches. Her fist blurred. The whistling of air as it was cut echoed around the room. That noise was quickly followed by multiple *bangs!* from her fist impacting against the punching bag.

Several yards away, a large sensor with a monitor attached to it counted the number of punches she released per second, along with how powerful each punch was based on the momentum at which she hit it. Her goal was to increase her punching speed.

Sweat poured down her body in rivulets. Her clothes caked to her skin. Despite how much sweat she worked up, her breathing remained even.

A loud beeping went off, her timer, which told her it was time to stop. She ceased beating the punching bag like nobody's business and turned to look at the monitor. Three hundred punches in a single minute.

She frowned. *My speed hasn't increased.*

She supposed she should have expected that. With only one hand to punch with, her punching speed had been reduced by half. She'd been working hard to get her speed back up to par, but it looked as if she had hit a wall. Five punches for every one second seemed to be her limit.

I suppose it could be worse, but still...

She looked down at her hand, wrapped in white training bandages. She clenched it into a fist, watching as the veins throbbed to life on her forearm. Her arm was covered in muscle. Her fingers and knuckles had calluses from constant training. It was a strong hand, a powerful hand.

It wasn't enough.

"Five punches isn't going to be enough to beat *him*."

Before her thoughts could linger, the sound of her intercom going off caused her to look over her shoulder. What could her aid want at this hour? Frowning, she walked over to the small speaker built into the wall and accepted the call.

"Yes?"

"Ms. Kuyo, a visitor wants to see you."

"I see." Kiara was not expecting anyone. "Did this visitor say what they want?"

"No, ma'am, and I've, well, pardon me for saying so, ma'am, but I've never seen him before. However, he says it's urgent that he speak with you."

"Hmm..." Kiara cocked her head to the side, doing far more than simply contemplating the situation. Something was wrong. She could feel it in her bones. After a second or two, she narrowed her eyes. "Very well. Tell him to head up to my office and that I'll be with him as soon as I take a shower."

"Of course, ma'am."

Sighing, Kiara ended the call and pressed several more buttons on the console. A large slot opened in the ceiling, which her personal punching bag disappeared into as it was hauled up by a series of silent pulleys. A section of the wall behind her timer also opened. The timer disappeared as it moved backwards on a series of treads, the wall sliding closed behind it. Once again, her personal training room looked like one large room with a blue mat covering the floor.

After taking a quick shower, Kiara dressed herself in a dark gray business suit. Like usual, the suit was missing its left sleeve. While some people were disturbed whenever they saw the stump that used to be her left arm, she rather liked the look. It might have made her punches slower, but she couldn't deny that she looked pretty damn badass.

Entering her personal elevator, Kiara only needed to wait for a few seconds before it took her to the floor containing her office. She exited swiftly, striding down the beige carpeted hall and reaching her office in record time. She reached out for the handle, ready to grip it—

—she paused. Her eyes narrowed. A split second later, she gripped the door and opened it, walking in with a nonchalant air.

A person stood in her office, his back to her. He was massive, towering over her like a *Titan* towered over a human. He was garbed in what she recognized as the robes of a Shaolin Monk. It was a long, yellow robe similar to a kimono, only looser and more flowing. The sleeves were rather voluminous, extending all the way to the floor. Short, dark hair covered his head.

Three bushy fox tails stuck out of his robes and two ears twitched on his head.

He turned to face her.

"You're the one who wanted to see me, right?" Kiara smirked as she spread her single remaining arm wide, as though inviting him to try something. "Well, here I am."

The man's face bulged. His eyes, which had been impassive a second before, suddenly became filled with an inexplicable rage. Kiara saw the whites turn red as blood vessels gathered within.

"DOOOOOOGGGGGG!"

The man unleashed a most unusual battle cry as he charged at Kiara, slamming into her and smashing them both straight through a wall.

***

"Go, Lindsay! GO!" Lilian cheered for Lindsay as her friend dribbled the ball across the soccer field. She would have cupped her hands to her mouth and used them as a microphone, but her hands were currently occupied with the large banner she had made.

"Come on, Lindsay! You've got this!" Beside Lilian, her mate also cheered their friend on. She smiled at how supportive he was. It was even better because they were cheering together.

"Come on, hotties! I wanna see those boobies bounc—BWAG!"

"SHUT UP, PERVERT!"

Lilian, Kevin, and Iris all turned their heads just in time to witness Christine bash Eric's face in. The boy crumbled to the ground, his head smacking against the metal bleachers on the way down. There was a moment of silence…

… And then they went back to cheering for their friend.

Lilian only knew a little about soccer from the time she had played a scrimmage with Lindsay and her friends; it was back before Kevin decided to be her mate. She knew that the ultimate goal was to score as many points as possible by kicking the soccer ball into the opposition's goal, but she knew little beyond that. Despite her basic knowledge, that didn't stop her from enjoying the sight of Lindsay playing her hardest.

A loud whistle echoed around the field. Lilian watched, confused when everyone stopped playing and headed back to their respective teams.

"What's going on? Is it already over?"

"No," Kevin answered. "It's just the ending to the first half. There will be a fifteen-minute break before the two teams start playing again."

"Oh." Lilian hummed in thought for a moment before smiling. "Why don't we go and see Lindsay? You know, to let her know that we're cheering her on?"

"Sure, let's do that."

"I guess we're getting up to greet the dyke," Iris mumbled.

Christine clicked her tongue. "Do you have to be so rude?"

"It's an expression of love."

The group stood up, leaving the unconscious Eric lying on the bleachers, and went down to where Lindsay's team was resting. They found their tomboy friend easily enough. She stood off to the side, drinking from a water bottle.

"Lindsay!" Lilian called out, causing the girl to turn around.

A grin sprang to her face when she spotted them. "Hey, guys! What do you think of the game so far?"

"It's exciting," Lilian said. "Not as exciting as watching my mate speed past everyone on the track, but still pretty exciting."

Lindsay twitched as a wan smile appeared on her face. "Yeah, I suppose it would be impossible for even something as exciting as a soccer match to beat anything your mate does."

"Very true." Lilian's sage-like nod made Kevin facepalm. "Now, if my mate was the one playing soccer, that would be a totally different story."

"Right." Lindsay sighed.

"Try not to look so depressed, dyke," Iris said in her usual rude voice. "Lily-pad's got the stud on the brain twenty-four seven. Nothing you, I, or anyone else does will ever be enough to compete with what he does. He could be staring at a wall, and she would think it was sexier than me stripping naked while pole dancing."

"Nice imagery there," Kevin muttered. To Lindsay he said, "try to ignore anything Iris says. She doesn't really mean it. She's just rude by nature."

"Oh, whatever, Stud." Iris draped herself across his shoulder, her right index finger making circles on his chest, her expression coy. "You know you love me—Goof!"

"Hands off my mate." Were Lilian's prim words as she smacked Iris down with a tail before anyone could notice. Iris fell to the ground, sprawled out, her black halter top askew, revealing more breast than it was supposed to.

Kevin felt a trickle of sweat leave a trail down the left side of his face. "Is it just me, or have we become a really violent group? Seriously, Eric's always getting beaten up by girls and we don't even bat an eye. Christine also tends to take her pound of flesh out of him, and you're constantly beating your sister whenever she gets, well, whenever she acts like her usual self."

"Hmm…" Lindsay actually thought about his words for a moment. "You may have a point. We have become pretty inured to violence. I wonder if this is what they call desensitization?"

Lilian shrugged. "Don't look at me. All I'm doing is protecting your chastity like you asked me to. If you'd prefer I let Iris molest you…"

"I appreciate you protecting my chastity."

"Ufufufu, the only one stealing your chastity will be me."

"And now I'm afraid."

Lindsay looked at Lilian and Kevin as they bantered, silently shaking her head. Something then tugged at her sleeve. Lindsay looked down at Christine, whose resigned expression caused everyone around to become curious. Kevin, who was still trading banter with Lilian, wondered what was going on.

"Look, I don't want you to think this means anything special, but you did really good out there… and stuff."

Christine glanced at Iris, who was dusting herself off. The vixen noticed her look, grinned, and sent her a thumbs up. Lindsay didn't see the thumbs up, since she was busy paying attention to her friend, but Kevin did.

Did Iris tell Christine to compliment Lindsay?

It seemed Iris was nicer than she let on, or maybe she was trying to amuse herself by setting those two up. That was something he could see her doing.

"Heh… thanks." Lindsay smiled at her friend, who looked away with a huff.

"Whatever."

Just then, something began falling from the sky. Kevin blinked as something white drifted lazily past his field of vision. He then looked up to see…

"Feathers?"

They were, indeed, feathers. Hundreds, maybe even thousands of feathers fell from the sky, whiter than snow, purer than fresh rain. They glowed in the dimming light of the sun, ethereal-looking and holding an otherworldly appearance as they descended from the heavens.

Kevin felt exhausted as one of the feathers hit his head. It sank into his bones, this biting sense of fatigue. He slumped down, his eyes involuntarily closing, his breathing growing deep. Sleep. He wanted to sleep.

"Beloved?" a voice called out, but it was far away, like a fading echo.

With his strength leaving him, Kevin pitched forward. He didn't hit the ground. Something caught him. He felt arms wrap around his middle, pulling him into a warm bosom. Having been buried in this chest many times before, he knew, instinctively, that this was Lilian's chest. He sighed and let the Sandman take him.

He was so sleepy.

***

"Beloved? Beloved, what's wrong? Beloved?!"

For a moment, Lilian felt panic as Kevin slumped into her chest and closed his eyes, his legs and arms going limp. She kept her arms around him, holding him close as she called out to him, hoping that he would respond. He didn't. He remained silent.

Questions assailed her mind. What was going on? Why wasn't her beloved responding? She calmed down when she felt his warm breath against her chest. He was still alive, his breathing deep and even, almost as if he was… asleep…

Wait.

With a jolt traveling from the crown of her head down to her tails, Lilian looked around her to see that everyone else had fallen asleep as well. The people in the bleachers were dropping like flies. So, too, were the soccer players and the coaches. The only people who hadn't fallen asleep were her, Christine, and Iris. Lilian absently noticed the long, black, white-tipped fox tail retract from Christine's back and slither back underneath Iris's skirt.

Much like Kevin, Lindsay pitched forward. The yuki-onna caught the girl before she could hit the ground, but because Lindsay was significantly larger and weighed more, Christine couldn't hold her up. The lolita-clad girl slipped onto her knees with a grunt. Unable to maintain her hold, Christine fell back, and Lindsay slipped from her grasp.

"I got her," Iris said, a single tail shooting from her back. She caught Lindsay, the tail wrapping around the limp girl before gently setting her on the ground.

"Good catch," Lilian said. Iris gave her a thumbs up.

"What the hell is going on?!" Christine scowled as she climbed to her feet.

Lilian wanted to know the same thing. Her attention was attracted to another feather, which fell right in front of her. She blinked when it fell to the ground and then evaporated into light particles. Unlike Kotohime, Lilian wasn't much of a sensor, but even she could tell that these feathers were created with youki. A lot of youki.

It has to be powerful to affect even Kevin…

She frowned. "This is…"

"Kitsune Art: Daoists Nirvana," a voice said behind them.

Lilian turned around, Kevin still in her arms. Someone that she vaguely recognized was walking toward them.

"It's a rather powerful technique, a sleeping enchantment that requires at least three tails to use. I wouldn't expect a simple two-tails like you to understand how it works."

The woman before her had blonde hair and blue eyes. Her body was garbed in a white lolita dress with a lot of frills and ruffled sleeves. Her slipper-like shoes made nary a sound as she stalked across the grassy field. She had a young face, childish almost, which created a juxtaposition with her prominent chest and wide hips.

The woman stopped several yards away from her, Iris, and Christine, who moved to stand protectively in front of Lindsay. She didn't take her eyes off this girl, who Lilian finally recognized. It was the new student they had been talking about earlier. Fan Shen-something or other.

"What the fuck are you doing here?" asked Christine. Lilian

wouldn't have posed her question quite like that, but she wanted to know the same thing.

"Yeah, what the fuck are you doing here?"

... Okay, so maybe she would.

Three fox tails suddenly sprouted from underneath Fan's dress. Her human-shaped ears became triangular and furred, moving up her head until they rested closer to her crown. She raised a hand slowly, dramatically even, as if she was about to make some great proclamation. She extended a single finger and pointed at Lilian.

"Lilian Pnéyma, by orders of the Bodhisattva, you are hereby sentenced to death, and I, Fan Shénshèng, shall be your executioner."

A Fox's Revenge

Chapter 2

Assassins of the Shénshèng Clan

Lilian stared at the woman who was pointing at her, not quite comprehending the situation. Kevin was still asleep on her chest. She kept her arms wrapped around him so he wouldn't fall to the ground. Yet even though she and her mate were in a position that would have normally been quite enviable, she didn't take her eyes off the three-tailed kitsune in white lolita clothing.

Christine and Iris weren't near her at the moment. Her friend was getting Lindsay to safety, and Iris had disappeared. Lilian knew that her sister hadn't abandoned her. More than likely, Iris was waiting in the wings, hidden away to provide backup should the situation become untenable.

"I'm sorry," she began after a moment, "but who are you and why are you going to kill me?"

The woman, Fan-something-or-other, tripped over one of her tails. Lilian almost winced when the woman slammed face first into the ground. The lolita-clad vixen shot back to her feet and hissed at Lilian like an angry nekomata.

"Do you really not know why I'm here to kill you?! Are you really that stupid?!"

"Hey!" Lilian felt a surge of irritation bubbling within her gut. "I am not stupid! The people who call someone else stupid are the real stupid ones!"

"I'm not here to banter with you, girl!" The kitsune stood up to her full height. "I'm here to get revenge for what you did to Jiāoào."

"Jiāoào?"

Lilian blinked. Why did that name sound so familiar?

"Are you telling me that you don't remember?" Fan narrowed her eyes at Lilian. "Jiāoào Shénshèng is my beloved younger brother and Father's heir. It was proclaimed by Lord Inari himself that Jiāoào would receive the ninth tail upon his ninth century of life, thus becoming the next Bodhisattva. However, thanks to what you did to him, my beloved brother can't even speak, much less lead a clan. He's become completely inert, incapable of interacting with the world around him, and it's all because of you!"

Jiāoào... Jiāoào... that was... who was that again?

Lilian scrunched up her face as she tried to recall someone who went by the name of Jiāoào. It took a while because, to be quite frank, she hadn't thought about him in a very long time. She only vaguely remembered the boy who had kidnapped her, and that was only because she had killed someone during that time. She still felt guilty about that.

"Oh! Now I remember!" Lilian would have snapped her fingers, but since her arms were full of Kevin, she didn't. "Jiāoào was that jerk who kept trying to marry me! Ha, yeah, I remember him. My beloved beat the crap out of that loser after he kidnapped me!"

Fan went still. Her head tilted down. Shadows played across her face, somehow ominous. Her lips twitched into a macabre grin.

A shiver ran unbidden down Lilian's back.

Maybe I shouldn't have teased her so much...

"Did you just call my beloved little brother a loser?" she asked, her voice grating, like a katana scraping against concrete. Her body shuddered from head to tails in what Lilian could only assume was rage. "That does it... I'm through talking to you. It's time for you to die, Lilian Pnévma! **Celestial Art: Spears of Light!**"

Light particles gathered around Fan's tails. Three spears composed of bright white light appeared, long and sharp, with wicked points that looked like they could easily cut Lilian straight through. They were shaped like a qiāng, a Chinese spear. Each one was over twelve feet in length and possessed a leaf-shaped blade at one end.

Lilian's spine tingled. She couldn't let those hit her. If she did, they would kill her for sure.

Fan grabbed each spear with her tails and tossed them at Lilian with unparalleled speed. The spears all converged on Lilian's location...

... And then went straight through her as if she wasn't even there. Seconds after, the spears struck the ground and exploded in rays of light. The light died down, revealing two small marks on the ground. As the Lilian and Kevin before Fan vanished, the real Lilian hid Kevin behind the bleachers, and then snuck around until she was behind Fan.

She already had her next attack prepared.

"Celestial Art: Flare."

Fan leapt backwards as two compressed orbs of celestial youki flew at her from the front. The balls struck the ground, and then vanished like they had never existed.

"What?!" Fan shouted.

Standing behind the woman, Lilian would have grinned if such an action was in her nature. Two orbs of compressed light emerged from her tails, flickering to life. These weren't illusions. This was her real attack.

Fan swiveled her head as though it was on a spoke, eyes widening when two more spheres just like the ones that had vanished came at her from behind. They converged, slamming into her with impossible force, and then detonated into two brilliant domes of light. Like an exploding star going nova, the light expanded into a single, giant dome with a ten-foot radius, consuming everything within its sphere of influence.

Lilian wiped some sweat from her forehead. It was a lot more difficult to combine attack, defense, and misdirection during real combat than it was during her spars with Kotohime. She had also put a lot of youki into that last attack, so she felt a bit drained. Still, she had to give herself a pat on the back. That was a jolly good show, if she did say so herself.

When the power from her attack died down and the dome disappeared, nothing remained of the spot that Fan had been standing on. It was just a ten-foot crater with a perfectly smooth surface.

"Did I get her?" Lilian wondered out loud.

"Kitsune Art: Buddha's Paradox."

Lilian stiffened when the world around her changed. The grassy soccer field melted away, the bleachers disappeared. Everything vanished and was replaced by a barren wasteland, a world of craggy surfaces, a place so desolate that no life could exist there.

Within the center of this world sat a man. He was a very thin man, his frame emaciated to the point where Lilian could see his ribcage. He also didn't have any hair. Adorning his thin body was a simple golden robe that seemed to shine with divine light. He sat in a lotus position, his body perfectly still, his breath coming out so slowly that Lilian wasn't even sure if he was breathing.

He opened his eyes, revealing that he had neither iris nor pupil, and suddenly, the entire world exploded with violent energy. Fierce hurricane-like winds ripped at Lilian's body. They swirled around her, tearing into her flesh and flaying her skin. Blood spurted from an uncountable number of wounds that appeared all over her as though invisible blades were cutting into her. She opened her mouth to scream, but all the air was sucked from her lungs, which soon collapsed as they were deprived of oxygen.

From that point on, Lilian's life was filled with nothing but pain.

***

Kiara grit her teeth. Pain lanced through her back and chest as the kitsune kept moving, shoving his shoulder into her as he slammed her through wall after wall after wall. Her ears were ringing as brick and mortar shattered all around her like fragile glass. She tried to ignore the sound of her building breaking apart, along with the feeling of her chest being compressed and her back being battered, but even she could not stop the yelps from escaping her lips.

Even so...

"Don't think something like this will be enough to put me down!"

With a roar, Kiara raised her arm and slammed her elbow into the crown of the kitsune's head. The ground beneath his feet cracked. His knees buckled. Then, with a loud rumble, he crashed face first into the floor, which broke apart underneath the power of her blow. The entire floor they stood upon caved in. She and her foe fell to the next floor down.

Like any good warrior, Kiara landed on her feet. She wasn't that injured. Her body had a few scrapes, and her back felt like a car had dragged her across the road by her feet, but it was nothing serious.

As an inu, her body was far tougher than most other yōkai, able to withstand incredible punishment like nobody's business and return it tenfold. That said, she was surprised. Kitsune weren't physically strong unless they were using reinforcement, yet this one had managed to make her feel pain, and she could tell that he hadn't used reinforcement at all.

A Fox's Revenge

There has to be some kind of gimmick to his strength?

They'd dropped into her training room, which was on the opposite side of her office. Sweat dripped from her forehead. Had she been any later in counterattacking, she would have been sent outside.

Fragments from the previous floor littered the blue mat. She grimaced as she realized how much it was going to cost to effect repairs. The fox who'd attacked her lay several feet away, face down on the ground.

"So," Kiara started in a conversational tone of voice, "you gonna tell me why you're attacking me, or am I gonna have to break my foot off in your ass and beat it out of you?"

The kitsune swayed as he clambered to his feet. She felt satisfaction upon seeing the blood that ran down the man's face. Yet despite the head wound she'd inflicted, he didn't appear all that affected by the damage.

"Dog… dog. Dog. Dog! DOOOOOGGGG!"

Kiara clicked her tongue as the man unleashed another one of those unusual battle cries of his and bull rushed her. Since she didn't feel like taking another one of his attacks head on, she dove to the left, seconds before he would have slammed into her. He smashed into the wall behind her, which exploded into hundreds of tiny fragments that peppered Kiara and forced her to raise a hand, shielding her eyes.

"DOOOOGGGG!"

The kitsune came at her again, and Kiara dove aside once more. Another wall was destroyed. Kiara felt a surge of irritation. Did this idiot not realize how much damage he was causing? It was going to take tens of thousands of dollars to fix those damn walls!

Deciding to teach the kitsune a lesson, Kiara widened her stance. She spread her legs wide and bent her knees at 45-degree angles. She tucked her fist into her torso and called upon her youki, which surged into existence, flaring around her body like fire. With her youki unleashed, Kiara felt power flooding through her veins. She channeled the red aura into her fist, which became engulfed in a bright red light that all but blocked her appendage from view.

"DOOOOOGGGG!"

The kitsune charged at her again. Time seemed to slow as Kiara centered herself. She studied her opponent. His dark hair flew back, his square jaw quivered in inexplicable rage, and his eyes bulged from his sockets. His eyes had become bloodshot, a dark and angry crimson filled with a hatred that could not be contained.

A Fox's Revenge

She didn't know if this rage was directed at her or if it was at all inu in general, though she did wonder why he had decided to attack her. Well, it didn't matter right now. All that mattered was putting this rabid yōkai down. She could worry about the how's and whys later.

"HYA!"

With a war cry of her own, Kiara unleashed a swift punch. The fist hyperextended. Red youki exploded from it, a cataract of overpowering energy that surged forth like a massive tidal wave. The mass of energy slammed into the four-tails and detonated with the violence of a maelstrom.

Kiara's world was engulfed in red light.

***

When Kotohime returned to consciousness, it was to see the apartment where she and her family lived in ruins. The entire building had been reduced to rubble. It looked like several giant hands had smashed into it from all sides. Now it was nothing more than a mountain of debris. Smoke rose from this mountain in plumes. Nothing was left.

"W-what...?"

Kotohime grunted as she pushed herself up. Her body was sore from where she had been smashed against the ground. If she hadn't enhanced herself with reinforcement at the last moment, she may have very well died.

She stood up, her body swaying back and forth precariously. Liquid stung her left eye, and it took her a second to realize that she was bleeding. It ran freely down the left side of her face, matting her hair to her forehead and forcing the eye closed.

A sound alerted her to something happening. A pained grunt caused her to turn her head. Her remaining good eye widened when she saw her sister being held in the grip of a giant kitsune with five tails. He had a hand around Kirihime's throat, clenching her esophagus hard enough to make her veins bulge. Kirihime struggled within his grip, kicking him with all her might and trying to slap him with her tails, but she clearly wasn't at one hundred percent. The tails were weakening. Kirihime's hands were slowing down. Her legs were starting to twitch and spasm. If this kept up, she would die.

Kotohime picked up her katana, which lay on the ground beside her feet. There was no time to think. All she could do was act.

"Water Art: Blade of the Water Lily."

Water coalesced around Kotohime's katana, hardening and increasing her blade's sharpness, as she shot forward.

"Ikken Hisatsu. Anawoakeru no Sen."

It didn't take her long to reach the man holding her sister. Before he could so much as think about using Kirihime as a shield, she thrust her blade forward hundreds of times within a single second. The kitsune dropped her sister and leapt back to avoid being impaled. Even so, blood flew from several shallow cuts that appeared on his skin.

With her wary eyes stuck on the man before her, who seemed in no rush to initiate more violence, Kotohime asked her sister: "Are you all right?"

"Y-yes…" Kirihime coughed, holding a hand to her throat. "I'm fine. I coated my throat with water and hardened it with my youki. Most of the damage is cosmetic." She indicated the bruises on her skin as though to emphasize her words.

Kotohime wasn't sure if she entirely believed her sister, but she also knew they didn't have the luxury of arguing.

"Sister… that man… he… My Lady… she… she was in the apartment…"

A sharp pain struck her heart. Like an icy fist, it gripped her and refused to let go. Yet even with the heartache filling her chest, she did not remove her eyes from the man, who continued staring at them with a silent gaze.

"I know… there isn't anything we can do for Camellia-sama right now." It hurt to say, but she had no choice. They needed to focus, or both of them would be killed. "All we can do is avenge her, and avenge her we will."

The sound of feet shuffling against the ground echoed all around her as Kirihime, stumbling like she had a concussion, stood back up. Kotohime didn't pay much attention to her sister. She couldn't afford to. To look away from an enemy was to present them with an invitation to attack.

She studied the man before her in more detail. He was quite tall, standing at least several heads above her. His body was composed entirely of muscle, the kind that she expected to see on an inu or an oni, not a kitsune. His hair was dark enough to be considered black, as were his eyes, yet the trace amounts of yōkai coming from him were celestial in nature. He had five tails.

She frowned as something clicked within her mind. "Are you a member of the Shénshèng Clan?"

The man's nod confirmed it. "I am indeed. My name is Li, and you are Kotohime, formerly known as Tsukihime, the Blood Moon Princess of the now destroyed Ślina Clan, and that is your younger sister."

"So you know who we are, which means you are deliberately targeting us."

"Not exactly. To be perfectly honest, I would rather not battle you at all, if I can help it," Li admitted easily, which put her on guard. The fact that he was so willing to let her know something like this made her wary. Why tell her anything? Why not just attack her? Unless she wasn't the target, which would mean…

"You're after Lilian-sama."

"Indeed we are," Li said. Kotohime's body tensed, but Lee moved faster than she could react and was suddenly standing just a few feet in front of her, his monstrous form staring her down with the kind of expression one might use when peering at an insect. "I would like to ask that you not interfere with my charge's mission. You can either remain where you are and wait, in which case, I shall not attack, or you can try to get past me, in which case, I shall put you and your sister down."

Kotohime glared at the one known as Li. "I choose neither of those options. As you are also a bodyguard, you should know that the duty of a bodyguard is to always protect their charge and ensure that person's continued safety. If the person you are supposed to protect is threatening the safety of the person I am protecting, then it means I have no choice but to go through you."

Li's silent stare would have unnerved most, but Kotohime was not most people. She met his stare evenly, her rage at the danger that Lilian and her mate were facing even now allowing her to meet the more powerful kitsune's look head on.

"I see. Very well, then…"

Releasing a deep breath as though expelling his emotions along with it, Li shifted his stance, widening it and adopting a strong combat stance used by Daoist monks. She recognized it as one of the more advanced forms of Wushu.

"… Get past me, if you can," he said, gesturing for her to bring it on.

***

It was unbearable. Every muscle in her body felt like it was being ripped apart at the molecular level. Her eyes had long since stopped being able to see. Her ears could no longer hear. Her brain was on the verge of shutting down. Everything hurt. Pain was all she knew. She just wanted the pain to stop. For everything to stop. Why wouldn't it stop? Why wasn't it stopping?!

"Lily-pad!"

Lilian gasped and, as suddenly as the pain had come, it disappeared.

"Lilian?! Lily-pad? Can you hear me? Are you all right?!"

"What... what...?"

Lilian blinked several times, eyelids rapidly fluttering as she looked around, her mind feeling sluggish as she tried to comprehend what she was seeing. She no longer stood in that barren wasteland. She was back on the soccer field, and her sister was standing in front of her. So was Christine. Both of them looked concerned. When did they... how did they... what was...

"A-an illusion," she rasped, her throat sore as though she'd screamed herself hoarse. "It was all an illusion."

"Tch!" Several yards away, Fan stood on the grassy field with her arms crossed in annoyance. "A few more seconds under that illusion and you would have been brain dead, just like my dear little brother."

Lilian grimaced as she realized how much trouble she was in. She had known there were some powerful illusions out there. Even so, she hadn't expected something like that. What made it worse was that the illusion she had been placed under wasn't even that strong, comparatively speaking. Fan only had three tails, after all.

That still left her with a problem. Her opponent had three tails, which meant she was not only far stronger than Lilian, but she also had more techniques up her sleeve. It was definitely a good thing that Christine and Iris were here. Then again, if they were here, then that meant...

"Where's Kevin and Lindsay?" she asked. Her ears were ringing and she had a terrible headache, the consequences of being trapped inside of that illusion for so long.

She couldn't remember what happened to Kevin. During the start of the battle, she had cast an illusion over herself and Kevin, set Kevin by the bleachers, and then—nothing. She'd been hit by Fan's illusion and everything after that was blank.

"Don't worry about the stud." Iris didn't take her eyes off Fan. "He and the dyke are safe."

"I wish you wouldn't call my friend a dyke, you stupid whore," Christine bit out harshly.

"That's not really an insult to me, you know," Iris shot back. "And such words mean very little when coming from a prudish loli like you."

"At least I'm not willing to jump everything with two legs and a dick!"

"Now, now, we both know that isn't true. The only dick I'll be jumping any time soon is the stud's, and that'll only happen if my Lily-pad joins in."

"Gods, you're so disgusting!"

Lilian almost sighed as the two began arguing back and forth. Didn't they realize that they were in the middle of a battle? They probably did, but they just didn't care. She really wished they would stop, though, as their bickering was giving her a headache.

That illusion messed me up more than I thought.

"ENOUGH!" Fan's enraged shout echoed across the field. "If you two are going to stand in my way, then I'll just have to kill you along with that damn bitch who refused my beloved brother!"

"I noticed you talk about your beloved brother a lot," Iris pointed out. "Are you some kind of brocon? Got a bit of a brother complex? I'm not judging, but I have to admit it's kind of weird to have a thing for your little brother."

"This coming from the skank who wants to get into her sister's pants," Christine pointed out.

"Ooh, you're getting wittier by the second."

"RAGH!" Fan screamed before her tails curled around her front, their tips converging into a single point. **"Celestial Art: Ch'ang-o's Celestial Canon!"**

Light gathered near the tips of her tails, forming into the shape of a sphere, which grew larger and larger until it completely blocked their view of Fan. Then, suddenly and without warning, it shrank, seconds before becoming a large beam of pure light that shot toward them with the speed of a *Gundam* undergoing atmospheric reentry.

Lilian reinforced her body and leapt away at the same time as Iris grabbed Christine and jumped high into the air. While they were in midair, Christine conjured half a dozen shards of ice, which she launched at Fan. The three-tailed kitsune was impaled by three of the six shards— or so Lilian thought.

When their foe vanished, Lilian's head swiveled in search of Fan.

She couldn't find the woman, however, as it seemed her foe had completely disappeared. It was only when a bright white light appeared behind her sister and her friend that she realized where her adversary was.

"Iris! Christine! She's behind you!"

"Celestial Art: Laozi's Chains!"

Lilian's warning came too late, or rather, Christine and Iris couldn't do anything because they were still in midair. A dozen chains shot from the ground, their ethereal bodies composed entirely of golden youki. They soared high into the air, over the heads of Christine and Iris, before falling back to spear the ground. The one dozen chains crisscrossed over each other, forming a net, which then retracted, taking the pair with them. Christine and Iris were slammed into the ground.

Their screams pierced the air as they were smashed against the ground. The earth around them dented. Cracks spread from the point of impact. Lilian gritted her teeth and angry tears sprang to her eyes as she listened to their agonized cries. She didn't have a chance to do anything for them, though, as Fan used her distracted state to attack her next.

"Celestial Art: Yin-Yang Entrapment!"

A circle appeared underneath Lilian, white on one side and black on the other, with a black and white dot inside of each opposite half. A *yin-yang* circle. She had absolutely no idea what it did, but she also had no intention of finding out. Reinforcing her legs, she launched herself out of the circle just in time to avoid a giant golden cage that appeared around it.

"Celestial Art: Taoist's Point!"

Lilian did not have enough time to fully evade the qiāng that Fan created and threw at her. It grazed the left side of her torso. She hissed in pain as foreign youki invaded the wound, burning her. It hurt a lot, more than she thought it would, considering she was also a Celestial Kitsune. She did her best to counteract the damage by sending her own youki to the damaged flesh, but even though her wound began healing, it still felt like something was burning her from the inside out.

"Celestial Art: Laozi's Chains!"

Before she had a chance to recover, two chains burst from the ground on either side of her. They wrapped around her arms, tightening until it felt like her arms were being squeezed into a thick paste, and then they retracted back into the ground, forcing her arms wide and pulling her down. Lilian struggled to escape from their indomitable grasp. She did everything she could, but no matter how much she fought against the chains, nothing happened. She was trapped.

Fan walked up to her. "You've given me quite a bit of trouble, girl. Far more trouble than a two-tailed brat like you should. However, it doesn't matter now. You should have known that a kitsune with two tails is no match for a three-tails like myself. That's how the world works."

Lilian glared at Fan as light coalesced around one of her opponent's tails, once again taking the shape of a qiāng, which her tail curled around.

"And now, Lilian Pnéyma, you will die."

"Yeah, I don't think so," Lilian said.

Fan hesitated at the confidence in Lilian's voice. That hesitation was all Lilian needed to launch her own attack.

"Celestial Art: Orbs of an Evanescent Realm."

Nine orbs of light appeared around Fan, surrounding her. Mere seconds after they were formed, the orbs shot toward the woman, converging on her. Fan leapt into the air just before they struck the area where she had been standing. This didn't stop Lilian's attacks.

Lilian hadn't been resting on her laurels these past few months, unlike a certain Void Kitsune. She had been following Kevin's example. Every day after school she'd trained with Kotohime for at least an hour, sparring against the much stronger and talented kitsune. Months of fighting. Hours of sweating and bleeding. Lilian had improved, bit by bit.

One of the areas where she had improved on was this technique: **Orbs of an Evanescent Realm.** When she had first created this technique, she could only control two orbs at any given time.

Now she could control all nine at the same time.

The orbs didn't collide. They curved, a full 90-degree tilt, and shot upwards, toward Fan. Lilian didn't know if her opponent was surprised, but regardless, Fan reacted with incredible speed, creating a pair of daggers from her youki. She used the golden daggers to try and cut through Lilian's spheres. In return, Lilian made her orbs dart all around the woman, making them flit in and out of Fan's vision, frustrating the woman as she slashed and hacked at them to no avail.

Of course, Lilian's technique was just a distraction.

"Void Art: Rain of Oblivion," another voice called out.

Fan looked up as nearly one hundred black flames appeared above her, their forms flickering with a strange sort of sentience and radiating an insatiable hunger that made her shiver. Even Lilian, who knew the creator of those flames, felt fear pierce her soul. For Celestial Kitsune like them, the sight of the Void, a power that negated the very concepts that created their world, was enough to make them tremble.

From where she and Christine were bound to the ground, Iris grinned. "It's time for you to burn."

The flames descended in mass, converging on Fan's location. Lilian was positive that this attack would do the woman in. She was floating in midair, with no way to dodge. She couldn't avoid this attack. The flames struck her without mercy, over and over, lighting her body on fire like a dark beacon. Fan screamed and screamed as the void fire ate her body.

Lilian looked down as Fan was eaten, feeling sick to her stomach, yet relieved that they had won. The chains around her body disappeared, and so, too, did the chains pinning Christine and Iris to the ground. She stood up, gingerly making sure that her arms hadn't been dislocated. She had reinforced them with youki to keep them from being pulled from their sockets, but that didn't mean having those chains yanking on her arms hadn't hurt.

Upon confirming that her arms were fine, Lilian looked up to ask Christine and Iris if they were okay.

"Are you two all right—gya!"

She didn't even get to finish her sentence when Iris pounced on her, sending them both to the ground. Lilian landed on the cold, wet grass, her back becoming slick with due. Iris, lying on top of her, began nuzzling Lilian's chest, liberally shoving her face into Lilian's superlative bosoms.

"Oh, Lily-pad, I'm so glad you're all right!"

"W-what are you—get off me!"

"I was so worried when I saw those chains wrap around you, though it also gave me an idea!"

"I don't want to hear your idea! Now get! Off! Of! Me!"

"I was thinking about how sexy you looked wrapped up in those chains. There was something innately appealing about seeing you chained to the ground, completely helpless and unable to resist. And that gave me the idea that maybe we could do a little bondage play. What do you think? Are you up for a little BDSM?"

"No! Why would I want to have you tie me up in chains?!"

"The stud might like it."

Lilian paused for a moment to consider that. Would Kevin like tying her up in chains and having his wicked way with her? She didn't know, though she couldn't deny that the idea was appealing, and it conjured some awfully sexy images.

She lay on the bed, her arms and legs chained up and tied to the bedposts. There was a ball gag in her mouth. It kept her from talking and caused drool to leak around the corners of her lips. The cold air from the ceiling fan overhead hit her bare skin, making her already hard nipples feel like they could cut through diamonds.
She was naked.
Straddling her hips was an equally naked Kevin, his defined chest, broad shoulders, and six-pack abs on display. She could feel his erection resting against her stomach. He wore a crooked smirk that she'd never seen on him before. However, she couldn't deny that he wore it well. He looked sexy as hell, like Gokudera Hayato, only hotter.
"I have to admit, you look absolutely ravishing like this, Lilian. I love seeing you lying helpless before me." Kevin reached out and grasped her left breast. A thrill of pleasure shot through her as he roughly fondled her tit; the act forced a moan from her mouth, muffled by the ball gag. Kevin saw this and leaned down, nibbling on her ear as he continued playing with her breast, whispering, "I'm going to explore every inch of your body, Lilian. Every nook. Every cranny. I'm going to play with you and make you cum repeatedly, and you won't be able to do anything but take it. What do you think of that... Lilian?"

"..."
"Hey, Lilian?"
"..."
"Lily-pad?"
"..."
"Would you wake up already?!"
"I think she's broken."
"Dammit, listen to me when I'm talking to you!"
"Don't worry, tsun-loli. I've got this. Oh, look. Kevin's running this way and he doesn't have his shirt on!"
"What?! Really?!"
Lilian turned about in search of her beloved mate—only to realize that she'd been had when she noticed that Kevin wasn't anywhere in sight. She tossed her sister a pout, crossing her arms under her chest and

puffing up her cheeks, which swelled like a pair of hot air balloons.

"That wasn't very nice," she muttered, her cheeks still fat from air.

"Sorry, but I had to get your attention somehow." Iris's devious smile told Lilian that her sister wasn't sorry at all. "Also, your nose is bleeding, just thought I'd let you know. And you're drooling."

"Eh?"

Lilian flushed in embarrassment when she realized that her sister was right. The warm feeling of blood trickling down her nose mixed with the coldness of saliva dripping from the corners of her mouth. She quickly wiped the blood and drool off, and then tried to ignore her sister's grinning face.

"W-whatever. Let's go wake up Kevin and Lindsay. Then we can get out of here."

"Oh, no. You three aren't going anywhere," a portentous voice echoed across the soccer field.

Lilian felt a thrill of shock run down her spine. There was no way that woman could still be alive! She had been consumed by the Void!

"Celestial Art: Yin-Yang Entrapment."

Another yin-yang circle appeared underneath her, Christine, and Iris —one that was far bigger than the previous circle. The circle glowed with a brilliant evanescent sheen before light erupted all around them, shooting high into the air, over their heads, and engulfing them to create a cage.

Lilian's body seized up. She didn't know what was happening, but it felt like every muscle in her body had stopped working, as if they'd all been frozen solid. Standing beside her, Christine and Iris also struggled to escape the strange confinement.

Fan appeared before them, walking into Lilian's field of vision. She was completely unharmed. The woman didn't have so much as a burn, ruffle, or even a smudge on her. She moved to stand in front of Lilian and her friends, and then turned to face them, hands on her hips and a smug expression etched across her face.

"I have to admit, I greatly underestimated you. You have proven to be far, far more trouble than any two-tails has a right to be." Fan frowned. "I suppose that is why Father did not object when my beloved little brother sought to mate with you. Though he should have known that the daughter of a traitor wasn't worth the risk, regardless of her talent as a kitsune."

It required a lot of effort, but Lilian forced her mouth to move. She channeled youki through her jaw and forced herself to speak. "How... how..."

"You are curious to know how I survived that last attack?" Fan's self-satisfied smirk pissed Lilian off. She wanted to wipe that arrogant look from the woman's face. "It's simple. You were never fighting me to begin with. Didn't you wonder why all my attacks were lacking in power? A kitsune with three tails has twice the amount of power that a kitsune with two tails has, yet all my attacks did the same amount of damage as one of your attacks. Why is that?"

Lilian thought about it. She hadn't noticed it when they were fighting, but now that Fan mentioned it, she had noticed a distinct lack of damage done by Fan's attacks. Back when she, Iris, and Kevin fought against Seth Naraka, all of the attacks launched by Seth—except those designed specifically to attack the spirit—had caused massive amounts of property damage. Yet this woman, who was also a three-tails, hadn't done nearly as much damage with her attacks. It was weird. Why would her attacks not cause as much environmental destruction? Unless...

"You were never fighting me to begin with."

Her eyes widened. "C... c... clo..."

"Give the girl a metal." Fan's mocking applause filled the nearly still atmosphere. "Yes, that is correct. I don't particular enjoy battles. Fighting is such an inelegant and ugly thing, something that a dog would do. That's why I created a light clone to play with you. I was hoping it would be able to kill you, so that I wouldn't have to sully my hands. However, you have proven to be stronger than I anticipated. A disappointment, really, but not totally unexpected. I believe those humans you are so fond of have an old adage: if you want something done right, you have to do it yourself."

Lilian listened as the lolita-clad vixen rambled on. This bimbo must have really enjoyed the sound of her own voice. However, Fan's continued talking also meant that Lilian had time to think of a way out of this.

She couldn't move, and her sister and Christine were also frozen, which meant they wouldn't be moving anytime soon either. If anything, they would have an even harder time than she did, as neither of them had celestial blood flowing through their veins. She was the only one who could break them out of this prison.

Unfortunately, she didn't know the first thing about this particular technique. Different clans used different techniques, which were based on the principles, theories, and religions of their home country. All of the Shénshèng Clan techniques were inspired by a combination of Buddhism and Taoist teachings. This changed the entire way they used youki. The flow, the way it was woven into their techniques, everything was completely different from the way she used her youki, which was far more unrefined and crude, since she didn't have anyone to teach her.

"Now, then, Lilian Pnévma." She was startled out of her thoughts when Fan raised a hand and pointed at her. "You, your friend, and your sister are going to die for me."

***

Kiara didn't know what to think.

There was a general rule about yōkai powers and how they worked. Inu were physically strong and had the ability to turn their youki into a powerful weapon, but they were susceptible to mind attacks and tended to act recklessly. Oni were brute strength personified but incredibly violent and nearly mindless. Yuki-onna possessed powers over ice but were weak against fire and heat. Tengu could fly and control air currents, but they could do little against electric attacks. Kitsune were masters at manipulation and illusions, and they had a versatile range of specialized techniques. That said, they were not physically powerful unless using reinforcement, and that ability had too many limitations to be truly useful...

... Or at least, that's how it was supposed to be.

"DOOOOGGGG!"

The fox's enraged battle cry echoed throughout the room as he slammed his fist into her face. The power behind his attack was unbelievable. Kiara could feel her jaw cracking under the assault as she was sent flying backwards, crashing through several walls, which did little to slow her down. It felt like she'd been hit by a speeding bullet train.

After smashing through what had to be six walls, Kiara found herself sailing through the air, staring up at a high ceiling. Thick metal girders and a massive network of rails and pipes, along with several fluorescent bulbs and ceiling fans, stared back at her. Then she found herself falling, crashing into something hard and blowing it to smithereens.

"M-Ms. Kiara!"

The frightened shriek had Kiara turning her head. Her receptionist, Michelle Blanchard, stared at her in horror, eyes wide and mouth agape. She then looked around and realized that she was at the front entrance to her gym. The passing of another second made her realize that what she had slammed into was the front desk, the pieces of which now lay scattered along the ground.

"Michelle," Kiara began in a controlled, even voice, "could you do me a favor and have everyone currently inside of the gym evacuate?"

"U-um, o-okay," Michelle said with a hurried nod.

"Thank you."

As Michelle ran off to begin the evacuation, Kiara stood up and brushed herself off. Then she tilted her head up to observe the hole she had made in her wall. Glaring at the damage done, internally calculating how much this was going to cost to fix, Kiara rushed forward and leapt back up to the floor she had fallen from.

Her foe spotted her the moment she landed in the hall.

"DOOOOGGGG!"

"Is that all this idiot says?" Kiara muttered to herself. Throughout their entire battle, he'd not said anything else. It was like the only thing he could do was yell "dog."

He came at her again, the kitsune whose name she didn't even know. Grimacing, she rushed him the same way that he did her. She couldn't allow him to move past this point, not until the gym was evacuated. She should have had everyone evacuate sooner, but this buffoon of a fox hadn't let her so much as sound the alarm.

She and the kitsune clashed again. Her fist burned with the red aura of her youki, slamming against the four-tailed avatar of rage. Kiara snarled as he met her attacks head on, literally. Her fist smashed into his head, yet he didn't budge. He didn't even flinch, as if he couldn't feel pain. What's more, it wasn't the kitsune giving ground; it was her. Despite putting all of her strength into that attack, she was the one sliding backwards.

Something is wrong here. Something is seriously, seriously wrong.

Kitsune weren't supposed to be this strong. Even Kotohime couldn't match her in a contest of strength. That fox was a damn good fighter, but she used finesse, not strength, to defeat her foes. Sure, she also had powerful specialized techniques that could wreak havoc on people, but the person Kiara was fighting hadn't used a single technique.

72

He was only using physical strength.

Realizing that, for whatever reason, her own strength wasn't getting the job done, Kiara decided to change tactics. She removed her fist from the kitsune's head. With her own strength no longer impeding her foe, he shot forward like a missile.

Kiara ducked before he could run over her like a stampede of angry onikuma. She grabbed his shirt as he passed her and, with a grunt of exertion, flipped the fox over her back and slammed him into the ground with all the force she could muster.

The results were catastrophic. The floor underneath them buckled, suddenly and swiftly. Cracks appeared along the floor's surface as the carpet was ripped apart like paper. Kiara leapt away from the kitsune just in time to avoid falling to ground level as the entire floor collapsed. Her opponent wasn't so lucky; he fell through the hole, falling fourteen yards down and crashing into the ground below.

"Hmm…"

Kiara looked down the hole to see that her opponent had crashed into several stationary bikes, smashing them beneath his frame. Her eyes narrowed when she noticed how the metal frame from one of the bikes had twisted and punctured straight through the kitsune's stomach. Despite the blood gushing from the wound, he didn't seem to notice the injury as he stood to his feet and swayed with a drunken gait.

So, he's physically strong, but he's vulnerable to piercing attacks… I see. So that's how it is.

Grinning, she leapt down the hole and landed several feet from her opponent. "I see what's going on now. You're one of those rare kitsune who have the ability to enter a berserker rage. It's a unique power that grants you incredible physical strength at the cost of taking away your ability to use normal kitsune techniques. However…"

Kiara shifted her stance as the kitsune's bloodshot eyes locked onto her. She hadn't believed his eyes could bulge any more than they already were, but she was proven wrong when they suddenly looked ready to burst from their sockets.

"DOOOOGGGG!"

His battle cry tore from his throat, the only thing his enraged mind would allow him to say. He rushed at her, not even bothering to pull out the bike handle that had speared him through his back and stomach. His four tails swatted the remaining bikes around him out of the way as he bull-charged her.

Kiara waited until he was nearly upon her before reacting. She sidestepped his attack, moving left. Then she latched onto his wrist and twisted his arm, using his own momentum to her advantage. The four-tailed kitsune was flung off his feet, tossed into the air, and flipped end over end. Kiara grunted as she exerted more force and slammed him into the ground.

The floor underneath him cratered. A shockwave from where he'd hit reverberated throughout the bike room. Stationary bicycles were sent flying in all directions. Some smashed against the walls, others the ceiling. A few even hit the glass mirror at the front of the room, shattering it with impunity and sending sharp fragments spraying across the interior like water from a fire hydrant.

Kiara let go of the kitsune's wrist and pulled her hand back toward her head. Blazing red youki covered her hand, straightened into a knife's edge, which she then thrust forward, piercing the kitsune's chest. Blood flowed from the wound, gushing out like oil from an abundant mine. The kitsune's eyes bulged further. His tongue lolled out of his gaping mouth, which had opened in a scream, even though no scream emerged, just a rasping sound that reminded her of a vacuum sucking in nothing. His body twitched and spasmed and jerked for several seconds. She watched with merciless eyes as his eyes rolled into the back of his head and his body went limp.

She pulled her hand from the wound on his chest. That last attack had pierced her opponent's heart. Her hand was coated in warm, thick blood.

The coppery scent made her nose wrinkle as she flung the ichor off her hand. As she stood to her full height, Kiara eyed her now dead foe with a thoughtful frown.

"However, all that strength is useless if you're too enraged to make rational decisions," Kiara finished her earlier thought. "Hmm... I could be mistaken, but the feel of his youki reminds me of the boya's mate. That means he's a Celestial Kitsune. Why would a kitsune who I've never met be after me?"

It was true that inu and kitsune usually didn't get along—her relationship with Kotohime and the vixens living with Kevin notwithstanding. Even so, no kitsune would be dumb enough to attack her in the open like this. The only reason she could think of for a kitsune to attack her was...

"Was if I was never the true target, and this person was merely sent

74

to dispose of me before I could potentially interfere with whatever their true objective is. Berserkers like this always have a handler, someone who keeps them on a tight leash. If that is true, then the one who was holding this one's leash let them loose on me and is likely attacking their true target."

She rubbed her face. She could already feel the headache coming on.

"And the only people I can see being their target is the kid and his girl. Dammit, boya, you really are a troublesome brat."

***

The longer the battle continued, the more Kotohime realized that she was in trouble. This man, Li, was simply too powerful. She and her sister had tried everything they could think of to defeat him, yet it all seemed to be for naught. Sword techniques were rendered useless, elemental attacks were impotent, nothing they did could even touch him. Outside of her surprise attack at the beginning, they had yet to so much as scratch him, whereas he'd already inflicted quite a bit of damage to both her and Kirihime.

"Ikken Hisatsu. Sen Suiryoku."

Kotohime reinforced her arms with youki, increasing the strength of her muscles and the speed at which she could move. Power pumped through her body as she attacked. Her arms became indistinct blurs, her blade mere flashes of light. She attacked the man from every conceivable direction, over and over, uncountable and untraceable. It was almost like she was attacking in several places at once.

None of her swings hit.

Her sword seemed to go straight through Li's body, as though all she was attacking were his afterimages. It was frustrating. No matter how many times she cut into him, nothing happened. What was going on? Why weren't her attacks working?

When her last attack missed, something large slammed into her chest. Kotohime didn't even have time to gasp in agonic asphyxia as her body was lifted off the ground.

"Sister! That does it! You're dead! **Water Art: Three-Tailed Crystal Whips!**"

Before Li could do Kotohime further harm, Kirihime attacked him. Three whips composed of water had formed on her tails, glittering aquamarine hardened into several sharp crystals attached together like

75

chain links. They moved in complex and never-ending patterns as Kirihime attacked Li from all sides: above, below, in front, behind, the left, the right. They were everywhere. Despite this, none of the whips hit. Li's body simply seemed to blur out of focus, and the whips passed straight through him.

Landing on the ground, Kotohime held a hand to her chest, wincing as she felt the nasty bruise forming on her skin. Her regenerative abilities, derived from her River Kitsune blood, would heal it, but if something wasn't done, she'd eventually run out of youki.

What sort of technique is he using?

She watched as Li seemingly phased through Kirihime's whips like a ghost. After dodging, Li hunched over and, like snakes attacking their prey, the five tails jutting from his tailbone leapt forward. They were heading straight for Kirihime.

Knowing that her sister couldn't dodge, Kotohime rushed forward, interposing herself between her sister and their opponent.

"Ikken Hisatsu. Tsukuyomi no Hogo."

Kotohime's sword became an indecipherable blur of silver. She wove her blade through the airspace between them, the silver edge flashing around her and her sister to create an impenetrable barrier. This was one of her most powerful defensive techniques—**Tsukuyomi's Defense**. No technique had ever been able to breach it, be they elemental or otherwise. It should have been enough to defend against a few reinforced tails.

It was not.

Kotohime couldn't figure out what happened. Her defense was perfect. Her blade created a literal wall that nothing should have been able to slip through. Yet somehow, someway, the tails that sought to attack her and her sister phased right through her defensive perimeter, slammed into her chest with incredible force, and threw her into Kirihime.

She and Kirihime flew backwards, slammed into the ground with bone-jarring force, and tumbled across the blacktop for several feet before coming to a stop. Pushing herself into a crouch, Kotohime gasped as she held a hand to her torso. That last attack had cracked a few ribs. Wincing, she slowly stumbled to her feet, and then looked at her opponent, who hadn't moved from his spot the entire time.

Something is going on here. That technique reminds me of the Ghost Step, but I know for a fact that this man is a Celestial Kitsune.

Ghost Step is a spirit technique. Is it speed? No. He's not moving at all. It's like his body simply phases in and out of existence. An illusion maybe?

"Are you all right, Kirihime?" she asked.

"Y-yes." Kirihime winced as she stood up. "I am fine, sister."

"Can you still fight?"

Out of her peripheral vision, Kotohime saw her sister's malicious grin, a smile that showed off sharp canines and was filled with the intent to cause harm. It only ever came out when she was in battle or hunting people for leather. Kotohime referred to this look as Kirihime's yandere smile.

"Are you really asking me that?" Kirihime licked off the blood that dribbled down her mouth. "I'm more than capable of still fighting."

"Good. Then let us try a different approach."

"Right. **Water Art: Drown in Despair.**"

Drown in Despair was one of her sister's illusions. As bodyguards, they tended to focus more on attacks that did physical damage, but like any good kitsune, they knew at least a couple dozen illusions. This particular one made someone think they were drowning. It affected the part of their brain that dealt with breathing, shutting off the connection between their mind and their lungs, and then projecting the illusion that they were wrapped in chains while sitting at the bottom of a lake.

"Water Art: Dance of Timeless Erosion."

Kotohime channeled youki through her tails. Water gathered around Li, thousands of crystalline droplets that glittered beautifully in the sunlight. These thousands of droplets soon began to spin around the man like a tornado, extending over his head and closing around him, encasing him inside of a dome of water that spun so fast it could slice straight through rock and steel. The dome then shrank, growing smaller and smaller, grinding down Li's body until nothing was left.

At least, that's what should have happened. What really happened was that Kotohime's attack phased right through Li, who stood in place, seemingly unaffected by her attack or Kirihime's illusion. His clothing remained unruffled and pristine. Kotohime couldn't see a single drop of blood anywhere.

"It was a good idea," Li said in the same calm tone that he had been using since the start of their fight. "Trapping me within an illusion, and then casting a technique meant to erode my body, grinding me into mulch similar to the way a river eventually eats away at the shore. On anyone else, I dare say this combination would have succeeded. However, such techniques will not work on me."

The way he made that statement, so calm and sure of himself, made Kotohime narrow her eyes. Li wasn't taking their battle seriously at all. He never attacked her or her sister outright. All he'd done was counter their attacks. Did that mean his technique was some kind of counter technique similar to the *Gyakujutsu* used by shinobi of Japan's *Meji* era to counter yōkai techniques?

I need to see more of this man's skill.

"Do you know why I am the one fighting you and not one of my associates?" Li asked suddenly, making her blink.

"Because you have five tails?"

"A good guess, but that's not entirely accurate." Li's facial expression did not change in the slightest as he spoke. It remained calm, impassive, like a block of ice shaped into the face of a person. "It is because among all those sent here to deal with your charge, I am the one most suited to combating yōkai that use physical and specialized techniques."

At the mention of her charge, Kotohime felt worry worm its way into her gut. She tried to keep calm, however, knowing that defeating Lilian would not be easy unless the kitsune fighting her had four tails or more. Her charge had Kevin, Christine, and Iris with her. She had faith that together they could, if nothing else, at least survive long enough for her to reach their side.

Kotohime took a calming breath as she slid into an *iaidō* stance. Beside her, Kirihime conjured a set of water daggers and twirled them around, her grin widening until it threatened to split her face in half. Kotohime felt a single drop of sweat trail down her face.

I am glad to see that my sister is at least having a good time, but I hope she remembers not to lose herself to her own battle lust.

"You may indeed be stronger than I," Kotohime declared in a confident voice. "However, it does not matter. Even if you manage to indefinitely hold off myself and my sister, you will not accomplish your goal."

For the first time since their battle had started, Li frowned. "And why is that?"

Kotohime's eyes danced with delightful mirth as she smiled at the man. "Because Lilian-sama is not alone, and I doubt whoever you sent after her can deal with someone who was personally trained in combat

A Fox's Revenge

by Kiara-san and Heather-san."

***

"Now, then, Lilian Pnéyma, you, your friend, and your sister are going to die for me."

The words rang with an ominous finality, echoing across the soccer field like a thousand voices declaring their inevitable end at the same time.

Lilian would have loved to say something, to tell this woman that she wouldn't be dying this day, but she couldn't. Her mouth had long since stopped working. Those last few single word sentences that she had been able to get out had zapped the last of her strength. Not even reinforcing her mouth with youki seemed to work.

Fan stood before her. The woman's dark eyes were alight with vicious mirth, a single finger still pointed at her. On the tip of said finger, a tiny light had appeared, a small sphere no larger than a thumbnail.

"**Celestial Art: Yúchángjiàn.** This is an assassination technique that I created after getting my third tail. I won't bore you with the details. Suffice to say, this technique seeks out and instantly pierces the heart of my target. It's fairly painless, which is why I don't plan on killing you first."

Fan smirked. Had her body not been paralyzed, Lilian would have shuddered. That expression made her heart constrict as though a snake were coiling around it.

"First, I'm going to kill your sister."

Lilian felt a chill settle within her, a frigid coldness that froze even the marrow in her bones. Her body shook. Her breathing stopped. Even her tails had become frozen over as though they'd been exposed to liquid nitrogen.

"Then I'm going to kill your friend."

Lilian's mind screamed at her, demanded that she continue struggling, that she break free from this entrapment technique. Yet her body still refused to move. Even when she pumped herself full of youki, she couldn't make her body do anything, not even twitch.

"After your sister and your friend are dead, I'll find that boy toy of yours and kill him in front of you. I'll be sure to kill him slowly, flaying his skin, destroying his organs. I'll make sure you get a front row seat to his screams, Lilian Pnéyma. You will watch as I destroy everyone you

79

love."

Something inside of Lilian snapped. Strength returned to her mouth, though the rest of her body still couldn't move.

"Don't..." She gritted her teeth. "Don't... touch... my mate..."

"Ho?" Fan's eyes widened slightly, but she recovered from her surprise with admirable alacrity. "So you can still speak, even though all of your muscles except your heart and lungs shouldn't be working. That mate of yours must be awfully important to you."

Cruel giggling filled the air. Fan's face twisted into a gleeful expression containing the first hints of madness.

"Maybe after I kill him, you will understand what I feel every time I gaze upon my beloved little brother as he lies in bed, his mind dead to the world. Then again, maybe not. I suppose it won't matter in the end. Now, then..."

Fan moved her hand until it pointed at something behind Lilian.

"... Time for your sister to die. **Celestial Art: Y—**"

Bang!

A loud noise like thunder rang out across the distance, interrupting Fan's technique. Lilian, Iris, and Christine suddenly fell to the grass as the **Yin-Yang Entrapment** dispersed, the circle beneath their feet fading. Lilian blinked several times, and then found her gaze shifting as a loud, ear-splitting scream pierced the air.

Fan was on her knees, holding her left hand in her right as dark, crimson blood seeped from a gaping hole in her palm. Lilian couldn't see much of the wound, mostly because the entire hand was covered in blood. It was like Fan had dipped her hand into a bucket of red paint. The three-tails stared at the injury in open horror as she continued to shriek in both shock and pain.

The woman's wailing was so loud that Lilian almost missed it, the sound of footsteps growing closer.

She turned away from the sight of Fan screaming incoherently and looked over to find someone she'd recognize even if her memories were suddenly erased.

Kevin walked forward, his steps steady and resolute. He held a gun in each hand. They were small, compact weapons, easily concealable within a pocket. Kevin had been keeping those guns concealed on his person at all times, ever since Seth had tried to kill her.

"B... Beloved..." Lilian's throat felt sore. It was probably because of how she had forced her muscles to move while caught within Fan's entrapment technique.

"Are you three all right?" Kevin asked as he stepped in front of her, Christine, and Iris. He didn't look back at them. His gaze remained focused on Fan, who had stopped screaming some time ago and was now glaring at him, her eyes a reflection of malice.

"We're fine, Stud," Iris said. "Though I think I'll be better once we get rid of this hag, and you, me, and my Lily-pad go back home and have ourselves a twenty-four-hour fuck-a-thon."

"Not happening," Kevin and Lilian declared at the same time, while Christine just muttered a harsh "perv" under her breath.

Iris pouted at them.

"Anyway," Kevin started again, "I'm sorry I didn't jump in until now."

"It's fine," Lilian said, simply grateful that she was no longer confined by that entrapment technique.

Christine seemed a bit surlier. "Why did you wait so long? You could have shot her once she had trapped us."

"I also had to check the perimeter to make sure she didn't have any back up. It would have sucked if I came to your rescue, only to get killed before I could do anything."

Christine conceded his point with a nod, though she still didn't look happy.

"I'm just wondering why you didn't kill her," Iris said. "A single shot to the head would have done the job."

Kevin didn't answer. Lilian knew why. He had told her that he would grow stronger, that he would fight when required, and that he would even kill if it became clear that there was no other way. But Kevin didn't like killing. He didn't want to kill. If there was a path that led to both sides coming out alive, then he would try to find it before resorting to murder.

"You…" Fan's voice was harsh, grating, and filled with murderous intent. "You damn… human… How did you break through my illusion? There's no way a lowly ape like you could have broken it!"

Lilian looked over at Iris, who simply shook her head. "Don't look at me. The stud had broken out of the illusion before I even got to him."

"There are only two ways for a human to break out of an illusion," Kevin said. "The first and easiest way is for a yōkai to inject the trapped human with their youki to disrupt the foreign energy used to create the illusion. The second way is to inflict pain on themselves, which disrupts

81

the neural pathways that your youki invades when you cast an illusion."

Lilian looked at Kevin more closely, finally noticing the blood dribbling down his mouth, which had quirked up into an awfully sexy smirk.

"Guess which method I used," Kevin said.

"D-damn you…" Fan gritted her teeth, the wound in her hand slowly healing. "H-how dare you…!"

"No, how dare you!" Kevin's snarl resounded across the field and set Fan back on her heels. "You think I'm gonna sit around and let you kill my mate? That I'll allow you to just waltz in and attack her for a reason as stupid as revenge?"

"S-stupid?!"

"Jiāoào deserved everything that happened to him," Kevin continued pressing his point. "Your younger brother was an arrogant, sadistic jerk who hurt others for his own pleasure. He was a spoiled brat who believed he was entitled to everything just because he came from a powerful clan. Being from a powerful clan doesn't give you the right to enslave others. No one has the right to treat others as if they're objects meant to be used for your own amusement! And I've got a newsflash for you, lady! It wasn't Lilian who beat the crap out of your younger brother! It was me!"

Fan's eyes went impossibly wide. Lilian almost laughed at the expression on the kitsune's face. She looked so stupid.

"Y-you…? A lowly human… impossible…"

Kevin's grin reminded Lilian of Kiara. It reminded her so much of the inu that she should have been disgusted by it, but she wasn't.

Beloved looks hot when he grins like that.

"It's very possible. Don't underestimate humanity. We may not have superpowers like you yōkai do, but we're more than capable of kicking ass when the situation calls for it."

Iris suddenly began clapping. "That was an awesome speech, Stud. You're becoming more shōnen with every volume."

"S-shut up," Kevin hissed, an embarrassed blush spreading across his cheeks. "I'm trying to be serious here!"

Iris crossed her arms under her chest and pouted, her powerful succubus eyes narrowing in seductive allure. "Hey, so am I. I'm seriously considering jumping your bones right now."

"W-w-w-what—shut up!" Kevin and Christine shouted at the same time.

"Aw, how cute. You two had a tsundere moment together."

"WE DID NOT! SHUT UP!" they shouted again.

Fan slowly struggled to her feet. Her right hand still clutched her left even though the wound had healed. Blood dripped off her fingers, the carmine liquid staining the grass. Lilian also stood to her feet, causing the three who were arguing to notice what was happening and follow her lead.

Fan's blonde hair fell over her face, casting harsh shadows and creating hard lines that distorted her features, making them appear more foreboding than such a cute face should be. Her three tails waved about behind her, writhing like the furious tendrils of an unfathomable abomination. Several droplets of blood trailed down her lips as she gritted her teeth hard enough to cut her gums.

"You... all of you..." The harsh, grating sound of Fan's voice caused Lilian's hackles to rise. "It seems I have underestimated you greatly. I played around too much and forgot my objective. That ends now. No more games. From this point on, I won't be toying around with you..."

Fan raised her head, and Lilian took an unconscious step back when she was greeted by the vicious snarl on the three-tail's face.

"... And mark my words: you four will die by my hands!" Fan shouted as though declaring their deaths to the heavens.

A Fox's Revenge

Chapter 3

Not Every Battle Ends in Victory or Defeat

"Celestial Art: Ch'ang-o's Celestial Cannon!"

A large beam of light erupted from Fan's tails. While Iris grabbed Christine and leapt away, Lilian wrapped an arm around Kevin's waist and jumped in the opposite direction. The beam of celestial energy tore across the ground, ripping up the grassy field, before striking the goal post on the opposite end and erupting in an explosion of particles.

Kevin eyed the large crater made by the blast, along with the trench that had been created when the beam seared straight through the ground. Its power reminded him of a high-intensity laser. Even though it hadn't touched the ground when it moved, the excess energy still reduced everything within a certain radius to their constituent molecules.

As they landed back on the ground, Kevin took aim with his guns and fired off several rounds. The thunderclap echoed loudly in his ears, but he tried to ignore the noise and merely focused on keeping Fan in his sights—at least, the figure that he thought was Fan. When his bullets tore through her like she didn't exist, he recognized the being before him for the illusion that it was.

"Celestial Art: Laozi's Chains!"

"Void Art: Flames of Oblivion!"

Several chains sprung from the ground and were subsequently burned by the black flames conjured by Iris. The sentient fire consumed

85

the celestial youki with an abnormal glee that caused Kevin to shiver. He never got used to seeing the Flames of the Void, which sought to erase all life and bring the world one step closer to the final oblivion.

Of course, the Void was anathema to celestial youki. The two were polar opposites. Thus, when the void fire met the celestial chains, a massive explosion of howling winds and overpowering energy sent everyone skidding backwards.

Kevin and Lilian shielded their eyes until the power died down, and then looked around. Aside from the new crater in the ground, only they, Christine, and Iris were present.

"Where did that bitch go?" asked Christine.

"She might be hidden under an illusion," Kevin said.

"No." Iris shook her head. "Illusions don't consume much youki, but they're a bitch to maintain, especially if she wants to use another technique like that cannon attack. She's probably just hiding right now."

"I've found her!" Christine called out, conjuring several shards of ice that flew toward the top of the bleachers, where Kevin could just barely make out the silhouette of a figure standing against the moon's backdrop.

"Celestial Art: Tsun Su's Shield!"

Several lines of light coalesced in front of the figure, moving in a circle until they took the shape of a giant yin-yang symbol. The ice hit the yin-yang circle and shattered like glass against it. The circle then morphed into a bright sphere, which shifted further still to form a sharp qiāng.

"Celestial Art: Taoist Point!"

The qiāng flew toward Christine who, unable to use any power beyond her ability to control ice, was as helpless as a human. The qiāng tore right through her like a hot knife through butter—or so it seemed. Rather than fall to the ground, Christine erupted into dark flames of the purest black, void fire, which exploded when the qiāng struck it.

When did Iris have time to cast an illusion over Christine?

Kevin was impressed by their teamwork. To not only create an illusion without anyone noticing, but for Christine to work with it required a lot of trust.

"Celestial Art: Orbs of an Evanescent Realm."

Nine orbs of bright celestial youki appeared around Fan seconds before converging on her location. The three-tailed kitsune leapt into the air. The orbs followed her.

What began was a game of cat and mouse. Fan landed on the ground and raced across the grassy field. She tried running over to them at first, but Lilian cut her off by sending four orbs in front of her, forcing the woman to swerve and then reverse course. Leaping and spinning and running, Fan kept moving as Lilian sent her orbs to attack the lady from all directions.

She conjured a pair of golden daggers of celestial youki and attempted to slice the orbs apart. It didn't work. Lilian's supreme control over her technique allowed her to move all nine orbs in a ceaseless pattern that couldn't be predicted. No matter how many times Fan swung her daggers, she hit nothing but air. The orbs surrounded Fan on all sides and every conceivable angle. She was trapped.

"Tch. **Celestial Art: Tsun Su's Shield: Version Two: Dome!**"

Left with no other recourse, she created another shield, a dome this time, which surrounded her entire body as the orbs struck it.

Explosion after explosion rang out, ear shattering and intense. Despite the amount of power behind Lilian's attack, Fan remained uninjured. The explosions ceased, yet the shield remained, pureness and unharmed.

"Void Art: Darkness Oblivione."

A sphere of crackling black fire appeared over Fan's head, massive in size, easily six times larger than Fan herself. With a grunt, Iris directed the giant sphere of darkness to descend. It fell on Fan without mercy. The shield that surrounded her fizzled out, and then the massive ball struck her. Fan's final scream of pain as she was consumed caused Kevin to grit his teeth. Even though he knew this woman was an enemy, he never enjoyed it when other people were in pain.

"Do you think we got her?" Lilian asked as the void fire disappeared, leaving behind a crater that was nearly twenty feet wide.

"I don't see how she could have escaped from something like that. Those screams of pain were certainly real enough." Kevin frowned as he studied the damage done to the surrounding area. This was going to take a lot of effort to cover up. Out of his peripheral vision, he spotted Christine and Iris walking toward them. He smiled, but then widened his eyes when he saw something bright traveling behind them. "Get down, you two!"

While Christine just looked shocked by his yell, Iris grabbed the girl and yanked her to the ground. It was a good thing she did. Several seconds after they both hit the dirt, a qiāng shot through the space they'd been standing on. It continued traveling toward him and Lilian, but they both moved out of the way quickly enough to avoid it.

Kevin threw himself into a shoulder roll, coming back up on his feet and aiming his guns at the spot where the attack had come from. He fired off a single round and watched as it splashed against a shield that suddenly flared into existence. He fired off six more rounds. Two of his shots missed, but the rest splashed against the shield. This had to be the real one.

I'm almost out of bullets.

He only had two bullets left in each gun, and he couldn't afford to reload while in the middle of combat.

"Lilian!"

"Right! **Celestial Art: Divine Spears That Strike the Earth.**"

Kevin watched as the woman, Fan, rushed out of her hiding place, dodging several thousand imaginary spears of light. He couldn't see them himself, the spears, as he was not the illusion's target, but he saw the effects it had on their opponent. Fan swerved and weaved through what she perceived to be a hailstorm of light spears that struck the ground and exploded, or so he thought. When one of the spears went through Fan and she disappeared, he knew that, once again, they had been fooled by an illusion.

"Dang it!"

Kevin rushed over to Lilian and tackled her mere seconds before another qiāng impaled the ground where she'd been standing. The spear exploded in a shower of light particles, which then took the shape of a rope that tried latching onto him and Lilian. He gritted his teeth as he held onto his mate and rolled them both across the ground, until they were out of the rope's reach. He then scrambled to his feet and pulled the redhead up with him.

"What the heck is going on here?" Lilian seemed frustrated by their lack of success in finding the real Fan. He couldn't blame her. Watching as all of their attacks were rendered useless by illusions bothered him quite a bit as well.

"I'm not sure." He surveyed the soccer field, wary for any potential attacks. "But something is definitely wrong. I know that my bullets hit a shield, which means she had to have been there."

Something was wrong. He didn't know what, but the more he thought about the battle thus far, the more certain he became. He was missing something. They were all missing something.

He studied the soccer field. Nothing seemed out of place. The damage done by their battle was still there. He could see the many pockmarks created by the various techniques all the yōkai had thrown around like so much candy. Holes and scorch marks and various scarring littered the ground. The large trench caused by that Fan woman's beam attack, along with the massive crater where the beam had struck the goal and exploded, remained. Likewise, the people on the bleachers were still passed out cold. Nothing seemed out of place...

... Until he looked down at his guns.

"An illusion," Kevin muttered in shocked realization.

Illusions were a result of the caster's imagination. If a yōkai could imagine it, they could cast it. However, illusions were rarely perfect. Since they were the product of imagination, if someone lacked knowledge about something, the illusion they cast would be imperfect.

Kevin's guns were a pair of SIG P938s. They were both black, had fairly standard features, and carried 7+1 round magazines. While the design on his guns looked identical to the ones he had been using, there was something missing from the guns in his hands.

These guns didn't have a place for his magazine clips.

"Pardon?" Lilian asked.

"We're in an illusion," Kevin said, loudly this time. "All this time, this entire battle, it's been nothing but an illusion."

Lilian's eyes widened. Kevin turned to shout at Christine and Iris, who were walking over to them.

"You guys! We're trapped within an illusion! You need to break out of it now!"

Following words with actions, Kevin bit down on his tongue hard enough to draw blood. His mouth was already filled with the coppery substance from the last time he'd dispelled the sleeping illusion, so the taste in his mouth didn't change. However, the sharp pain disrupted his neurological pathways, which had the consequence of shorting out his five senses and breaking him free from the illusion—just in time to hear a terrified scream.

Kevin spun toward the source and stared in uncomprehending shock at what he saw. Christine sat on the ground, on her butt, her hands behind her back and being used as support. She was staring up at Iris in wide-eyed horror.

Iris had a qiāng composed of celestial energy sticking out of her back. It looked like it had been thrown at her from behind. The tip protruded from her chest, blood dripping along the blade's edge, almost as if it were made of steel instead of youki, and an increasingly large red stain spread along her shirt and trailed down her stomach.

The twin-tailed succubus stared down at the qiāng's tip, blinking several times, as if she couldn't figure out what it was doing there. She then looked at him and Lilian. Their eyes locked for a moment before she looked down. As she stared at Christine, her lips twitched into a surprisingly warm smile. She opened her mouth, though whether to speak or something else, Kevin didn't know. Iris released only a strangled gasp as blood dribbled down her chin.

And then she pitched forward, collapsing to the ground like an android that had run out of power.

"IRIS!"

Lilian rushed forward, her panicked and horrified yell proceeding her. Kevin swore as he followed her. He aimed his guns in the direction the spear had to have come from and fired off a round. Fan rushed out from behind the bleachers. He unloaded the rest of his rounds at her, but while his aim standing still was pretty much ten for ten, he couldn't aim while moving yet. His shots went wide. Even so, the three-tailed kitsune still put up a shield. Perhaps the sound made her react on instinct.

"Iris! Iris! Iris!"

His guns clicked empty. He knelt next to Iris at the same time that a shocked Lilian fell to her knees and tried shaking her sister awake.

"Christine!" His shout made the yuki-onna's head snap over to him. He reloaded his guns with two spare magazines. "Keep that woman away from us with suppressive fire! Do it now!"

Christine's eyes were still wide, but she obeyed his command. Hundreds of ice shards appeared all around them and peppered Fan, forcing her to retreat. They speared the ground like stakes, constantly following the path she took, leaving her unable to cast any of her techniques.

"Lilian! Lilian, listen to me!" Lilian looked at him, her eyes wide. "You need to take Iris and head over to Sonoran Junior High. It's the closest school to the soccer field. Christine and I will cover you. Go now! Hurry!"

Lilian still looked downright terrified. Her eyes were wide. Her face was pale. She was shaking. Even so, she listened to him. Her tails extended and wrapped around Iris, lifting her into the air. He couldn't see the blood soaking into her red fur, but he could see it splashing against the grass. Iris's arms and legs dangled like wet noodles as Lilian rushed off, her reinforced legs going far faster than he would ever be able to run.

"You're not getting away!" Fan shouted, but she was forced to retreat when Christine fired more ice shards at her. It became even more impossible for her to do anything when Kevin began firing at her as well.

"Christine, fire at the surrounding lights while I keep her busy!"

Christine didn't say anything, but the ice shards she created suddenly changed targets. Instead of racing off to try and impale Fan, they struck the many lights surrounding the soccer field, shattering them and casting the field into near total darkness. Even kitsune could not see in the dark. Their vision was only as good as a human's. Like Kevin, she probably only saw silhouettes.

A silhouette was all he needed.

A single gunshot rang out. A howl of pain followed. Kevin saw the silhouette stagger, proving that he'd hit his target somewhere. Knowing better than to push his luck, he put the safety on one of his guns, pocketed it, and then grabbed Christine by the hand and ran off.

Fan's enraged, pain-filled screams chased after them.

***

The Sonoran Junior High campus wasn't like the one for Desert Cactus High School. Where the high school was composed of multiple buildings of varying sizes, Sonoran Junior High was a single building. Constructed from a combination of red brick and cement, the building was shaped like a giant rectangle. It was a three-story structure that looked kind of imposing in the darkness of night.

Lilian ignored the imposingness of it as she rushed into the building, breaking through the door and hurrying inside. Her tails were coated in warm liquid. She raced down the halls, panicking as she tried to find the nurse's office. Having never been to this school before, she didn't know where anything was. But she had to find it! Iris's life blood was being drained even now. If she didn't find some place where she could at least try to patch her sister up, then Iris would die.

Nurse's office. Have to find the nurse's office!

The beating of her own heart was abnormally loud as she searched in vain for the nurse's office. She found a library, several classrooms, and even came upon the gym, but the nurse's office was nowhere in sight.

Where is it? Where is it?!

"Lilian!"

The shout came just as she was passing a hall she'd already been down. She saw Kevin and Christine. Kevin gestured for her to follow him, and she did not hesitate to do so. They ran down the hall, taking several twists and turns, their footsteps bouncing around them as they ran across the tiled floor. The many windows they passed allowed moonbeams to shine in, which reflected off the white tiles. Numbered doors were on their left.

"In here!" Kevin shouted.

They reached what could only be the nurse's office; it was a decently sized room composed of white tiles and white walls. Blue padded seats rested against one of the walls and a long counter with a single sink and several cupboards sat against another. There were two doors. One led to what looked like an office with a desk and swivel chair. The other led to a room with a bed. It was the room with the bed that Kevin directed Lilian to.

"Set Iris on the bed."

As Christine went over to the chairs set against the wall, Lilian did as she was told, though she nearly cried when she saw how terrible Iris looked. Iris's entire front and back were soaked in blood. Her skin had become much paler. Iris had always been pale due to her void blood, but now her skin tone was a ghostly white.

"Lilian, grab several rags—they should be over in the cupboard above the sink. Soak them in warm water and come back. Also, be sure to grab the disinfectant."

Lilian nodded and hurried off toward the table with the sink. She searched the cupboards and quickly found what Kevin wanted. After setting aside the disinfectant, she put the rags under the sink, and then, not even bothering to wring them out, she rushed back into the room.

Kevin had taken his shirt off. She normally would have admired his broad shoulders and defined muscles, but she couldn't take any enjoyment out of the sight. He'd wadded up his shirt and was using it as a means of applying pressure to Iris's wound. When he saw her standing there, he gestured her over and began instructing her.

"Help me clean off the blood around her wound."

They worked together, wiping away the blood, which seemed almost futile since Iris was bleeding so much. They still did the best they could. Most of the blood was coming out of her back, so they were eventually able to clean the wound on her front. As he set aside the rag and began disinfecting the wound, Kevin called for Christine.

The little yuki-onna looked shell-shocked. Lilian couldn't blame her. She might have been a yōkai, but just like Lilian, she wasn't inured to violence. She was probably even worse off than Lilian, who had been in several violent confrontations already and had even been forced to kill another in self-defense.

"Christine, do you think you can cauterize these cuts with your bakeneko power?" he asked.

"I-I can't," Christine mumbled, looking away. "I haven't been able to use my bakeneko powers since that incident with Heather and Lindsay."

"I see. In that case, I'm going to pinch Iris's wound shut," Kevin told her. "When I do, I want you to freeze it closed. It's not the best solution, but it will keep her from losing any more blood until I can find a needle and thread to sew the wound shut."

Christine swallowed heavily. "C-couldn't Lilian just use her celestial powers to heal her?"

"I-I can't," Lilian whispered, her voice sounding anguished even to her own ears. "Iris is a Void Kitsune. Our powers are polar opposites of each other. If I tried to heal her, it would make her injury worse."

Christine dithered. "I-I don't... I'm not sure if I—"

"You can do it," Kevin interrupted the girl. "You can do this. I have faith in you."

"B-but what if I make it worse? What if I accidentally freeze her heart or something?"

"If you don't trust in yourself, then trust me. I know that you can do this, so you should trust me when I tell you that you can do this."

"O-okay. I'll try."

Christine walked between Lilian and Kevin. The spear had penetrated Iris just below her left breast. It looked like a large slit. The skin had peeled open like a red flower, revealing blood and muscles and bones. Kevin pinched it shut. Christine then placed her hands over the wound and channeled her youki.

Ice slowly formed over the frayed edges of torn skin. Iris didn't even let out a whimper, which worried Lilian because it meant her sister couldn't feel what was happening. That was never a good sign. She placed her hands on her knees and clenched the fabric of her skirt. Rarely had she ever felt more helpless than she did now.

"Okay," Kevin said as he removed his hands from Iris. A thin layer of ice had formed over the wound, keeping it shut. As he shook his hands, which had turned a pale blue, Kevin continued speaking. "Let's seal her back now. Lilian, help me push Iris onto her back."

***

After they cleaned Iris's back and sealed the wound shut with Christine's ice powers, Kevin left the two yōkai alone. He told them that he was going to try and find a needle and thread to sew Iris's wounds shut. They could hear him pulling out drawers and opening cabinets in the next room over.

Lilian sat on the examination bed next to her sister's prone body. In an effort to keep herself distracted, she'd taken to wiping off the rest of the blood covering Iris. A little way to her left, wringing her hands together as she sat on a padded blue chair, Christine appeared to be experiencing a combination of shock and stress.

Iris was lying on her back again. Her torso was exposed to the elements. Lilian gently wiped away the blood that had gotten on her stomach and breasts. As the carnelian liquid was wiped off, pale white skin became visible. Iris's skin was cold and clammy. Lilian tried to pretend this didn't mean her sister was knocking on death's door, and instead tried to imagine what her sister would do if she were awake right now.

She'd probably be moaning in orgasmic bliss and saying something about how her Lily-pad had finally accepted her love.

The amusing thought only lasted for a second before the situation sent her crashing back to reality. They'd been attacked by a member of the Shénshèng Clan, and Iris had almost died. She might still die if they didn't do something soon.

Once she finished wiping off all the blood, Lilian stood up and took the rags to the sink. Kevin nodded at her, but that was the only greeting he gave. He was still busy searching for a needle and thread. Lilian couldn't even bring herself to nod back; she merely dumped the rags in the sink and turned on the faucet.

"It doesn't look like there's a needle and thread here," he said at last. "I'm going to search the home ec room. They might have some."

"Okay."

Kevin hurried out of the room. The door closed behind him. Lilian turned off the faucet and returned to the room where her sister lay comatose. She sat back down on the bed and grabbed one of Iris's hands.

A stifling silence filled the air. With nothing to do but think about their situation, Lilian found her mind locked within a fierce struggle of self-recrimination. If only she'd been stronger. If only she'd been more capable. If only she hadn't let Iris fight with her. Lilian's mind tormented her with all the things she could have done to prevent this from happening.

"I'm sorry."

The silence was broken. Lilian turned to Christine. The yuki-onna was gripping the fabric of her lolita dress. Her head was bowed, hair falling in front of her face. Her shoulders were trembling.

"I'm… I'm so sorry," she whispered again.

Lilian tilted her head. "For what?"

"It's my fault Iris got hurt." This was the first time Lilian had heard Christine call Iris by name. She would have been shocked had their situation not been so dire. "When Kevin started shouting at us, I couldn't do anything. We yuki-onna are susceptible to illusions because our only ability is conjuring ice and affecting the temperature. Iris broke me out of the illusion and pushed me out of the way. She… she took that attack for me."

Lilian felt like she should have been mad at Christine. A part of her wanted to blame the yuki-onna for what happened to Iris, but she couldn't.

"That sounds like something Iris would do," she said, looking back at her sister. "While she might not seem like it, Iris is a really good person who cares deeply for her friends. When we were living in Greece, Iris would always protect me from the men and women who lived in the village next to our clan's estate, even if it meant getting hurt. This isn't your fault."

Christine looked up at her, and Lilian finally saw the tears that had gathered in the yuki-onna's eyes. That's when she understood.

Despite how they acted around each other, Christine and Iris were friends. They argued and fought and bickered like really foul-mouthed children, but they also hung out together, did things together, had fun together. Their constant fights, reminiscent of the way she and Christine used to fight over Kevin, was just what they did. It didn't mean they weren't close. If anything, it proved to Lilian that Iris and Christine were good friends because they weren't afraid to fight.

"Come here." One of Lilian's tails extended and coiled around

95

Christine's wrist. The snow maiden squawked as she was pulled to her feet and over to Lilian.

"W-what are you… oh…"

Christine soon found herself sitting on the bed with Lilian, trapped in a one-armed hug. Her head rested against Lilian's right breast, and Lilian used her free hand to tenderly pet Christine's hair.

"Everything's going to be okay," Lilian said softly. "You'll see. Kevin will return to patch up Iris. Then we'll find a way out of this mess."

The first tear to fall was soon followed by a second and then a third. Christine's tears chilled her skin. Lilian tried to ignore the coldness that seeped into her as the tears soaked her clothes and frosted over. Yet even as she comforted her friend, offering her platitudes and reassurances, Lilian wasn't sure if she believed them herself.

She felt like a hypocrite.

***

Kevin returned to the nurse's office almost five minutes later. He entered the room where Lilian and Christine sat with Iris, a case in his hands. He stopped when he saw them both sitting on the bed, the yuki-onna holding Lilian like a lifeline while she tenderly stroked the girl's hair.

"Did something happen?" he inquired.

"No." Lilian shook her head. "Nothing happened."

"I see."

Kevin didn't ask any more questions.

Perhaps he's more focused on helping Iris.

Kevin moved over to the bed, Lilian and Christine scooting away so they could make room for him. He set the case, a small plastic box with a clear lid, on the bed, and then opened it. Gleaming within were several silver needles plus numerous multicolored threads.

"Christine, can you get another rag?" asked Kevin.

"Um, okay."

Christine stood up and walked toward the door. Kevin could have asked Lilian, but she knew why he asked Christine. Giving the girl something to do would help calm her down.

"Make sure to soak it in hot water," Kevin added.

"I got it."

"Oh, and be sure to wring it out thoroughly, too. It'll be hard to sew

97

Iris's wounds shut if her skin is wet."

"Right."

"Lilian," Kevin said softly as Christine left, the sound of running water soon echoing from the other room. "After the ice around Iris's wound melts, I'm going to need you to pinch it shut while I sew it closed."

"Whatever you need me to do, Kevin, I'll do it," Lilian told him. "Right now, I think following your lead is the only thing I can do. You're much calmer and more level-headed than I am at the moment."

"Am I?" Kevin asked. "I suppose... I suppose that is good to know."

Lilian frowned at Kevin's words. She took a moment to study him, and then began noticing things she hadn't noticed before. The way his left leg shook. The minor tremors in his hands. His unsteady breathing. His pale skin with trace amounts of cold sweat clinging to it. That's when she realized the truth.

He's just as frightened as I am. He's scared too, but he's not showing it because of me and Christine. He's presenting a strong front because he knows that someone needs to be strong in this situation.

It should have been obvious, really. How could anyone not be scared by what had happened? Kevin especially should have been frightened out of his mind. He was a human, albeit, one who'd been through a lot more than most humans. But even though he was scared, even though he was worried, he was doing everything he could not to show it, so that she and Christine could have a pillar of support to lean against.

Despite the situation, Lilian's heart felt like it was going to burst. "I love you, Kevin."

Kevin looked startled for a moment, but his face soon softened, and he stared at her with adoration clear in his eyes. "I love you, too."

Christine returned with a rag that was so hot steam wafted from it. She gave it to Kevin, who used the steaming hot rag to melt the ice that kept Iris's wound shut. Blood started leaking out, but Lilian acted quickly, reaching out and pinching the skin shut with reinforced fingers.

They worked in silence, her and Kevin. She kept the skin pinched closed, trying not to grimace as Iris's warm blood stained her fingers. Kevin quickly threaded a needle and—after taking a slow, calming breath—got to work.

Lilian did everything she could think of not to quake at the sight of the needle puncturing her sister's skin. Being a kitsune, she'd never seen this method of treating an injury. Before, whenever she'd been injured, it would always be either Kotohime or herself who healed the wound with their techniques. This method seemed so primitive in comparison. It didn't seem like it could help.

However, help it did. Kevin stitched the wound closed, the thread crisscrossing to form multiple X-patterns until he reached the end. Then he pulled on the thread, tightening it as one might tighten his shoelaces, before snipping the end and tying it so it wouldn't come undone. After that, Kevin rolled Iris onto her front, and, repeating the same process as before, he sewed the back shut as well.

Kevin released a slow, shuddering breath as he finished sewing the injury on Iris's back. A single glance at his hands revealed how horribly they were shaking. Even so, he didn't let her or Christine know how he felt, merely putting the needle and thread back into the case and closing it. He then stood up and woodenly walked out of the room before returning several seconds later with a blanket that he laid over Iris.

"Okay," he said, a minor tremor in his voice. "There isn't... there's not much more we can do for Iris right now, except to find a way out of this situation and get her to Kotohime or Kirihime. I might have sewn the wounds shut, but Iris probably has internal injuries too. I can't heal those."

"What about that woman?" Christine asked in a surprisingly soft voice. Lilian imagined the snow maiden was feeling subdued by everything that had happened.

"She's obviously going to be coming after us," Kevin said. "We'll need to deal with her if we want to make a clean getaway."

Lilian felt something heavy push down on her shoulders, a metaphorical weight that made them droop. "By deal with her, do you mean...?"

"I... if that is what it takes." Kevin's shaking worsened for a moment, but he quickly mastered himself, clenching his hands until his knuckles turned white. "Iris's life is more important to me than hers. If I have to kill that woman in order to save Iris, then so be it."

Lilian wondered if the sharp pain in her chest was caused by his words or Iris's perilous predicament. She knew that Kevin hated killing. Despite everything they had been through, despite having already taken two lives, he was still just an abnormally kind high school student. Killing was anathema to him.

Yet she knew that he would. For her, for Iris, for any of their friends, Kevin would kill his heart and take the life of another. It made her feel guilty.

Kevin wouldn't be forced to kill if he and I never met.

Almost before the thought had fully formed, Lilian shook her head to dispel it. She couldn't think like that. Kevin had accepted her. He had decided to become her mate of his own volition. Even after being forced to take his first life, Kevin still remained by her side, still continued to accept her and return the love that she felt for him. Allowing herself to wallow in guilt would be doing him a disservice.

"We need a plan to deal with Fan," Kevin started. "So long as she's around, we'll never be able to get Iris somewhere she can get proper treatment."

He reached into his back pocket and pulled out a folded sheet of paper. Carefully unfolding it, he set the paper on the floor, allowing her and Christine to see what it was—a map of the school. As he sat down, Lilian and Christine shared a look before also sitting on the floor.

Lilian sat cross-legged as Kevin began making marks on the map with a marker that he pulled out from his other pocket. The map was pretty basic. It showed all the rooms on each floor and their room number, but it didn't reveal anything more than that. According to the map, there were three floors plus one basement.

"I found this map while I was searching for the needle and thread," he explained. "I've already come up with a basic plan that should work against our opponent. She's injured, probably upset from letting us escape, and I doubt she'll be thinking clearly. That should work to our advantage. Here's what we're gonna do. Lilian, I'm going to need some of your hair…"

***

Kotohime could almost feel her ribcage collapsing as Li smashed a fist into her chest. Her feet left the ground and her body soared backwards. She managed to swing her legs around, flipping until her feet were oriented toward the ground.

Her landing left much to be desired.

Kotohime's geta sandals had long since been lost. She winced as her now bare feet skid along the hot black top. She winced again when she took in a breath and gurgled up blood, which dribbled down her chin. A third wince came when she sent youki to her fragmented ribcage.

While she felt her ribs reform and snap back in place, the dwindling of her reserves was a cause for concern.

Several feet away, Kirihime lay unconscious against a broken wall. Her hair had fallen in front of her face and her eyes were closed. From where Kotohime knelt, she could see the blood leaking from her sister's mouth. Kirihime's French maid outfit had long since been reduced to tatters.

She turned her gaze away from the sight of her sister and onto her opponent. Li remained pristine. His clothing had yet to receive a tear, and he didn't have so much as a smudge marring his skin. The wounds that Kotohime had dealt during her surprise attack were all healed.

It must be some kind of specialized technique.

That was the only explanation she could conceive. Kotohime knew for a fact that he wasn't using illusions. She would have sensed the invasion of foreign youki long ago. That could only mean that some kind of special technique was being used to make his body become incorporeal.

But there was a problem with this line of thought. Only Spirit Kitsune had the power to make themselves incorporeal. The very act of making oneself incorporeal meant that the person in question was turning themselves into an intangible being akin to a disembodied spirit. In other words, a specter. The **Ghost Step**, the most basic Spirit Kitsune technique taught to kitsune that have gained their third tail, could accomplish this task, though with limitations. However, Celestial Kitsune could not learn spirit techniques. Therefore, he could not be using **Ghost Step** or any other spirit technique to do this.

So how is he doing this?

"You will never find out the secret behind my technique," Li informed her as if reading her thoughts. "You are a skilled kitsune, Kotohime. Your talent with a blade is unmatched and your techniques are incredibly destructive. However, that is your only talent. Fighting. One such as yourself, who has dedicated her life to combat, cannot even begin to fathom the nuances of my technique."

The way this man spoke irritated her. It told her that he wasn't taking this fight seriously. Even now he continued to stand in that one spot. He had yet to so much as lift his feet! And he only ever attacked after her attacks failed.

That's what had gotten Kirihime. She had charged headlong into battle with Li, her weapons passing right through him like he didn't exist. Then he had delivered a brutal palm thrust at her head, and Kirihime had found herself being slammed into the mountain of rubble that had once been their apartment. She'd been unconscious before she hit the ground.

All around them were the ruined remains of the parking lot. While their battle had not expanded far, the damage done by Kotohime's techniques had been catastrophic. No fires burned, but many cars lay in ruins, twisted lumps of metal. The walls surrounding this part of the complex had crumbled as if a tsunami had engulfed them. The ground was full of holes from her powerful water techniques. It was a wonder no one had seen their battle and come to see what was happening.

She stared at the man whose immaculate appearance taunted her, as if telling her that she was powerless against him.

"I will ask you one more time." Li's voice was still calm. His tone hadn't changed throughout their entire battle. "Do you concede?"

"Concede?"

This would have been the moment where Kotohime raised a hand, hid her smile behind the sleeve of her kimono, and then giggled demurely as she politely told him to fuck off. As both her sleeves and, in fact, most of her kimono, had been ripped to shreds, she didn't do that.

Instead, she stabbed her katana into the ground, using it as a crutch as she stood up. Despite the battle that had been waged, her blade remained immaculate and unsullied. This sword was the kind that could not be broken, not by the likes of this man.

I wish I had my wakizashi.

Her wakizashi had been lost during the initial assault. The explosion had flung it away from her. It was probably buried somewhere in the rubble.

Her legs wobbled and shook. Her knees wanted to give out. Her body felt like it had been repeatedly bashed against an impenetrable barrier by a battering ram.

It was the consequence of her River Kitsune blood. She could heal her wounds, mend her muscles, repair her organs, but that didn't mean she had no limit. Muscles would eventually wear down from natural causes, bones eventually ached from overuse. While the wounds inflicted upon her had healed, she could do nothing about the damage that came from straining herself.

She refused to acknowledge this weakness. She raised her head and glared at Li through the bangs falling around her eyes. Slowly, painfully, she raised her sword and slid into a basic *kenjutsu* stance.

"I refuse."

"I see." Li sighed, and for the first time since their battle began, he seemed disappointed. "I do not like violence. I fight when the tasks that I am given require fighting, but it has never been something that I enjoyed. That being said, I will not shy away from combat when left no other option."

The atmosphere shifted, becoming tense. Kotohime felt it immediately, the killing intent. It was hard not to. Throughout their battle, Li had never once released any killing intent, almost as if he hadn't felt any desire to kill her. Now she could feel it. He was about to get serious. This wouldn't be her attacking and him counterattacking. She could tell. He was going to try and kill her.

"You have left me with no other recourse," he continued. "If you will not acknowledge your defeat gracefully and back down, then it means I must put you down."

Kotohime's muscles tensed—

—and in between the second it took for her to tense up, Li moved. There was no warning, no hint that he had made the transition from point A to point B. One second he was standing several yards away. The next second he stood right in front of her.

Kotohime's eyes widened. He stared down at her, and for the first time since Corban had died, she felt utterly helpless. This man was going to kill her, and she could do nothing to stop him.

"Forgive me. Know that killing you brings me no pleasure. I only do this because you have left me with no other option," he said, raising his fist and bringing it down more swiftly than she could comprehend—

—Only for the fist to inexplicably stop not even an inch from her nose. Kotohime stared at the appendage, which trembled and shook, blinking.

"What the heck…?"

It took her several seconds to realize why Li's fist wasn't moving; it was because of the long black tail that had wrapped around Li's forearm and wrist, keeping it from turning her face into mulch.

Li seemed shocked as well.

"What is this?!" he cried out. He didn't get the chance to say anything else, as the tail coiling around his entire forearm lifted him up and tossed him away. He landed several yards from Kotohime, but he made no move to close the distance again.

"Haaaaa…"

Kotohime blinked. What was that noise? It sounded like… yelling?

"… waaaaAAAAA!"

The apartment complex to her left exploded in a shower of brick and mortar. Debris rose into the air, shooting off in every direction and pelting the ground. Kotohime did her best to protect herself, raising her arms, shielding her face from the debris. Fortunately, most of what hit her was small and didn't hurt very much.

When she could feel nothing hitting her anymore, she lowered her arms to see what had caused the sudden explosion. She then promptly wondered if she had become unknowingly trapped in an illusion, or perhaps her lack of youki had induced delusions of some kind, for those were the only explanations she could think of to explain what she was seeing.

Camellia stood in the epicenter of the ruined apartment building, completely unharmed, minus the dirt covering her toga. Her ears twitched and her tails flexed. She seemed to be observing the area with the curious gleam of a child.

Their eyes locked.

The sunny smile on Camellia's face was so out of place, so contrasting to the devastation surrounding her, that Kotohime almost face planted. The only reason she didn't was because faceplanting was not something an elegant *yamato nadeshiko* like herself did. Ever.

"Ah, Kotohime! Morning!" Camellia greeted with her ever-childish grin, though Kotohime did notice that she hadn't been called "Koto-Koto" or something equally childish.

"It's evening, Camellia-sama," Kotohime muttered.

"What happened here?" Camellia either ignored or hadn't heard the words. She surveyed the remnants of their apartment building with curious eyes. "Everything looks like it went doki-doki boom."

Kotohime didn't know what *doki-doki boom* meant, but she had neither the desire nor the inclination to figure it out. Fortunately, she didn't have to.

"Camellia Pnéyma," Li said, staring at the woman who merely blinked in return. "Once known as the Dancing Lily of the Netherworld, but has since been reduced to someone with the mentality of a child. I do not know how you survived my attack, but please do not interfere any further. If you do, then I will have no choice but to kill you as well."

Camellia said nothing. She looked at Li for a second longer, and then went back to staring at her surroundings—until her eyes caught sight of Kirihime. She slowly walked over and knelt in front of her maid, her left hand going to the woman's shoulder, trying to shake her awake.

"Kiri-Kiri? Kiri-Kiri, why are you lying around like that? What's that red stuff coming out of your mouth? Why aren't you answering me?"

The slew of childish questions that Camellia unleashed made Kotohime grimace. It was sad, Camellia's complete lack of understanding. Due to her degraded mental disposition, she couldn't understand concepts like internal bleeding and damage induced by blunt force trauma. She didn't know why Kirihime wasn't responding to her. Had she not already understood and accepted that this was how Camellia was, Kotohime would have wept.

Kotohime was given no more time to ponder Camellia's sad fate as Li suddenly appeared before her within a split second, the five-tailed kitsune's hand already coming in to impale her through the chest. He was too fast. Kotohime had no time to dodge.

The hand was stopped.

Once again, the culprit was one of Camellia's tails. Li tried to get out of their hold, but for some reason, he couldn't phase through Camellia's tails like he had Kotohime's attacks. This strange turn of events seemed to baffle him as much as it did Kotohime.

"W-what the... why isn't my ability working?"

"Are you the one who hurt Kiri-Kiri?" Camellia asked, and Kotohime sensed, more than saw, the intense shifting in Camellia's demeanor. "Did you do this to her?"

Camellia stood up and turned around. Her face still looked childish, cheeks puffed up almost humorously, and yet...

... There was something about Camellia that put Kotohime on guard. Some indefinable change had taken place within the woman. She didn't know what it was, but Kotohime could sense that something about her charge's mother was different.

Li also seemed to sense this difference, for he took a halting step back. "I only did what my lord bade me to do. We cannot have you interfering with our—guah!"

Kotohime felt a ripple of shock tear through her when another of Camellia's tails slammed into Li with force. A ferocious shockwave erupted from where the tail smacked against his stomach. A mere split second later, Li plowed straight into an apartment building several dozen yards away. Like a house of cards, the building collapsed, burying Li under several tons of rubble. Dust billowed out from the wreckage, and when it cleared, it revealed Li, lying beneath several massive chunks of concrete, his body reminiscent to a broken doll.

"Ug... uu..."

Embedded into the apartment ruins, Li struggled to push the debris off him and stand up. Blood leaked from his mouth. His monk robes were torn, revealing the ugly black bruise on his stomach that he had received from Camellia's tail. He placed his hands against the broken wall, as though to push himself up, but another tail slammed into him, and instead of getting up, he released a cry of pain and collapsed back into the building. The tail retracted.

Kotohime tore her eyes away from the sight of Li and looked over at Camellia, who was... powering up?

"HAWAAAAAA!!!!!!!"

Yes, Kotohime idly noted. Camellia was, indeed, powering up. She was crouched down in a stance that Kotohime had seen on the television on many occasions since arriving at the Swift residence. Her knees were bent at 45-degree angles, hands clenched into fists and tucked into her side. A strange, silvery aura engulfed her body, howling in torment like a thousand damned souls. Kotohime could almost see them within that aura, the faces of people whose lives had been lost, the wandering spirits damned to spend an eternity on earth. They surrounded Camellia, creating an aura almost similar to the one Kiara created from her youki.

The aura vanished, or rather, the ectoplasm that had formed the aura gathered to a single location: Camellia's hands, which her five tails were entwined around like furry gloves. The coalescence of spirit matter compressed into a tiny sphere, which grew to the size of a baseball. It then began howling with the horrid ring of a thousand voices all crying out at once.

"Hawaaaaa..."

Kotohime blinked when Camellia began to speak. Of course, she wasn't speaking actual words but her catchphrase.

"Hawaaaaa..."

Over by the building, Li had finally managed to stand up. He held his left arm to his stomach. A lot of blood spilled from his mouth, denoting to severe internal injuries, perhaps even a ruptured lung. Still, Li moved, stumbling out of the collapsed building like a drunken sailor.

"HAAAAAA!"

It was at that exact moment, just as Li emerged from the building, that Camellia unveiled her attack. She thrust her hands and tails toward Li like she had no doubt seen *Son Goku* do at least a thousand times already. A giant beam of energy blasted out, a cone of pure destruction that slammed into Li, whose entire body disappeared as the chaotic energy engulfed it.

The beam didn't stop with Li. After consuming his body, it plowed through the wall behind him, and then continued to strike an apartment several dozen yards away, which promptly exploded in a torrent of spiritual energy.

Kotohime covered her eyes with an arm as the winds howled and screamed. Dust flew in her face, making her cough before she covered her mouth with her other hand. She could feel her body sliding back as it was struck by the relentless forces battering her. Blood leaked from the bottom of her feet as the black top rubbed her skin raw.

Then it was over. The winds stopped. The howling stopped. Everything stopped. All that remained was a heavy stillness.

Kotohime uncovered her face. The world around her looked like something from an apocalyptic manga series. The buildings of their complex were all ruined. Even the ones further out had been destroyed by the backlash of Camellia's attack. A large trench at least eight feet across and four feet deep started where Camellia stood and disappeared beyond several decimated buildings.

After gazing at this new world in shock, Kotohime turned her head to Camellia. The five-tailed, toga-wearing kitsune had not moved from her place next to Kirihime. The aura had died down, and she looked a little tired. However…

She also looked excited.

"Begone evil of the Megaverse," Camellia intoned, striking a pose and pointing at the spot where Li—and an apartment—had once stood. "In the name of the moon, I will punish you! Tee-hee!"

Silence. Several crickets began chirping. A tumbleweed rolled across the battlefield, and then several snakes hissed as they slithered by. It looked like they were chasing after the tumbleweed, though it was anyone's guess as to why.

Kotohime stared at Camellia for a few seconds longer, slowly raised her right hand…

… And promptly palmed her face.

"I knew it was a bad idea to let Camellia-sama watch anime with

Kevin-sama, Lilian-sama, and Iris-sama."

***

Fan glowered as she limped her way into the school building. This was the place where she had pinpointed that blasted Lilian's location. Grimacing as she made her way down a bland hall, Fan pressed a hand to her leg to keep it from wobbling.

While the wound on her hand had healed, the one on her leg was being stubborn. The bullet had hit her knee cap. She had managed to heal the wound itself, but the bullet was still inside; it kept grazing against her joints, sending jolts of agony straight to her brain and making her knee threaten to buckle.

She couldn't believe that she had been injured by a human! Twice! She'd not been injured at all during her entire battle with Lilian and the other two yōkai, yet some measly human had managed to injure her two times! It was absolutely absurd!

"Damn that human," she growled, the grating noise bubbling from her throat. "When I get my hands on that pathetic ape, I will make him rue the day he was born!"

She looked down the hall. White tiles covered the floor. Plain white walls surrounded her on two sides, along with a checkered ceiling above her. Several windows on one side allowed sparse amounts of moonlight to filter inside, illuminating the interior. A row of doors were on the other side, with a numbered plaque hanging from each one.

Frowning, Fan began wandering the halls, searching the rooms. Each room was empty. They contained no signs of life, just the desks and tables that she had come to expect from a human educational institution. While Fan had been able to pinpoint Lilian and the others' location to this building, she didn't know where they were hiding. That meant she had to search the entire building from top to bottom.

"I can't believe Father gave me such a demeaning task," she muttered to herself as she checked a classroom. It was empty. She moved on. "This is absolutely humiliating. I shouldn't be here. I should be spending time with my beloved little brother, trying to help him recover."

She scowled some more after checking another empty classroom. Where were her targets?! As she turned around, about to continue traveling down the hall, she caught sight of something red out of the corner of her left eye. She swiveled her head just in time to see red hair fluttering around a corner.

"There you are," she growled. "Lilian Pnéyma, your time is up!"

Fan limped after the fluttering red hair. Because of the wound on her leg, which aggravated her even now, her target always managed to stay ahead of her. The few times she caught sight of the blasted girl, it was to see her hair fluttering as she disappeared around a corner. For a moment, she thought that she might be chasing after an illusion, but she could sense no foreign youki inside of her.

She continued tailing after the girl, who would be suffering a most brutal death when she caught up, and eventually came to a flight of stairs. She peered down the stairs. The door at the end was partially open. Scowling to herself, she limped down the stairs and flung the door wide before walking through.

The room was strange. Pipes hung along the ceiling and traversed the walls, a network of steel grids running in a variety of directions, crisscrossing and intersecting to conceive an unnaturally symmetrical web. Large machines thrummed and vibrated with life. There were all kinds of contraptions, strange metal boxes, small fans, rumbling cylinders. An annoying *hiss* filled with air.

There was very little light to see with. What light there was only served to cast shadows around the room, which moved and twisted, creating macabre images that parodied life.

She ignored the unsettling pit that swelled within her chest. Her target was somewhere in here, and she would find that little wretch and kill her—no, she would beat her to within an inch of her life, find that blasted human, and kill him in front of her. Only then, after that damn scarlet woman watched the life drain from her mate's eyes, would Fan kill her.

Fan walked past a metal fence, the lights shining through the chain links playing off her face. She turned her head left and right, eyes constantly sweeping the perimeter. A noise caught her attention. She looked to her left—

—and froze.

She met a pair of blue eyes.

He stood in front of a metal door that was partially open. In one hand, he held one of those human weapons: a gun. In the other were several locks of long red hair, which fell from his fingers and fluttered to the ground.

It was as she watched the silken strands of crimson fall to the floor that she realized something.

She'd been tricked.

"You!" Fan shouted in rage. "I'm going to murder you!"

The boy just looked at her, his blue eyes resigned. "Not today, you're not."

The calm response Fan received pissed her off so much. She saw red. She started channeling youki through her tails. She was going to erase this ape from the face of the earth!

Said ape raised his gun and fired. Out of instinct, Fan switched from attack to defense. **Tsun Su's Shield** appeared before her, a brilliant barrier shaped like a yin-yang symbol, a powerful shield which no mere human weapon could hope to penetrate.

Unfortunately, she didn't realize until too late that she wasn't the target.

Ping!

Fan turned around just in time to see a spark ignite as the bullet struck one of the pipes. Not even a second later, the pipe exploded, igniting a chain reaction that caused more pipes to detonate, gouts of flame shooting out in thick plumes. She didn't even have time to yell before her world was consumed by hellish fire.

***

After exiting the boiler room via an escape tunnel, Kevin proceeded through a dark corridor that led to an emergency exit. He ran swiftly. The world exploded around him. Faster. Faster. The sweltering heat caused his skin to break out in a sweat. He ran faster still. Several times a gout of flame would explode to his left or right, forcing him to cover his face, lest it get burned. Move faster.

There was an emergency exit at the end of the tunnel: a ladder with a hatch. Sonoran Junior High was an old building. He didn't know what it had been before becoming a school, but he knew that the building must have been something else at some point. It was the only explanation for why they had an emergency exit like this. The hatch was already open and all Kevin had to do was climb up the ladder.

The cold night air felt almost welcome on his skin. His world opened, revealing that he was several hundred yards from the school. Desert landscape greeted his eyes. Large saguaros loomed over him like silent sentinels. Tiny bushes and barrel cacti sat by his feet. He couldn't see Lilian or Christine, but if they had followed his plan, then they

110

should have been at Desert Cactus High School by now.

With the Sonoran Junior High building exploding in plumes of fire and smoke behind him, an exhausted Kevin set out in the direction of Desert Cactus High School.

A Fox's Revenge

Chapter 4

A Troubling Situation

Lilian walked through the desert with Christine. The cold night air hit her skin, causing goosebumps to break out and shivers to run down her back. A pair of even colder arms were slung limply over her shoulder as she tightly gripped the bum of her insensate sister, whose unconscious body she was carrying.

Iris's legs were limp, swinging back and forth like pendulums on either side of her. Shallow breaths, so light that Lilian almost mistook them for a soft breeze, hit the back of her neck. It worried Lilian how unresponsive Iris was.

"Do you think Kevin is all right?" Christine asked, snapping Lilian out of her thoughts.

They'd left Kevin behind to deal with Fan while they had vacated the building according to his plan. Lilian didn't much care for this plan. She wanted to help defeat Fan, but Kevin had made a strong argument about why she couldn't. The most important thing was getting Iris somewhere she could be treated. That meant one person staying behind, one person carrying Iris to safety, and the other protecting the one carrying Iris. Even if Lilian didn't like it, she understood that this was the best course of action.

"Of course Beloved is all right," Lilian stated. "Beloved is strong. Some three-tailed kitsune with a chip on her shoulder isn't going to get the best of him."

Christine stared at her for a moment longer, then turned her head. "Yeah... I guess you're right."

Silence reigned after that. The school buildings belonging to Desert Cactus High soon loomed before them. People became visible as they neared the front gate. Crowding around the school entrance were several dozen, maybe even over one hundred people. Lilian was surprised, but after a moment of staring, she recognized some of those people from their uniform: light blue shorts and a white shirt with blue trim. It was the uniform worn by the girls' soccer team.

One of the people wearing the girls' soccer team jersey saw them and called out. "Christine! Lilian! There you two are! Where have you been? I was—what happened to Iris?!"

Lindsay ran up to them, her exuberant expression upon seeing them quickly morphing into shocked concern when she saw the pallid and unconscious form of Iris on Lilian's back.

"Lindsay," Lilian greeted. Christine remained silent.

Her face turning pale, Lindsay stared at the trio. "W-what happened? Why do all of you look like you were dragged through the mud? Is that blood on your clothes? Where's Kevin?"

Lilian raised a hand to avoid the series of rapid fire questions her friend sent. She needed to reinforce her other arm with youki to keep Iris from falling. Lindsay quieted down.

"I can't answer any of those questions. Not here."

Lindsay appeared nonplussed. "What? Why not—" her eyes widened "—is it because of...?"

"Yes." Lilian nodded. Lindsay looked from her to Christine. After a second, the yuki-onna nodded once, and Lindsay turned back to Lilian, though her gaze immediately flickered to the one on Lilian's back.

"And Iris...?"

"She's... alive." Lilian grimaced. "Which is something I should be thankful for. Beyond that, there isn't much I can tell you."

"I-I see." Lindsay closed her eyes, and Lilian knew that her friend was thinking. When she opened them again, it was to penetrate her with a stare. "Where's Kevin?"

Lilian hesitated. "He's still back there."

"You mean you left him?" Lindsay's shocked expression morphed into a scowl. "How could you? I thought he was your mate!"

"Do not take that tone with me," Lilian snapped. "Kevin is my

114

mate. No one is more worried about him than I am, but Kevin said he had a plan to... deal with the situation. He said that Iris was our first priority. He told us to leave and get in touch with Kiara. I trust him, so I'm not going to question his judgement."

Lindsay reared back as if her words were a physical blow, or perhaps Lilian's glare and tone merely surprised her. "I... I'm sorry. I shouldn't have said that. I know you love Kevin and would never leave him behind without a good reason."

"It's fine." Lilian took a deep breath. "I'm sorry for snapping at you. With everything that's happened today and Kevin still not here... I guess I'm feeling more than a little anxious."

"I'll bet." Lindsay gave her a sympathetic look before glancing at Christine. "Are you all right, Christy? You've been pretty quiet."

"I'm fine," Christine said, her voice softer than Lindsay had probably ever heard it.

Lilian's heart went out to the gothic lolita. While they were both yōkai, Christine had never really been involved in the yōkai world. She'd experienced the violence at the Comic-Con in San Diego, but it probably hadn't seemed as real. She, Lindsay, and their human friends had escaped before things got really dicey.

This battle had been personal. Even the previous fight that she had been in with the mind-controlled Heather hadn't been this bad. That woman they fought, Fan, had really been out to kill them. That kind of thing tended to frighten most people, which she imagined Christine must have been feeling now that things had calmed down. The shock of what happened was probably hitting her all at once. Matters likely weren't helped by the fact that Iris had been injured protecting her.

This is my fault. I got her involved in this.

Guilt. Lilian felt guilty for bringing all this trouble upon her friends, for making Christine experience the violence of their world. All Lilian wanted out of life was to live with her mate and have fun with her friends. She didn't want to have anything to do with the yōkai world, but it looked like that world was refusing to let her go, and now her friends were being dragged into her problems.

"Are your parents here?" Lilian asked in an effort to ignore the way her stomach churned.

Lindsay shook her head. "No... Dad's at work. Mom was going to come to the game, but... well, she got called in for a surprise meeting with her friends in the Aesthetics Appreciation Club."

A small trail of sweat dripped down Lilian's face at Lindsay's mention of that club. "No offense, Lindsay, but I really don't like your mom very much."

"Ah-ahahaha." Lindsay raised a hand to rub the back of her neck. "Yeah, I'm really sorry about her. She and her friends are kinda... weird."

Weird didn't even begin to cover Lindsay's mom. She and her friends had formed a group called the *Aesthetics Appreciation Club*, which was just a pretense for a bunch of middle-aged women to drool over pictures of boys' half their age, sometimes even younger. It was disturbing. Then again, Lilian didn't really have any place to talk, since she was 160 years old and dating Kevin, who was only fifteen.

"Shut up!" Lilian glared up at the sky. "I don't wanna hear another word out of you!"

"Uh, Lilian, who are you talking to?" asked Lindsay.

"No one," Lilian said morosely. "Would you mind if I borrowed your phone? I need to make a phone call."

***

Kevin was tired. His body ached, his clothing was ruined, and the burns on his arms and legs, courtesy of the explosion he had created, stung. He wanted to sleep. Yet he knew that he couldn't, not yet, not until he had confirmed Lilian's and Christine's safety and made sure Iris was being cared for.

Stumbling toward Desert Cactus High School, Kevin arrived at the school gates to a surprise. A large number of students had gathered alongside their parents near the school entrance. With them were two police cars, their red and blue lights flashing. Four policemen stood within the crowd, which he realized must have been all the people who were knocked unconscious by Fan's illusion. It looked like they were taking statements.

This doesn't look good.

Worry wormed its way into his gut. Who had called the police? Would they take him in for questioning? What would they discover if they went over to the battle sight or, heaven forbid, the junior high? His worries caused him to stop for a moment, images of himself being arrested for causing all this trouble flittering through his mind like transient claws scraping the inside of his head.

"Beloved!"

The moment passed when Lilian rushed out of the crowd and ran over to him. He had barely a second to notice that Christine, Heather, and Lindsay were also present before his arms found themselves full of one gorgeous fox-girl.

Kevin didn't even get a moment to speak before a pair of soft, warm lips were upon him, kissing him with an intensity that contained more than simple passion. It was as if all the worry Lilian felt was being placed within her kiss. He felt Lilian's desire through her lips, felt her need to know that he was all right, her fervent wanting of reassurance.

He didn't allow himself to think as he kissed her back. He wrapped his arms tightly around her waist, pulling her flush against him as two deceptively strong arms went around his neck. Just as Lilian did for him, Kevin put all the feelings he had, his relief at seeing her safe, at them both being alive, into his kiss.

They only broke apart when oxygen became a necessity; her mouth left his, her tongue retracted, the string of liquid that connected them breaking. Lilian then pressed her forehead against his. She closed her eyes and took a slow, deep breath.

"I'm so glad," she whispered. "I'm so glad you're okay."

"Yeah," Kevin muttered. "Sorry for worrying you."

Lilian shook her head, and her eyes opened once more to stare into his. "I knew you would be okay. I had confidence in you. I knew you would win, but I just..."

She trailed off, but that was okay. Kevin understood. Even though she had confidence in him, that didn't stop her from worrying about him. A parent might have confidence in their child, but that never stopped them from fretting when their child did something potentially dangerous, be that playing sports or whatever. It was the same thing, though Lilian's worry seemed a lot more intense, but he was probably being biased.

Unwinding themselves from each other, Lilian sought his hand. It was a gesture that he reciprocated. They walked over to the group of three, who stood near one of the police cars. As they stopped in front of the group, Heather crossed her arms and smirked.

"Well, look at you two, acting all lovey-dovey with each other immediately in the aftermath of an unmitigated disaster," Heather said, grinning as though unaffected by the confusion and fear that permeated the people present.

Kevin rolled his eyes. "Lilian and I are dating, you know. Acting like a couple is expected of a couple."

"Hmm... touché."

"Are you okay, Kevin?" Lindsay asked.

"I'm fine," Kevin reassured her before something tugged at his sleeve. It was Christine. "What's wrong, Christine? Are you injured?"

Christine shook her head, then looked at the ground. "I'm... really glad you're okay. I-I was worried... um..."

Had the situation been different, Kevin might have expressed shock. Christine never really displayed worry for others. He knew that she could get worried, but she would normally deny ever being worried about someone else. That she was admitting she had been worried concerned him.

"I think she needs a hug," Lilian whispered in his ear.

Kevin glanced at her out of the corner of his eye. She nodded and gestured with her head, indicating what she wanted him to do. Knowing better than to go against her, as she knew women better than he did, Kevin followed her advice and pulled Christine into a one-armed hug.

"I'm sorry for worrying you," he said to the stiff-as-a-board Christine.

"T-that's right. Y-you should be sorry," Christine muttered. It sounded like she was trying to sound angry, but there was a hiccup in her voice, and she was burying her face in his chest. "Jerk."

Resisting the urge to chuckle, Kevin reached up and ran his hand over her head. Her hair was soft like powdered snow. For just a moment, he thought he heard purring, but then Christine pulled back, wiped her eyes, and glared at him.

"If you do something dangerous like that again, I'll kill you dead, got it?"

He smiled. "I got it."

"Good," Christine muttered.

With that small episode over, Kevin looked around, a sudden bout of worry wiggling inside of his gut when he realized they were missing someone. "Where's Iris?"

"I called Kiara a little while ago," Lilian informed him. "She showed up with an ambulance in tow and they took Iris."

"I'm surprised you didn't go with her."

"I wanted to," Lilian allowed. "But I... I was worried about you, so..."

Kevin understood. She wanted to be with Iris, but worry for her mate overrode worry for her sister. It was just another part about being

Lilian's mate that made him feel guilty. Because he was the most important existence in her life, everyone else, including fraternal twin sisters, took a back seat.

"Let's go see her, then." He wrapped an arm around Lilian's waist to draw her close. She accepted the embrace and returned it, seemingly taking solace in his presence and scent. He looked at Christine, who he knew was worried about Iris as well. "All of us."

Christine looked at him. She didn't say anything, but the nod she gave let him know of her desire to ensure that Iris was okay.

"By the way, where's Eric?" asked Kevin.

"He already left," Heather said. "He wanted to stay, but I called his dad and sent him home."

"Gotcha." Kevin nodded.

"It's probably a good thing," Lindsay said. "Eric's presence would only complicate things."

"Ah… yeah, that's true…"

"I apologize for interrupting," a masculine voice said, making Kevin and the others turn to the police officer walking up to them. "While I have no intention of keeping you from your friend, we do need to ask some questions to the young man who just arrived."

"Uh, w-well, I suppose I could," Kevin stumbled over his words. Oh, crap! He knew that he shouldn't have just walked over here after everything that had happened. Now they were suspicious of him! He was going to get sent to jail!

"Don't worry, son." The police officer placed a hand on Kevin's shaking shoulder. "I won't be asking anything too invasive. It's simply standard procedure to question everyone who was present during the vandalism."

"Vandalism?"

Was that what the cops were calling the damage done to the soccer field? Vandalism? Surely they weren't that dumb. Nothing about that soccer field looked like it came from vandals. There had been craters and holes all over the ground. Craters and holes!

As Kevin stared at the officer, wondering if this man was an idiot, he caught sight of something that startled him. It hadn't been noticeable at first because he'd been worrying himself sick, but a closer inspection revealed that the officer's pupils weren't the standard round shape. They were cat-like slits.

A yōkai...

A Fox's Revenge

Kevin knew that there were many yōkai working in various professions undercover: newscasters, reporters, doctors, they were all over the place. Their job was to cover up incidents like this, so the human population would never catch on to their existence. He knew that, but even so, he'd never expected to meet one of those yōkai.

I shouldn't be so surprised.

His shock must have shown on his face because the officer winked as he led Kevin away from the others and began asking standard questions—or at least, that's what it appeared like to everyone else.

"You should know that right now the story we're giving everyone is that vandals somehow managed to get their hands on small-scale explosives and tore the soccer field apart," the officer said. "However, claiming the field was vandalized won't hold up in a major investigation. That's why we'll be tampering with the memories of everyone here."

That was standard procedure, Kevin knew. When something happened that couldn't be explained easily or in a way that was believable, yōkai altered the memories of the people present.

Kevin swallowed. "W-why are you telling me this… uh, sir?"

The officer played with the rim of his police hat. Kevin noticed that his fingers were clawed. His race struck Kevin like a bolt of lightning.

Nekomata.

"Because you, Ms. Diane, and Ms. Grant are exempt from this rule. I am merely informing you of what we plan on doing. That way, if anyone speaks about what happened, you don't say something incriminating. Altered memories are delicate. Even after the memories have been altered, it is possible for the tampering to be broken by someone saying something that contradicts the alterations made."

Months ago, Kevin would have asked why they didn't just erase the memories, but he already knew the answer. One couldn't erase what happened here. If a bunch of people suddenly lost their memories of an event that other people knew had happened, it would cause a panic, which might end with the existence of yōkai being revealed.

"Oh." Kevin breathed a sigh of relief. "I understand."

"I'm glad you understand. Now you'd best head back to your friends. I hear one of you was put in the hospital, and it looks like your mate is getting anxious."

Kevin looked behind him to see Lilian shivering in place. To any normal person, it would have looked like she was cold. To Kevin, it looked like she was two seconds away from pouncing on him.

He turned back to the police officer, whose eyes with slit-like pupils flashed yellow under the moonlight.

"… Right."

Kevin adamantly told himself that he was not sweat dropping.

***

Alexander Ramirez watched as the human boy named Kevin entered a small car with his mate, the other two humans, and the yuki-onna. As the car thrummed to life and drove away, no doubt in route to the hospital, he released a hefty sigh.

That boy had clearly been through a lot. They all had, but it was more obvious in the boy. As a police officer and a yōkai, he knew what signs to look for, and he'd seen them in that boy's eyes. Kevin Swift had killed. Not only had he killed, but he'd resigned himself to the inevitability that he would have to kill again.

This is the reason yōkai aren't supposed to reveal their existence to humans.

While it was true that many yōkai lived among humans, that didn't mean the yōkai and human worlds were connected. They were more like parallel worlds that just happened to share the same plain of existence, rather than being two separate dimensions. These two worlds occasionally intersected, but for the most part, they were separate worlds unto themselves.

The yōkai who lived within human society were a part of human society. Rather than simply existing alongside humans, they co-existed with humans. Of course, because of humanity's irrational fear of the supernatural, yōkai living amongst humans had to hide the fact that they were yōkai.

That was why yōkai like him were around. He was damage control. It was the job of him and those like him to ensure no human discovered their existence. The only reason Kevin and his companions hadn't had their memories altered was because Davin Monstrang had told everyone that they were not to be touched.

He had no idea what made this group of humans so special, but when the man up top gave an order, that order was obeyed.

"Hey, Alex." An officer walked up to him. "We've found something that you may want to see."

Alexander looked at the officer, his fellow yōkai undercover, and took careful note of the man's uncomfortable shifting. Whatever his fellow nekomata wanted to show him must have been something big.

"Lead the way."

It turned out what his fellow officer, one Jackson Polluck, wanted to show him was off campus. They strode through the desert, away from the high school and over to the junior high—or the ruins of what had once been a junior high school.

Even though he'd seen plenty of destruction in his life, Alexander still gawked in surprise at the demolished building. The entire structure had collapsed. Rubble lay strewn across the ground, ranging in size from large chunks of wall to small glass shards. Several fires still burned brightly, lighting up the night sky, while plumes of smoke blotted out the stars. It reminded him of the buildings that had been bombed during Pearl Harbor.

"What happened here?" he demanded.

"From what we can gather, the boiler room exploded, which set off a chain reaction causing all of the gas pipes running through the building to detonate as well," Jackson informed him.

"I see…"

He'd already taken statements from Lilian Pnéyma and Christine Fraust, so he knew that a yōkai had fought them. He was surprised the yōkai in question had been a kitsune, as they were well known for their dislike of combat, but he guessed there were some clan politics involved, perhaps a feud between one or more of the Thirteen Great Clans. Without knowing the full details, he couldn't really make any accurate judgements.

"That isn't all, Alex," Jackson said conspiratorially. "We've just received word that two other battles have taken place. One was at Mad Dawg Fitness. According to eyewitness reports, Kiara F. Kuyo was also attacked by a kitsune."

Alexander turned to Jackson.

"A kitsune." Blink. "Attacked Kiara F. Kuyo?" Blink. Blink. "In broad daylight?"

"Yes."

"They must have had a death wish."

Something strange was going on. Why would a kitsune attack Kiara, of all people? She was one of the strongest yōkai in Arizona. Attacking her was foolhardy unless…

"These events are related somehow…"

"Did you say something, Alex?"

"No." Alexander shook his head. "Continue please."

"Right. The last attack happened at Le Monte Apartment Complex. We have no clue what happened there, but over half of the complex is in ruins. Our sensor on sight detected massive amounts of celestial and spirit youki, along with youki that we suspect belongs to a River Kitsune."

"Casualties?"

"We've confirmed two dead—an elderly couple. A dozen more were injured. All of them have been sent to the nearest hospital."

"So you're telling me that we've had three battles happen in one day, and at least one of those battles ended with people either dead or in the infirmary?"

"That about sums it up, yes."

Alexander sighed. He so did not need to hear this right now.

"Monstrang's going to have someone's head for this."

He surveyed the demolished school again, already imagining the headache it was going to cause. A battle on a soccer field they could cover up. A school building being blown sky high would be much harder to cover. Either way he sliced it, he and the rest of the Saint's Bureau Office were going to have a long week.

Alexander was about to start issuing orders—when a sharp pain erupted from his back and stomach. He looked down to see something sticking out of his belly. It looked like a spear with a leaf-shaped blade. It wasn't made of solid mass. Its form was ethereal, composed of golden energy.

"Wha…"

Alex saw more than felt his legs give out. He collapsed to the ground, falling on his side, his arms and legs curling around his stomach. Several feet away, Jackson also crumpled to the hard earth, his eyes sightless and glassy, a spear impaling his chest.

The sight of his dead partner was the last thing Alexander ever saw.

***

When Kevin arrived at the hospital with Christine, Lilian, Lindsay, and Heather, it was to find several people already there. Kiara, Kotohime, Kirihime, and Camellia were all present.

They were just outside of the room where Iris no doubt resided. Kevin noticed that it was the same room she'd been placed in after being attacked by Jiāoào's servant on October of last year. Kotohime sat in *seiza* by the door, her katana in hand and her eyes closed. Kirihime was sitting on a padded bench opposite the door, while Camellia slept on the next seat over, her head resting on the three-tail's lap. Kiara was leaning against the wall, her only remaining hand tapping against her knee. She looked up as they walked over.

"Hey, boya. It seems you're always getting yourself into trouble."

"I'd love to deny that accusation, but for some reason can't." Kevin walked up to the group alongside everyone else. Lilian and Christine were on either side of him. Lindsay stood next to Christine, while Heather walked ahead to stand beside Kiara.

"Heh, you'll have to tell me all about what happened later on, then."

"I can do that."

"Lilian-sama, Kevin-sama." Kotohime opened her eyes. Kevin noticed that she wasn't wearing a kimono, but a gray business suit instead. He wondered why. "I am pleased to see that you and your friends are safe. I was worried when I realized that you were also being attacked."

"Wait, so you were attacked, too, Kotohime?" Lilian sounded shocked.

"Indeed." Kotohime's grave nod emphasized her point. "Our foe was most formidable. Had it not been for Camellia-sama intervening when she did, I dare say that man would have defeated me."

"Mom did...?" Lilian gawked at Kotohime, then looked over at her mom.

"Hawa-hawa-hawa... zzz... hawa-hawa-hawa..."

Kevin also looked at Camellia, who lay with her head on Kirihime's lap, snoring away. The fox in the French maid outfit petted the woman's hair while wearing a gentle smile. There was a snot bubble coming out of Camellia's nose.

Lilian looked back at Kotohime. "Are you sure you weren't under some kind of illusion? I love Mom, but she's kind of, well... she's kind of useless."

"Ouch." Lindsay winced. "That's a harsh thing to say about your own mother."

"It's kinda true, though," Kevin told her. "Trust me, Camellia has trouble just getting dressed in the morning, and she's always tripping over her own two feet. I should know. I usually end up with her breasts in my fa... ace..." He trailed off as he remembered how such instances had been happening far less lately. "I wonder..."

124

"Kevin?"

"It's nothing." He waved off Lindsay's concerned glance.

"I am as surprised as you are," Kotohime admitted. "Camellia-sama may have once been a formidable kitsune, but she has not been capable of combat since giving birth to you and Iris-sama…"

As Kotohime trailed off, Lilian's expression turned worried. "How is Iris?"

"We're not sure yet," Kiara told them. "My personal physician is currently checking her over, but he hasn't come out to give us his diagnosis."

"Were you able to heal her injuries at least?" Kevin asked Kotohime, who shook her head.

"I am afraid not—at least, not fully. While I did indeed manage to heal the injury and internal damage, because of the primitive sewing job, I suspect she will likely have a scar."

"O-oh." Kevin clenched his hands. He was the one who'd sewn her wounds shut. If she gained scars from what happened, it would be his—

"Stop that," Lilian demanded.

"H-huh?"

"That." Lilian gave him a look. "You're blaming yourself for what happened to Iris, aren't you? You're probably thinking something like 'It's my fault that Iris is going to have scars,' right?"

"W-well, it is, isn't it? I mean, I'm the one who—"

"It's not your fault." Christine's soft voice startled everyone present. She'd barely spoken two sentences since leaving the Sonoran Junior High building. "You saved her life. If you hadn't sewn her wounds, she would've died before she could get treatment."

Kevin looked away, wondering why his face felt like it had been hit with a flame thrower. "I-I only did what I thought was best at the time…"

"And it likely saved her life." The door to Iris's room opened and Kiara's physician walked out. "Had you not sewn her wounds shut when you did, Ms. Pnéyma would have bled to death."

Kiara's physician, a strange man whose face reminded Kevin of a toad, glanced at everyone present. He was the same doctor who'd first fixed up Iris back when she'd been attacked by Jiāoào's servant. Iris had received a scar from being stabbed back then as well. This would make her second scar—fourth if he decided to consider the entrance and exit wounds as separate injuries.

125

"There." Lilian beamed at Kevin. "You see? If it wasn't for you, Iris would have died."

Kevin returned her smile with an uncertain one of his own. "Yeah… I guess."

"How is Lady Iris?" Kirihime asked, speaking up for the first time.

The doctor's mood visibly shifted to one of concern. "Unfortunately, while Ms. Pnévma is alive, she is currently unresponsive."

"What do you mean?" Kotohime frowned at the doctor.

"What I mean is that her body has shut down. It is similar to being placed in a coma, but also different."

His words alarmed all those present. Lilian looked particularly horrified.

"So she's… so my sister is…?"

"I'm afraid so." The doctor nodded. "I believe the reason for her body shutting down is due to how she was attacked."

"This isn't something we should be talking about out here," Kiara interrupted. "Perhaps we should talk about this somewhere else, maybe inside of Iris's room? That way, Lilian and the others can see her while we talk."

The doctor paused for a moment before slowly nodding. "Yes, I believe that would be okay."

Everyone was directed into Iris's room. Kirihime woke up Camellia who, after several "hawas," followed them inside.

Plain white walls greeted them. Iris was lying on a bed near the window. Dressed in a white frock, her pale form was deathly still. Lilian broke off from Kevin and rushed to her sister's side. He followed silently, placing a hand on his mate's shoulder as she grabbed one of Iris's hands and brought it to her face.

"Her hand is so cold," she whispered, pressing Iris's palm against her cheek. Kevin could do nothing but give the redhead a comforting squeeze, offering his silent support, even though he felt like crying himself.

"H-hawa… I-Iris…?"

Camellia walked up to her daughter's side. The look on her face was telling. Despite her mentality being that of a child, Kevin knew that somewhere in there, locked away behind a prison of insanity, was the woman who'd birthed Lilian and Iris. She had to be in there.

There's no way tears like that can be faked.

126

"You said something about the manner in which she was attacked being the reason she won't wake up," Kotohime softly prodded the doctor to explain.

"Yes, I did." The doctor turned to Kotohime. "While I was scanning Ms. Pnéyma, I noticed that traces of celestial youki are still inside of her body. As you know, celestial and void powers are polar opposites, anathema to each other in every way. When Iris was stabbed, the celestial youki injected into her played havoc on more than just her body. It damaged her psychologically, mentally, perhaps even spiritually. It wouldn't be inaccurate to say that having a power that is so diametrically opposed to her own has caused Ms. Pnéyma's mind to become locked away."

So Iris's mind was essentially locked inside of her body? Kevin supposed such a thing wouldn't be improbable when dealing with yōkai. After all, if people could affect the mind through illusions and enchantments, then locking it away shouldn't be outside of the realm of possibility either.

"When will she wake up?" Kotohime asked.

"I can't say with any certainty. The problem is that her mind has been locked away by a foreign power that is the exact opposite of her own. In a case such as this, it's a matter of willpower. She could wake up as soon as tomorrow. Consequently, it may be years before she awakens."

Kevin heard the unspoken *"She might never wake up"* in the doctor's words. Lilian obviously could, too, because she stifled a sob. Christine, who had walked over to the other side of the bed, shed silent tears, and all the while, Lindsay stood behind the yuki-onna with a helpless expression.

"I see," Kotohime said. "Is there nothing you can do?"

"I'm sorry," the doctor replied, "but I've done all I can. The rest is up to her."

***

"I see. So you two are leaving?"

Kevin stood in the hallway with Christine and Lindsay. Heather stood several feet away, giving them a moment of privacy. She was going to take them home. Lilian was still inside of Iris's room with the others, refusing to leave her sister's side.

"Yeah." Lindsay's apologetic smile looked tired thanks to the bags

A Fox's Revenge

under her eyes. "There isn't much we can do. Half the stuff that doctor was talking about flew straight over my head anyway." She shook her head, her smile becoming strained. "Yōkai. Kitsune. Celestial. Void. You sure have gotten yourself involved into some pretty messed up stuff."

"I guess I have." Kevin ran a hand through his hair. "Sorry for getting you mixed up in all this." He looked at Christine. "Both of you."

"Psh! What are you apologizing for?" Lindsay crossed her arms. "It's not like you're the one who decided to stick around. Don't forget that I could have stopped hanging around you guys after I found out about this whole yōkai thing. I chose to stay because you, Lilian, and Iris are my friends. I'm not gonna just up and abandon you."

Kevin gave her a grateful smile. "Thanks."

"You're welcome." Lindsay grinned back before surprising him with a hug. "You take care of yourself and that mate of yours, got it?"

"I will." Kevin returned the hug.

As Lindsay stepped away, Kevin looked down at Christine. The tiny snow maiden remained silent. He didn't know what was going through her head, but the lack of violence and *tsundere* moments from her bothered him.

Deciding to test his luck, he pulled her into a hug. Christine stiffened in his arms, but he ignored that and wrapped his arms tightly around her. She felt so small, so much more fragile than Lilian or Lindsay. It made him want to protect her.

"You take care of yourself, all right?" he said.

Christine remained silent, her arms not moving. For a moment, Kevin wondered if she would headbutt him or maybe try to freeze him in a block of ice. The moment soon passed, and a pair of tiny arms wound around his waist, while small hands gripped the back of his shirt.

"Kay." Christine's voice was abnormally soft. "You take care of yourself, too. I don't want the person I lo—one of my friends dying because he decided to do something stupid."

"Heh, now that's more like the Christine I know. I was beginning to get worried."

Kevin's heart lightened just a bit when he noticed the steam rising from Christine's head. It was a good sign.

"D-don't think hearing that makes me happy." Her voice came out muffled, since her face was buried in his chest. "I-I don't care if you're worried about me… idiot."

"Don't you mean *baka*?" Kevin couldn't help but tease. Christine responded by headbutting him in the chin. "G-gu!"

"Idiot!"

Christine glared down at Kevin, who'd fallen onto his backside, blinking up at her in dazed confusion. Above him, Lindsay shook her head.

"That was a dumb thing to say, Kevin."

"U-ugh." Kevin wondered why he was suddenly seeing two. "You should have told me that beforehand."

"You should have known what would happen beforehand."

Kevin could say nothing to dispute that.

***

Kevin reentered Iris's hospital room. Kotohime and Kirihime were still present. The kimono-clad bodyguard had taken to sitting seiza on a tatami mat that she had acquired from somewhere—her Extra Dimensional Storage Space, he concluded. Kirihime slept sitting on a padded chair, her hair falling in front of her face as her head tilted down. He noticed that Camellia had switched to her fox form and was lying on Iris's bed, her five tails lying limply behind her. Lilian still sat in the chair next to her sister, her hands holding onto one of Iris's like it was a lifeline. Kiara and Heather had already left.

The hospital was letting them stay the night. Technically, that was against policy, but Kiara's physician apparently had some clout. He'd told them not worry about anything, that he would take care of any complaints.

"Lilian." Kevin placed a hand on her shoulder. "How are you feeling?"

Lilian didn't look away from her sister. The despairing look on her face pulled at his heartstrings. "I feel guilty."

"For what happened to your sister?" he asked.

"For everything. Even before I came here, Iris was also getting herself injured because of my problems. What's more, Christine was nearly killed, and you... you've been forced to kill someone again, all because I didn't have the power to do it myself."

Kevin understood her guilt well. He also felt guilty over what had happened, though his reasons were both similar and different than her own.

"I don't think you have anything to feel guilty about. There are times when things happen that are beyond our ability to control. I imagine someone coming to try and kill you is one of those things. It's not your fault someone wanted to take your life. If anything, the one to blame in all this is your matriarch for having tried to play matchmaker by marry—mating you off to that spoiled brat."

"I guess." Lilian finally glanced at him, a half-smile touching her lips. "Though I don't think you have any right to try and console me."

Kevin's own smile was quite wry. "I suppose trying to convince you that you shouldn't feel guilty is hypocritical of me, but my point still stands."

Lilian's smile brightened just a bit. It was too bad the look only lasted for a second.

She went back to staring at her sister, whose still form had not moved an inch. With the moonlight shining in through the window, Iris appeared almost ethereal. Her skin had grown impossibly pale, to the point where it seemed translucent. It presented a stark contrast with her black hair.

"Things were so much simpler when it was just you and me," Lilian said softly. "Back when you had first rescued me and my biggest worry was trying to make you fall in love with me. Now we've had to deal with everything from members of another kitsune clan to assassins. Every time something happens, we're faced with more dangers than before. Iris was almost killed this time, and there's a good chance she'll never... that she won't..."

Kevin moved to stand directly behind Lilian. He leaned down, wrapping his arms around her as he set his chin on the crown of her head.

"She'll wake up," he reassured her. "You know how stubborn Iris is. She's not gonna let something like this beat her. She still has to seduce you into her bed."

Lilian, shedding silent tears for her sister, snorted. "That's true. She won't let herself be taken down until she's at least had a threesome with us."

"Right."

"If she beats this," Lilian continued softly, "I think I might actually let her join us in bed."

"Please don't joke about something like that."

"Sorry, Beloved."

Despite playing off Lilian's words as a joke, part of him wondered if she might truly mean them. Kevin knew about what Iris and Lilian did before him. It bothered him to think about their past.

Many clans often married within their clan. Since kitsune didn't need to worry about genetic defects, and, in fact, kitsune mating within the clan kept their blood pure, it was more common for them to mate within the clan than outside of it. Kotohime had lectured him on this subject before, so he understood this from a purely academic standpoint.

It still bothered him. Maybe it was because he was human, but he didn't approve of it. He didn't think it was right—even if Lilian and Iris were the same gender.

"We should probably get some sleep," Kevin said.

"Yeah," Lilian agreed.

Kevin paused, sighed, and then said, "You should sleep with Iris tonight. I'm sure she'd appreciate your presence."

Regardless of his thoughts on Lilian and Iris's relationship, he, above everything else, wanted his mate to be happy.

"You're probably right."

They separated. Kevin straightened up, while Lilian got out of her seat, grabbed her shirt, and lifted it over her head. Her breasts popped free, bouncing several times like they were made of jello. She disliked bras, so she barely ever wore them. Then she unzipped her jean skirt and slid it, along with her underwear, down her hips.

He knew this was a kitsune quirk. Lilian, like most of her species, didn't really like clothes. Being supernatural creatures that had been born as foxes, the concept of clothing only came to them because of their association with humans. To them, nudity was their natural state of being.

As she stood there before him, stark naked, Kevin admired her incredible figure and inhuman beauty. Her shapely ass, wide hips, and slender shoulders were a sight to behold. The delicate curvature of her spine as it connected her slender neck with her magnificent derriere still astounded him. Beyond that, her two red tails and fox ears gave her an exotic appearance. Kevin wondered if he would ever get used to this sight.

Probably not.

Lilian crawled into Iris's bed, moving under the covers. Once she got comfortable, she turned around to look at him.

"Are you coming in?"

"E-eh?" Kevin blinked. "Ah, well, I was actually planning on just finding a place on the floor…"

"Don't be silly, Beloved," she said. "There's no way I'm not sleeping with you just because Iris is using this bed. Besides, it's not like this will be any different from every other night."

"I guess that's true," he conceded. Iris snuck into their bed often enough that Kevin was never surprised to wake up with another occupant beside him and Lilian.

"Right. So, get in here."

Sighing, Kevin decided to do as he was told. Even if he were inclined to put up a fight, he was too tired. It was no surprise, considering what he'd been through.

Kevin slowly divested himself of his clothing, until he was down to just his boxers. No matter how much time passed, or how many times Lilian pouted at him, he still refused to sleep nude like her. He wasn't comfortable being naked.

He slowly crawled into the bed and was about to spoon with Lilian —

"Other side."

—When the girl spoke up.

He looked at her. "Pardon?"

"Get in on the other side. Iris is really cold, and I need your help warming her up."

"So, I'm being turned into a heating unit now?"

"Just for now."

Kevin wondered if he should be annoyed about being demoted from mate to heating unit. Probably. But he was too tired to care. He crawled into the bed from the other side. Lilian was already resting her head on Iris's breasts, her arms and legs entwined around her sister. Kevin did the same and realized that Lilian was correct; Iris's body was, indeed, much colder than normal. It made him think of a corpse.

If I couldn't feel her breathing...

He followed Lilian's example and wrapped an arm around Iris, pulling himself close and using his body heat to help warm her up. Just as he was about to close his eyes, Kevin could have sworn he saw the twin-tailed succubus's lips curve into a delightful smile.

I wonder if I'm being too soft, he thought before drifting off.

***

Fan winced as she quietly limped her way up the steps to the modest condo that she lived in with Guang and Li. The stairs shook and jangled, metal clinking together. She winced with every step she took, gritting her teeth as pain lanced through her. Her entire body felt like it had been set on fire.

"That's because it was set on fire, you idiot." Fan scowled.

Right. Her entire body had been set on fire.

"Oh, shut up! I don't wanna hear another word out of you!"

But then I wouldn't be able to—

"I SAID SHUT UP!"

…

"Better."

… Meanie.

"What was that?"

…

Fan scowled, but even that scowl faded into nothingness. Maintaining facial expressions hurt. Everything hurt. It was all thanks to that damn human.

"The next time he and I meet, he's going to die slowly and painfully."

Climbing the flight of stairs took a lot more effort than it should have. Her legs felt like gelatinous liquid. Her arms and face stung as the cold night air hit her burns. Having expended almost all her youki to protect herself from that last explosion, she had almost none left, and, therefore, couldn't heal herself.

That fact irked her. To think she'd been driven to this point by a lowly ape. It was humiliating!

She opened the door and entered her condo. The door clicked shut behind her. Upon stepping further inside, she realized that she wasn't alone.

"Li," she greeted the man standing in the center of the living room… and then stopped when she noticed something was wrong. "Y-your arm!"

Li glanced over at her, his silent eyes purveyors of worry as he glanced at the burns on her arms, legs, torso, and face. He then looked at his own arm—or rather, the spot where his arm should have been. It wasn't there anymore. His entire right arm was gone.

"There was an… unforeseen incident during my battle," he informed her. "In all honesty, I am quite lucky to have escaped at all."

"A-are you going to be okay?" she asked.

"I believe I am the one who should be asking that. You appear to have suffered a lot."

"Oh, stuff it." Fan knew she looked awful. She didn't need Li rubbing it in.

"To answer your question, I should be fine. I lack the youki necessary to regrow my arm, but I should be capable of it after a good night's rest." While his facial expression didn't change, his eyes contained a glimmer of worry. "And yourself? Will you be all right?"

"I'll enter a healing trance tonight." Fan waved a hand dismissively, or rather, she tried to. She winced halfway through. "It shouldn't take too long for me to heal these. They look bad, but most of them are only second-degree burns."

"I am pleased to hear that."

"Where's Guang?"

"Guang has been... defeated."

Fan sucked in a breath. "So he's dead?"

When Li remained silent, Fan closed her eyes. She'd never really cared about Guang, but he had still been one of her bodyguards. Hearing that he'd died struck her surprisingly hard.

"I see. I guess we'll have to avenge him, perhaps after we kill the Pnéyma girl and her human boy toy."

"Actually, Lord Bodhisattva has asked that we return home."

"W-what?" Fan allowed her startlement to show on her face. "But we haven't killed Lilian Pnéyma or her mate yet!"

"That is true, but it seems your father has changed his mind regarding her. That, or he simply wishes for us to return."

Fan bit her lip. She didn't like Arizona. She didn't like being so far from her beloved younger brother. At the same time, Lilian Pnéyma and her mate had humiliated her. It would be one thing if she'd been defeated by a yōkai who was stronger than she was, but to be beaten by a two-tails and a human was shameful. She wanted to kill them, and not just because of what they'd done to her beloved younger brother. Not anymore. It was even more personal now. At the same time...

"F-fine," she conceded to Li. This was an order from her father, and one did not disobey the will of the Bodhisattva, not even his daughter. "When do we leave?"

"We leave first thing tomorrow morning."

Fan nodded, right before casting Li a suspicious glance. "We're not going to be traveling on one of those metal death traps again, are we?"

Li's silence was telling.

A Fox's Revenge

"… Dammit…"

A Fox's Revenge

Chapter 5

Leaving

It was the day after the multiple attacks on herself and her charge's family. Because she didn't have any clothes of her own anymore, as they had been destroyed when their apartment blew up, Kotohime was wearing one of Kiara's business suits. Dark gray. Slacks and a long-sleeved shirt. The shirt had the top three buttons undone because her chest was too large to fit in it. How Kiara could stand to wear these things was beyond her.

She stood in the office of Davin Monstrang. She was alone this time. Kirihime had remained at the hospital with Kevin, Lilian, Iris, and Camellia.

Kiara was with them. She had arrived early that morning. Since Lilian had been their target, they had deemed it prudent for at least two of them to remain by Lilian's side at all times.

Sitting behind his desk, Davin Monstrang remained silent. Kotohime tried not to squirm. She was a warrior, a swordswoman renowned throughout the yōkai world for her talent with a blade. Even so, she couldn't stop the small chill that traveled down her spine as he stared at her from behind his large, interlocked hands.

Davin Monstrang was a large man, though perhaps calling him large did him an injustice. His sheer size made him look like he could squash a bull with nothing but his girth. Numerous chins, thick brow ridges, and a lack of eyebrows made up his most outstanding features. His buzzed head had two small bumps on either side of his forehead. He wore a garish orange Hawaiian T-shirt that clashed horribly with the Spartan decorations of his office.

"This is the sixth time you've come to me after a major incident has occurred," Davin Monstrang grunted. "It's troubling how every problem that has happened recently seems to be caused by the Pnéyma Clan."

"You have my most sincere apologies." Kotohime bowed before the man, a deep bow from the waist. "I wish I could claim otherwise, however, it is just as you say. It seems the troubles of the Pnéyma Clan have finally caught up with us, and Arizona is getting swept up in our issues as a result."

Davin grunted. "Don't forget the brat. He's also become swept up in your problems."

"Kevin-sama has willingly involved himself with us," Kotohime rebutted. "While you may not approve of a yōkai becoming romantically involved with a human, the fact remains that it was his decision to become involved with us. Anything that happens to him now is a direct result of this acceptance."

"This has nothing to do with a human and a yōkai becoming romantically involved," Davin said. "I promised his mother when she came to me that I would do everything in my power to protect him. That is a promise I have done my utmost to keep."

This was Kotohime's first time hearing about this. She had no idea that Davin Monstrang and Karen Swift were acquainted, though that did explain why a yōkai of Monstrang's position was working out of a newspaper distribution center. Kotohime would confess to being curious. However, she also knew better than to pry.

Davin grunted. "I didn't call you here to discuss the brat's love life. Things with the Pnéyma Clan are becoming volatile. First there was that business with the child from the Shénshèng Clan, and then there was the attack in California." Kotohime opened her mouth, but Davin's raised hand stopped her. "I am not saying that was your fault. However, you cannot deny that your involvement caused a lot of damage and threatened to reveal our existence to the humans."

Kotohime did not like how he said that, but she also couldn't deny the truth to his words. Their battle with Luna had caused a lot of damage, which had easily been seen by a number of humans. Only the timely intervention of Kuroneko had kept humanity from learning anything.

A Fox's Revenge

"And then there was also that incident with the kitsune assassin and his accomplice. They enchanted an entire school full of children and used them to attack the brat and your charge. We were lucky the most anyone suffered from that catastrophe was a few broken bones, and that only those who already know of our existence remember what happened. This time, we weren't so lucky."

The chair emitted a harsh squeal as Davin leaned back. Kotohime worried that it might break, but she said nothing for fear of sounding rude.

"The soccer field belonging to the Peoria school district is in ruins and Sonoran Junior High has been completely destroyed. What's more, there is no way we can keep news like that from the public. Several people who live in the vicinity of the school saw it go up in flames, and we've received reports of people seeing figures fleeing from the scene. Can you guess what those eye witness reports claimed these figures looked like?"

Kotohime shifted to hide her discomfort. "I can take a guess, yes."

Davin blew out a smoky breath. "That's why I've decided that it would be for the best if you and the Pnéyma Clan leave the states for a while." Kotohime's eyes widened, but before she could protest, he said, "I'm not saying it's permanent, but with everything that has happened here, and with the recent news that I've gathered, it would be best for everyone involved if you found yourselves a more secure location that is not within the United States."

Kotohime understood what Davin was asking—no, demanding. It was a pretty way of saying, *"We can't protect you and your group, so I'm telling you to leave."* Basically, she and the three Pnéyma Clan members had become too troublesome for Davin to tolerate.

"I… I understand," Kotohime said at last. "What about Kevin-sama?"

"The brat?" Davin inhaled a deep breath of air and blew it out. Rings of smoke emitted from his nostrils. "It's not really my choice anymore, is it? Even if I told him to stay here, he would not listen, and I can't force him to stay. I might have made a promise to his mom, but I'm not going to stop him from making his own choices."

Kotohime breathed a sigh of relief. "Thank you, Davin-dono."

"Don't thank me. I'm simply foisting responsibility of the brat onto you. From now on, you're going to be in charge of him, and you're going to have to tell his mother about what happened here."

Despite Davin's words, Kotohime could feel nothing but relief as she gave one final bow and left his office. Even if they had to leave the country, at the very least, Lilian would have her mate. She knew that her charge was going to need him in the coming days.

***

While all the rooms belonging to members of the Pnéyma Clan came equipped with their own bath, the guilty pleasure of the clan was most definitely the matriarch's. Of course, calling it something as mundane as a bath would have been doing it a disservice. Bathhouse was a more appropriate term.

The bathhouse of the matriarch was large. With a ceiling that rose high above her head, decorated with mosaic tiles to look like the clear summer sky, and a bath the size of an Olympic swimming pool, even terms like large and grand did little to describe it. Arrayed around the room, protruding from the walls, were several waterfalls situated between majestic Corinthian columns. Many tales abounded among kitsune of the legendary orgies that had taken place in this bathhouse.

Delphine believed that the term "legendary orgies" was misleading. That said, she would not deny that several of her sons and daughters had been born in this very bathhouse.

Poke.

Sitting idly, whiling away the time with a glass of wine that floated on a tray in front of her, Delphine studied the bathhouse that she had created so many centuries ago…

Poke.

How many of her daughters had been conceived in this bathhouse? Three? Four? How many of her numerous sons? She supposed it didn't matter, but thinking about it amused her nonetheless…

Poke.

Her mind idly wandered to Camellia. What was she doing now? Was she safe? Given her mentality, there was a good chance that she had gotten into trouble. If only she had never allowed Demetry to marry Camellia…

But then I wouldn't have Lilian and Iris.

Poke.

Lilian and Iris were a study in opposites. Where Lilian was open and enthusiastic, Iris was mysterious and alluring. If people likened Lilian to a fresh spring breeze, then Iris was the searing summer heat.

140

Light and Dark. Naïve and cynical. Yes, the only way those two could have been more different was if Lilian had some modesty and shyness to go along with that irrepressible personality of hers. As it was, Lilian and Iris were still vastly different from each other.

Poke.

There is also that sister complex that Iris has. Delphine frowned. *I do so hope that she doesn't decide to follow in her half-sisters' footsteps. I do not need another set of lesbian twins.*

Poke. Poke.

Delphine sighed as she finally decided to address the person who was poking her left boob.

"Is there something I can help you with, Jasmine dear?"

Jasmine Pnéyma was Delphine's youngest. The girl had only gained her second tail thirty years ago, and she looked a lot like Delphine did at that age. Her silvery hair was styled in braids, and her emotionless carmine eyes were nearly identical to her mother's. There were only three differences that were worth noting.

Height and bust were the first and most obvious variations between mother and daughter. Having only become a supernal being thirty years ago, Jasmine held the appearance of a thirteen-year-old girl. As such, she didn't have much in the way of a chest, nor was she very tall.

The last difference was not something that could be seen except by those who were observant. Demeanor. Whereas Delphine preferred to greet the world with a deceptively sweet smile that made her seem more approachable than she truly was, her youngest wore a facade of emotionlessness. She knew the girl had emotions; Violet seemed able to rile her up with little effort. However, by and large, the quiet beauty often remained impassive, even in the most extreme of circumstances.

Currently, her youngest daughter was poking her left boob while staring at it with inscrutable eyes.

"Do not worry, Mother," her daughter said in a bland voice. "I am merely trying to ascertain how it is possible for someone to have titantic titties such as yours. I am quite certain that these magnificent melons defy the laws of nature, physics, and probably a few other universal concepts."

Were Jasmine anyone else, Delphine would have worried about how she said all that with a completely straight face.

"If you are worried about whether or not yours will grow to be this big, then I would not worry. You are still young, and mine did not get this big until I reached 160." Delphine watched, amused as Jasmine ceased her poking to cup her own breasts, which could barely even be called such. "Oh, dear. Are you embarrassed? There is no need for that. Even without breasts, you are awfully cute."

"I am not embarrassed." Jasmine began rubbing her chest up and down. "I am merely wondering if rubbing my measly baby bumps will cause them to grow bigger. I heard of a secret method about making your boobs grow from Holly."

"I see." Delphine had heard of that method, too, and she already knew it to be a lie. She wouldn't tell Jasmine that, though, as watching her youngest grope herself amused her. "Well, far be it for me to stop you. Perhaps if you keep that up, yours will grow to be as big as mine one day."

"I do not believe I want massive mammaries like yours," Jasmine declared, her vacant carmine orbs not changing in the slightest. "They must be the cause of unbelievable back pain."

Delphine pouted at her daughter. "I rather resent that." Her expression returned to its placid demeanor as she sipped her wine. "I will have you know that I have never suffered back pain once in my life."

"Hn."

Just then, something appeared before them. Its long, pipe-like body, ethereal form, and large eyes denoted it as kudagitsune. Delphine recognized the youki signature of the one who summoned it, and a smile crossed her face.

"Oh, my. A message for me?"

The kudagitsune held a message aloft for her to take, which she did, unfurling the scroll and holding it above the water while she read. The message was short and to the point. At the bottom was Kotohime's signature in kanji.

"Hmm. It seems there is some excitement going on in North America as well."

"Mother?" Jasmine's lips twitched into the slightest of frowns.

Delphine smiled at her youngest. "Jasmine, would you be a dear and inform Violet that I would appreciate her company for lunch?"

Jasmine twitched at the mention of Violet, but she did not do anything else. She stood up in the water, which stopped at her navel, and bowed.

"I will do as your command, Mother."

"Thank you." Delphine smiled as her youngest exited the

bathhouse. When the girl had disappeared, she turned back to the scroll. Her smile widened. "It has been so long since I've seen my daughter and granddaughters. It will be nice to see them again." The smile stretched from ear to ear. "And, of course, I am looking most forward to finally meeting Lilian's mate."

***

"WHAT DO YOU MEAN OUR APARTMENT WAS DESTROYED?!"

Kevin winced as his mother yelled at him over the phone. He jerked the cellphone away from his ear, waited until he was sure she was finished yelling, and then put it back to his face.

"There was a, uh, an accident. One of the other residents left the stove on, or something, and our apartment blew up. In fact, most of the complex was destroyed."

"Are you okay? What about Lilian? Is she okay? Kotohime?"

"Everyone is fine," Kevin assured his mother. "We weren't there when the apartment exploded."

"That's good." His mother sighed over the line. *"No, wait, this isn't good! Our apartment was destroyed! What are we going to do?! Where are you going to live?! Do you want me to come home?"*

"No!" Kevin nearly shouted. He received a raised eyebrow from Kiara, which made him flush and lower his voice. "I mean, don't worry about us. Kiara's been kind enough to let us stay with her. She's even agreed to help set us up with a place to live until the apartment complex is repaired."

"Oh, well, okay, I guess."

Kevin had the distinct feeling that his mom was disappointed, but he tried not to think about that.

"Anyway, I was just calling to let you know that."

"All right, honey. You be good okay, and be sure to thank Kiara."

"I already have. Don't worry, Mom. I'm not you."

"Now that's a mean thing to say to your mother."

"And no less true. Anyway, gotta go."

"All right. I love you, Kevin."

"Right. Love you, too."

Kevin hung up the phone with a sigh. Pocketing it, he turned to face Kiara.

"Sounds like you've got everything with your mom squared away," she observed with a cool gaze.

"I don't like lying to her like this." Kevin rubbed his face. "It feels wrong."

"Of course it does." Kiara snorted. "No one likes lying to their loved ones. However, sometimes we don't have a choice."

"I know. It still doesn't seem right."

Kiara shrugged, as if to say, *"That's how it is."*

"Do you have everything packed?" she asked.

Kevin nodded. "Yeah, not like I have much that needs to be packed anyway. Everything I owned was in the apartment. All I have now is the stuff I bought the other day."

He hefted the two bags containing his and Lilian's clothing. Since he and Lilian had nothing to wear, he'd gone out and bought them some clothes the previous day. Lilian did have a few more items than him, but most of that was the lingerie she stored in her Extra Dimensional Storage Space.

"In that case, come with me. I've got something to give you."

Kiara turned on her heel and walked away. Curious, Kevin followed her, walking along the light beige carpet of her expensive condo.

His instructor in the art of badassery lived in a ritzy place. The condo that she owned had two bedrooms and two bathrooms, with an additional office and a small training room. It was a lot larger than most condos, being about the size of a one-story house.

It wasn't the size that made this place so incredible, but the appliances that decked the place from top to bottom. Everything Kiara owned was top of the line. She had the latest and greatest in technological innovations, be it her desktop with its multiple monitors and ridiculous processing power, or her surround sound system that could be accessed from anywhere, or be localized to specific rooms. If that wasn't enough, then running through most of the house, visible through small glass slits along the floor, was a small stream that constantly recycled water via the waterfall in her living room.

He and those who lived with him had been staying there for the past few days, though he was the only one present at the moment. Kotohime and the others had left already. They were probably visiting Iris at the hospital right now. It was where they went every day after breakfast.

Kiara led him into her office. A combination of wood and glass made up the floor, allowing him to see the stream of water beneath him as he walked inside. The room had its own fireplace on one side of the wall and a gigantic bookshelf sat on the other. Most of the books were physical training manuals and health books. On the opposite end of the room from the door was a large desk made of walnut. Also…

"Is that a poster of Wolverine?" Kevin asked.

Kiara stopped. "You mean Hugh Jackman? Yeah, it is."

"Why is he half naked?"

"Why shouldn't he be half naked?"

Kevin had nothing to say to that. Kiara walked behind her desk, which had a safe secured inside of the wall.

"I had these custom-made for you," she told him as she placed her hand on a small scanner. The safe unlocked with a hiss. "I didn't plan on giving them to you until you could move and shoot at the same time, but given what happened, I figured now would be as good a time as any."

Before Kevin could ask what she was talking about, Kiara turned around. There was a case in her hands. It wasn't very big, maybe a little under a foot in length and half a foot in width. The wood gleamed of fresh polish, and its dark red contrasted with her light tan skin. He stared at the case, then at her.

"Well?" She smirked. "What are you waiting for? An invitation?"

Kevin took the case. It was heavier than he expected. Placing it on the desk, he undid the bronze latches that kept it closed and slowly opened the lid. Purple velvet lined the case. It shimmered with an effervescent sheen, which refracted off the two objects resting within.

They were guns. One shone with the brilliant gleam of freshly polished silver, and the other was so black it seemed to reject light's touch. Both were larger than the average handgun. The barrels were not only bigger but also a lot longer than a standard 9mm.

"Are these Desert Eagles?" he asked, wondering if the shock he heard in his voice was just his imagination.

"They are not," Kiara said, "but they're based on the Desert Eagle's design."

"They're heavy," he commented as he picked them up, testing their weight. They were probably five pounds heavier than a Beretta.

"Of course they are. Those are experimental guns based on blueprints that were created by the Sons and Daughters of Humanity." Kiara's feral grin made Kevin realize that he was staring at the guns with a gobsmacked expression. He tried schooling his features, but he still couldn't mask his shock. "Surprised? So am I. Apparently, before she left them, Heather raided one of their safe houses where several weapon

designs were kept. She gave these blueprints to Davin Monstrang as a form of appeasement when she asked for amnesty."

"I see. Yeah, I suppose that makes sense. I always wondered how someone who once worked for an organization like that was allowed to live in Arizona and work as a school teacher."

Kevin looked back down at the guns. Despite their weight, they fit comfortably within his hands. Their grip possessed small grooves that conformed to his fingers, and the triggers were within easy distance of his trigger fingers.

"Those guns are special," Kiara continued, causing him to look up. "I don't understand how they work, but they apparently fire youki instead of lead bullets."

"What?"

Kiara took in his nonplussed reaction and grinned. "Yeah, I made the same face when they told me that. The engineer who helped design my personal training equipment built these. He told me that these guns fire youki bullets."

She reached back into the safe and pulled out another box, which she set on the desk and opened. This one contained the same velvet lining, but instead of weapons, there were nearly a dozen magazine clips.

Kiara held out one of the clips—only this looked nothing like a standard magazine. It held the same general shape, but this contained numerous glowing red lines that ran along it like veins. He also noticed a single tiny hole located where the bullets would normally be ejected. Kevin took the clip from her and examined it.

"This is your ammunition," she told him. "The magazine is reusable. Whenever it runs out of energy, all you need to do is have a yōkai fill it with their youki, and it can be used as many times as you want."

"That's pretty cool," Kevin muttered. "I wonder why the Sons and Daughters of Humanity didn't use these weapons at the Comic-Con?"

"Because it isn't practical," Kiara said. "No yōkai would ever willingly charge their weapons for them, and according to Heather, they haven't been able to replicate youki with their experiments. From what I've been told, these designs were originally scrapped due to that reason."

"Makes sense."

Kevin loaded one of the clips inside of the silver gun. Nothing happened at first, but when he flicked the safety near his thumb, red

147

veins like lines from a circuit board lit up along the gun's surface. He guessed that meant the gun was powered.

"My engineer has made one dozen magazine clips for you," Kiara continued. "I've filled half of those with my own youki. They should last you a good while. We've run tests. Using my youki for these will give you about one hundred shots before you run out of bullets."

"That's quite a bit. Most magazines only allow twelve to sixteen shots before you need to reload."

One hundred rounds for a single magazine was massive. It meant he had 200 bullets if he used both at the same time. With that much ammo, it was unlikely that Kevin would ever have to reload during combat.

"Right." Kiara nodded. "Anyway, I would suggest asking Kotohime, Camellia, and your mate to fill up the other six cartridges for you. Different types of energy will produce different effects, and since different yōkai have different weaknesses…"

"It'll be good to have as many types of ammunition as possible in order to exploit those weaknesses," Kevin finished.

"Exactly." Grinning her feral grin, Kiara ruffled Kevin's hair. "I've taught you well. Now come on. We need to head out. Your mate is probably anxiously waiting for you."

***

After placing his new guns and the container filled with magazine clips in his bag, Kevin got into Kiara's car. He then proceeded to scream like a little girl as the one-armed inu drove with the maniacal talents of a psychotic daredevil. It was definitely a good thing that the hospital was only a ten-minute drive—ten minutes because Kiara apparently mistook the gas pedal for the breaks.

It was a windswept Kevin who was dropped off in front of the hospital. The front doors to the large white building slid open to admit him. He stumbled into the waiting room. Several people looked at him as he entered and just as many ignored his existence; some sat on the chairs lining the walls, while others stood, arms crossed and uncaring. Several sick people coughed into their hands. Kevin also saw a number of individuals who were nursing injuries, though none appeared severe.

His feet tapped against white tiles as he walked up to the receptionist, a woman with a cat-like grin and sharp, amber eyes.

"I'm here to see Iris Pnévma," he said.

"I figured as much," the woman replied, lips peeling back into a grin. "You've been coming and going for the past few days. You don't need to bother signing in. You remember the way, right?"

"Yeah."

"Then just head on down. No sense wasting time here. Your mate probably wants to see you anyway."

Kevin twitched at the mate comment, but he didn't allow himself to feel startled. He was growing used to discovering that the people around him were yōkai in disguise.

He passed through a door next to the receptionist's desk. Walking down a hallway, he moved past numerous doors on his left, each one numbered. Sunlight sprinkled in through several windows arrayed at evenly spaced intervals on the hall's other side. Upon reaching the room he knew Iris resided in, he stopped.

Voices were coming from the other end.

"I don't wanna go!" Lilian shouted.

"Look here, girl, you're being unreasonable," a voice that Kevin had never heard before said. "This is an order from your matriarch. You have to go."

"No!"

"Lilian-sama, please do not be stubborn about this."

"Quiet, Kotohime. You kept this from me. How could you?"

"Because I knew that Lilian-sama would react exactly as she is right now if she were to learn about where we are going beforehand."

"Stop acting like a brat," the new voice said. "I don't know why you're so dead set on not returning home, but you've got no choice in the matter anymore. Shit's hitting the fan. I don't know if you've heard, but our clan is officially at war with the Shénshèng Clan."

Kevin froze by the doorway as he continued to listen in. War? Lilian's clan was at war? Since when?

"W-what?" Lilian asked.

"Come on, girl, use that head of yours. Did you really think Mom would allow what happened to you to go unpunished? Tensions have been rising between the Shénshèng Clan and our clan ever since that pampered little brat tried to kidnap you. Now that we have proof of the Bodhisattva's intentions to off you, Mom has formally declared war as of two days ago."

"I-I didn't know that."

"Of course you didn't know that." Kevin could almost hear the eyeroll in the other person's voice. "There's no way you could have,

149

busy as you are enjoying life with your mate. Ha, really, you have it so easy."

"W-whatever." He could detect Lilian's embarrassment through her tone. "I still don't want to go."

The voices seemed to trail off. Kevin was about to press his ear against the door and listen in further—

"HAWA!"

"M-My Lady!"

—when two shouts from behind made the hair on his neck bristle.

Kevin spun around just in time to receive a face full of tits. His back slammed against the door, swiftly depriving him of oxygen and forcing the door open. He and the person whose jugs were asphyxiating him tumbled into the room, where he landed on his back, and the person who crashed into him landed on top. His face was still shoved between the pair of massive mammaries, which were quite familiar to him.

It's been awhile since this has happened.

"Owie…" He heard a familiar voice above him. "That really hurt. Hawa, maybe I shouldn't run down the hall like that."

"M-Mom?! What are you doing?! Get off my mate!"

"Hawa?"

The breasts were removed from Kevin's face, allowing him to breathe again. He sucked in great, gulping heaps of oxygen. The person on top of him sat up and looked down. She tilted her head for maximum adorableness.

"Oh, Kevin-kyun." Camellia's bright smile reminded him of rainbows. "What are you doing down there?"

Kevin's right eye began twitching. "You ran into me."

Camellia's *moé* levels reached a new plateau when she placed a finger on her lips. "I did?"

Kevin wasn't affected. "You did."

"Oh." A pause. "My bad. Tee-hee."

Kevin watched Camellia rap the knuckles of her right hand against her head with a blank look. He knew that letting her watch anime with him, Lilian, and Iris had been a bad idea. At the same time…

She isn't referring to herself in third person…

"It's fine." He sighed. "Would you mind getting off of me?"

"Ah, right. Sorry."

Camellia climbed off him and stood up. Kevin sat up, only blinking when Camellia extended a hand, which he took, allowing her to pull him to his feet. She then walked over to Iris's bed, sat down, and grabbed her daughter's hand.

Kevin ignored the incongruity of Camellia's actions and turned to face the other people in the room. Kotohime and Lilian stood before him. There was also another person in the room, someone that he'd never seen before.

She didn't look a day over eighteen, but considering she had three tails sticking out from underneath her outfit, appearances didn't mean much. And speaking of her outfit, Kevin wondered just why in the heck she was wearing a toga. Was this something that all women in Lilian's clan wore? Her long silver hair was carefully tied with bandages, ending in a dolphin's tail near her feet, which were clad in sandals. Her chest was quite small, and there was also...

"Holy crap, you're tiny."

This girl was short, barely coming up to his chest.

Kevin received a fist to the gut for his words. He wheezed as the air was violently expelled from his lungs, and then dropped to his knees and curled his arms around his stomach as the fist retracted.

"B-Beloved!"

A worried Lilian knelt next to him, rubbing his back and sending trace amounts of celestial youki to help ease his pain.

"Cocky brat." The woman who'd planted her fist in his gut crossed her arms and glared at him. "You think you can look down on me just because of my height? Get real! Say crap like that again and I'll neuter you."

"But I need that part of him!" Lilian exclaimed. "How else is Beloved supposed to give me kits?"

"Glad to know you care about me so much, Lilian," Kevin muttered.

"Like I care about that," the woman said. "No one messes with the meister, especially not some cocky little human brat."

"Messes with the meister?" Kotohime made an odd face.

"G-gu... whatever." Kevin stood up with Lilian's help. That punch really had hurt. "Sorry for calling you short."

"Apology accepted." Kevin didn't like the woman's smile. Not one bit. "Not like your words matter anyway. You're just a perverted brat, after all."

"P-perverted brat?!" Kevin nearly shrieked. "I am not perverted!"

"Say that when your face isn't getting shoved into someone's tits."

"That wasn't my fault!"

The woman waved her hand dismissively as if swatting a fly. "Semantics."

Kevin gawked. This woman, she was so—wait.

"Just who the heck are you anyway?" he asked as he suddenly realized that he didn't know this woman.

"I'm glad you asked." She placed her hands on her hips and puffed out her nonexistent chest. "You should be honored. I don't normally deign to introduce myself to lowly humans, much less a brat like you." Kevin scowled, but she ignored him. "Feast your eyes upon the greatest, most beautiful kitsune you'll ever meet. I am the magnanimous, the all-powerful, the incredible—"

"That's my aunt, Violent," Lilian said, causing all the wind to get knocked right out of the woman's sails. Kevin watched as, somehow, despite standing still, the three-tails tripped and fell, her face smacking against the ground with a loud *crunch!*

"D-dammit, girl, you're not supposed to interrupt me when I'm doing my introduction!" The woman stood up. Her nose was bleeding, but she wiped off the blood and snapped it back into place. "And it's Violet! Vi-o-let!"

"Ufufufu, my bad." Lilian gave her aunt an innocent smile that wasn't all that innocent.

Violet growled. "Don't lie. You're not sorry at all."

"So, what were you guys talking about?" Kevin asked, taking absent note that Kirihime had joined them and now stood by her mistress's side. Camellia was still holding Iris's hand, not paying attention to anything else.

"We were just discussing travel arrangements, Kevin-sama," Kotohime informed him. "We'll be leaving shortly for—"

"I'm not going," Lilian interrupted before her maid-slash-bodyguard could continue. She crossed her arms and sent everyone her most powerful pout, complete with jutting lower lip. Kotohime and Violet looked resigned and annoyed respectively.

"Going where?" asked Kevin.

"Back home, of course," Violet said.

"You mean back home to Greece, don't you?" He looked at Lilian, then Kotohime. "The Pnévma Clan's home?"

"Indeed."

"Heh, give the brat a cookie. That's right, we're heading back to the

Pnévma Clan's ancestral home. It's getting too dangerous for our family to be out in the world at large. The men of our family are staying where they are, but you guys have been ordered to come back."

Kevin raised an eyebrow. "Am I included in this group?"

Violet gave him a look that made Kevin wonder if he'd just asked a stupid question. "You are Lilian's mate, aren't you? Of course you're coming. Mom wants to meet you."

At the mention of Violet's mom, Lilian hissed and wrapped her arms around one of his. Kevin studied her for a moment, then addressed Violet. "I'm guessing your mom is the matriarch of the clan?"

"That's right."

"I see." Kevin slowly turned around and walked toward the door, pulling Lilian along with him. "Excuse me, you two, but I'd like to speak with Lilian alone for a moment."

"Of course, Kevin-sama." Kotohime bowed her head.

"Whatever." Violet waved them off. "I don't care what you do, though I hope you can make this stubborn child see reason."

"I'll show you stubborn." Lilian scowled.

Kevin didn't allow Violet time to retort. With Lilian's hand in his, he walked out the door and down the hall, taking several turns until he found a small waiting room off to the side.

Several chairs sat in the center of the room. A TV hung overhead, playing the news, which featured a report on the destruction of Sonoran Junior High. There were two vending machines resting against the wall. One of them sold drinks, the other snacks.

Kevin studied Lilian, whose agitation showed clearly on her face. Even if he hadn't known her as well as he did, he would have still been able to tell that she was displeased.

"Are you all right?" he asked.

"No, I'm not all right," Lilian's reply was short, showing just how bothered she was. "I don't wanna go back to Greece."

"Because you don't want to see your family." Kevin nodded. He knew the story. Lilian had never really gotten along with her family, or so she always said. "Are they really that bad?"

"Yes," Lilian said quickly. "They are. I've never gotten along with my relatives. Ever since I gained my second tail, my family members have treated me and my sister like we're pariahs. Every day that we lived there, Daphne would treat me like I was a burden. She took every opportunity she could to let me know how fortunate I was that the great, wonderful matriarch was benevolent enough to let myself and Iris stay with them, of how lucky we were that we hadn't been banished from the clan. The males of our clan treated us like crap, and the women pretended we didn't exist. It was horrible there. I don't want to go back."

Kevin noticed that she only really spoke about Daphne specifically. He wondered if the others treated her better. They might have. Surely not everyone in the clan treated her and Iris like crap. While Lilian was no liar, he also knew that she sometimes exaggerated when it came to stuff she didn't like.

Lilian had never spoken about her life in Greece at great length. He knew she disliked remembering those times, and so he went out of his way not to bring them up. Also, if he was being honest, he never really believed her past would become relevant. It had nothing to do with her life now—or so he thought.

It's funny how life works out sometimes.

Kevin pulled Lilian into a hug. He felt her body melt against his. Her arms came up and wrapped around his waist as she tucked her head under his chin. He took a moment to relish in the feel of holding her against him. It felt right somehow, like this was how things were supposed to be.

"I know you don't want to return home," he said. "Believe me, I understand where you're coming from, but I'm not sure we have a choice anymore. We can't stay here. If we did, we'd just be bringing our friends more trouble. What if the next assassin who comes after us decides to use Lindsay or one of the others as a hostage? We'd be helpless."

"I know," Lilian's muffled voice spoke against his chest. "I know that. I just…"

"You don't get along with your family, but you don't have to worry about them. I'll be with you, and I won't let Daphne or anyone else talk down to you, okay?"

Lilian's grip on him tightened. "Daphne can be pretty scary, you know."

"Pfft!" Kevin scoffed. "After the things I've seen, I doubt anything can frighten me anymore, and even if it did, you're my mate. As your mate, it's my job to stick by your side and help you out."

"I guess," Lilian mumbled. She paused. "I'm being silly, aren't I?"

"A little," Kevin admitted. "But that's just a part of who you are, and if you weren't the person that you are now, then I wouldn't love you as much as I do."

Lilian looked up, her captivating emerald eyes peeking out from beneath a curtain of shimmering crimson hair. A soft smile caused her lips to curve so beautifully it reminded him of a painting.

"I see. Thank you, Kevin."

Kevin returned her smile with an easy one of his own. "You're welcome."

***

After returning to the room with a more compliant Lilian in tow, Kevin informed everyone that they would be going to Greece with them, much to the amusement of Violet.

"Heh, sounds like someone's been whipped by their mate. Isn't it supposed to be the other way around, girl?"

After he prevented Lilian from strangling her aunt, the group prepared to leave. Several doctors came in and tried to place Iris on a stretcher—tried because Lilian nearly threw one of them out of the window when he attempted to cop a feel of her unconscious sister. After kicking the doctors out, he and Lilian set Iris on the stretcher, and Kevin pushed Iris out of the hospital.

They were directed toward the back of the hospital, where two cars waited for them. One of them, a limousine, sat in the parking lot with someone who Kevin could only describe as a bishounen standing by the already open door. He soon discovered that the pretty boy was actually one of Violet's many half-siblings.

"Wait, so there are male kitsune?" Kevin asked in shock. *The young man twitched.*

"Of course there are male kitsune," the bishy snapped. *"How do you think kits are made? Do you think we just spring up from holes in the ground?"*

"Sorry." Kevin shook his head. *"Let me rephrase that. I meant, there are male kitsune in this story?"*

"Bastard!" The bishy growled, then paused to look at him in shock. *"Wait, you can break the fourth wall?"*

Kevin blinked. "The fourth what now?"

"The fourth wall! You know, the wall that separates our world from

reality?"

"I have no clue what you're talking about."

"Oh, for the love of—what a useless human!"

"Oi! You take that back right now, Sparkles! I'm not useless, you third-rate side character!"

"A side character, am I?! You clearly don't know who you're talking to, brat! I'm the great—"

"No one cares who you are," Violet interrupted them. She then gave Kevin an appraising look, as if she suddenly saw him in a whole new light. *"Not bad, brat. Not bad at all."*

Kevin sent her an expression so dry that deserts looked wet in comparison. *"Hearing you pay me a compliment fills me with dread for some reason."*

Violet just laughed.

Iris was placed into the ambulance that they had somehow acquired —Kevin suspected enchantments were involved. Lilian had wanted to travel in the ambulance with Iris, but Violet gave her an emphatic no. This would have probably ended in another fight had Kotohime not intervened.

"Do not worry, Lilian-sama. Camellia-sama and I will travel with your sister and look after her in your stead." Her dark eyes gleamed sharper than the katana in her hand. *"I am certain that if any perverts are in the vehicle with us, my blade will convince them to keep their hands to themselves."*

He and Lilian climbed into the limo after that, followed by Violet and Kirihime. Kevin had never been in a limo before, but he had to admit that the one they rode was nice. The interior was spacious and all the seats were made of dark leather and felt really cushy. He and Lilian sat on one side, while Violet and Kirihime sat on the other. He noticed that the woman dressed as a French maid looked uncomfortable.

She probably wants to be with Camellia.

"Is that one of those cell phone thingies?" Violet asked as Kevin pulled out his Android.

"Uh, yeah?"

"Cool." Violet's eyes sparkled with disturbing fascination. "I've heard of those, but I've never seen one before now."

A Fox's Revenge

Kevin looked at Lilian, who correctly interpreted his facial expression.

"Most of the female members of our family aren't allowed to interact with humans, remember?" she said. "Violet is no exception to this. While she's done more traveling than me, I doubt she's ever interacted with humans for any serious length of time. I'm actually surprised granny sent her to retrieve us."

"You shouldn't speak like that about your betters, girl." Violet crossed her arms and gave Lilian a pious glare "Just because I've never lived among humans for any length of time doesn't mean I'm ignorant."

"And yet you've never seen a cell phone before," the redhead pointed out.

Violet blushed. "Shut up!"

"Could you not shout please," Kevin said. "I need to make a call."

"Calling our friends?" Lilian asked.

"Yeah, I… want to say goodbye."

Lilian's eyes grew soft and compassionate. "I understand. Would you mind if I said goodbye, too?"

Kevin smiled. "Not at all."

After placing the call to Lindsay's house, Kevin put the phone to his ear, listening as it rung. The ringing stopped when someone picked up and a soft voice said, *"Hello?"*

For a moment, he didn't recognize the voice. It was so quiet and not at all like the person it belonged to that he needed a second to analyze who it was.

"Christine?"

"Yes?"

"Sorry, I almost didn't recognize you."

"… Kevin?"

"That's right. I should have figured you'd be at Lindsay's house. Is she also with you?"

"… She's taking a shower."

"I see. Is everything okay, Christine?"

"I'm fine."

"You sure? You sound kind of—"

"I said I'm fine!"

"O-okay. Sorry for asking. We haven't spoken much since… after what happened. I'm just worried about you."

"I-I know. Sorry for snapping at you. I'm just… stressed right

158

now."

Kevin wanted to ask Christine what was wrong. He wanted to help her. Unfortunately, they were on a timetable, and even if they weren't, Kevin didn't know how much help he could be. What sort of comfort could he give to a girl who confessed to him and got turned down?

"It's okay. Listen, I have something to tell you. I wanted to tell Lindsay, too, but I guess you can tell her when she gets out of the shower. Lilian, Iris, and I are… going away."

There was a pronounced pause.

"What?"

"There's been some trouble between Lilian's family and the family belonging to that girl who tried to kill us. It's become too dangerous for us to stay here. We'll be leaving for Greece soon… I don't know when we'll come back."

"O-oh…"

"I'm really sorry we're leaving you like this."

"N-no, it's fine… i-it's not as if I care that you guys are leaving me alone or anything."

"Christine?"

"A-anyway, I've gotta go. Goodbye."

"Go? Christine, wait! Lilian wanted to… say goodbye." Kevin took the phone from his ear and looked apologetically at Lilian. "She hung up on me."

"It's okay, Beloved." Lilian wore a sad smile that looked out of place on such a normally vibrant face. "We probably should have expected this. Christine is also going through a tough time right now. We should be supporting her, but instead we're leaving. I understand if she doesn't want to talk to us."

Kevin saw the despondency on Lilian's face, the sadness in her eyes. He reached out and wrapped an arm around her, pulling her close and letting her use his shoulder as a pillow. She leaned into him.

Violet made gagging noises.

Lilian smacked the woman with her tails.

***

Shinkuro stood on a balcony overlooking a massive garden. Down below a variety of color spread out before him. Thousands of different flowers were arrayed to create a vibrant image. He recognized all the flowers within, having personally planted and cultivated them for over

1,000 years.

"How long has it been since our clan has fought a war?" he asked of no one in particular. He received an answer anyway.

"Not for at least seven centuries, Father."

Standing several feet behind and to his left was his eldest son, Chao.

Like his father, Chao had blond hair, but his was cut short. His light blue eyes complimented his fair skin, and his bearing was strong and regal. He would have made a perfect heir—too bad Lord Inari had declared that Jiāoào would gain the ninth tail instead of him.

"Seven centuries," Shinkuro murmured to himself. "Seven centuries without war. I suppose it was inevitable that we would fight after such a long period of peace."

"Indeed. I have no doubt that we will crush the Pnévma Clan beneath our heels."

Shinkuro sighed. "That attitude is likely the reason Lord Inari decided that you would not be my successor."

He didn't need to turn to imagine the scowl on Chao's face. "Jiāoào was even more arrogant than I am, Father."

"True, but Jiāoào was also young and had room to grow. You have gained your eighth tail already, and you have still not grown since you became a true kitsune."

Before Chao could say something to dispute him, a young servant arrived and bowed before them. His bald head and orange shaolin monk robes denoted him as a member of the branch family.

"My Lord, I know that you said you wish not to be disturbed; however…"

"You are right. Father did say he didn't want to be disturbed," Chao said, his voice a low growl. "And yet here you are, disturbing him. I hope you have a good reason for it."

The servant quaked as Chao stared him down. Shinkuro felt a sense of tiredness come over him. When would his son learn?

Shinkuro turned to face the man, who stiffened as he came under the effects of the Presence of the King, the aura that Shinkuro acquired after gaining the ninth tail.

"Be at peace, Chao," he said.

Chao's startled glance spoke volumes to him. "But Father—"

"If he has risked my wrath to disturb me, then he obviously has a good reason for doing so." He looked down at the man and consciously willed his presence to lessen. "Well, child? For what reasons have you disturbed my musings?"

"Lady Fan and Lord Li have returned from the United States, My Lord. They are waiting for you in the receiving room."

"I see. Thank you for informing me. You are dismissed."

"Yes, My Lord."

As the servant bid a swift retreat, Shinkuro turned to his son. "You must learn patience, Chao. Had I let you continue tormenting that boy, it would have taken even longer to get that information out of him. I have been waiting for Fan and Li to return and have no wish to delay our meeting."

"I understand... Father."

His son clearly didn't understand, but he chose not to say anything. If time and age did not bring understanding, then few things would.

Shinkuro walked the halls of his home. The freshly polished stone floors gleamed with the shine of marble. Red walls decorated with artwork stood on his right. The left was open, with only a guard railing and red columns to block his view of the massive gardens that surrounded his residence. He soon entered the mansion proper, passing by many doors, his son's footsteps echoing behind him, until he reached the receiving room.

Fan and Li were waiting for him, kneeling in the center of the receiving room, their heads bowed in deference even though he had yet to arrive. That was good. That was proper. That was the way they should be.

He walked past his daughter and grandson, up the dais toward his chair, and gracefully seated himself. Chao stood two feet behind and to his left, as always. Only once he was situated did he speak.

"Li, Fan, I am pleased that you have answered my summons so promptly. Please, raise your heads."

They did as told.

"Father," Fan said. "If it is not presumptuous of me, may I ask—"

"No, you may not ask," Chao said with a scowl.

Fan glared at him. "I wasn't talking to you. I was speaking with Father!"

Sensing the argument and seeking to end it before the situation became worse, Shinkuro released his power. The trio stiffened. A cold sweat broke out on their brows. Shinkuro watched with indifference as they began to shake. Only when he felt they'd had enough did he reel his powers back in.

"I did not ask you two to come here so that you, Fan, could argue with your elder brother. Nor did I allow you to follow, Chao, so that you could antagonize your younger sister. I understand that arguing is a part of being siblings. However, neither of you will argue while in my presence again. Are we clear?"

"Yes, Father," Fan said, her voice meek.

"I understand, Father," Chao said.

"Good. Now then, Fan, ask your question."

"Thank you, Father." Fan wet her lips. "I just wished to know: Why did you pull us away from our mission? I thought you wanted Lilian Pnéyma dead."

"I did indeed." Shinkuro nodded. "While it would be a pity for such potential to be wasted, I deemed her death necessary after the damage she inflicted upon my son. However, I am beginning to think that I may have acted too hastily. Tell me, Fan, what do you know of psychology?"

"Um, very little, Father."

"I thought as much. You do not pay much attention to humanity, so I do not blame you for this. I myself do not think much of the species. That being said, I have had my best healers, and even some healers from the still warring Mul clan, attempt to cure Jiāoào of his ailment. It seems, however, that whatever is affecting my son and leaving him in this sorry state is not any enchantment or illusion, as I first suspected."

He paused at his daughter's expression.

"Something you wish to share with us, Fan?"

"N-no, Father," Fan stuttered. "It is just... I was simply remembering something a human once told me."

A human?

Shinkuro shifted in his seat, resting his head against his left hand. "And what did this human tell you?"

"He said that..." Fan swallowed. "... That he was the one who defeated Jiāoào, not Lilian Pnéyma."

Shinkuro leaned back in his chair, silently contemplating this information. "So I see. Tell me, this human, his name would not happen to be Kevin Swift, would it?"

Fan looked visibly startled. "Um, yes. Yes, it is."

"Peculiar," he murmured softly to himself.

"Father?"

"I know of this Kevin Swift that you speak of. He is of little

162

consequence right now, however. The fact remains that Jiāoào's current state is not the cause of a technique, but a result of him withdrawing into his own mind. Perhaps his humiliating defeat at the hands of a human is the cause. Regardless, I have recently heard that sometimes it is possible for people to be drawn out of their mind by hearing the voice of someone important to them. Jiāoào has always been rather taken in with Lilian Pnévma, despite my wish to see him with someone else."

Fan scowled at the mention of Jiāoào's infatuation with the Pnévma girl. His daughter had been even less approving of that relationship than him.

I would have preferred having the Pnévma girl mate with one of the branch members. Fan probably simply wishes she were dead.

"Then you are saying that you no longer wish Lilian Pnévma dead, Honored Grandfather?" asked Li, speaking up for the first time.

"That is, indeed, an accurate summation of my desire," he told the son of his second eldest. Zhìlì had birthed the most children among his three sons. In fact, most of the branch members came from his second eldest son. "I have other designs for Lilian Pnévma now, and I shall require your help to see my vision realized."

***

"I didn't know that your family had their own private jet."

Kevin knew that the Pnévma Clan was powerful within the yōkai world, and the kitsune world in particular. He even knew they had a lot of money. However, knowing of their wealth, of their power, and seeing the evidence of it, were two completely different things.

Violet shrugged. "After hearing about how convenient planes are, Mom decided to buy one for the express purpose of traveling to places where we haven't set up a Shrine Gate."

Shrine Gates were small shrines known as toris that connected the territory of a kitsune to somewhere else. Kitsune territories, he'd been told, were built within a temporal dimension, a plane of existence that had been phased out of the real world. It basically took the concept of an Extra Dimensional Storage Space, and cranked the power and sheer absurdity of it to over 9,000.

"Oh."

After arriving at the airport, Kevin and the others had been directed toward the Pnévma Clan's private jet, a Boeing. Soft carpet ruffled against their feet. Low lighting. Varnished wood walls. Several lounge chairs sparsely populated the interior, which made Kevin feel like he was in a five-star resort's luxury suite. It even had a bolted down table and its own bar.

They placed Iris on a bed located within the back of the plane, which was where he and Lilian sat. While he tried not to pay attention to his mate tenderly stroking her sister's hair, it was difficult, especially when he noticed the despondency she wore like a glove. On any other occasion, he might have found it ironic that Lilian was now the one giving her sister affection. Not now. He couldn't find the humor in it.

"Yeah," Violet continued their conversation. "Because we weren't granted permission to set up a Shrine Gate in the United States, we have to use other methods of transportation. Ships take too long, and they can't reach certain parts of the United States anyway, so Mom decided to buy a jet."

Kevin shook his head at the ridiculousness of someone just deciding to buy a jet. He knew they were rich, but really, who the heck threw that much money into something like this? And from the sound of it, the matriarch had bought this on a whim.

"It was actually this very jet that brought Mom, Iris, Kirihime, Kotohime, and I to the United States," Lilian added, looking up from her sister. "Granny bought this about a year after I met you."

"Huh, interesting."

Kevin looked around the interior some more. Kotohime was sitting on a couch. She had a cleaning kit out and was lovingly cleaning her blade in a most disturbing manner. Kirihime stood behind Camellia who sat at the bar... writing?

Kevin blinked, then rubbed his eyes. Yes, Camellia was, indeed, writing something. He didn't know what, but he could see that she had a pen in hand and was very clearly moving it across a sheet of paper. At least, he hoped she was writing on paper. He didn't want to think about how hard it would be to get pen out of that wood.

"Where'd your brother go?" asked Kevin when he noticed that the bishy was missing.

"Men aren't usually allowed in the same place with us," Violet said. "Even at home, they aren't allowed in the Pnévma Clan grounds unless the matriarch requests them. Right now, only about three Pnévma males are living there, and they're merely there to serve as bodyguards and servants."

"Oh." Kevin took a second to absorb that. "Then why am I here?"

"Because you're my mate," Lilian said. "I'm not going to let some stupid rule keep us apart."

"Actually, it's because you are not a member of the Pnéyma Clan," Kotohime said. "The Pnéyma Clan's rules only apply to members of the clan. As an outsider, you are exempt from these rules." She paused, tilted her head, and then added, "Of course, you being Lilian-sama's mate is the only reason you're even here to begin with."

"Uh huh…" Kevin had nothing to say to that.

"I apologize for the wait, Lady Violet," a voice said over the intercom. *"But I thought you would like to know that all of our preparations have been made, and we will be departing shortly."*

"Thank you. Please carry on."

Kevin wondered if he should tell Violet that the woman speaking couldn't hear her, but he decided not to.

"So, was the person we heard over the intercom your maid or something?" he asked instead.

"Naw, I don't need a maid." Violet waved a hand in the air. Her left leg bounced as she set it on her right knee. "That girl is just one of the kitsune who works for the Pnéyma Clan. She lives in the village that Mom built some eight hundred years ago. She used to work at the resort, but ever since Mom bought this jet, she's been its pilot." Violet grimaced. "I feel kind of bad for her, though. Learning how to fly this couldn't have been easy."

The plane soon began to move. Kevin ignored the rumble and light shaking as tires rolled across the bumpy road toward the takeoff strip. The bed didn't have a seatbelt, but the takeoff seemed smoother than normal airplanes, so he didn't fear falling off. He felt the hand in his grip tighten, and he looked at Lilian to find her clenching her teeth.

"You okay?" he asked.

Lilian shook her head. "I'm a kitsune. You know that we prefer remaining grounded."

Kevin nodded noncommittally and squeezed her hand back. Lying on the bed that he and Lilian sat on, Iris jostled only slightly.

He glanced around some more. Kotohime looked tense, as did her sister, but they were old enough to control their fear. Camellia wasn't even bothered. She hummed a happy tune as she continued to write. Weird. As for Violet…

"You're afraid of flying, aren't you?" Kevin asked. Violet blushed, then sputtered.

"W-w-wha—afraid?! Hell no, I'm not afraid!" Violet pointed at herself with a thumb. "This Lady Violet is afraid of nothing! Especially not stupid metal death traps that—kya!"

The plane accelerated. Violet threw her hands up in the air and fell from her seat.

He shook his head. "Not afraid, my ass."

Lilian giggled. Violet glared.

"What was that? You got something to say, girly?"

"... No."

"Good. Then why don't you keep q—"

There was a moment of weightlessness as the plane suddenly left the ground.

***

The airport was always a bustling place, with hundreds of people congregating there, using it as a hub to get where they wanted to go. Today was no different. The walkways were congested with dozens of people, all of them vying to reach their destination. Children walked with tiny strollers. Adults in business suits strode forward on long legs, a case in one hand and a phone in the other. Parents. Grandparents. So many people were there, and all of them wanted to get where they were going fast.

"KYA!!!"

A blood-curdling scream stopped everyone in their tracks. People looked around, as if expecting to find the source of that scream right next to them. When, after several seconds had passed, nothing happened, the people went about their business, the scream forgotten.

Life at the airport continued on as normal.

***

Flying in a private jet was vastly different than flying in a regular plane. For one thing, there was no need to fasten the seatbelts—because there were no seatbelts. There was also no tiny aisle that people were forced to walk through if they wanted to get somewhere. Then there were the free drinks and food, which were actually good drinks and food and not the salted peanuts and soda they gave people on regular planes. It was definitely way better than flying coach.

Kevin stood in the middle of the plane—on his hands. He was doing a handstand, or rather, handstand pushups, though his were a little different from regular handstand pushups. Kiara often made him do these as a means of simultaneously working on his balance, strength training, and muscle coordination—and because she enjoyed torturing him, he was sure.

"Ninety... two..."

Sweat dripped down his bare torso, slick like oil. His face felt red. He could feel all the blood rushing to it. It was a light-headed feeling, like when you've sucked in too much helium. He imagined stoners felt this way when they were high.

"N-ninety-three..."

Sitting on a couch several feet to his left, trying not to show how nervous she was about flying, Violet watched him work. He could feel her eyes on him as if they were lasers.

"You know... I didn't notice this before, but he's kinda ripped, isn't he?"

"Indeed." Kotohime was still cleaning her katana. She sat on the couch near the front, her practiced motions only slightly jittery. "Kevin-sama has been undergoing intense physical training in order to fight against yōkai alongside Lilian-sama."

Violet raised an eyebrow. "A human is trying to become strong enough to fight yōkai? Is he stupid?"

Kotohime indicated the negative with a headshake. "Not at all. Kevin-sama has simply realized that in order to stand by Lilian-sama's side, he must become stronger. It would not be wise to underestimate this human, Violet-sama. Kevin-sama has already defeated Jiāoào, a nekomata assassin, and a three-tailed kitsune—with Lilian-sama and Iris-sama's help, of course."

Taking a deep breath, Kevin bent his legs at the waist, until his body formed the shape of an L. Gritting his teeth, he raised them back up, and then lowered his body, while at the same time moving forward. The end result was that his body was parallel with the floor. He pushed himself back up to a handstand position.

"Nine... ninety-four..."

Violet whistled. "Really? That brat already defeated several yōkai?"

"This brat... can hear you... you know?" Kevin grunted as he finished his one hundredth push up. Grunting, he placed his feet on the ground and stood up.

"So?" Violet raised an eyebrow at him. "What makes you think I care if you can hear our conversation. Compared to this Lady Violet,

167

you're just a good for nothing human brat."

"Tch." Kevin clicked his tongue. This woman's constant arrogant and demeaning remarks annoyed him, but he wouldn't let himself fall prey to her taunts. He would be the bigger person. "Whatever. Does this jet have a shower?"

"It's down the hall at the back," Violet said. "Like, all the way at the back. It'll be on your right."

Kevin looked toward the back, where a small hallway eventually ended and split in two directions. One side had the sign for a restroom. The other said shower.

"Right. Thank you."

He walked over to the bed. Lilian was lying on top, sleeping next to her sister. Like a crimson curtain, her hair was splayed out, starkly visible against the white backdrop of the bed sheets. She lay on her side, her legs slightly curled. She was also naked, and lying on top of the sheets, so he could pretty much see everything. He touched her shoulder and gently shook her.

"Lilian. Lilian."

Lilian cracked a single eye open.

"Kevin." Her voice held the slur of someone who'd just woken up. "Are we there yet?"

He shook his head as she sat up and stretched. "No, but I was planning on taking a shower and wanted to know if you'd like to join me."

Her eyes brightened at the idea of joining him. She opened her mouth, no doubt to tell him that he shouldn't have even asked, when she paused. Her head turned, gaze traveling down, and suddenly, Kevin realized something.

"You don't have to if you don't want to. I'll understand if you want to stay with your sister."

Lilian hesitated for a moment, then slowly shook her head. She graced him with a smile.

"It's fine. Iris isn't going anywhere." She didn't quite sound like she believed her own words. "I'd love to take a shower with you."

"Kay. Come on, then."

Kevin allowed her to take his hand and pulled her up. He then began leading her to the back.

"Don't do anything I wouldn't do!" Violet called out. Lilian turned around long enough to pull her right eyelid down and blow her aunt a raspberry. "Little brat!"

"Please calm down, Violet-sama." One of Kotohime's tails wrapped itself around the tiny kitsune and kept her from leaving the couch. "Getting yourself so worked up will give you ulcers."

"Shut up, Kotohime! Let go of me! I need to show that brat who's boss! Let! Go!"

The last thing Kevin saw was Violet struggling to break free of Kotohime's tails.

The shower wasn't much, just a tiny cubicle big enough to fit maybe four people. Despite that, Kevin still thought it was awesome that a private jet had its own shower.

"You're really sweaty, Beloved," Lilian noticed.

"That's because I was exercising."

"Ah."

Being the only one not naked, Kevin quickly stripped out of his clothes and put them in a cabinet that contained several towels. He then turned on the shower—

"IYAN!!"

—and was blasted by freezing cold water.

"Hahahaha! Looks like I forgot to tell you that the water's cold when it first starts! How do ya like that, brat?!" Violet shouted.

"D-damn that, w-woman." Kevin shivered as he was left with no recourse other than to stand in the freezing cold shower. If he moved, then Lilian would be the one getting the spray of chilling water. "I sometimes forget that you kitsune are tricksters."

A pair of warm arms wrapped around his middle and a full-bodied figure pressed into his back. He could feel Lilian's nipples slowly harden against his skin. It was electrifying.

"I'm sorry about her." Lilian pressed her lips against the junction between his shoulder blades. "While all kitsune enjoy pranking to some degree or another, Violet tends to prank constantly. They're usually just small and annoying ones, kinda like her."

"I HEARD THAT!"

"NO, YOU DIDN'T! SHUT UP!"

Kevin ignored the outraged cry coming from the lounge. Hearing Lilian shout at her aunt amused him enough that he didn't feel as annoyed. The water was beginning to warm up anyway.

"All right." Lilian pumped herself up. "Time to wash your back."

Despite having been dating Lilian for nearly nine months and being this intimate with her for about seven, he still couldn't get over how far they'd come. Many eons ago—ten months ago—the very thought of doing this with a girl, any girl, would have made him pass out from embarrassment.

Kevin stood slightly hunched over, his hands pressed flat against the wall. Lilian was gentle as she scrubbed his back with a luffa that had been hanging off a rack near the door. It felt nice, even better than the hot water cascading down his back and shoulders.

"Lilian?"

"Hmm?"

"Do you remember when I mentioned training with you?"

Lilian paused, then resumed cleaning his back. Her hand went lower.

"I do. It was a few days after that three-tails tried to kill us. You mentioned how it would be a good idea for us to learn teamwork; that way we could overcome people more powerful than us. I believe your words were 'We'll be far stronger working together than we would fighting as individuals.'"

"At the time, you said that you didn't think you were strong enough on your own," Kevin recalled Lilian's answer. "You told me that you wanted to get stronger as an individual first, then work on fighting together with me."

"That's right." He couldn't see it, but Kevin could tell that she was nodding.

"Do you feel strong enough now?" The luffa stopped moving. "I'm only asking because I think it might be a good idea if we started learning how to fight together. I… I don't want what happened during our battle with that Fan woman happening again. Had we—you, me, Christine, and Iris—worked as a team right from the start, we may have come out of that battle relatively unscathed."

"Yes," Lilian said softly. "I suppose you're right. Perhaps if we'd been able to cover each other's weakness like a four-man cell should, we wouldn't have been so overwhelmed at the beginning, and Iris would have… she wouldn't…"

Kevin turned around and pulled Lilian into a hug. He ignored his growing arousal in order to comfort the girl in his arms. He still wasn't ready to have sex. He couldn't, not until he became strong enough that he could truly stand beside her. Even if he was ready, he didn't want their first time to be while she was grieving over her sister.

"Don't think about that right now. If there is one thing that I have learned from Kiara and Kotohime, it's that regretting what happened in the past is pointless. We can't undo what's already been done. The only thing we can do is learn from our mistakes and never repeat them."

"You're right." Lilian nuzzled against his chest. He could feel the smile as her lips kissed his skin. "You know, it really is amazing to see how mature you've become."

"You think so?"

"Oh, yes." Lilian's smile shifted. A pair of soft hands landed on his butt. "You've become a much more mature person. Really, you've truly grown... in more ways than one."

Kevin yelped when Lilian pinched his backside. It stung, but then she began rubbing the spot she pinched, which he had to admit felt nice.

He placed a hand under Lilian's chin and tilted her head up. Half-lidded pools of emerald stared up at him from above an enthralling smile.

"I believe," he began in a very serious manner, "that it is my turn to clean you."

"So it is," Lilian agreed, right before he pushed Lilian until her back was against the wall and his lips had consumed hers in a fiery kiss.

It would be nearly an hour later when they emerged from the shower because the water had gotten cold.

Violet would complain about the amount of noise they made.

***

It took about nineteen hours to get from Phoenix to Greece. Due to the time difference, they arrived at five a.m. That was around eight p.m. in Arizona.

The island where the Pnévma Clan lived had an unusual shape, longer than it was wide, with numerous small peninsulas and several sheer cliffs. There was a massive mountain situated in the center. Located at the mountain's peak was a crater.

Because the Pnévma estate didn't have a landing strip of its own, nor did the village next to the estate have one, their jet had to land on a strip near the resort.

Kevin looked out of the window to see the resort, a large series of buildings shaped like traditional Greek architecture with a modern touch. From an aerial view, he could see that all the buildings were built within a circle. A series of walkways and gazebos connected them. The beach was within a few minutes walking distance on one side, and vast, tropical forestry lay on the other. The landing strip was a little ways from the resort. There were several other jets parked there.

"It's because of all the humans who like to come here," Kotohime explained when he asked her about it. "Most humans arrive on the Pnéyma Clan's private cruise line, Spirited Away, but some prefer traveling to the resort via plane. That's why the Pnéyma Clan bought its own airline."

Kevin wondered if the sweatdrop on his head was natural. Not only did they have a private jet, but they had their own airline as well? What the heck?

"My mother and I came here on a plane," Kevin said. Lilian, who sat by his side, glanced at him. "I don't remember much about that time, but I remember that much. I think it was because her company was paying for us, but we didn't come here on a ship."

"Ufufufu, that is most interesting."

"Whatever," Violet said bluntly. "Like I care about—HIIII!"

Kevin stared at Violet as she fell on her hind quarter when the jet touched down on the landing strip. It was a bit bumpy, but nowhere near as bad as a regular plane.

"Not afraid of flying, huh?" Kevin couldn't help but tease. This was payback for constantly calling him a brat!

"I-I'm not!"

"Of course you're not." Kevin nodded.

"I'm telling you, I'm not—"

They hit a small bump.

"—KYA!"

"And I completely believe you," Kevin said, straight-faced.

"S-stupid brat!"

They eventually stopped, and the flight attendant who'd served them drinks and food also helped them exit the jet. Kevin was amused to note that Violet couldn't get out of the jet fast enough.

He hefted his and Lilian's bags. Because his was heavier thanks to his new weapons, he carried that on his back. Behind them, Kotohime and Kirihime prepared Iris's wheeled stretcher, while a silent Camellia watched them.

"You ready to visit your relatives?" he asked Lilian, who shook her head.

"No, but... so long as I'm with you, I'll be okay."

173

Kevin offered his mate a comforting smile as she grabbed his free arm. They exited the boarding ramp, the two maids seeing to Iris's safe disembarking behind them. Violet was waiting near another vehicle.

It wasn't a car.

He stared at what appeared to be a very large horse-drawn carriage. It looked like the kind of thing he'd expect to see in *Cinderella*, a large white carriage inlaid with gold. Several different types of flowers were imprinted along its length. Two kitsune females stood in front of the double doors, which were already open and waiting for them.

"You expect us to get there by carriage?" he asked, now incredulous.

Violent hopped into the carriage. "What's the problem, brat?"

"Uh, how about the fact that we've got seven people, and that thing doesn't look like it can fit more than four at most?"

"It's bigger than it looks."

"Then how about one of us is comatose and we've got nowhere to put her?"

Violet poked her head out of the door and scowled at him. "Stop being such a baby and get in here!"

"Come on, Kevin." Lilian tugged on him. "We don't really have time to argue."

"Ha… I guess." He sighed. "Really, though, this is so stupid."

"What was that?!" Violet demanded.

"I said you're the most magnanimous woman I've ever met."

"Your sarcasm is unwarranted, brat."

"Kevin-sama," Kotohime interrupted before he could retort. "I do apologize for the inconvenience, but do you think you could…"

"Yeah, I got it." He sighed again. He could already tell that he would be doing a lot of that. Sighing, that is.

Kotohime gave him a gracious smile. "Ufufufu, Kevin-sama is too kind."

"Coming from you, that sounds more like an insult than a compliment," Kevin observed.

Sliding one arm under Iris's legs and the other under her back, Kevin lifted his mate's sister into a bridal carry. He then proceeded into the carriage, closely followed by Lilian, Camellia, Kotohime, and Kirihime. On the way in, he noticed something odd.

Are those two women glaring at me?

"P-please be careful with Lady Iris, Lord Kevin," a worried

Kirihime said as he entered the cabin, which served to bring Kevin's focus away from the women staring daggers at him.

"Don't worry, I'll be careful," Kevin assured her.

Iris's legs swung limply as he maneuvered them into the carriage. He was glad this thing had a double door. Otherwise he would have probably knocked Iris's head against the doorframe.

There was still the problem of seating arrangements, though. He'd been right when he spoke of how small it was. They could barely fit six people, never mind finding a spot for Iris. He ended up sitting against the doorless side of the carriage with Iris resting firmly in his lap. Her legs rested on Lilian, who sat next to him, while Camellia took the last place on their side. Kotohime, Kirihime, and Violet sat on the other side.

As the carriage started moving, Kevin tried to ignore the small, shapely rear that pressed firmly against his crotch. He felt guilty for allowing himself to become aroused by the situation, not just because Iris wasn't his mate, but also because she was unconscious. It was hard, however. Regardless of her state of being, Iris held an erotic and enthralling beauty that no one could match. She was, as Eric had once put it, sex on legs.

"Muuu…"

An odd noise caught his attention. Kevin turned his head. Lilian was staring at him, her cheeks swelled up like a balloon about to burst.

"Uh… is something wrong, Lilian?"

"I wanna be the one sitting on your lap."

"I-I'm sorry." Kevin felt oddly embarrassed by her blunt admission, or maybe it was because they hit a small bump and Iris's bum rubbed against him. It could have been either reason, really. "You know I'm not really comfortable like this."

"You look pretty comfortable to me, brat," Violet piped up. Kevin tossed her a glare.

"Ufufufu, indeed. Seeing you holding Iris so tenderly against you as she sits on your lap is enough to make one wonder…"

Kevin switched his glare from Violet to Kotohime.

"… All my hate."

They eventually left the resort behind and entered a small off-beaten path that had no markings and no directions. Kevin looked out the carriage windows to see nothing but foliage on either side.

"Isn't there supposed to be some kind of barrier put in place here?" he asked suddenly, turning to Lilian. "I remember you telling me there was a barrier that made humans walk around in circles."

"The barrier has been taken down," Violet said before Lilian could speak. "I'm sure you noticed how there were no humans at the resort. With the current hostilities between our clan and the Bodhisattva, we've ceased all our business operations on the island. Since no humans are here, we've temporarily taken down the seal that keeps humans out in order to strengthen the ones that protect against yōkai intrusions."

"Huh." Kevin went back to staring out the window. "That makes sense."

He saw a shift as he observed their surroundings. The foliage grew less dense and a roadway appeared. Dirt eventually shifted into cobblestone, and they arrived at what looked like a small, Greek village taken straight from the time when Leonidas was alive.

"Wow. When you said this place was old-fashioned, you really meant it."

"I told you," Lilian said, also peering out the window. She snorted in what Kevin interpreted as disgust. "Even after nine years away, this place still hasn't changed."

The village, which Kevin learned from Kotohime was called Psyxé, was built near the large mountain, which gave off a chilling vibe. Square buildings made of weathered stone stood on either side of the road. Small stands where men and women with fox tails and ears sold their wares were spaced between buildings. Kitsune walked to and fro, their outfits ancient and outdated. Most were still wearing togas, though a few wore slightly more modern clothing, as in, not togas but still not stuff worn by people in the 21st Century. Kevin felt like he'd somehow stepped several thousand years back in time.

Several kitsune stopped as their carriage strode past. While many bowed, just as many pointed and began whispering. He couldn't hear what they were saying, but for whatever reason, the stares really bothered him.

They eventually left the village. It took Kevin a moment, but he soon noticed that they were traveling up the mountain that Psyxé was next to. The path they took was winding and long. It reminded him of the one time he and his mother had hiked the Grand Canyon. Of course, he called it hiking, but they had actually been riding on donkeys.

The world changed again as they entered a cavern. The sunlight was blotted out, but several fluorescent bulbs, which he soon realized were mushrooms of some kind, lit the rocky interior before them.

"We should be arriving at the Pnéȳma Clan's ancestral home soon," Lilian told him.

Almost as if her words were prophetic, they exited the cavern and came upon a gigantic stone wall. Unlike the village, the wall looked brand new, as if it had been built just yesterday. They passed a portcullis, which opened the moment their carriage exited the cavern, and Kevin received his first glimpse of the Pnéȳma Clan abode.

Massive didn't begin to cover it. His vision was filled with nine sprawling buildings built like ancient Greek architecture. Each structure had a pathway leading up to it, a beautifully laid cobblestone walkway surrounded by the loveliest of gardens. Several streams ran through the garden. There were also a number of small ponds. He didn't recognize any of the flora, but he couldn't deny its beauty. An array of colors like those of a rainbow assaulted his sight.

In the center of all this was a massive building. Corinthian columns lined it on all sides, their surfaces gleaming with an unusual luster. The triangle-shaped roof was a standard of Greek architecture. He could see intricate motifs within the triangular frame; a fox with nine tails was surrounded by a variety of people with foxy appendages. All of them were bowing before the nine-tailed entity in worship.

"Woah…"

"Heh." Violet smirked at him. "You humans are always so easily impressed."

Kevin rolled his eyes but didn't say anything.

The carriage rolled to a stop. The small jostling caused Iris to slide, but he had secured his arms around her waist to keep the fox-girl from falling. The doors soon opened, which he was thankful for. Sitting with a girl who wasn't his mate on his lap made Kevin feel guilty. After making sure Iris was secure in his arms, he carefully exited the carriage with the others.

Someone was waiting for them.

Kevin found himself glancing at yet another woman of indescribable beauty. Her tall stature put her at least a head and shoulders above him. Her long hair shone silver in the light and was tied into numerous intricate braids. She wore a toga that resembled a dress. Its single shoulder meant he could see a good deal more than he probably should, and a slit running up one side revealed gorgeous thighs and calves. Seven beautiful silver tails swayed behind her. He also noticed, almost absently and with an air of resignation, that she, too, had really large breasts.

Is every kitsune I meet going to have big boobs?

The woman before them was scowling, and it took Kevin a second to realize who that look of annoyance was directed at.

"Lilian." She sniffed. "I see that you have gotten yourself and your no-good sister into a good deal of trouble. As always, you have proven yourself to be completely incapable of doing anything other than causing a ruckus."

"Daphne." Lilian clenched her fists. They were shaking. "Don't you have something better to do than taunt me? Like actually being useful for once?"

"I am plenty useful." Daphne scoffed. "You're the one whose uselessness knows no bounds. Constantly causing trouble for our matriarch, always daydreaming. Our matriarch gave you one task, and you proved yourself to be so useless that you couldn't even fulfil that one, simple role."

"I'd like to see you try mating with that brat!" Lilian bared her teeth at the woman.

Kevin sensed an argument of epic proportions brewing. It may have had something to do with the bolts of lightning that sparked between the two, shooting from their eyes as they glared at each other. Either way, he decided that it might be time to intervene.

"So, you're Daphne?" He stepped in front of Lilian. "It's a pleasure to meet you. Kotohime has told me a lot about you."

Daphne blinked several times, as if not sure what to make of his presence. Then she looked down at Iris, who lay resting in his arms, her face buried in the crook of his neck. Kevin felt really uncomfortable when her penetrating stare met his gaze again. He wondered what she was thinking—then retracted that thought when he realized that she was probably thinking something bad about him.

He was proven right several seconds later.

"You must be Kevin Swift. Lilian's mate." Daphne sniffed as if dismissing him. "That useless human who kept us from reaching an accord with the Shénshèng Clan."

Kevin twitched.

I don't think I like this woman very much.

Lilian didn't either. "Don't insult my mate, you two-bit hag!"

"How dare you call me that!" Daphne's glare became furious. "I am not a two-bit hag, you little brat! I'm—" she paused, then took a deep breath and began again. "I am not going to argue with you about this. The matriarch wishes to see you. You would do well to be on your best behavior. And could someone take Iris to Camellia's abode?"

"I shall take Iris-sama off your hands, Kevin-sama," Kotohime said. Kevin frowned as he allowed the woman to take the girl from him.

"You were having fun at my expense in the carriage, weren't you?"

The way Kotohime hid her smile behind the sleeve of her kimono told Kevin all he needed to know. "Ufufufu, Kevin-sama, you wound me. Do you truly believe that this humble Kotohime would leave you in charge of Iris's wellbeing in order to watch you squirm in discomfort due to the uncomfortably erotic situation that it would cause?"

Kevin snorted. He didn't know what was worse: the fact that he understood Kotohime's humor or the fact that he was beginning to appreciate it.

With Iris off his hands, Daphne led him, Lilian, Camellia, and Kirihime into the sprawling Greek temple. Violet left them, saying something about how she needed to get back to training.

The inside was every bit as ostentatious as the outside. White marble flooring danced with a brilliant shine from light filtering in through a series of sunroofs. Imposing columns decorated either side like giant sentinels. A glance up revealed a painted roof depicting scenes of a nine-tailed fox committing various acts; lounging, frolicking, being worshipped. This place really did seem more like a temple of worship than a person's home.

They were led down a flight of stairs lit only by a series of well-placed oil lamps. The hallway they soon entered reminded him of a video game he had once played, *God of War*, except without all the blood and body parts. He glanced at Lilian to see how she was holding up.

She's nervous.

Lilian had always been an open book. Despite being a kitsune, the redhead had never been good at masking her thoughts, feelings, or intentions. It helped that he knew pretty much everything about her—the consequence of living with her for ten months.

He reached out and grabbed her hand. Lilian appeared startled for a second, but she quickly tossed him a smile and laced their fingers together.

The room they were eventually led to looked like a combination of throne room and temple. It was about half the size of a football field. It was also pretty much empty. The only thing of note, aside from the ridiculously giant columns and various murals on the walls, was the dais, on which an ornately decorated throne made of gold sat.

Sitting upon that throne was a woman.

Beautiful could hardly begin to describe her. Her silver hair fell about her head like a cascading waterfall, glittering as though it was studded with gemstones. Her skin held a pearlescent sheen that radiated an inhumanly perfect quality. Much like Daphne, she, too, wore a toga, though hers was several levels more immodest and revealed far more than it should. The nine tails behind her back writhed as if they had minds of their own. Each one was bright silver, each one seemed to glow with a power that was not of this world. There was only one thing that garnered more attention than her tails and immodest outfit.

Make that two things.

Those are huge.

Kevin would see a lot of crazy ass shit in his life. Heck, he would do half of that crazy ass shit himself. However, in that moment, at that time, Kevin knew for a fact that he would never, *ever*, see another pair of boobs larger than the ones that woman was sporting. Gigantic didn't even begin to cover them.

Those pneumatic knockers look lethal. I'd better be careful not to pull a Rito Yuki on her.

"My matriarch," Daphne intoned in a formal voice as she knelt and bowed her head. "I have brought Camellia and her family to you, as requested."

So, this is the matriarch. Kevin eyed the woman. Aside from her inhuman beauty, she didn't have much in common with Lilian.

"Indeed, you have." The woman's pleasant smile bothered him, though he couldn't explain why. "Thank you, Daphne."

"Of course." Daphne stood up and walked up the dais to stand by her mother's side. The matriarch, who Kevin knew as Delphine Pnéyma, glanced at those gathered below her.

"Momma!" Camellia suddenly shouted.

Kevin blinked. *What the heck?*

Delphine's amused smile turned surprisingly tender. It looked, honestly, a lot like a loving mother gazing at her most beloved child.

"Camellia, dear, how have you been?"

Camellia's sunny grin was quite childish. "I've been well."

"Hmm." Delphine studied her daughter for a little while longer. "You seem different than the last time we met."

So it isn't just me who sees it.

"Hawa?" Camellia tilted her head.

"Well, maybe not so different," Delphine muttered before gazing at Kirihime, who stiffened under the woman's eyes. "And you, Kirihime, thank you for looking after my childish daughter."

While Camellia pouted, Kirihime curtsied. "M-My Lady Pnévma, I am not worthy of such praise."

"Now, now." Delphine's carmine eyes held a gleam of amusement. "There is no need to be humble. I know it must have been difficult to protect someone who is so carefree. You have done an admirable job."

"T-thank you."

"I do not see Kotohime or Iris." The fox-woman seemed disappointed. "A pity." Her gaze then turned on Lilian, who gripped Kevin's hand fiercely. "Lilian, I am very pleased to see you again."

"Granny—hurk!"

"Muu." Delphine pouted at Lilian, whose entire body suddenly went rigid. "Must you always refer to me by that atrocious title? I would much prefer it if you called me... Big Sister."

Big Sister? Kevin made a face. *What the heck?*

"And I see you have brought your mate with you."

His and Delphine's eyes locked.

And in that moment, Kevin felt it.

Power. Unending power. It was like a tide threatening to sweep him away and drown him. He'd never felt something like this before. He felt cold, like death had suddenly embraced him from behind.

His free hand clenched into a fist, while the one holding Lilian's hand gripped hers almost painfully. He wanted to look away from this woman, whose terrifying beauty bothered him and whose body seemed to radiate power. He wanted to, but he couldn't. He was held in place by some unidentifiable fear that he could not describe. It consumed his very consciousness.

And then, Delphine's smile warmed, and the feeling of power left more quickly than it had come. Kevin's body sagged. He took several deep breaths. It was only after doing so that he realized he had actually stopped breathing for a second. A cold sweat broke out on his forehead.

What was that?

"It is a pleasure to finally meet you," Delphine said.

Kevin shook himself from his fear. "It's, um, nice to meet you too, I guess."

"Such a disrespectful tone." Daphne sneered.

"Now, now, my darling daughter," Delphine chided her eldest. "You must forgive young Kevin. He is, after all, a human, and this is his first time ever meeting someone like myself. It is only natural that he would be a bit overwhelmed."

Kevin didn't know if he'd just been insulted or not, and honestly, he didn't even know if he cared.

"Well, now," Delphine clapped her hands, "you must be tired from your long journey. Why don't I have someone show you to your abode?"

The great bronze doors that they had entered suddenly opened again, and in walked the bishy who Kevin had first met before getting on the jet. Like the others, his hair was silver, bearing the same family trait as everyone in the clan except for Camellia and her daughters. He, too, wore a toga of pure white. His arms, which swung back and forth as he walked, were covered in layers of hard muscle. They looked decorative, like they were meant to be admired and not used.

"Caleb here is currently serving as an attendant," Delphine said.

That would explain why he's allowed in the estate.

"He will show you to where you will be staying," she concluded.

"Follow me, please," Caleb said politely, even though it looked like someone had shoved a lemon down his throat.

With nothing else to do, Kevin, Lilian, Kirihime, and Camellia followed the man as he led them out of the room.

***

Caleb led their group to one of the many buildings that lay sprawled around the estate. There were eight buildings, not including the largest one, the temple-looking one, that sat in the ancestral home's center. That made for a grand total of nine overall. He wondered if the number of buildings had been done on purpose, or if it was all just a happy coincidence.

It didn't take long for him to realize that the building they were led to was actually a house. It was built like a standard ancient Greek abode. The dwelling was shaped like a square, composed of limestone bricks and red roofing. Unlike the modern houses that he was used to, this one consisted of long hallways with doors that led into various rooms, which were centered around an open courtyard. The floor inside was also composed of stone, but resting over it was a blue rug that decorated much of the interior.

A Fox's Revenge

Kotohime was waiting for them inside. She bowed when they arrived. "Camellia-sama, Lilian-sama, Kevin-sama, I am glad to see that you have arrived safely."

Kevin frowned. "Why wouldn't we arrive safely?"

"Ufufufu, no reason." He did not like Kotohime's laugh nor how quickly she spoke. "Now then, you and Lilian-sama should unpack. When you have put away all your belongings, please come back downstairs. Breakfast should be ready in just a bit."

It felt weird having breakfast when they would have normally been asleep. That was what happened when one traveled, he supposed. He was going to have major jet lag tomorrow.

"Where is Iris?" Lilian asked.

Kotohime placated the girl with a placid smile. "Do not worry, Lilian-sama. Iris-sama is residing within her bedroom."

Lilian nodded stiffly, then tugged on Kevin's hand and led him up the stairs. A hallway with a series of doors greeted them, and his mate pulled him along to one specific door. Lilian took a deep breath, as though steadying herself, and then she opened the door and went in.

The room was rather plain. Kevin didn't know what he had been expecting, but, well, a room completely unadorned with decorations was not it. This room had nothing save a divan, a closet, and a dresser.

Lying on the divan was Iris.

Lilian walked over to the divan, where she sat down and reached out a trembling hand to her sister. Kevin walked up behind her as his mate stroked Iris's hair. He couldn't see her face, but he could see from the way her body shook that Lilian was close to tears.

"It's really odd," Lilian began in a whisper. "Iris has always been there for me, protecting me, loving me, fighting for me when no one else would. Yet I could never do the same. Whenever Iris had nightmares, I couldn't stop them. When the Void whispered to her, I could never do anything. All I've ever been able to do was stand on the sidelines and watch as she suffered alone. Now she's been poisoned by the same type of youki that I have, and I can't do a single thing to help her." A sob wracked Lilian's body. "Why? All I wanted was for us to have a normal life. Is that too much to ask?"

Kevin didn't hesitate to wrap his arms around Lilian as she cried. He didn't know if she'd been holding this in until they were alone or if this was just a spontaneous burst of tears, but he supposed it didn't matter. He held Lilian tightly as she cried out her sorrows and

184

frustrations until they finally subsided.

"Feel better?" he asked.

Lilian sniffled as she wiped her eyes. "A little."

"I'm glad. Why don't you show me your room?" Kevin suggested.

"M'kay. I can do that."

Taking him by the hand, Lilian walked to the door. She paused to take one last glance at her sister before heading to another door, which opened into a room that made Kevin blink.

It looked like a typical room, minus the stone floor and the divan that acted as a replacement for a bed. A large bookshelf to his left was filled with manga. There was a huge collection of various series, some of which he didn't even know existed.

He had known that Lilian was obsessed with manga. She read the stuff all the time, and she was even learning how to draw her own manga. For some reason, though, he had assumed her love for manga came after meeting him, but now it looked like it had come long before they had ever met.

Manga wasn't the only thing in this room, he realized upon glancing at the walls. Numerous posters hung from each wall. All of them were of various manga that she must have read.

"Is that a Rurouni Kenshin poster?" he asked, pointing to one poster in particular.

Lilian glanced at the poster and smiled. "Yes, it is."

Kevin nodded as he looked at the poster next to it. He deadpanned. "And that... that's a hentai, isn't it?"

Indeed, right next to the Rurouni Kenshin poster was another poster. This one was of a naked woman spread eagle on a desk. Behind her was another woman, also naked, and holding a ruler as though it were a paddle with which to smack people with.

"Erm..." Lilian went into her version of deep thinking, complete with a hand on her chin. "Would you be upset if I said yes?"

"No." He ran a hand through his hair. "But it does make me wonder about your preferences." He glanced back at the bookshelf. "Still, I didn't realize you had such a large collection of manga."

"Ah, well, before you and I had ever met, manga was my only escape." Lilian smiled as she walked over to her bookshelf. Kevin followed her. "This was even before Jiāoào became obsessed with me. I didn't have much hope back then. The negotiations between Granny and the Bodhisattva were proceeding smoothly and it looked like I would be mated off to some old fart. Kotohime noticed my growing depression and went to the human world and bought me several manga volumes of *Ranma ½*. I absolutely loved them. They allowed me to escape my own bleak future, if only temporarily. After that, well, I just kept asking her to buy more and more, until I had filled up this entire bookshelf."

Kevin nodded as he looked over the manga on her shelf. A number of them were manga from the 80s and 90s. He recognized a few like *Rurouni Kenshin* and *Dragon Ball*, but there were some that he'd never seen before. He made a note to read those when he got the chance. As he continued glancing over the manga, he noticed something. While there were a lot of mainstream series, there were also a good deal of other manga that were, well, they certainly weren't mainstream.

"Urusei Yatsura, Ranma ½, Bastard... Municipal Force Daitenzin... Ragnarock City... Adventure Kid... High School DxD... To LOVE-RU Darkness... Kanokon..." Kevin felt a growing sense of unease as he read more titles. "Lilian?"

"Yes, Beloved?"

"Why is it that more than ninety percent of your manga collection are either harems or hentai?"

"Well..." Lilian took a moment to think before answering. "After meeting you, I had Kotohime get me all of the manga that boys like to read. I used them as reference guides when learning how to seduce you."

"I figured it was something like that." Kevin pressed a hand to his face. Looking back, it was so obvious that she had been trying to recreate scenes from harem manga and hentai *doujinshi* that Kevin felt like smashing his face against a wall. How he had missed the signs was something he would never understand. "Anyway, let's get unpacked and then head down for breakfast."

"Okay."

As they unpacked their belongings, Kevin wondered about what life had in store for them. Whatever awaited them, he was really, truly, honestly praying that it wouldn't lead to anything like the situations found in the manga on Lilian's shelf. He didn't have much hope.

The life of a harem protagonist is fraught with peril.

And tits.

But mostly peril.

Chapter 6

The Consequence of Feeling Helpless

Kevin and Lilian slept well through the morning. By the time Kevin woke up, it was around three p.m.

Stretching his arms and legs, Kevin blinked several times to rid himself of the blurriness. Sunlight shone in his eyes, threatening to burn his retina, but he ignored that in favor of lamenting his own tiredness. He loved traveling, truly, but he despised jet lag with a passion.

I should build a teleportation device.

He glanced down his chest at the red hair of his mate. She'd been every bit as exhausted as him, maybe even more so. Traveling across the globe, meeting her relatives, these actions must have taken their toll.

He rolled them over, so that Lilian was lying on her back. His hands were on either side of her head. Lilian's eyes remained closed. Her parted lips breathing in and out, causing her bare chest to rise and fall. With her hair splayed out like a fiery halo, she appeared reminiscent of an angel.

Feeling an overwhelming urge as he stared at her lips, Kevin didn't hesitate to lean down and kiss them. Lilian stirred as his lips touched hers but didn't waken. He pulled back, but only for a second, before kissing her with a little more force, while pressing his boxer-clad body against her bare one.

"Hn."

A delicate sounding moan was muffled by his mouth. A pair of hands became buried in his hair, pulling him down to press deeper against Lilian's waiting lips. He groaned as a warm, wet tongue penetrated his mouth. It rubbed against him, caressing his tongue and stirring up the increasing amount of saliva between them. One of his arms slid underneath Lilian's back, pulling her with him as he sat up.

They continued to kiss, but with Lilian now straddling his lap. He was rock hard, the pitch tent in his boxers was wedged firmly between her butt cheeks. She slowly rocked her hips, making him gasp and lose ground, allowing her tongue to probe further into his mouth. He felt his boxers grow wet, both from his own precum and from the lubrication Lilian released as he rubbed against her.

"Lilian," he groaned as the kiss broke and Lilian began licking the sweat that accumulated on his neck. His hands went to her cheeks, which he grasped firmly and helped her move against him. "You're going to kill me one of these days."

"That's not something you should tell me, Beloved." Lilian's voice came out muffled, but even so, he could pick up the heady tone lacing her words. "If you say something like that, I might decide to stop. I'd feel awful if my mate died because of something I did to him."

"Then… I'll be sure to shut up."

Kevin felt a knot coiling in his lower abdomen. It felt like a damn trying to hold back several billion tons of water during a level-five hurricane, while sixteen battering rams were bashing against the other side.

Knowing that he wouldn't last much longer, he pulled a hand away from her butt and reached down between them, fingers sliding across her stomach, through sparse amounts of red pubic hair, and finally pressing against the small button that he was looking for.

Lilian stiffened in his arms. Her legs clamped around his waist like a vice and shook violently, as did her arms. He felt her feet locking together as her heels pressed against the small of his back. A set of teeth clamped down on his trapezius, sending mixed signals of pleasure and pain straight into his brain. His mind nearly shut down as the dam broke, tipping him over the edge and causing him to explode.

Kevin almost collapsed back onto the bed, but he quickly placed a hand behind him to keep from falling. Lilian quivered in his remaining arm, her own arms going slack, along with her legs.

"B-Beloved…" She sounded tired.

"Mm?"

"I-I love you so much."

Kevin chuckled. "I love you, too."

***

Christine sat within her shower, her knees curled up to her chest. The hot spray from the showerhead rained down on her, causing her bangs to become matted to her forehead and cheeks. Despite the water being on its hottest temperature, she could find no comfort in it.

She and Iris were walking toward Kevin and Lilian. There was no sign of their enemy, who had seemingly disappeared. While Iris looked smug, somehow, as though she had chased the woman off herself, Christine felt wary. The hairs on the back of her neck were prickling.

"Hmph, she probably ran away," Iris said.

Christine sent her a sidelong glance. "She had us on the ropes. I doubt she ran away."

"Whatever, she's not here anymore, and that's what matters." Iris waved a dismissive hand in the air. She then sent her an appreciative look. "You surprised me there, tsun-loli. I hadn't realized you were so good in a fight."

Christine was glad it was so dark. She didn't want Iris seeing her blue face.

"D-don't think I enjoy having you c-c-c-compliment me! And of course I can fight! I might not have been in a lot of battles like you and Lilian, but I'm still a yōkai!"

"Heh." Iris ruffled her hair in a condescending manner. "True enough."

Christine scowled and was just about to swat Iris's hand away when three things happened in quick succession. The first was that Kevin began shouting something about them being trapped in an illusion. The second was the electric jolt of foreign youki entering her body. The third was a momentary feeling of weightlessness as she was shoved onto the ground.

Growling at the pain lancing up her backside, she looked up to give Iris a piece of her mind—

What…?

—only to stare in shocked horror as she saw a light spear piercing

189

the fox-girl's back. Iris stared at the spear's tip, which went straight through her back and out of her chest. She blinked. Then she switched her gaze to Christine.

Iris smiled at her. Blood dribbled from her mouth and dripped down her chin. A crimson stain expanded from her shirt. Yet she still smiled at her.

And then she collapsed.

Christine's own horrified and enraged cries drowned out the sound of gunfire.

"She pushed me out of the way," Christine muttered, the sound of her soft voice echoing due to the room's acoustics. "We always argued, and I kept calling her such horrible names, and yet, she took an attack that was meant for me."

Alone in her shower, Christine's tears ran down her cheeks and mixed with the water.

***

It was nearly half an hour later that Kevin and Lilian decided to get up. Kevin soon discovered the wonders of Greek bathhouses. It looked similar to a Japanese hot spring, if only in the vaguest sense. The bathhouse was shaped like a rectangle, made of limestone tiles. Steaming water bubbled from an unknown source, while steps descended into the bath, which stopped at about waist height.

"This estate is built on a natural hot spring," Lilian told him as they cleaned themselves off. "That's actually the reason Granny turned this island into her territory. The natural hot spring is half the reason humans come to the resort. Well, that, and they also get to enjoy all of the hospitality that a kitsune clan has to offer."

After getting cleaned and dressed, they tried to decide on what to do. Both of them were pretty ravenous, and not just because of their previous activity. They'd skipped breakfast and lunch to sleep in. Kevin's stomach gurgled unpleasantly, letting him know that he needed sustenance.

"Would you mind if we explored the village?" asked Kevin.

Lilian bit her lip. "You mean… you want to see Psyxế?"

"If you're not comfortable with that, we don't have to," Kevin said. "I'm sure we can find something else to do…"

"No." Lilian shook her head. "I don't mind showing you around.

If... if it's just for a little while, I'm sure everything will be okay."

"If you're sure," Kevin said.

"I'm sure," Lilian told him.

"Ufufufu, so you two are going into the village?" Kotohime asked as he and Lilian walked over to the entrance and put their shoes on. Dressed in a mauve kimono, the woman had appeared from behind them as if by magic.

"That's right." Lilian stood up and clenched her fist. Kevin thought he saw fire igniting behind her irises. "I've decided that we're going out to lunch and then I'm gonna show him around. The village might be a snorefest, but Beloved's never been in an all-kitsune village before, so it should be interesting."

"In that case, I shall accompany you."

Lilian crossed her arms and pouted at the swordswoman. "I don't need someone constantly watching me, you know. I'm perfectly capable of taking care of myself."

Her short response was met with Kotohime's placid smile.

"I do not doubt that Lilian-sama and Kevin-sama are more than capable of looking after themselves. However, as your bodyguard and maid, it is my duty to ensure that you are safe at all times. Besides..." Kotohime continued when Lilian opened her mouth, "... it is just as you said. This is Kevin-sama's first time visiting a kitsune-only village, and you know how some of the kitsune in Psyxé are, do you not?"

Kevin did not like Kotohime's words. He also didn't like the way Lilian's eyes widened in realization. Not one bit.

"You're right," Lilian said, growling. "Those dirty vixens might try something with my beloved. They're a threat to my beloved's purity."

"I'm pretty sure that my *purity* has been all but decimated by you and your family," Kevin retorted.

Lilian ignored him. "Very well, Kotohime. I shall place you in charge of keeping any potential vixens away from us while I show Beloved around."

Still smiling pleasantly, Kotohime bowed before Lilian. "I live to serve, Lilian-sama."

"Come on, Beloved." Lilian grabbed his hand. "Let's go."

Kevin sighed as he dutifully allowed the girl to pull him along.

***

Lindsay was worried.

A Fox's Revenge

Being a human, and one whose involvement with the yōkai world was minimal at best, she didn't understand what her friends were going through. All she knew was that Lilian and Kevin had left the country due to some blood feud or something, and that Christine had become abnormally quiet ever since.

School was out. It had ended later in the year than usual, June, due to the still as-of-yet unexplained destruction of the gym last year. She wondered about that, but figured Kevin and Lilian were somehow involved. It only made sense. Because school was no longer in session, Lindsay had decided that she and her friend should go out.

It wasn't the pleasant experience she'd been hoping for.

She walked alongside Christine. The mall was decently crowded, though because of the early hour, it wasn't too congested. They hadn't done much, merely walked around the mall. The silence between them was almost deafening.

This is really awkward.

Lindsay looked at the girl by her side. Her outward appearance was no different than before. Her black lace bodice was affixed to her torso. Her black skirt descended past her knees, swishing as she walked. Black slippers lightly tapped against tile, and the ruffles on her sleeves rustled as her arms swung back and forth. Nothing seemed to have changed.

Lindsay knew differently. Christine's steps were stilted, stumbling almost. Bags hung under her eyes. She walked with a noticeable hunch, her shoulders slouched and tired. Lindsay also noticed the redness in the little yuki-onna's eyes, a clear sign that she'd been crying sometime today.

"… Christine?"

"Mm?"

Lindsay hesitated. Should she talk with her friend to find out what was wrong? Would Christine get angry at her? Would her friend clam up? Even if the yuki-onna was willing to speak, how could she, a mere human, help when she barely understood what was happening in her friend's life?

"Let's get something to eat." Lindsay grabbed her friend's hand and smiled down at the yuki-onna. Christine blinked several times as if she was processing her words. She didn't say anything, but after a moment, she gave her a nod of assent.

As she led the girl to the food court, Lindsay lamented.

I'm such a coward.

A Fox's Revenge

***

Kevin noticed the looks almost the moment they arrived at the village.

He, Lilian, and Kotohime had taken another carriage back into the village. It was a fifteen-minute trip from the ancestral home, which Kevin learned was actually built within the crater on top of the mountain. That explained why they had passed through a cavern to get there. The walls had blocked most of his view, but he had noticed the giant mountain range on all sides of the ancestral home.

After their carriage parked near the village entrance, they disembarked and entered the village itself.

The stares started almost the second they began walking around.

Kevin had become immune to stares. Indeed, with a mate like Lilian, whose inhuman beauty caused heads to turn wherever she went, he'd been pretty much forced to learn how to ignore people staring at them. The additional presence of Camellia, Christine, Lindsay, Iris, Kotohime, and Kirihime to his entourage had all but obliterated his ability to perceive stares…

… Or so he thought.

He glanced around at the people they passed. Almost everyone had stopped to look at them. At first, he assumed they were looking at Lilian or Kotohime. That was the first thing everyone else looked at back home. Only after thorough observation and making eye contact several times did he realize the truth. They weren't looking at his companions; they were staring at him.

I don't know why, but for some reason, these stares are really beginning to bug me.

Lilian seemed annoyed by the stares too. Her arms were wrapped around his right and she glared at pretty much every female who passed them.

"Ufufufu." Kotohime chuckled. "Lilian-sama seems very territorial today."

Kevin watched Lilian's cheeks swell like a bullfrog.

"I just don't like the way these vixens are looking at Beloved," Lilian defended her actions. "These girls aren't like Iris. They don't care for my mate and me. They're just a bunch of hussies."

"I'm not sure they're interested in screwing me," Kevin said. "I think they're just curious about why there's a human in their presence."

Lilian's scoff told him how ridiculous she thought that notion was.

"Kevin," she began, "these women are kitsune, not nekomata. We might be slightly curious creatures, but by and large, our thought processes run more along the lines of how we can manipulate others for our own purposes over satiating our curiosity."

"You know, I get very worried when you say things like that," Kevin observed idly.

"Ufufufu, do not worry, Kevin-sama. Lilian-sama has no talent at manipulation. I am sure you have realized that by now after all of her failed attempts to seduce you."

Lilian's face turned red. "T-that was a mean thing to say."

Kevin ignored Lilian as he nodded in assent. "I did notice that. I mean, I'm sure that walking around the house naked would be enough for most teens, but it's not really what I would call seductive."

"Not you, too, Beloved," Lilian bemoaned.

"Sorry." Kevin tossed her an apologetic smile. "I couldn't help myself."

"Mou. You're not sorry at all."

***

Fan climbed the stairs to one of several spires that made up her father's home. She had been thinking about her father's plan for the Pnévma girl ever since he had told them of it. She personally hoped to see it fail. Not because she didn't want to see Jiāoào return to normal; she just didn't the one who accomplished that feat to be Lilian.

I should be the one who heals his damaged mind.

The stairway slowly wound in a clockwise motion. Her hand trailed along the guardrail. There were no exits in his spire. No floors. Just a top and a bottom. A beginning and an end. Behind her, the surprisingly silent footsteps of her bodyguard, Li, echoed with much less noise than her own.

Intricately woven tapestries greeted Fan as she reached the top. They covered the wall in stately designs fit for royalty. Her younger brother always did have a habit of enjoying the finer things in life.

Father must have put these here in the hopes that it would help Jiāoào recover.

She looked around the room. Royal purple carpet covered the floor. Furnishings fit for a king were arrayed around the interior, a dresser made of a rich dark wood inlaid with golden designs, a nightstand of the same color. They gleamed brightly under the natural sunlight filtering in through the window. A potted plant sat upon the windowsill, a snapdragon, its blood red petals looking very much like a dragon.

Beside the nightstand was a large bed. A canopy hung above it, sheets of transparent silk hanging from it, swaying in the gentle breeze. Bedsheets the color of amethyst covered the bed, which could easily fit five people. It only had one occupant at the moment, and he rested upon several large, fluffy pillows that matched the sheets.

"Jiāoào…"

Fan traveled over to the bed on shaky legs and sat down beside her younger brother. His eyes were open but stared at nothing. He didn't react when she sat next to him, not even so much as a twitch. It broke her heart to see him like this.

"What do you think of Honorable Grandfather's plan?" asked Li.

Fan twitched. "No offense to Father, but I think it's a horrible plan."

"But if it works…"

Fan scowled at Li. "What makes you possibly think something like that could work? The entire idea is a human concept."

"Don't underestimate humanity, Lady Fan," Li warned. "It was, after all, a human who bested you. And if I am right, then it was the same human who bested you that also bested Jiāoào. That should tell you something."

"Even an insect will get lucky sometimes," Fan said. "Either way, there is absolutely no way that Pnéyma girl will be capable of helping my beloved younger brother. I doubt he even likes her after what happened between them."

"I wouldn't be so sure of that. The young lord was rebuffed by Lilian Pnéyma many times, yet he always came back to her over and over again."

"There's no need to inform me of what I already know," Fan snapped.

Li shrugged. "Considering your words, I had assumed you'd forgotten."

Fan clicked her tongue and looked back at her beloved younger brother. It was hard to forget about how he'd obsessed over that Pnéyma girl. Ever since he first saw the little trollop, he had been infatuated with her. She still remembered the first time he'd come back from the Pnéyma Clan's ancestral home after traveling there with Father. He had mentioned meeting an *angel with hair made of fire*. She remembered how her heart shattered when he told her that he was going to mate with her.

Her brother had slowly pulled away from her after that. It was heartbreaking. They used to be so close before that girl interfered. Before that, she had been his everything! He'd always stuck by her side until then, spending time with her, sleeping with her, bathing with her. After that girl showed up, however, he'd stopped doing that.

"You're my sister," he would say. *"I can't be close to my sister when I'm trying to get a mate. I need to be seen as desirable, and having my sister fawn over me isn't what women look for in a man."*

After that, her brother had become obsessed with looking manly. He'd studied everything he could about how real men should act, reading books and trashy human novels on manliness. He had soon determined that real men were players and had a harem of women at their beck and call. He'd gone behind Father's back and acquired a number of slaves, which she knew he kept in a safe house. He would always disappear there when Father was away on business.

Fan hadn't said anything. It hurt. It broke her heart. Before that time, Father had planned on having her be the one to mate with Jiāoào. Seeing her brother who had, up until that point, been her whole life, leave her in the dust to play with slaves was the third most painful memory in her life.

I'm sure that Shílì had something to do with my brother's change.

She didn't know when Shílì had first appeared, and he never showed himself to anyone, but Fan knew. One of her brother's maids had been her spy, so she knew about the Void Kitsune who'd appeared before him one day. Even so, she hadn't said anything. Shílì was too good at disappearing, so she hadn't been able to bring his existence up to Father.

I should be the one healing him, not that trollop!

That's right. She should be the one who healed him. She was sure that she could find a way, one that not even her father had thought of. And once she healed her beloved younger brother, he would remember the love they had once shared and denounce his desire to mate with the trollop. Yes, she could see it all now:

Jiāoào's eyes slowly fluttered open, much to Fan's surprise and joy. He looked around, irises flickering back and forth, before they landed on her.

"Fan," he said, his voice raspy from disuse. *"Did you save me?"*

Fan gave her beloved younger brother her gentlest smile. "I did."

"Thank you." He smiled at her. "And... I'm sorry for ignoring you the way I did. I know that it was wrong, but I... I was just so embarrassed."

"It's okay." Fan reached out and cupped his face with the tenderness of a lover. "I understand that boys will be boys. So long as you have learned your lesson, that is all that matters."

"I have." He nodded seriously. "Don't worry, Fan. I know the truth now. You are the only woman that I will ever need in my life."

Fan's heart lightened at his words. The ice that had formed since he had met that atrociously boorish Pnéyma trollop melted. Everything was going to be better now, she just knew it.

"Come on, my beloved younger brother, let's take a bath together."
"Okay."

"Huhuhuhu…"

"Fan, your true self is showing."

"Ge!"

Fan snapped out of her daydream at the sound of Li's voice. She tossed him a vicious look, while trying to mask her embarrassment… and also surreptitiously wiping away the drool from her mouth before he noticed.

"A-anyway!" Fan stood up and dusted the nonexistent dust off her stately robes. "I do not believe Father's plan will work. Therefore, we must discover another method while Father is speaking with the, um, the…"

"The Vættir Clan."

"Right." Fan nodded. "While father is meeting with the Vættir clan, you and I will research a way to cure my beloved younger brother."

"I do not know if this is a good idea." Li sounded most reluctant.

Fan ignored him. "Quickly, to the Bat Cave!"

"Don't you mean the library?"

Fan blinked. "Did I not say library?"

"No," Li's tone was surprisingly dry, "you did not. You said Bat Cave."

"O-oh." Fan coughed into her hands, embarrassed. She must have been truly preoccupied to break the fourth wall that badly, and what the hell was a bat cave anyway? "My bad. Let me try that again. Now, quickly, to the library!"

Li sighed. "As you wish, Lady Fan."

***

As they were no longer confined to a carriage, Kevin had a lot more time to study the layout of the village. It really did look like the ancient Greek settlements he'd read about in history books. All of the buildings were made of stone. They had no glass in their windows, and most places didn't even have doors, just square-shaped holes in the wall, though some were covered by curtains.

While the design of the buildings was outdated by about 800 years, Kevin did notice that they possessed some technology.

Lilian led him into one of the few cafés Psyxế possessed. No bell chimed to let the owner know that customers had entered. Stone flooring presented a stark contrast to what he was used to seeing on a café floor. There were no decorations on the gray stone walls and the wooden tables looked old. However, while much of the building seemed ancient, Kevin noticed a relatively new cappuccino maker.

Of course, by relatively, he meant it looked like something from the early 50s.

A person walked up to them, a woman, whose brown hair shimmered and whose three tails waved behind her as she walked. She was pretty, but Kevin had noticed that every kitsune was pretty, so that didn't mean much. Compared to vixens like Lilian and Iris, this woman was almost plain.

"Hello," the woman greeted before stopping. She looked at Lilian, blinked, and then rubbed her eyes. "Lilian?"

Lilian shuffled. "Berenise, hello."

Berenise frowned. Her eyes flickered to Kevin, then Lilian, and then to Kotohime. Kevin thought he saw her eyes flash with emotion, but then she placed her hands on her hips and grinned.

"Well, I'll be. It really is you. I'd heard rumors that you ran away from home."

"Is that so?" Lilian muttered. Berenise either ignored or didn't hear the words. She turned to Kevin.

"And who is this handsome young man?"

Lilian held his arm closer. Kevin sensed her getting territorial again. "This is Kevin, my mate."

Berenise looked nonplussed. "Your mate? You have a mate?"

"Yes."

"Since when?"

"Since nine months ago."

"Oh, well, congratulations are in order, I guess." Again, that emotion flashed in Berenise's eyes. Kevin felt like he should know it, but he couldn't figure out what it meant. "I'm glad to see you've found your mate at such a young age. You know that most of us don't find our first mates until we're a bit older. I had to go through ten mating periods before I found my mate."

Kevin felt his cheeks burn at the mention of mating periods. He remembered Lilian's first ever mating period last year. She had very nearly raped him. She probably would have raped him if it hadn't been for some quick thinking on his part.

Lilian also blushed, clearly remembering her loss of control during that time.

"Ufufufu," Kotohime giggled quietly.

"Quiet, you," Kevin and Lilian said at the same time.

"Ara, ara." Kotohime hid her mirthful smile behind her kimono's left sleeve. "You said that at the same time. How adorable."

"It is awfully cute," Berenise agreed.

"W-whatever," Lilian quickly changed the subject, "anyway, we were hoping to get something to eat here."

"Of course." Berenise's demeanor subtly shifted into something a little more professional as she curtsied. "Come on, let me get you three seated."

They followed Berenise further into the tiny cafe. Kevin noticed that a few other people were there aside from them. He saw a group of young kitsune girls who looked around Lilian's age. They stared at him as he walked by, then began whispering and giggling to each other, while also stealing more glances at him. Kevin didn't know whether to blush or roll his eyes.

It seems all girls act the same regardless of race.

"Here's the menu. Let me know when you're ready to order." Berenise handed him and Lilian a menu. Kotohime declined one, claiming she'd already eaten. She also declined a seat, instead electing to stand behind Lilian, her katana held firmly in her left hand, as always.

"This place is actually kinda interesting." Kevin glanced through the menu. All the dishes were written in Greek. He couldn't read Greek.

"You think so?" Lilian also glanced at the menu, though she clearly could read it, unlike him.

"Yeah, I mean, it feels almost like I've stepped into the past or something. I think that's pretty cool."

"The novelty will wear off soon, trust me on this." Lilian closed the menu. Kevin did as well. Not like staring would help him understand the language. "It seems new and exciting right now, but eventually, you'll realize how boring it is. You'll see that there's nothing to do here except wander around, and that will eventually become boring because there isn't all that much to see anyway."

"I could probably find some interesting wildlife," Kevin pointed out, causing Lilian to smile and shake her head.

"You and your animal fetish."

"What's that supposed to mean?"

Lilian's grin told him that trouble was coming. "It means you. Like. My. Tails."

Kevin almost stiffened when one of Lilian's tails caressed his leg. He did stiffen when it tried going down his shorts. Only quick-witted thinking on his part let him fend her off.

"We are so not doing this here," he told her. Lilian giggled, making him decide to change the subject before she could embarrass him further. "Still, though… I know you don't really like this place, but for a human like myself, it's pretty interesting."

"I guess it would be," Lilian conceded. "I prefer being back home in Arizona. There's just so much more to do there. I get to go to school and spend time with our friends. We can travel to the mall and see movies or have fun at the arcade. Plus there's all the anime that we can watch at home. You can't do any of that here."

Lilian brought up some excellent points. Kevin did recognize that there wasn't much they could do there. There were only a hundred or so buildings in the entire village, and most of those were probably houses. This cafe was apparently one of two, and there were only about a dozen or so stores that sold clothing, which, judging by what everyone wore, consisted mostly of togas.

At the thought of home, Kevin felt a small ache appear in his chest. Was Christine okay? How was Lindsay doing? Were Alex and Andrew keeping Eric on a tight leash? Did Kiara and Heather miss him? He'd never really thought about it before, but these people had become inextricably linked to his life. Now they were gone—or rather, he was gone, and he didn't know when he and Lilian would go back.

"Are you okay, Beloved? You grew quiet all of a sudden." Lilian placed her hands over his.

Kevin snapped himself from his thoughts and smiled. "I'll be fine. I guess I'm just feeling a little overwhelmed by everything that's happened is all. I don't think it really hit me until just now that this is really happening; that we're really here in Greece, living with your family."

"Kevin..."

Kevin wondered if the sudden weaknesses in his legs was natural.

"I... to be honest, while I've been made aware about the dangers of the yōkai world, I never really believed it would have anything to do with us. I mean, yeah, we had to deal with that kitsune who kidnapped you, and we got involved with that disaster in California, and the assassin Seth Naraka when we came back home, but all those events happened in the human world. I guess a part of me always assumed that any yōkai problem we had would be dealt with in the human world, too, but now we're here, and I... I feel like I've suddenly realized that this is all real."

"Oh, Kevin." Lilian's warm hands on his felt pleasant. They were like a small buoy keeping him from getting lost at sea. Kotohime gave him a compassionate glance as well.

"Does that make me weak?" Kevin asked.

Lilian looked appalled that he would ask something like that. "Of course not. Why would you say something like that? There's no shame in being afraid. I've been afraid plenty. When that Fan woman attacked us and hurt Iris, I was frightened out of my mind. You were the one who took command back there. You were the one who saved my sister and killed Fan. You are really, really strong. You're just feeling a little overwhelmed by everything that's happened. To be honest, I am, too. Even though we spent twenty hours on a plane doing nothing, we never really had a chance to just absorb everything that's happened. I don't know about you, but I've been trying to not think about all this because I feel like my mind would break if I did."

Lilian's words went a long way toward reassuring him. He knew that he was being stupid. They'd already been through so much. He'd been almost killed numerous times, yet here he was, his feelings overwhelming him as if he were a lost child. It made him feel pathetic, but it also made him feel human.

"Yeah, I guess you're right." He sighed, then smiled. "Sorry for acting so pathetic. I think I just had a Yuki moment there."

Lilian shook her head and gave him her own reassuring smile. "It's okay. We all get like this on occasion. And don't compare yourself to that fruit cake. Yukiteru Amano is a complete beta, and while you might not be a prime example of an alpha male, you're definitely not some whiny little brat like him."

"Ouch." Kevin winced. "I don't know who I should feel sorrier for: Yuki or myself."

"Muu." Lilian pouted at him. "That was a compliment, Beloved. I was complimenting you."

"Didn't sound like a compliment," Kevin muttered. Kotohime giggled. "Quiet, you."

"Ara, ara." The woman with the katana merely gave him a placidly amused smile.

***

After eating at the small café, Kevin, Lilian, and Kotohime left to wander the village some more. The female kitsune who'd been watching them from several tables over also left. When Kevin turned his head, he saw them out of his peripheral vision.

Are they following us?

"Lilian-sama…"

"I know."

"Shall I…?"

Lilian closed her eyes and sighed. "No, let me deal with this. I can't… I can't run away from this forever."

Kotohime, who walked several feet behind and to their left, bowed her head in acknowledgement. "Very well. I'll leave things to you. Please be sure to call me if you need help."

"Will do."

Kevin blinked when Kotohime slowly withdrew, heading into an alley between two buildings. He frowned. Glancing once more at the group of girls behind him, he understood that his belief had been correct. They were following him and Lilian.

"Lilian, what's going on?"

"I'm sorry, Beloved." The disheartened expression on her face bothered him. "I was hoping this wouldn't happen, but it seems that even several years isn't enough to erase some grudges."

Before Kevin could ask what she meant, the girls finally caught up to them. There were six of them. All of them wore togas. Five of them had two tails, like Lilian, but one of them, the ringer leader, Kevin guessed, possessed three.

"Lilian Pnévma," the ringleader said, flicking her long brown hair over her shoulder. "I didn't think you'd return after being sent away. You've got a lot of nerve coming back here."

While she appeared outwardly calm, Kevin was certain that Lilian's mind was a flurry of activity.

"I'm sorry." Lilian smiled. For some reason, it reminded him of Iris. "Have we met before?"

"Tch!" The woman spat on the ground. "I see you've grown more arrogant since getting sent off. Did living in the human world make you forget about all the fun times we've had?"

"I don't recall having any fun with you," Lilian declared. "Perhaps your memories are fuzzy."

"Is that so?" The woman's lips pulled back as she grinned. Her canines were sharp. "I think you're the one whose memory is messed up. Shall I remind you of all the good times we've had together?"

Kevin didn't know exactly what was happening here, but he once remembered Lilian telling him that she wasn't well liked. He had assumed it was her family that she'd been talking about. However, it looked like she had also been bullied by the girls in her village.

Well, whatever. He didn't care about the details. These people were picking on his mate. That was unacceptable.

"I do not know what business you have with my mate," he began, stepping in front of Lilian to address the woman, "but I suggest you speak to her with more respect."

The woman looked shocked. Perhaps she was surprised that a human was addressing her in such a tone, or maybe she was simply shocked that someone was talking down to her at all. It didn't really matter.

A smile appeared on her lips. "Ho? It seems you've got some bark to you, child." The smile disappeared. "I don't like men who bark at me like some kind of rabid dog. I think we should fix that."

Kevin twitched as a sense of vertigo came over him. The world around him darkened as everything, the buildings, the stalls, and the people, disappeared one by one, until only the woman remained. It was like he had tunnel vision.

Enchantment.

As the name implied, enchantments were a method of controlling, or rather, enchanting a person into doing a yōkai's bidding. They were generally cast by producing pheromones laced with youki. Depending on the strength of the yōkai in question, an enchantment could do anything from making someone mildly aroused to turning them into that yōkai's willing slave.

Kevin had let Iris cast enchantments on him as a part of his training. Her enchantments were strong—stronger than this three-tails. Ignoring the effects were easy.

"Lilian," he said in a steady voice. "This woman is casting an enchantment on me. Does that count as assault?"

A hum off to his left told him that Lilian was thinking. "Yes, I believe it does."

"Good."

Kevin had always been told by his mother to never hit girls, and he used to follow that rule—until Heather started beating the crap out of him on a daily basis. While Kevin often duked it out with his sparring partner, that didn't mean he would hit a female at random. Violence wasn't in his nature.

However, it was a different story if he was attacked first.

Kevin stalked toward the woman, whose enchantment still affected him. He could feel it pressing against his mind. He could feel it making his heart beat rapidly in his chest, like the double bass pedal to a metal band. And since he could feel it, Kevin could ignore it. These feelings weren't real.

"How are you still standing?" the woman asked, taking one step back for every two steps he made. "You should be kneeling before me! You should be licking my feet! Why are you still standing?!"

"I'm not in the mood to answer your questions," Kevin told her, quickening his pace. "You've made me rather angry. I think it's time to punish you."

"W-what do you plan on doing?" asked the woman as she continued to retreat. "Y-you wouldn't hit a woman, would you?"

"Oh, you don't need to worry about something like that." Kevin smiled. "I believe in gender equality."

The woman's fair skin turned white as a sheet. She kept going until her back hit a wall. Kevin rushed forward. The woman shrieked as he threw a punch—

He stopped his fist just before it could graze her nose. The woman's eyes went crossed. Her knees trembled. An acrid stench filled the air.

A Fox's Revenge

The three-tails had pissed herself.

"I do not know who you are," Kevin said. "Frankly, I don't really care. Mess with my mate again, and I really will hit you."

Pulling his fist away, he ignored the woman as she sank onto her hands and knees. He turned away and walked back over to Lilian.

He paused.

"I'm not sure why you said you weren't strong enough to start training our teamwork. Seems to me like you're plenty strong."

Lilian stood in the center of a pile of bodies. The five girls who had been with the three-tails were lying around Lilian, moaning and groaning. All of them sported bruises. Two of them were drooling and possessed glazed eyes, showing that they'd been felled by an illusion.

"These vixens aren't very strong," Lilian replied. "Well, they seemed that way when I was younger, but that's because I was weaker back then. Most kitsune don't know how to fight."

Her words were difficult to accept at face value, but that wasn't because he didn't believe her. Thus far all of the kitsune they had met until now knew how to fight. Luna, Seth Naraka, Fan, Kotohime, Kirihime, that blond fop who beat him at the Comic-Con, all of them could fight. Given how often he'd fought against a kitsune, it was easy to assume that every kitsune could fight.

Kevin understood that this wasn't true. The kitsune he'd fought, the kitsune he knew, they were the minority, a small percentage of the kitsune population. It was also because they were violent that Kevin had confronted them. If they hadn't been, if they were like these girls, then he probably would have never met some of them.

"Yeah, I guess you're right." Kevin walked up to her. At the same time, Kotohime landed on the ground next to them. He assumed she had been watching them from one of the buildings.

"That was an excellent display of prowess, Lilian-sama, Kevin-sama," she said with her perennial smile. "However, I believe we may want to leave now."

"Why is that?" asked Kevin.

"Because you two have attracted a crowd," Kotohime informed them.

Kevin and Lilian looked around. Their battle, if it could have been called such, had not gone unnoticed. A large crowd had gathered around them. Many kitsune were staring at them, whispering and pointing. From the way their noses and lips had curled, he assumed they were making snide remarks.

I see why Lilian didn't want to come here now.

"I think you're right," he said. "We've overstayed our welcome. Lilian?"

The relieved smile on Lilian's face told him all he needed to know. He regretted asking her to take him down to the village now. At the same time, he was glad this had happened. It gave him a new perspective from which he could look at his mate with.

"Yes." She grabbed his extended hand. "Let's go back to Granny's."

***

Sitting on her dais as she mused about life and other trivial issues, Delphine sneezed.

"Kuchu! Kuchu!"

It was a surprisingly cute sneeze.

"Are you feeling ill, Mother?" asked Daphne.

"No." Delphine wiggled her nose in another gesture of surprising cuteness. "I think someone was just talking about me. Heheh, I hope it's a hot guy!"

Daphne merely stared at her mother with her best "WTF?" expression.

"… Right."

***

Jasmine was a very fastidious kitsune, though she preferred to consider herself more the type of kitsune who simply strived to be the best she could. Perfectionism, she understood, was a fallacious concept. Even the gods were not perfect. This she knew from the one time she'd seen Lord Inari after the annual kitsune poker night.

It had not been a pretty sight.

One of her many habitual patterns was that Jasmine liked routines. Doing the same thing every day at the same time every day, going through the motions, as it were. It kept things relatively easy. She didn't have to devote much time to thinking about her day, which left more time for other pursuits.

Like figuring out why her mother's titanic lumps of fat defied the laws of physics and the very fabric of reality.

Jasmine also considered herself an intellectual. Perhaps it was the result of her young age, though she liked to think otherwise, but she was a curious kitsune. When there was something that she couldn't figure out, she enjoyed researching whatever that something was until she understood every facet about it, inside and out.

She sat on the porch of her abode. The sun had finally begun dipping below the horizon. From where she sat, Jasmine could see it beginning to hide behind the Omichlódis mountain, the very mountain in which her home sat. Colors filled the sky, splashes of pinks, swirls of purple, streaks of red. They congealed with an artistry that no painter, be they human or yōkai, could recreate.

She paid little attention to the sight, however, as sunsets were only of mild interest. Her focus was instead on her book, one on human psychology, which she'd convinced her shadow to travel into the human world and acquire for her. While she didn't much care for the primate race in general, she would admit that their pursuit of knowledge was worthy of admiration. They had some truly fascinating ideas.

After flipping the page of her book, Jasmine paused in her reading to take a sip of her tea. She blinked several times and then looked up because her eyes were getting a tad sore from having stared at pages of text for several hours.

That's when she saw *him*. His messy blond hair gave him a carefree look, a sort of devil-may-care appearance. Hiding behind his bangs were eyes of a bright azure. He was blessed with sun-kissed skin, and she could tell from the definition in his arms and the broadness of his shoulders and chest that he was in good shape. He had no tails and no ears. Jasmine had never seen a human before, but in that moment, she knew, beyond a doubt, that this young man was human.

"Ayane?" she spoke into thin air. "Who is that?"

Jasmine did not look behind her, but she knew that her shadow had appeared. She also knew that, were she to turn her head, her shadow would be kneeling submissively before her. As expected of a kunoichi.

"That is the human, Kevin Swift, Jasmine-denka," Ayane told her. "According to the information that I have already gathered, he is Lilian-sama's mate, de gozaru."

The young man walked next to a familiar redhead. Lilian. Jasmine didn't have many dealings with the other girl. They had never spoken before, and Jasmine preferred to keep it that way, for the time being. She didn't hate the older kitsune, of course. However, Lilian and her sister were trouble.

At the same time…

"I see," Jasmine murmured. "So, he is, indeed, a human, just as I expected."

"Shall I gather more intelligence on this human, de gozaru?"

Jasmine considered having her shadow do the preliminary intelligence gathering on Kevin Swift. She'd already managed to gain some useful information, it seemed, and she could probably do a better job than Jasmine herself. However, the intellectual in her would not allow someone else to study something that fascinated her.

"... No," she said after a moment. "I would rather study him myself."

"As you wish, de gozaru."

She felt, more than heard, her shadow disappear. Without paying the human a second glance, Jasmine went back to her reading.

***

Christine arrived at her empty home several hours later. A glance at the clock revealed it to be 12:25 p.m., considerably earlier than she usually arrived home when going out with Lindsay. Thinking on it, it was not actually all that unusual for her to not arrive home until the next day. She normally spent the night at Lindsay's house after they went out.

Lindsay...

She knew that her friend was worried about her. She also felt horrible for worrying one of the few people who accepted her. While she never really showed it, she did care about her friends, and Lindsay was definitely one of her best friends. She didn't want to worry the human girl, but it wasn't something that she could help.

Iris smiled at her. Even as blood dribbled down her chin, even as she collapsed, she still smiled at her.

The problem she was confronted with was something that Lindsay couldn't help with. This issue was outside of human boundaries. It delved into a world beyond the comprehension of an athletic tomboyish schoolgirl.

Christine sat on the bed, her hands hovering over Iris's chest, her youki willingly coursing through her as she covered the stab wound in ice.

What's more, this wasn't something that she wanted her friend becoming involved in. She already had one human friend neck deep in the violence of her world. Kevin. The boy who, even now, she loved more than anything, the boy she would probably never stop loving thanks to her curse.

But even though she worried for him, Christine knew that Kevin, at least, could handle himself. She'd seen proof of that during their fight with Fan. Christine didn't know if she would be able to deal with someone like Lindsay, a regular high school girl, also becoming embroiled in the world of yōkai.

She watched with a sense of helplessness as Kevin and Lilian worked together, slowly sewing Iris's wounds shut.

However, something had to change. She knew that. More and more yōkai incidents were occurring in heavily populated human centers. Christine didn't know if her situation was an isolated event, though considering how she and her friends had run smack dab in the middle of a war between kitsune and kappa in California, she didn't believe so.

She and Lilian ran down the tunnel, reaching the hatch that would lead outside. As she began to climb, she remembered how Kevin had all but commanded them to leave. She understood his reasons, but even so, hearing him tell her to leave Fan to him, to take Iris and run, pierced her heart more surely than any javelin ever could.

The world was changing. Perhaps it was a sign that the yōkai world wouldn't be able to hide for much longer. Having lived in the human world all her life, she didn't know much about that. What she did know was that she couldn't afford to be weak anymore.

After taking a hot shower, Christine went into her room, a towel wrapped around her small body, and stopped in front of her phone. It was an old phone, a landline phone, and one that she'd never used— mainly because there had never been any reason to. Now there was. She picked up the phone and dialed a number that she had never used but had memorized by heart.

It only rang once before someone answered it.

"Hello?" an old, wizened voice came from the other end.

Christine took a deep breath.

"Orin, I need your help," she said without inflection, doing the one thing she thought she would never do.

With this, life as she knew it would never be the same again.

***

Kevin woke up in the middle of the night. He could hear the sounds of nightlife filling the air, a soothing lullaby of natural music. The chirping of crickets was soft and gentle. An owl hooted somewhere in the distance. Running water mixed in with animal music, a steady flow from the slowly moving creeks that meandered through the ancestral home.

Lilian was still asleep. She lay on her side, her nude body conforming to his. He was tempted to let himself be lulled back into the dreams of Morpheus... unfortunately, nature was calling, and he was loath to disobey that particular call.

After extricating himself from Lilian, who frowned at the loss of his body heat and snuggled against the spot he'd been resting in an attempt to reclaim it, Kevin went to take a leak.

The restrooms in this dwelling were odd devices. Honestly, it was just a hole cut into a rock bench with fast flowing water underneath. Not exactly what he would call the most modern of crappers.

It was absolutely ludicrous how outdated these kitsune were. He understood that, due to their longevity, change among yōkai came slowly, but come on! The Pnéyma Clan owned a freaking resort with all the luxurious amenities of a five-star hotel! Surely they could pioneer those inventions and use them in their everyday life? Or was the idea of using human technology for themselves just that abhorrent?

"If there is one thing that you should know, it is that we yōkai are prideful creatures. We have, for many eons, been at the top of the food chain. Even as far back as the seventeenth century, we were still more powerful than humanity in spite of their overwhelming numerical superiority," Kotohime lectured him as he sat in the living room of their apartment.

"What does that have to do with why yōkai disdain from human technology?" he asked.

"It is not that we disdain from it. There are many instances where we will use human technology—and as you know from interacting with people like Kiara-san and Lilian-sama, there are some of us who have

210

cast aside our pride for the sake of progress. However, by and large, most yōkai dislike using human technology. For them, the act of using something created by humans is the same as admitting that humanity has surpassed yōkai."

"Has it?"

"Not really, but then, yōkai are no longer at the top either. It is hard to say who is the superior species now, especially as there are so many different types of yōkai, and we do not get along very well. However, that is a lesson for another time. The knowledge that I wish to impart right now is that yōkai do not like using human technology. They will use it when necessary, but only when necessary, and it will be done with great reluctance."

"Is Lilian's family like this, too?"

"In some ways. Pnéyma-denka is a very forward-thinking kitsune. She does not disdain herself from using human technology when it is convenient for her. Psyxé, the village located next to the Pnéyma Clan ancestral home, has some human technology that the matriarch has declared useful, and many young kitsune from the village are trained to use human technology so they can run the resort located on the island's shores. She also has a bad habit of buying certain human luxuries that interest her. However, while Pnéyma-denka is often considered a forerunner in using human technology, she falls under the category that I like to call 'why change what works?'"

"So, basically, you're telling me that the Pnéyma Clan will use technology to do things that they cannot do on their own, but not for something that would just be more convenient for them?"

"Exactly."

Kevin shook his head. He remembered his conversation with Kotohime nearly four months back, when she had begun teaching him about the specifics of the Pnéyma Clan. He hadn't really believed her words back then. Now her words were coming back to bite him in the metaphorical, and literal, ass.

After finishing his business, Kevin was about to head back to bed when he spotted Kotohime out of the corner of his eye. She stood outside on a balcony that overlooked the Pnéyma grounds. Her kimono lightly fluttered in the breeze. Kevin wondered if the woman ever wore anything else.

"Kotohime," he greeted as he moved to stand beside her.

A Fox's Revenge

"Kevin-sama," she greeted him with a nod and a smile. "What are you still doing up?"

"I could ask you the same thing."

"Touché."

Kevin looked out at the grounds of the Pnéyma Clan ancestral home. The streams that ran through the grounds shimmered with moon and starlight. The silhouette of plants swayed as a breeze blew through the grounds, which also buffeted his hair.

Yet even though everything seemed peaceful, Kevin could not help but feel uneasy. This place sent chills up his spine. Perhaps it was simply the realization that he was the only human on an island full of yōkai, but he didn't think so. There was just something about being here, in this place, that put him on edge...

... He felt like he was standing before the gates to the Underworld.

"I believe you should know, Kevin-sama," Kotohime's voice startled him out of his reverie, "that I, much like Lilian-sama, do not believe that you are weak. Weak would be not accepting the reality of your situation and living in denial. Weak would be not doing something to help those you care about because you are too afraid. That is what it means to be weak, and you, Kevin Swift-sama, are not that."

She was referring to his earlier conversation with Lilian.

"I guess."

Kevin gave her a tentative smile. It was returned by Kotohime's own brilliant beaming, which reminded him of the moon. He looked back out at the grounds, his mind in contemplation.

"I know that I've gotten stronger, that I'm a stronger person now than I was before meeting Lilian." He looked down at his hands. "But still, sometimes I feel like no matter how hard I work, it will never be enough. I ask myself things like 'How can I be strong enough to protect Lilian against yōkai when I can barely defend myself?' Or 'How can I become strong enough to defeat yōkai when I'm just human?' I try not to think that way, but sometimes I can't help it."

Kotohime nodded at him, her manner understanding. "That is natural. As a human, your mind is probably overwhelmed by everything you have seen. You've accepted that we are yōkai, that we have powers that you cannot comprehend, at least consciously. However, choosing to accept something and truly accepting something is not always the same thing. It will probably be many years before you truly accept the differences between humans and yōkai."

212

Kevin nodded noncommittally. He knew that she was probably right.

"Still," Kotohime continued musing, "you have done an admirable job thus far, and I expect that, given time, you will succeed where many other humans have failed." She ruffled his hair. "After all, you have become quite the capable young man. You actually remind me a bit of my last mate."

Kevin studied Kotohime out of his peripheral vision. She never really talked about her past, though he knew some of it. He remembered their conversation back at the hotel in California, where she'd told him about how she and her sister had been members of the Ślina Clan.

"Would you mind telling me about your mate?" he asked. Kotohime looked at him. He could see her pondering the question.

"I do not see the harm," she said slowly. Her eyes turned toward the sky, glazing over with past remembrance. "I remember... I met him shortly after the Ślina Clan was destroyed. My sister and I were on the run. We were being chased by members of the Mul clan. Luna Mul was actually the one in charge of chasing us down. She had only been a four-tails at the time."

Kevin had not thought of Luna Mul very much. He tried not to think about her. As the first person he had ever killed, thinking about her made his stomach churn. Even though he did not regret killing her, he despised how that act had destroyed whatever was left of his innocence.

"I had been injured back then," Kotohime continued. "My sister had only been a two-tails and was not skilled enough to heal me. I had lost a lot of blood. I remember slipping in and out of consciousness. To be honest, I still do not remember much of what happened to this day. What I do know is that we somehow managed to evade our pursuers, but I collapsed from exhaustion and injury. It was during that time that Corban found us."

Kotohime's lips curved with a gentleness that he rarely saw. Her smile was breathtaking.

"He had nursed me back to health and treated my injuries. He didn't care that I was a kitsune. All he saw was a person who needed help. I knew right then that he was going to be my mate."

It always astounded Kevin to hear about how kitsune fell in love. They weren't like humans, who generally needed time to learn more about a person before they fell in love. With kitsune it was a near instantaneous thing. It was instinct, just as Lilian had told him several days before they started dating.

"You should know that Lilian-sama gets her taste in men from me." Kotohime sent him a sly grin.

"I've noticed." Kevin's voice was just a touch dry.

"Now then, Kevin-sama really should be getting to bed. I am sure that Lilian-sama is missing his warmth."

"Right." Kevin yawned. "Good night, Kotohime."

"Good night, Kevin-sama."

Chapter 7

Meeting the Clan

Kotohime stood in the courtyard, left hand on the hilt of her katana, right hand resting at her side, posture relaxed. Standing several feet away, Kevin and Lilian eyed her like prey who'd been cornered by a predator. That made her smile.

One second passed. Kevin and Lilian shuffled their feet. Two seconds. They exploded into action.

Kevin rushed forward at an impressive speed—for a human. He reached into his holsters and pulled out his guns, which were currently using magazine clips that Kotohime had charged herself. He fired off several shots. Bright blue spheres of compressed water youki sped toward her. Kotohime used her sheathed katana to block each one, all except the last, which she had to dodge because she'd misaimed her katana.

No, that wasn't misaimed. Kotohime narrowed her eyes as Kevin closed the distance and attempted to pistol whip her. She blocked it with her katana. *I sense foreign youki. I see. Lilian used an illusion to bend the light and trick me into thinking the bullet was off by just a few centimeters. Clever.*

After his attempt at beaming her across the face with his pistol failed, Kevin paused as though he didn't know what to do. Kotohime kicked him in the chest.

"Celestial Art: Orbs of an Evanescent Realm."

As Kevin skidded across the ground, nine orbs appeared around her. Kotohime eyed the spheres of celestial youki and shifted her stance, feet sliding along the ground as she lowered her center of gravity. As the spheres shot forward, she tucked her sword into her wrist, grabbed the hilt, and then moved. Her body spun as she released her katana from its sheath with a near silent *hiss* of steel, swinging it with the full force of her youki-reinforced arms.

"Ikken Hisatsu. Senpū."

Kotohime normally used her whirlwind technique in conjunction with one of her water techniques. However, for what she wanted to use it for now, this would work fine.

She spun a full 360 degrees. Her blade flashed out, appearing as nothing more than a streak of light. It sliced straight through all nine orbs like they were made of paper. The spheres, unable to maintain cohesion, dispersed into millions of light particles that rained down around her.

The sound of a gun going off caused Kotohime to turn. Her katana, back in its sheath, lashed out and smashed apart each bullet as it came. She also made sure to disrupt any foreign youki in her body, just in case Lilian and Kevin tried to trick her with another illusion.

A lull entered the battle. Kevin and Lilian stood still as though they weren't sure how to proceed. Kotohime waited patiently for them to make their next move.

"Kitsune Art: Extension."

"Celestial Art: Flare."

Two red tails with white tips shot at her. The tips were alight with two small, yet incredibly bright orbs of golden energy.

She knew of this technique; it was one of several that Lilian had created during their spars. It was a very basic technique. All Lilian did was create a sphere or two with her youki and compress it to the point where it was ready to burst. Despite its simplicity, it was a rather ingenious use of her limited powers.

The intensity of the technique depended on the amount of youki Lilian packed into it. Kotohime knew from watching the redhead experiment that this technique could be powerful enough to leave perfectly rounded craters in the ground or weak enough to merely blind her foes by burning their retina with intense light. Judging by the amount of youki Kotohime sensed, Lilian intended to blind her, probably in order to give Kevin an opening.

She wouldn't let that happen.

"Kitsune Art: Transient Counterforce."

Transient Counterforce was one of her personal techniques. She had created it many years ago when she'd only been a three-tails. It had been her desire to create a technique that could negate other techniques.

Its application was simple. All youki had a flow, and if she could find the flow, she could disrupt it with her own youki, thereby destroying the technique before it could hit her. **Transient Counterforce** was simply applying her youki through her tails and attacking the youki fueling her enemy's technique where that flow was weakest. The stronger the technique, the easier it was to break.

A barrier appeared before Kotohime. The two red tails struck the barrier. Lilian's **Flare** dispersed before it could hit her. Kotohime then took two steps forward. She attacked with her sheathed katana before Lilian could react.

"OWCH!"

Lilian yelped as Kotohime smacked the fox-girl's tails. A kitsune's tails were sensitive, both to pleasure and to pain. When she attacked the girl's tails, the extension technique was disrupted and Lilian's concentration was shattered.

"Lilian!"

Kotohime turned on Kevin as Lilian's pained cry distracted him. She had to give him credit. Despite being distracted, he managed to avoid her initial blow, redirecting her sword swing with the black gun in his left hand. This did not deter her, though, and she quickly spun around and attacked the opening in his right flank. She blinked when he redirected her again.

How did he do that?

Frowning to herself, Kotohime upped her speed, attacking Kevin with greater and greater ferocity. Her frown grew when he avoided all her attacks, deflecting them with one of the two guns in his hands. A thrust aimed at the opening in his chest was smacked away by the silver gun. An overhand slash aimed at the hole near his left shoulder was dodged when Kevin sidestepped it, then hit her sheathed katana with the tip of the black gun. Over and over again Kotohime aimed at the openings in his stance, and over and over her attacks were deflected.

Lilian's body stiffened

This is...!

Growing curious to see how far she could push Kevin, Kotohime reinforced her body with youki. Her speed increased, as did her strength. Her physical abilities soon exceeded those of human limitations, and they continued to climb higher and higher. There should have been no way that Kevin could keep up with her.

Yet keep up with her he did.

His breathing had grown ragged by now. Sweat dripped from his brow and caked his clothes to his skin. He was beginning to give out...

... and yet he was still keeping up with her.

I see... this style... ufufufu, how interesting...

Kotohime slashed diagonally and upward at Kevin's right hip. It was blocked, redirected over Kevin's head, and avoided. Undeterred by her failed attack, she followed through with a thrust toward the opening under his left armpit. It, too, was avoided when Kevin twisted away from her.

She upped the ante, using her speed, which exceeded human capabilities, to get behind him and attack his spine, the only hole currently in his guard. Kevin still avoided it. He spun around almost before she began to move, almost as if he knew what she would do before she did it. Using the gun in his left hand, he smacked her sheathed katana away.

"Celestial Art: Underground Chambers Prison."

"What?"

Kotohime looked down in surprise when something wrapped around her ankles. Chains. Chains made of celestial youki. They wound around her ankles and calves, coiling like a snake strangling a mouse.

"Gotcha!"

She looked up to see a black gun pointed directly at her face. Her body moved without conscious thought. The gun fired a round of blue energy that soared over her head—

"GYA!"

—and struck Lilian, if that scream was any indication.

"Oh, crap! Lilian!"

Before Kevin had time to rush to his mate's side, Kotohime thrust her blade forward, finally connecting. The tip of her sheathed katana struck Kevin square in the jaw, launching him into the air and sending him crashing to the ground mere seconds later.

"Kevin!"

A Fox's Revenge

The chains around her calves dispersed. Lilian rushed toward her mate, who sat up, looking dazed and confused, as if he'd just been punched in the face several times by *Mike Tyson*. Considering she struck him in the jaw with her sheath while using reinforcement, he probably had a broken jaw. Whoops.

"Are you okay?" Lilian knelt by Kevin's side. He tried to open his mouth and speak, but only gibberish came out. He definitely had a broken jaw. "Hold on. Don't try to speak yet. **Celestial Art: Divine Tongue.**"

As Lilian began licking the spot where she'd struck Kevin, Kotohime raised her hand to hide her mouth behind the sleeve of her kimono. It was not to hide her snort. She was a yamato nadeshiko. She did not snort.

Only Lilian-sama would create a healing technique that requires her to lick her mate.

"You taste salty," Lilian murmured in between licks. She shifted position, straddling Kevin's legs to better lick the spot that Kotohime had hit. Kevin said nothing, merely groaning in mixed pleasure and pain. One of his hands had grabbed a handful of Lilian's rear.

"If you two are quite finished," Kotohime said in a loud voice, which she made sure contained the proper combination of amusement and exasperation. "I would like to give you my assessment on your abilities and teamwork."

Kevin and Lilian were quick to stand up after that. While Lilian tossed her a small, displeased glare, Kevin's cheeks were stained a very mild red. Kotohime shook her head and withheld a giggle.

"Now then, I can say with honest certainty that you two work quite well together." She smiled when Lilian and Kevin broke out into matching grins. "I suppose I should not be surprised by this. Despite having only fought together twice, you both know each other well, and you clearly understand how the other thinks."

Kotohime paused, collecting her thoughts.

"That being said, there is still much room for improvement. While you have good teamwork, it takes too much time for you to implement your plans. All of your attacks are simple and straightforward, which makes them easy to see through. I also have yet to see you string together any combinations. This is common among people who are relatively new to battle. You unleash one attack and expect it to hit, and when it doesn't hit, you're thrown off your game and become susceptible to counters. You will need to work on correcting this."

Kevin and Lilian looked at each other. Kotohime wondered what silent conversation they were having, though she could take a few guesses. She coughed into her hand, bringing their attention back to her.

"That being said, your last attack was truly inspiring. You, Kevin-sama, kept my full attention with that unusual style of yours. Meanwhile, Lilian-sama used **Chameleon Masquerade** to sneak behind me and bind me with **Underground Chambers Prison**, which gave Kevin-sama the opportunity to fire at me when I couldn't counter. Had I been a three-tailed kitsune, or even a four-tailed kitsune with little combat experience, that attack might have worked."

Kevin's and Lilian's faces brightened. Kotohime decided to crush their happiness right then and there.

"Of course, because Lilian-sama deemed it necessary to sneak up behind me, she ended up getting hit with Kevin-sama's bullet when I dodged. That shows a complete lack of awareness on both your parts. You're lucky that we were using my youki, otherwise Lilian-sama could have been killed."

Kevin paled while Lilian flushed.

"I had to get behind you," the redhead muttered. "**Underground Chambers Prison** only works at a certain distance, and since you and Kevin were moving so much, getting behind you was the most sure-fire way to make sure my technique worked."

"In that case, you need to work on your technique," Kotohime informed her. "It's clearly incomplete if it requires you to be a certain distance from your opponent."

Lilian crossed her arms under her chest and pouted. "I'll have you know that I'm rather proud of that technique."

"Proud or not, it doesn't change the fact that it needs more work."

"... Mugyu."

"Don't use other people's catchphrases, please." Kevin sighed.

Just then, the door to their abode slammed open. Kevin and Lilian spun around in surprise. Kotohime blinked when Daphne stormed into the courtyard.

She was scowling.

"So this is where you've been. Didn't I tell you the other day that you were to head over to my abode first thing in the morning? Come here now. It's time for your lesson."

"Ara, ara." Kotohime hid her smile as a horrified look crossed

Lilian's face.

"Oh, no." The girl shook her head. "I'm not attending any more of your lessons. Never again."

Daphne stalked forward as Lilian hid behind Kevin. "I have no particular desire to teach an ungrateful girl like you either. However, our matriarch has commanded me to restart your lessons."

"No way. I'm not going."

"You don't have a choice in the matter!"

Lilian shrieked when Daphne's seven tails suddenly extended, swerving around Kevin and wrapping around the redhead like a person being rolled up in a futon because the one putting it away didn't realize there was someone still sleeping in it. The two-tailed vixen struggled and squirmed to no avail. All seven of Daphne's tails had engulfed her and only her head remained visible. She wouldn't be getting out of that unless Daphne let her.

"Beloved, help! This evil woman is going to torture me!" Lilian cried out as Daphne began walking away.

"Oh, be quiet," Daphne snapped. "Believe me, the last thing I want to do is waste my precious time teaching a girl who refuses to further advance our clan. Now do me a favor and keep that mouth of yours shut."

Lilian started yelling out a surprising amount of expletives, but she soon found her ability of speech hampered when a ghostly white ball gag randomly appeared and was shoved into her mouth. Even then, the girl continued shrieking through the gag until she and Daphne left, the door slamming shut behind them.

An odd stillness settled upon the courtyard.

"Well," Kevin tried to shake off the awkwardness of watching his mate getting ball gagged by her own aunt, "I think I'm going to take a bath."

"A splendid idea, Kevin-sama." Kotohime nodded. "Do you have any plans after that?"

"I'm sure I'll figure something out," he told her, waving goodbye as he headed for the bathhouse.

***

Jasmine had always been an early riser, which was good because she had plans that day, and the sooner she got started on those plans, the better.

221

As the sun streamed in through the window, she opened her eyes… to find another pair of eyes barely a fraction of a centimeter from her own.

"Yo," Violet greeted.

"GYA!"

Shocked beyond belief by the sudden appearance of her immediate older sister's face, Jasmine did something she would lament later on; she tried to sit up.

The sound of two heads smacking together was followed by two voices crying out in shock and pain. While Violet's head snapped backward, Newtonian physics determined that Jasmine's head would slam against the bed. Wincing as she rubbed the new bump on her forehead, Jasmine glared at the woman straddling her.

"What are you doing here?" she snapped.

Violet smirked. "I was just making sure I got to be the first person to greet my lovely little sister."

Jasmine glared at her for a moment longer, then turned her head to glare at her shadow. "Why did you let her do that?"

Ayane sat on the floor two meters away in a seiza. She was sharpening a kunai. A bright red sports bag sat by her side.

"Violet did not have any killing intent, so I didn't see any threat in her actions."

"That's right, there's no threat here." Violet pointed at her chest with a thumb.

"Alexi didn't see any threat either."

An awkward silence hung in the air. Jasmine eventually shook it off. She glared at Violet.

"Out."

"Aw, come on!" Violet pouted at her. "Don't you want me to help you get dressed?"

Jasmine's glare gained several levels of animosity. "Out! Now!"

"Okay, okay. Yeesh, what an unlikable girl you are." Violet sighed as she climbed off her sister. She threw her hands behind her head and grinned. "Whelp! I'm off to go train. Smell you guys later!"

Jasmine stared at the door as it closed behind her older sister. She then turned her expressionless gaze to her shadow.

"Aren't you supposed to stop people from creeping up on me like that?"

Ayane never stopped cleaning her kunai. "Correction: I am

222

supposed to protect you from those who would threaten your life or endanger your well-being in some way, shape, or form. Violet-sama's actions, though mischievous, had no malevolent intentions behind them."

Jasmine stared at her shadow for several more seconds. When it became readily apparent that Ayane would not be saying anything else, she climbed out of bed and decided to get dressed. She had important research to do today.

***

Kevin wandered the grounds of the Pnévma Clan's ancestral home. He didn't really know what else to do. Lilian was taking lessons of some kind from Daphne. Kirihime and Camellia were looking after Iris, and Kotohime was...

"Is there a reason you're following me?"

"Ufufufu, surely you jest, Kevin-sama. With Lilian-sama taking lessons from Daphne-sama, I have decided that I can best serve my charge by protecting her mate. I thought that would be obvious."

... Following exactly five steps behind him and slightly to his left. Kevin had learned that this pacing was how bodyguards walked during the Shogun era of Japan. It was so that if the bodyguard needed to fight, they could draw their katana without bisecting the one they were guarding.

"Right. I suppose that makes sense." Kevin had kind of been hoping for some time alone, but he didn't exactly mind the maid-slash-bodyguard's companionship. She was unobtrusive enough and only spoke when spoken to, just like a bodyguard, he guessed.

The gardens on the Pnévma grounds lay sprawled out before him. Kevin had learned after wandering for a bit that the Pnévma Clan's ancestral home was a lot bigger than his initial assumptions. According to Kotohime, the entire grounds had a one-kilometer radius, which explained why all the buildings were spaced so far apart. It took nearly fifteen minutes just to walk from his dwelling to the one that the matriarch resided in.

"Ne, Kotohime?"

"Yes, Kevin-sama?"

"Do you know anything about the flora in this garden?"

"Not really." Kotohime surveyed the garden with her keen, hawk-like eyes. "While I have taken great pains to learn flower arrangements, I have never studied gardening in depth. I only know a few of the flowers located in this garden. The rest are unfamiliar to me."

Kevin nodded as he looked around. He knew a lot about animals, but nothing about plants—unless that plant happened to be something that an animal inhabited. He recognized a few of the trees. Towering cypress trees provided several spots of shade amongst grassy knolls surrounded by flowers. The leaves of olive trees swayed in the unusually eerie breeze. He even saw a sakura tree sitting on a small island in the middle of a pond connected to the garden via a bridge.

He shook his head at the oddity of a sakura tree in a Greek garden.

"Kevin-sama." Kotohime's tone contained a hint of mirth—and warning, but mostly mirth.

"We're being followed, aren't we?" he said.

"Indeed. It seems the youngest of Pnéyma-denka's daughters, Jasmine-sama, is following us."

Kevin didn't know who Jasmine was by anything other than name. He continued walking while scanning the area. It didn't take long to spot the head of silvery hair peering at him from behind a bush. When the girl realized that she had been spotted, she quickly ducked down, as if that would somehow make him not know she was there.

He released a weary sigh.

"You can come out now." He turned toward the bush, which rustled several times. "I know you're there, so just come on out." Still no answer. "I'm not gonna bite, you know?"

"Be careful not to disappoint her, Kevin-sama." Kotohime hid her smile behind the sleeve of her kimono. Kevin felt like there was some hidden meaning to her words.

"Hush, you."

Kevin waited to see if Jasmine would come out. When, after several seconds of silence had passed, nothing happened, he grew annoyed.

"Look, you can either come out right now, or I can drag you out!"

"Oh, my. Such a dominating personality, Kevin-sama. Ufufufu."

Kevin ignored the maid-slash-bodyguard in favor of the girl who stepped out from behind the bushes. Long silver hair framed a face that Kevin felt could only be called cute. Her pale skin contrasted well with her Apollonian carmine eyes. He could see the resemblance between her and the matriarch, even though this girl was really short and flat as board.

"So, you're Jasmine, huh? Lilian's younger aunt?"

"That is correct. I am Lilian's younger aunt and the youngest of Mother's children."

Even her voice is emotionless. Creepy.

Kevin smiled at the girl. "It's nice to meet you."

"A pleasure."

As the girl continued staring at him, Kevin became really uncomfortable. There was just something about her gaze that threw him off. It must have been how impassive her expression was.

"So…" he scratched the back of his neck, "was there something you wanted from me?"

"You are the first human that I have ever met. I would like to ask you a few questions, if you would permit it."

Having spent so much time with Lilian, Kevin could understand Jasmine's curiosity. From what Kotohime had told him, most of the main family of the Pnévma Clan, that is to say, all of the matriarch's daughters, weren't allowed to interact with humans. They were trained to handle the Pnévma Clan's day-to-day operations, but they only dealt with other yōkai, if they were even allowed out of the grounds. The girl's curiosity was understandable.

"I guess I could answer a few questions," Kevin said. Jasmine's facial expression didn't change much, but she seemed pleased, or at least, he thought she was pleased. It was really hard to tell.

"Thank you," she said… and then she randomly pulled out a clipboard from her Extra Dimensional Storage Space, along with a pen. Kevin found it disturbing to see a girl who looked so young reach into her shirt. "First question: when was the first time you masturbated?"

"W-what the heck?!" Kevin tried not to blush. He failed. "What kind of question is that?!"

"It's a very important question. Now please answer."

"Screw that," Kevin spat. "There's no way I'm going to answer such a personal question. I don't even know you!"

"Ufufufu, so cute, Kevin-sama."

"You be quiet!"

Jasmine frowned at him. Her two tails writhed in agitated fury. It was the only sign of her displeasure.

"You will answer my question," she intoned solemnly, and the next moment, Kevin felt something enter his mind. It was gentle and soothing, like a loving whisper. It told him to answer all of Jasmine's questions, that he wanted to answer her questions.

Kevin put some extra vitriol into his glare.

"I suggest you stop that right now." Jasmine blinked. The feeling disappeared. "You tried to use an enchantment on me just now, didn't you?" Another blink. Kevin nodded. "I guess I should tell you this before you decide to do something like that again, but enchantments don't work on me, so I would strongly suggest that you not try placing me under one."

That was only partially true. Kevin was highly resistant to enchantments. Ever since he started training to become stronger, he'd had Iris and Lilian cast enchantments on him in order to up his resistance, working his resilience toward being enchanted as he might work out a muscle.

On a side note, some of the crap that Iris had made him do when her enchantments did work was downright embarrassing. He still felt his face heat up when he remembered how she'd made him run around the South Pavilion Mall completely naked. He was very grateful toward Kotohime for erasing the memory of everyone who saw him.

While it had taken a lot of work and put him in a lot of embarrassing situations, Kevin could now say that he was quite resistant to yōkai trying to enchant him. According to Kotohime, it would take an enchantress—a kitsune who specialized in enchantments—with at least four tails of power to enchant him.

Jasmine blinked some more. Kevin had the distinct impression that she was shocked.

"Do you have any more questions? Preferably ones that don't have me talking about my private life?"

"… I do have a few."

"All right then." Kevin breathed. "Ask away."

"What is your favorite sauce…?"

Kevin smiled. That was a weird question to ask, but one that he was actually willing to answer.

"… And which part of the body would you prefer to lick it off of?"

An awkward silence followed. Kevin must have heard wrong. He heard her that wrong, right? Yes, this was all in his imagination. It had to be. It... just... had to... be...

He stared at the young girl before him, whose inexpressive face was reminiscent of a statue, his own expression slowly deadpanning.

"I'm leaving now," Kevin declared, turning around and walking off, leaving the young girl to stare at his back.

A Fox's Revenge

***

I want my mate.

Lilian barely managed to withhold her sigh. She sat on a fluffy pillow while Daphne paced in front of her, the woman's droning voice scratching her ears as she lectured her about the history of human weaponry.

"The hand cannon is considered by many to be the first projectile weapon ever created by humans. It was invented in the late thirteenth century, and was a very simple, if effective, weapon," Daphne was saying, but all Lilian heard was, *"Blah, blah, musket, blah."* Who the heck cared when humans first invented weapons? That didn't apply to her.

If Daphne wants to really teach me about humans, she should talk about when manga was first invented. At least that would be interesting.

Lilian gazed around the room. It was a very plain room, boring and dull, with drab colors and no decorations to speak of. Hmph. This room was exactly the kind of room she would have expected from someone like Daphne. What a boring old hag.

"Are you listening to me?" Daphne snapped. Lilian gave her least favorite aunt a bored glare.

"No," she said bluntly. "I'm not listening to you. I don't care about when humans invented guns. How is that going to help me? What does that even have to do with helping your oh-so-glorious Pnévma Clan?"

"You are mated to a human," Daphne tried to explain patiently. Tried. And failed. Lilian saw the clear signs of irritation, the dark red veins throbbing on her aunt's forehead. "For some reason, our matriarch has decided to allow this foible of yours, and let you continue being with that *boy.*"

Lilian nearly hissed at the way Daphne said "boy," as if she were swallowing poison. "That boy has a name. It's Kevin. You should use it."

"I do not care about his name. He is a human, and humans are beneath us. Just what you see in a human child, I will never understand."

"I wouldn't expect an old hag like you to understand anyway."

"What was that?" Daphne shrieked.

Lilian leapt to her feet. "You heard me. Or has your hearing gone as well, you ugly old prune?"

"An ugly old prune, am I?! That does it!"

Lilian was unprepared for when Daphne grabbed her cheeks and

227

began pulling on them, hard. Her cheeks stretched obscenely as if they were made of rubber.

"Ow, ow, ow! Wet go of ma face, you ol' hag!"

"Not until you apologize for your rude behavior and remarks!"

"Wike hell I'm apowogizing!"

"Then I'm not going to stop!"

Lilian struggled to get out of Daphne's grip, but she found the effort futile. She soon realized that her oldest aunt was using reinforcement on her. Unfortunately, that meant Daphne's strength far exceeded her own. Even if she used reinforcement herself, it wouldn't matter. When it came to reinforcement, it was all a matter of power, not application, and seven tails worth of power trumped two.

Desperate times called for desperate measures!

Lilian reached into her Extra Dimensional Storage Space and quickly pulled out the object she wanted. She then shoved the object in her aunt's face, causing it to explode, which elicited a shriek of surprise and pain from Daphne, who let go and staggered back.

"W-what the heck is this?! Why does it sting so much?! And what is that horrid stench?!"

"Ha!" Lilian stood up and pointed at her aunt, who was busy trying to clean out her eyes. "How do you like my pepper bomb? Pretty neat, huh? I made it using a combination of pepper and lysol. Of course, I wanted to give it some extra oomph, so I also added some sulphur to the mix."

"Y-you little brat!" Daphne's banshee-like wail cut through the room. "I'm going to murder you!"

"That's only if you can catch me!" Grinning, Lilian rushed to the window and jumped onto the sill. She turned around to cast a glare at Daphne, who was still futilely trying to find her. Even though she knew the old hag couldn't see her, she still pointed at the woman. "Remember this day as the day that you almost caught Captain Lilian Pnéyma!"

Cackling like a madwoman, Lilian leapt out of the building.

Daphne's angry ranting followed her.

"Now to find my beloved." Lilian grinned as she bolted away.

**

Violet was training. It wasn't like there was anything else to do in this place. The Pnéyma Clan ancestral home was pretty boring, all things considered. Nothing ever changed. She honestly understood why Lilian

228

hated living there.

The morning air was warm, a result of it being summer and the generally warm Mediterranean climate. Her toga had become sweaty and kind of gross, but she didn't care. She continued her training, punching and kicking away at the training dummy that she had created from a log and some really thick rope.

She knew that her style of combat differed from the rest of her family—which was sort of an oxymoron when she thought about it, as no one in her family actually enjoyed fighting.

Unlike most kitsune who believed finesse and elegance to be the fundamental and most important facets of combat, she believed in power. She put her whole weight into every punch she threw. Each strike rang with a clear, resounding *smack!* as she beat on the training dummy. It rattled and shook under her fists. Such a satisfying feeling.

"Whoo! You go girl! Kick that log's ass!"

Violet sighed at the familiar voice. She turned around.

"Hello to you, too, Aster—tch!" She looked away. "Do you two really have to walk around like that? It's unsightly."

Aster and Azalea looked at each other's nude bodies, grinned, and then turned back to Violet.

"Nope."

"Nothing unsightly here."

"Not the least bit unsightly."

"We're about as unsightly as you are tall."

Violet gritted her teeth at the comment on her height. She knew that she was short, dammit, but they didn't have to rub it in!

"I don't have time to deal with you two." Violet turned back to her training log. "And you two might not think there's anything unsightly, but we've got a guest staying with us, and it's a man, so you may want to put some clothes on."

"A man?" The twins blinked as one, for they were one. "A man is staying with us?"

"That's what I said."

The sisters turned to each other.

"What do you think, my love? Should we put some clothes on in order to appear presentable to a man?"

"Hmm… I don't know. I mean, it's not like this guest is the only man around. Granted, the rest are Mom's brats so they are family, sorta, but I don't really care about a man."

"On the other hand, do we want him to see us like this?"

"Good point."

Violet listened to her sisters's constant chattering. The more they spoke, the more annoyed she became. Her annoyance soon reached its peak, and she whirled back around to toss them her most vicious snarl.

"Can you two take that somewhere else?! I'm trying to train here!"

"You call hitting that log training?" one of them asked. Violet couldn't tell which, as they both looked the same.

"Now, now, my beloved sister," the other chided. "You know that she's a failure as a kitsune. This is probably the only type of training she can do."

"I don't want to hear that from a pair of useless lesbos like you!"

Before the lesbian twins could retort, a loud explosion caused the earth to rumble. Violet grimaced as she turned to a dwelling a few hundred meters away. Smoke puffed out from the windows, black and acrid. Violet could see several anguished faces within the smoke, the remnants of souls as they dispersed into the wind.

"Looks like the idiot scientist and her daughter are at it again," one of the twins said.

"I wonder what she was trying to do this time?" the other pondered.

Violet shook her head, deciding that, whatever her older sister was up to, it was clearly nothing good. It also didn't involve her, which was all the more reason to ignore the constant smoke pouring from the house. This happened on a regular basis anyway.

She turned to get back to training, but paused when she saw a figure running across the garden toward her older sister's dwelling.

"Hey, sis, who is that?" asked one of the twins.

"That's the guest," Violet told them, sighing. The brat was heading right into the mouth of danger without even realizing it. Could she just leave him to his fate like that?

Yes. Yes, I can.

"So that's the guest, huh?"

"Which clan is he from?"

"Why is he hiding his tails?"

"What is he even doing here?"

"I can't answer any of your questions when you bombard me like that." Violet glared at them. "One question at the time." The twins became silent. "First, he's not from a clan. Second, he's a human, so he doesn't have tails. Third, he's here because he's Lilian's mate."

The twins blinked. "Not from a clan?"

"There's a human in the Pnévma estate?!"

"Wait a second—when did Lilian get a mate?!"

"I have neither the time nor the inclination to answer your questions." Violet turned back to her log. "If you want to know the answer, why don't you go talk to him yourself? Now leave me alone. I have to get back to my training."

***

Kevin coughed up several lungs worth of smoke as he burst into the modest abode. He stuck his mouth and nose into his shirt, but that didn't seem to help much. His eyes also stung something fierce as the acrid stuff aggravated them.

Maybe this wasn't such a good idea. Oh, well. Too late to turn back now.

He stumbled through the house. He was in a hall—or he thought he was in a hall. He couldn't tell because of the smoke.

Using the wall to keep himself from walking into anything, Kevin slowly, carefully, moved through the house. Soft carpet crunched under his feet. It felt like there were several dozen twigs or something creating a layer over the carpet. Paint chips, maybe? He ignored that in favor of continuing to walk forward—at least, until he nearly fell down a flight of stairs.

Because he still couldn't see anything, Kevin needed to walk down the stairs slowly. It was actually worse going down. The smoke seemed much thicker, and he realized that it was coming from down below. He had to close his eyes lest the smoke burn them.

He eventually made it to the bottom after a few missteps. The air was much clearer down here than it was at the top of the stairs. He wondered about the oddity of that, but decided not to contemplate such a thing in favor of continuing.

"Well, shoot. It looks like that didn't work either," a voice said. "I wonder if the reason we failed to produce a **Spirit Guardian** is due to a miscalculation between the amount of mountain and spirit youki we used."

"That could be it," another voice, similar to the first but much younger, said. "But I could have sworn my calculations were on the dot this time. I used the exact same method that you showed me, Mother."

"You must have extracted the mountain youki from Violet

231

incorrectly, then. That's the only explanation I can think of for why you weren't able to create a **Spirit Guardian**." The voice sighed. "Oh, well. We can just extract more youki later, though we need to be careful. I don't want Mother finding out about what we're doing."

"Neither do I." Kevin sensed the shudder in the younger voice.

He finally rounded the corner and found himself standing at the edge of a circular room. It looked like a giant cylinder. The stone floor was covered in what he mistook for soot at first, along with several large blocks of what appeared to be stone. In the center of the room were two females.

The taller of the two looked like the other one's older sister. They both had silvery hair, though the shorter girl's hair was cut to her shoulders, while the older woman had long hair tied into a messy ponytail. They also both wore glasses, which he found odd because he didn't think any kitsune needed glasses. He also couldn't see their eyes because of the light reflecting ominously off of those same glasses. He also noticed that both of these women were quite beautiful—even if they were covered in that strange soot that wasn't soot.

Just then, the taller one's foxy ears twitched. Her six tails became livelier. Then, as if sensing his presence, she turned her head in his direction.

"Oh, crap!"

Kevin knew he was screwed only seconds after he said that.

***

Lilian searched for her mate. She hadn't had much luck so far, though she'd managed to find Kotohime. According to her maid-slash-bodyguard, Kevin had rushed off somewhere, though the kimono-clad femme didn't know where. The woman had apparently lost him when he scrambled through a copse of trees.

"He is surprisingly agile," she had said in her defense.

"Ha... I finally manage to escape from that old hag so I can spend some time with my mate, but he isn't even around when I want to see him," Lilian complained to no one in particular. She just felt like announcing her complaints out loud. "Shut up."

...

"He couldn't have gotten too far," Kotohime placated her. "He took off in this general direction, and I am sure we would have seen him by now if he changed directions. And if we don't find him, you could always wait in the house. I am sure that Iris-sama would appreciate it if you visited her."

Lilian wondered if Kotohime was trying to make her feel bad. After they'd arrived here, she'd gone out of her way to avoid visiting Iris. She didn't like seeing her sister in such a sorry state. It tore at her heart. If she visited Iris now, she was afraid that her mood would drop, and she'd become depressed again.

I need to stay strong. I don't want to visit Iris and start crying. The next time I see her should be a happy occasion. I want to see her smiling.

"But I wanna spend some time with my mate." Lilian pouted at her maid.

"You spend plenty of time with Kevin-sama." Kotohime's voice reminded Lilian of a desert. "In fact, I would say that you spend more than enough time with him."

"You can never spend too much time with your mate, Kotohime."

"If you say so, Lilian-sama."

"I do say so."

Just then, Lilian sensed something, a disturbance in the force.

"My 'Kevin is about to have his chastity stolen' senses are tingling," Lilian muttered.

Kotohime gave her a sidelong glance. "That is a very specific sense, Lilian-sama."

"I developed in case I needed to protect my mate's chastity from ravenous vixens."

"I'm not sure he has any chastity left after what you and Iris-sama have done to him," Kotohime mused to herself.

"Come on!" Lilian ignored her maid and rushed through the copse of trees in the direction that her *"Someone is about to rape Kevin"* detector told her to go.

***

Kevin really wasn't sure how he'd gotten himself into this situation—oh, wait. That was a blatant lie. He knew exactly how he'd gotten into this situation. Damn him and his stupid superhero complex!

He was strapped to a bed, not an examination table like he'd expected to see in a normal lab, but an honest-to-gods bed. And it wasn't just any bed. Oh, no. It was one of those love beds. The glimmering soft fabric of the comforter was a passionate crimson, and his head rested against several heart-shaped pillows. The bed itself was also shaped like a heart. He had no clue how the kitsune got an honest-to-gods love bed in here—

—Oh. Wait. That was also a blatant lie.

Damn these foxes and their Extra Dimensional Storage Spaces! Who pulls a freaking bed out of their cleavage?!

The cold air hit his bare skin. He was completely naked. There was nothing covering his modesty. He wasn't sure if the air was causing his goosebumps, or if it was because of the leering looks of the fox-girl and fox-woman.

"This is perfect," the fox-woman purred, pushing her glasses up the bridge of her nose with her middle and index finger. The light gleamed off her lenses, blocking her eyes from view and making Kevin shudder. "I have always wanted to study a human."

"Woah, woah, woah! Hold on!" Kevin tried to reason with them. "I don't know what you're planning on doing to me, but whatever it is, I want no part in it!"

A reasonable argument indeed.

"Ho… do not worry, young man. I guarantee this won't hurt a bit. You'll probably even enjoy it," the woman reassured him.

Kevin was not reassured at all. Not one bit.

"Ivy?"

"Yes, Mother."

"H-hey, why are you getting on the bed?! And wait, did you just call this woman 'Mother'?! She's your mother?!"

"Indeed, I am Ivy's mother." The glasses flashed again. Kevin wondered how such an innocuous action could look so sinister. "Does that surprise you?"

"Kinda." Kevin squirmed when the younger female straddled his stomach. "I thought you were her older sister."

"Hn. What a flatterer, you are. Too bad for you I'm not interested in having sexual intercourse at the moment. Otherwise, I would be the one on top of you now."

Kevin tried not to blush. He failed epically. His entire body felt like a furnace.

"I-intercourse?!" he squeaked.

"Indeed, intercourse is when—"

"I know what intercourse is!" Kevin shouted mere seconds before Ivy disrobed, revealing her milky skin and admirable breasts. If he had

to compare them to a fruit, he would've said they were about the size of large grapefruits. "Don't take your clothes off!"

Ivy paused to tilt her head. She looked genuinely confused.

"But I have to take my clothes off. We can't engage in sexual intercourse if I don't," she said as if she were speaking to a child.

"Did you ever think that maybe I don't want to have sex with you?" Kevin spat, the skin on his face threatening to melt from the heat he was releasing. "Now put your clothes back on!"

"Mother." Ivy turned to look at her mom. "He does not seem to wish to have intercourse with me. What should I do?"

"How about getting off me for starters," Kevin quipped.

"Hmm, this is most unusual," Ivy's mother said. "I have never heard of a man who is unwilling to engage a female in intercourse." The glasses were pushed up again. They flashed. Again. "However, for the sake of science, we must press on, even if the partner is unwilling."

Ivy followed in her mother's footsteps, pushing her glasses up the bridge of her nose. Unlike her mother, she grabbed her glasses from the side to adjust them. They still flashed just as ominously, however, letting Kevin know that he was screwed.

"Right. For science."

Ivy resumed her activities, and as she slid her white cotton panties down her legs, Kevin discovered that her hair was naturally silver. He might have felt curious, were he not two seconds away from being raped.

Oh, Lord! This is it! Today's the day I become a man! His mind wailed uselessly. *But I don't want to become a man! Not to these people! God! Odin! Zeus! Allah! Kami! If you're going to make me a man today, then could you at least make my partner Lilian?!*

He was beginning to seriously regret his no-sex policy.

Ivy placed her hands on his chest and raised her hips. Kevin tried to get out from underneath her, but those straps were tied on way too tightly. He could barely move, much less get out from underneath someone.

I need a miracle.

Kevin prayed with all his might for someone to help him out of this predicament.

Fortunately, it seemed as if the gods had heard his prayer.

"Water Art: The Moon Goddess's Surging Waterfall."

Just before Ivy could actually go through with the deed, what appeared to be several thousand gallons of water smashed into her. The woman was blasted off him with the force of a cannon. She went soaring away and crashed into a wall, which crumbled around her the moment she struck it.

"W-what the—" The fox-woman seemed shocked. "That technique is—"

"Celestial Art: Celestial Cannon."

A beam of pure light lanced out from the entrance and struck the woman full on. She, too, went soaring backwards, crashing into a wall that cracked and dented under the force of her body slamming into it. She then slid down the wall and fell onto her butt, completely unconscious.

"Beloved!

Kevin felt a surge of joy. Not only was he saved, but he'd been saved by the only two people he could trust in this mad house. He turned his head to see Lilian rushing up to him, her smile joyous. She came up to the bed...

... and then she stopped.

Her eyes widened. She looked at him up and down, from head to toe, and then stopped at about his middle. It took him a second, but Kevin eventually realized what had caught her attention.

"Uh, Lilian?" Kevin became worried when he saw her staring at his uncovered instrument of DOOM. She wasn't saying anything. She was just staring. "Um, Lily?"

Several seconds later, Kevin became covered in blood as Lilian was launched backwards by her own nosebleed. She flew across the room, out into the hall, and crashed into the wall, where she proceeded to slowly slide down. She didn't get back up.

Kevin slowly turned his head toward Kotohime. The left sleeve of her kimono was already raised and her eyes held a mischievous twinkle that he knew all too well. She was definitely smiling behind that kimono.

"Not. A. Word," he muttered bitterly, trying, and failing, to not blush.

***

After finding his clothes, getting dressed, and waking up Lilian from her nosebleed-induced coma, Kevin ran out of the crazy scientist duo's dwelling like a child with the Pedobear chasing after him. He, Lilian, and Kotohime eventually managed to get lost within the clan grounds. He had absolutely no clue where they were.

He lay on the grass, staring up at the canopy overhead. Leaves created strange shapes out of the shadows. Several birds chirped, the sound of their song echoing through the small grove.

Lilian lay next to him, snuggling against his side. He could feel her curves pressing into him, feel her breasts pushing against his chest. He had wrapped a single arm around her, hand idly stroking her shoulder, which she seemed to enjoy.

"I'm sorry to say this, Lilian, but your family is crazy."

"You think so?" Lilian murmured.

"I know so."

"Mm, yeah, I guess you're right. They've always been a little weird."

"Of course, considering how weird you are, I don't suppose that's saying much—owch!" Kevin glared down at her. "You bit me."

"You were being mean." Lilian's mischievous green eyes glinted as she looked at him.

"Hm." Kevin let his head fall back on the ground. "Yeah, I guess I was. Sorry about that."

"It's okay." Lilian kissed the place on his shoulder that she bit. "I still love you."

Kevin felt his lips quirk into a tiny grin. "Good to know."

Silence descended upon them. The quietness of the small copse was broken by the babbling of a brook. Kevin thought he heard a bullfrog, though he might have been mistaken. He didn't think bullfrogs lived in Greece, but there might have been some other species indigenous to this country that sounded like one. It would be interesting to go exploring to find out what wildlife lived here.

"So those two were Holly and her daughter Ivy," he said after a moment. "I remember you telling me about them a while back."

"I remember, that was back when you still liked Lindsay." Lilian cuddled closer and buried her nose in the crook of his neck. "Ivy is one of the only members of our family aside from myself who knows how to cook. I'm not sure where she picked up the skill, since her mother is definitely not the cooking type, but I guess she has a natural talent for it or something."

"You learn something new every day."

Kevin closed his eyes. Lilian's warm body lulled him more surely than any lullaby. He felt the temptation to just let himself drift off into slumber.

"Oro? What's this?" a strange voice asked. Kevin's eyes snapped open. Right in front of him, filling his vision, were two ruby red eyes staring at him.

"Uh." Kevin tried not the scream. "Hi?"

"Hello," the woman replied with good cheer and a kind smile. "My, but this is a surprise. Hm, hm. You're a human, aren't you? I thought we'd stopped letting humans onto the island. How did you get here?"

"Uh, I came here with Lilian."

"Lil—oh!" The eyes widened as they looked down. "It is Lilian!" The eyes went back to him. "I was so surprised to see an unfamiliar face that I completely missed Lilian lying with you. Hm, hm. You two look awfully comfortable. Is there something going on between you?"

"I'm her, uh, her mate."

"Really? Mukyu, really?"

The eyes were practically shoved into his face. She was so close, he could feel her nose touching his. Kevin was beginning to get freaked out.

"Uh, yes?"

"Oh, isn't that lovely?" He breathed a sigh of relief when the eyes backed up. "I had always wondered if Lilian would find herself a mate. It's most reassuring to know that she's finally found someone to love. Maybe now Momma will stop trying to mate her off, and she can come live with us again."

Realizing that he wouldn't be falling asleep any time soon, Kevin sat up—tried to sit up. Lilian was sleeping against him, he realized, and she must have been sleeping deeply indeed to not wake up with all this noise.

After a moment's thought, Kevin slowly scooted back until he was resting against a tree. Then he lifted the still-sleeping Lilian and moved her until she was resting between his legs, her back against his chest, and his head atop of hers. He encircled his arms around her waist. Lilian, as if sensing the new position, snuggled against him.

Now that he wasn't lying down, he finally got a good look at the woman who'd discovered them. She was definitely a member of the Pnévma Clan. He could tell by her silvery hair and red eyes, which seemed to be a trait shared by most members of their family except Camellia, Lilian, and Iris. Her soft skin and the toga she wore made him think of Artemis, the legendary Goddess of the Moon and leader of the Huntresses. She had five silver fox tails.

Even though it was getting pretty redundant by this point, Kevin noticed that she was also quite gorgeous.

"You're one of the matriarch's daughters, right?" he asked while idly playing with one of Lilian's hands.

"Oro, that's right." The woman's smile had a very soothing quality to it. "I'm Marigold. It's very nice to meet you, um…"

"Kevin."

"Kevin," she tested the word, then nodded in approval. "Hm, hm. That's a very good name, mukyu."

Kevin knew that if he were to wipe at his forehead, he would come away with a large glob of sweat. What the heck did "mukyu" mean? What kind of catchphrase was that?

"You have some, uh, very interesting catchphrases." The woman opened her mouth. "And please don't say it's a part of your character concept. Lilian already used that joke in Volume One." He paused, his face scrunching up. "Volume One?

Marigold's childish huff reminded him of Camellia. "Fine."

"Thank you."

Marigold regarded him for several seconds. He didn't know what she was looking for, but she nodded after a moment, and then popped a squat barely a foot from where he sat. It was at this moment, just as Marigold sat down, that Lilian chose to wake up.

She let out a loud yawn, her hands stretching above her head. She almost hit Kevin in the face. Fortunately, he had some quick reflexes and knew her habits. Thus he avoided having her palm in his jaw.

"Lilian, good to see you're awake."

"Morning, Beloved. I—ah! Marigold!"

"Oro. Hello, Lilian," Marigold said with a cheerful smile.

"When did you get here?"

"I've been here for a few minutes now. You were just asleep."

Lilian looked up at Kevin. "Why didn't you wake me?"

"Because you look adorable when you sleep, and I didn't have the heart to wake you."

"Muu, I suppose that's a good enough reason, but you owe me some kisses later."

"Okay," Kevin agreed. There were worse things that he could think of doing than kissing his girlfriend.

"Oro!" Marigold clapped her hands together. "You two get along so well."

"Of course." Lilian puffed her chest out like a peacock strutting their stuff. "Kevin is my mate. It's only natural that he and I would get along together."

"So lovely." Marigold crossed her legs, placed her elbows on her knees, and rested her cheeks on her hands. "Would you mind telling me how you two got together? I would love to hear a good romance story, mukyu."

"Sure." Lilian's bright smile gained another level of luster.

Lilian seems to get along with this woman. I guess not every member of her family is estranged to her.

Lilian soon began to tell the story of how she and Kevin hooked up —with many embellishments and twice the *ecchi*, which surprised Kevin because he didn't think their life could sound more erotic than it truly had been. Some of the things she said made even him blush. Marigold, whose face was an atomic red as she listened, looked like she might pass out. At the same time, she had leaned in as though hanging off Lilian's every word.

Kevin didn't say anything to dispute her. Lilian was clearly reveling in telling someone how they got together, and he was loath to say something that might take away the smile that had blossomed on her face.

He rested his chin on Lilian's shoulder and looked at her out of his peripheral vision. His heart grew warm as he watched her talk animatedly to her five-tailed aunt.

She truly has the most wondrous smile I've ever seen.

It was a smile that he would do anything to protect.

A Fox's Revenge

Chapter 8

There's Something Seriously Wrong with This Family

"So… this is it? You're really leaving?"

Christine grimaced at Lindsay's crestfallen expression. It was 8:25 a.m., the morning after she'd called Orin and asked for his help. She'd had to call Lindsay and ask if her mom could drop her off at the airport. Lindsay had gone with her. Her friend's mother was also at the airport. She was currently standing behind a large column, drooling over a young man several yards away.

I wish that woman wasn't Lindsay's mom.

They were in the airport terminal for her flight, which would begin boarding soon. She could see the airplane through the glass window. Several people were disembarking from it, exiting through the jet bridge.

"I-it's not that I want to leave or anything," Christine tried to reason with Lindsay. "This is something that I have to do."

"But… but why?"

"Because I'm… because I'm weak." Christine swallowed at the admission. It was always hard to admit to one's own weakness, and she knew that she had a harder time of it than most. "When that woman attacked us, I barely did anything. Iris and Lilian did most of the heavy lifting, and Kevin is the one who saved us in the end. And because of me, Iris was… she was…"

243

Christine hated thinking about what happened to Iris, not only because it showed how much she truly cared for the perverted fox, but also because it showed her how useless she was.

She clenched her hands into fists. "If I'd just been stronger, if I could use my powers better, then Iris wouldn't have been injured because of me. I need to get stronger, and my benefactor, Orin, he can help train me. He can make me stronger."

Lindsay's face contorted into something that was too powerful to be called sadness. That word didn't do it justice. Tears leaked from her eyes, falling down her cheeks. Her arms were shaking from the overwhelming emotions that must have been raging through her.

"Everyone's going away," she whispered. "Iris, Lilian, and Kevin have all left, and I don't know when they'll be back. They didn't even say goodbye, and now you're leaving too. I don't want you to leave."

"Lindsay…"

"I know that you're a yōkai or whatever, and I get that some major battle took place, and that you feel weak because of it. You and Lilian and Iris and even Kevin live in a different world than me. I understand that, but I still don't like it. How can I when it's taking all of my friends away from me?"

Christine felt her desire to leave and grow strong falter. Her friend was truly distraught. Could she really leave Lindsay like this? She closed her eyes. Yes, she could. It hurt, but…

"Look, I understand how you feel," Christine said. "But I need to do this. Every time we got into trouble, the others were always the ones to deal with it. Despite being a yōkai, I could never do anything. I…" She felt her face turn blue from embarrassment, but she quickly carried on. "I don't want the boy that I lo—my friends to fight these battles without backup. That's why I have to do this."

More than anything, Christine didn't want Kevin to fight without her help. He might have rejected her feelings, but that didn't change how she felt for him, even if she tried to pretend that she was okay with them just being friends.

"I get that," Lindsay murmured softly. "I understand that you want to protect your friends instead of being the one who's protected. I feel that way a lot whenever I hear about the things that are happening to Kevin, Lilian, and Iris. But, you clearly don't understand how I feel."

Okay, now that actually kind of irritated her. Christine was trying to be understanding toward her friend, but Lindsay was being really stubborn, and what the hell did she mean by that? She didn't understand how Lindsay felt? Christine understood plenty.

"Oh, yeah?" Christine gave her friend a minor variation of the stink eye. "Then why don't you enlighten me? What am I not understanding?"

"You're not understanding this."

Christine hadn't been sure what to expect this morning. A tearful goodbye? A hope to see you soon? She didn't know as she'd never really done goodbyes before, though she imagined such affairs were often sad.

What she didn't expect was for her friend to kiss her.

She blinked several times as Lindsay's face closed the distance. The other girl's eyes were closed. Christine needed several seconds to register the warm feeling of her friend's lips pressed onto hers. She needed several more seconds to register what it meant. By the time she'd processed what was happening, it was already over.

Cue blush.

"W-w-w-w-what the fuck do you think you're doing?!" Christine's face felt like a giant blueberry popsicle as humiliation and anger warred within her. She pointed a quivering finger at Lindsay, who looked just as shocked and embarrassed as she felt. "You k-k-k-k-kissed me!"

Lindsay froze at the accusation, then straightened, her eyes glinting with determination.

"That's right. I did. And you know what? I'm going to kiss you again."

"Buwa?"

That was the only thing Christine was allowed to say.

Because Lindsay kissed her again.

***

It was later in the day, and Kevin had nothing to do. Daphne had found Lilian and dragged the girl off, kicking and screaming, once again, which meant he no longer had his mate with him. Marigold had also wandered off somewhere. She had said something about flowers and left. That meant it was just him and Kotohime.

"I'm bored," he said.

"Ufufufu, bored already? Weren't you the one who kept insisting that this place was interesting?" asked Kotohime.

"Well, yeah, but that was when Lilian was with me. Now there's nothing to do except read manga." He paused. "Which I could do, but that would kinda defeat the purpose of exploring a new place."

245

"Ufufufu, if you say so."

Kevin sighed as he kept walking aimlessly. It was while he wandered to nowhere in particular that a strange sound caught his attention. Multiple strange sounds. He cocked his head and listened to the noises, a series of grunts, screams, and something being smacked really hard. Curious, he followed the sounds to their source.

It was Violet, the short aunt of Lilian, who was currently pounding the crap out of a poor log. She launched her fists forward. They slammed into the wooden log, shaking the entire thing down to its foundation. Sweat flew from her skin and her toga had become partially see-through. Also…

What. The. Heck?

Violet's chest looked a lot bigger now than he remembered. Wasn't she supposed to be flat? Those things looked almost like watermelons!

The girl eventually stopped punching the log. Her fists were bruised and bleeding, but she didn't seem to care. She wiped the sweat from her forehead, and then looked down as though just now realizing something.

"Aw, man!" she grumbled. "My chest bindings are all wet. Freaking great. Now I've got to get some new ones and rewrap my chest."

It was at this point that Kevin decided to step in. "I had no idea you wore chest bindings. I guess that explains why you looked flatter than a billboard the last time we spoke."

"Unyaaa!" Kevin stumbled back as the woman shrieked. She whirled around, a hand rising to her chest. "You! Don't freaking sneak up on me like that!"

"Sorry," Kevin apologized. "I didn't mean to scare you."

"S-scared?" Violet laughed. "Who said I was scared? I ain't scared of nothing!"

Kevin turned to Kotohime. "She was scared, right?"

"Indeed she was, Kevin-sama." Kotohime nodded. "She was positively frightened."

"Thought so."

"You two shut up! Shut up right now! I wasn't scared at all!"

Kevin could have continued to tease her, and in fact, he was tempted to keep it up. He decided not to. There was something else that he wanted to talk about.

"Are you training?"

"Of course I'm training," Violet grunted. "What's it look like I'm doing?"

"Hitting a log really hard."

"Thank you for that enlightening observation, Captain Obvious," she snarked.

"Your sarcasm is unwarranted."

"Your presence is unwarranted."

"All right. Fine," Kevin said. "I'll leave. It's not like I want to hang around a midget with knockers the size of her head anyway."

"What was that?! You wanna go, brat?!"

"Bring it on, shorty!"

Violet charged at Kevin, who sidestepped her as she threw a punch. To add insult to injury, he stuck his leg out as she stumbled past him, which, of course, caused her to trip and fall face first into the dirt. Kevin withheld a chuckle as Violet lay on the ground, her butt sticking in the air.

"Do you like eating dirt?" he asked, taunting her.

"Grrr!!!" Violet leapt to her feet and spun around. The murderous look on her face would have been frightening on, say, Kotohime. On her it just looked silly. "I'm gonna kick your ass!"

"I'd like to see you try!"

Kevin cracked his knuckles and grinned. This was going to be fun.

***

While many of her brethren looked down on humans as being inferior, Kotohime had always admired humanity's tenacity and their ability to adapt. Humans had gained great power. They weren't the supernatural abilities of yōkai, but their technology was to the point where even a nine-tails had to be wary of them.

Kevin was a great example of human adaptability. When she had first met him, he was a wishy-washy teenager who smacked of harem protagonist tropes. Of course, he still smacked of harem protagonist tropes, but that was neither here nor there. Since their meeting, Kevin had changed. He had accepted Lilian, he was learning how to fight against yōkai, he had already killed two yōkai, and he was currently kicking Violet's ass.

"Hold still, you!"

"Why should I hold still? It isn't my fault you're too slow to hit me."

"Damn you!"

Kevin was running roughshod over Violet. Of course, he wasn't hitting her. In fact, he hadn't attacked once since the battle had started. He was simply letting Violet wear herself out, dodging or redirecting her attacks. He used the same style on her that he'd used on Kotohime earlier. Kevin presented openings in his defense, which even an amateur like Violet could see, and used those openings to force Violet into subconsciously attacking them, making her easy to predict.

"Why! Can't! I! Hit you!?"

"Because you suck, that's why!"

"Grr! Shut up! Shut up shut up shut up and let me fucking hit you!"

"Yeah... no."

As Kevin continued to taunt, tease, and toy with Violet, Kotohime sat underneath the shade of a tree and quietly cleaned her katana.

"Ufufufu, I'm so happy that Kevin-sama and Violet-sama are getting along so well," she said to no one in particular.

***

An hour after picking a fight with Violet, Kevin left the three-tailed vixen huffing and puffing as she lay on the ground. That chick had more stamina than he'd expected. While he wasn't too winded because dodging her required so little effort, he had been forced to expend a lot of energy.

Kevin chuckled as he thought about Violet's reactions to his teasing. He wondered if Iris and Lilian were bad influences on him. He was sure that teasing someone over their height and chest size was not something that he would normally do, but it was definitely something that Iris would have done.

Well, whatever. Violet got some combat experience, so she can't complain.

"You seem pleased with yourself, Kevin-sama," Kotohime observed.

Kevin smiled. "You can tell? I guess I just feel relaxed now. It's as if all my stress went away by beating up Violet."

Hiding her mirthful smile behind her kimono, Kotohime said, "I'm pleased to hear that, but do try not to pick on Violet-sama too much. She's had a rough life."

"I'll do my best."

"Thank you."

Pushing through a line of trees, Kevin halted when a wall suddenly appeared before him. He didn't know which building this was. That

A Fox's Revenge

being the case, he followed the wall until he reached the corner. He paused again.

There were voices coming from around the corner.

"Look who came crawling back to the Pnévma Clan," a male voice sneered. "Did you and your sister miss me so much that you couldn't stand to be away for a moment longer?"

"As if," Lilian's voice reached him. "*One Piece* will end before I ever miss your ugly mug, Palladius."

Kevin pressed his back against the wall. He peered out from around the corner. Lilian was standing several feet away. There were two bishounen next to one. He recognized Caleb, but the other person was unfamiliar to him.

"Little cunt!" Not-Caleb snarled. "I should teach you a fucking lesson in manners!"

"I don't think you should be doing this," Caleb told the man.

The other kitsune scowled at him. "You think I fucking care what you think? Shut up, dickweed." He turned back to Lilian. "Now that your sister isn't here to protect you, I'm going to have some fun."

Before he realized what he was doing, Kevin leapt out from around the corner, unsheathing his guns and unloading a torrent of bullets into Not-Caleb. The kitsune was so surprised that he couldn't do anything as he was hit in the chest and shoulders by several water youki bullets. There was no blood. These bullets were low intensity. Even so, the man's body jerked back and forth as though he was having muscle spasms.

Kevin stopped shooting. As the man stood there, swaying like a drunkard who'd downed an entire keg by himself, Lilian twisted her tails together, turned them into a giant fist, and slammed them into Not-Caleb's crotch.

"Gomu Gomu no Pistol!"

The high-pitched squeal that followed made even Kevin wince. The man collapsed to the ground while holding his nutsack. As Kevin walked up and got a good look at the man, he noticed that the kitsune's eyes were rolled into the back of his head.

"Beloved!" Lilian leapt at him.

"You need to be careful, Lilian," Kevin said as he hugged the vixen back. "Using someone else's attack name could get us in trouble for copyright."

"Whatever. It was just once."

"You say that now, but… in any case, what happened here?"

"This jerk thought he could try to take advantage of me since my sister is in a coma," Lilian said with a scowl. "I'm kinda surprised. I thought he'd try to go after Iris since she's an easier target right now."

Kevin wrinkled his nose. "I'm really beginning to lose respect for your family."

"If it helps, most of us aren't like him," Caleb said, gesturing to the unconscious kitsune. "Many of us don't like Lilian or Iris, but we won't hurt them either."

"I'm not sure that's any better," Kevin said. "Anyway, what should we do with him?"

"Why don't you leave him to me, Kevin-sama, Lilian-sama?" Kotohime suggested.

"Um, we'll leave him to you then," Lilian agreed.

Kevin took one look at Kotohime and shivered. He didn't want to know what she planned on doing to this guy. He really didn't.

***

Many still considered Paris to be the capital of the fashion world. Karen Swift would not deny this. Having traveled the world over as a fashion journalist, she could say with all honesty that Paris did indeed have the latest in fashion trends.

Having just finished spending the past several hours at yet another fashion show with one of *Vogue's* photographers, Karen walked the streets of Paris. Lights flashed all around her. Cars drove by on the road. Despite it being 10:37 p.m., there were still hundreds of people walking down the streets, enjoying a night on the town. Karen watched the people walk past her with envy. She'd not been able to go out like that since graduating from high school. Not since…

Best not think about that.

Karen hastened her pace. The Four Seasons Hotel George soon loomed before her, a large U-shaped building of at least seven stories. She entered the lobby and was greeted to a beautiful marble floor with unique designs. Several glass vases filled with colorful flowers sat arrayed around the room. Expensive artwork lined the walls and beautiful statues sat on pedestals.

She ignored the ostentatious decor in favor of hopping on the elevator and traveling up to her room. The elevator pinged and the door opened on the third floor. She stepped into a well-lit hallway. Beige carpet met her heels. Keen eyes surveyed the white walls with several paintings hanging from them in between each door. She reached her door and was about to slide her card through the keycard slot... when she paused.

Karen had an outstanding sixth sense. She could tell when something was wrong, even if there was no evidence to suggest that something was out of place. It was a skill that she had developed early on in life, about a year after high school, in fact.

Something was definitely wrong now.

Taking a slow breath, Karen reached into her purse and pulled out a small gun. It was a personal defense gun that she'd had custom-made for her several years back. Black and sleek, it had a slim design that allowed her to easily slip it into her purse without anyone being the wiser. It only had nine bullets, though, so she needed to make each shot count.

With her gun in her right hand and the card in her left, she unlocked the door and gripped the handle.

One. Two. Three.

She flung the door wide open and stepped swiftly inside, her gun already sweeping the room for potential hostiles. It didn't take her long to find the anomaly in her room. He stood with his back turned to her, hands clasped behind his back. He wore a large black trench coat that went down to his knees. She saw his face in the window's reflection and her blood ran cold.

"Ethan Paine."

She quickly pointed the gun at him—only to be forced to leap back when something dropped from the ceiling. A dark cloak fluttered around the crouched figure. Gleaming black metal and a red visor glowed with malevolence as it penetrated her with a glare.

"At ease." Ethan's gruff voice made her ears prickle.

The figure straightened, mechanical joints whirring as it moved. It stood to its full, intimidating seven plus feet of height, towering over the much smaller Karen. It stared down at her, then moved to stand beside Ethan, a silent guard.

"I see you've finally created them." Karen's voice was cold. "You were always going on about creating a warrior capable of fighting against yōkai, though I never expected your perfect warrior to be a robot."

"Humans are simply too fragile to stand up against the threat of yōkai incursion without aid." Ethan still had not turned around. "These

Yōkai Killers will be the first line of defense for humanity."

"I see you're still going on about how yōkai are threats against humanity."

"Of course." Ethan finally turned to face her. "My beliefs will never change. I am surprised to see that yours have. Was it not a yōkai who took your family from you? And yet now you are allowing an entire family of yōkai into your house, letting them get close to our son—"

"My son," Karen snapped, shutting the man down before he could truly start. "You gave up any right you had to call him your son after what you did to him, after what you did to us. You are no father of his."

"It's just as well." Ethan dismissed her words, causing Karen to grit her teeth. "Anybody who willingly cavorts with yōkai is no son of mine."

"Why are you here?" Karen asked. "I know you, and I know that you know better than to show your face to me. You wouldn't come here unless you had a damn good reason, so let's hear it, and make it quick. My patience isn't what it used to be."

"Are you sure you want to threaten me?" Ethan growled out in a low voice. "My guard is quite zealous when it comes to my safety. It has a series of very powerful overrides installed that not even I can stop when activated. Threaten me any more than you already have and those overrides may activate."

"Your guard is just a hunk of metal," Karen determined. "Steel and circuits. Once you know how something like that works, it's no longer a threat."

"Don't be so sure. You may be a whiz when it comes to technology, but our science department has made leaps and bounds since you left us. I doubt even you could discover a weakness within this killing machine."

Karen stared at Ethan with a hard look. A trickle of sweat trailed down her brow, but she dared not wipe it away. She kept her gun pointed at Ethan, whose scarred visage remained impassive.

"However, I did not come here to fight with you today," Ethan continued. "I have merely decided to give you this one chance to save yourself and your son. Times are changing. The world is changing. Yōkai activity is increasing by the day. It won't be long now before the yōkai menace becomes a threat that the governments of the world will no longer be able to ignore. And when that time comes, all those who side with yōkai will be terminated."

"And you're giving me this warning in order to have me tell Kevin that he should stop seeing Lilian. Is that it?"

"By the time I finish telling you everything I know, you're not going to want that kitsune or her family spending any more time with your son anyway."

Karen's eyes narrowed. "What do you mean?"

"I mean that your son was nearly killed one week ago when a group of yōkai attacked the Pnévma Clan and destroyed your apartment."

"W-what?" Karen stared at the man, shock raging through her body. Only her knowledge of how dangerous Ethan was kept her from dropping her gun. "What are you talking about?"

In response to her words, Ethan took out a small disc from a pocket inside of his trench coat. "This disc contains the video of a battle that my subordinate recorded. Your son was involved in it and was nearly killed multiple times." He set the disc on the table, which also had her laptop. "Watch this, and you will understand why peaceful coexistence between humans and yōkai is nothing but a pipe dream."

Ethan walked past her, his metallic guard following behind him, the whirring of its joints echoing loudly in her ears. She heard the door shut, and the sound of footsteps and whirring servomotors soon receded. Karen listened, not moving until she was sure that Ethan and his abominable contraption had left.

Slowly making her way over to the table, she picked up the disc and looked at it. She then sat down, turned on her laptop, typed in the password, and inserted the disc.

And then she saw it, her son's battle against a yōkai, a kitsune with three tails using celestial techniques. She watched as he, Lilian, Christine, and another girl that she didn't know, fought against the three-tails, which culminated in the girl she didn't know getting stabbed through the chest, and her son and his companions retreating.

She brought a trembling hand to her face, her mind unwilling to believe what her eyes were telling her. This wasn't a fake. Ethan knew better than to give her falsified video content. That meant this was real. That battle had been real.

As the video ended, Karen scrambled to pull her cell phone out of her pocket. She quickly hit the speed dial to call her son, then put the phone to her ear.

The wait felt like forever. With every ring in which the phone went unanswered, her mind became plagued with worry. Images of her son being killed in a similar manner to that girl filled her thoughts. She knew that she had never been a very good mom, that until his middle school year, she'd barely even tried acting like a mom, but she still loved Kevin dearly. The thought that he might be hurt, or worse, dead, caused an icy fist to clutch her heart in an iron grip.

The ringing stopped.

"H-hello?"

Karen almost sobbed in relief as her son's sleepy voice filled her ear. She'd never believed something so mundane could be so cathartic.

"Are you sleeping in, Kevin?" She teased her son. "It's already two in the afternoon. Shouldn't you be up by now?"

"Two in the—oh, right. I guess it is."

"Is everything all right over there?" she finally asked.

"Hm? Of course. Why wouldn't it be?"

"I just… I was wondering if there was anything you wanted to tell me."

"Can't say that there is." Her son yawned again. *"Why? Is there something you wanted to talk to me about?"*

Karen bit her lip. What should she do? Should she tell her son that she knew about his battle with the kitsune? Should she reveal that she knew about the existence of yōkai? Did she really want that knowledge, which she had kept hidden from him for years, getting out? Did Kevin even need to know?

He was safe. Whatever had happened to him, he was safe and clearly not worried. Perhaps… perhaps it would just be better to let sleeping dogs lie.

"Oh, no. Nothing in particular," Karen said. "I just wanted to call and see how you were doing. You know how we mothers worry for our children."

***

"You know how we mothers worry for our children."

Kevin listened to his mom on the other end, wondering about the real reason she had called him. Worried for her child? Was that really the best excuse she could come up with? In all the time that he'd been living on his own, his mother had only ever called him on three occasions, and all of them were to tell him that she would be arriving home late from whichever country she was currently visiting.

"Really? You don't strike me as the worrying type."

254

His mother huffed. *"Now that's just rude. You know that I worry for you all the time. I just don't show it because I have confidence in your ability to take care of yourself."*

"I guess."

"Anyway, now that I know everything is okay, I'll talk to you later. Oh! I should be coming home in about a week or so. I was wondering if you, Lilian, and Kotohime would like to go traveling for summer vacation? Maybe we could visit Germany or something."

"Uh..."

Well, crap. This was not good. What should he say now? *"Sorry, Mom, but I'm not actually in the country. In fact, I'm currently staying with my mate's family in Greece. Please don't come looking for me."* He couldn't see that going over too well.

"Um, I'll have to get back to you on that."

"Hmm, well, okay. But let me know where you'd like to visit soon. It takes a lot of time to book reservations, and you know how I like getting a good hotel room to stay in. Although, I suppose now we'll need two, huh?"

More like four, but he wasn't going to tell his mom that.

"Right. So, uh, goodnight, Mom."

"Night, Kevin—wait. Isn't it supposed to be noon over there?"

"What's that? *Kkrrrch!* I can't hear you, Mom! I think you're breaking up. *Krrrcch!"*

"Are you making strange noises to try and make it sound like the signal is being lost?"

"… No. Anyway, goodbye, Mom."

"W-wait! Kevin—"

Kevin hung up with a sigh. That was too close. He'd almost given away the knowledge that he was no longer in Arizona, or even the United States, for that matter. The last thing he needed was for his mom to discover that he'd left the country and start snooping around. His mom was a journalist; there was no telling what she would find out.

He set the phone back on the small table in his and Lilian's room, then looked over at the redhead whose bed he shared.

Lilian was asleep. She'd woken up briefly when his phone started ringing, but that was only to tell him to either answer his phone or have it destroyed *Gomu Gomu* style, which he took to mean she'd use extension to crush his phone—and probably the table.

Shaking his head, Kevin slowly walked back toward the bed—

Kevin blinked rapidly several times as, before he could take another step, something covered his head and he inhaled some kind of strange, sickly scent. His body involuntarily relaxed. His mind went hazy. His vision went dark.

Kevin knew no more.

**

Kevin awoke to the sound of voices. They were distant at first, muffled, as if he were underwater, but they quickly became sharper.

"Jasmine-denka, I have brought the young man, just as you requested."

"Thank you, Ayane. Were you seen?"

He tried to move, but neither his arms nor his legs would budge. He eventually realized that his arms were tied behind his back and his legs were similarly bound. Whoever had done the tying also knew their knots. He couldn't even move his wrists to loosen them.

"I am sure that Kotohime noticed my presence. She is most observant. However, no one else saw me, and she will not interfere unless Kevin Swift is placed in danger."

"Good. Now, can you please remove that bag from his head."

"Of course, Jasmine-denka."

The bag was lifted from his head, and Kevin was greeted by a decently lit room. He stared up at what he could only guess was a ceiling for several seconds, which made him realize that he was lying on the floor. A glance around revealed a modestly sized, if barren, room. There wasn't much in the way of decor; a bookshelf sat on one side, a desk with several scrolls and calligraphy brushes sat in another. There was a divan with an almost naked little girl sitting on it, and a nightstand stood by... the... bed...?

... Wait. What?

Kevin turned his head back to the little girl and gawked. He recognized her from just this morning. It was Jasmine, the youngest of Delphine's daughters. She sat on the divan, her tiny feet placed firmly on the ground, hands resting in her lap. She wore only a towel, and her hair was dripping wet. Pearlescent drops of water ran down her bare shoulders and elegant neck.

"Jasmine?"

"Good evening, Kevin Swift."

"What am I doing here?"

"That should be obvious," she said in a tone that made him feel like he'd asked something stupid.

He sent her the driest look he could muster under the circumstance. "Humor me."

"Very well." Jasmine acquiesced easily enough. "You are here because I had my shadow bring you here."

"Shadow?" Kevin looked around, his eyes flickering back and forth. He couldn't see anything, however, making him wonder if she was talking about a person, or if she was being literal.

"Yes, Ayane is my shadow and protector. She has protected me ever since I gained my second tail."

"She sounds like a kunoichi or something."

"That is it exactly. Ayane grew up in a village that trained kunoichi. She was one of their top ranked assassins until being defeated by Mother. Ayane asked to be killed, but Mother instead told her to serve the Pnéyma Clan. She has been a faithful retainer of our clan ever since then."

"Ah." That was actually a pretty interesting story. Maybe it was just because he had watched too much *Shinobi Natsumo*, but he'd always been interested in ninja, and kunoichi specifically. "Cool, cool. Now, do you think you could untie me? As much as I love lying on the cold floor, unable to move, I'm beginning to lose circulation in my wrists and calves."

The girl studied him with her expressionless look, then nodded. "That is a reasonable request. Ayane, please remove his bindings."

Kevin felt his bindings fall away. He rubbed his wrists in an attempt to get the blood flowing back into them. His legs also seemed fine. Once he was sure everything was in good working order, he stood up.

"That's a lot better. Thank you."

"You are most welcome."

Kevin stared at the girl who stared right back. He felt kind of bad for thinking it, but this girl really freaked him out. Despite having essentially had him kidnapped and brought before her, her facial expression hadn't changed one bit. It remained as bland now as it had when they first met.

"Right, so, uh, perhaps you could tell me why I'm here now?"

"Of course. I had you brought here because you fascinate me."

"Uh…" Kevin didn't know if he should feel flattered or freaked out. "Perhaps you could elaborate?"

"I suppose that would be the appropriate thing to do." Jasmine nodded. "As the first human that I have ever met, you interest me a great deal. I am also intrigued by your ability to shrug off my enchantment like it was nothing. Furthermore, you are a man, and from what I can tell with my inexperienced eye, a very handsome one. To put it in simpler terms, I want you—"

Kevin knew that most men would probably be feeling very flattered right about now. Indeed, having a female praise him would have normally made him feel flattered, too—and embarrassed, but mostly flattered. However, three things kept him from feeling flattered. One: this girl had kidnapped him. Two: he already had a mate and didn't need another one. And three: the person claiming that she wanted him looked like a thirteen-year-old girl.

"Uh, look, Jasmine, that's, well, it's really flattering to know that you want me to be your mate and everything, but I already have a mate, so…"

"Mate?" Jasmine blinked. "I did not have you brought here so that I may ask you to be my mate. You spoke before I could finish."

"Oh?" So she didn't want to be his mate? If that was the case, then he guessed it was okay. After all, she couldn't ask for something more awkward than that. "So, what did you want from me, then?"

"I want you to be my master."

"Heh?"

Okay, so maybe she could ask him something more embarrassing. Just who the heck said something like that? And with such a straight face!

"Um, when you say master, do you mean…"

"I mean that you shall be my master, and I shall be your humble and most devoted slave from this day onward."

"G-gu!"

Kevin was beginning to regret asking.

"L-look…" Kevin backed away from the little girl who now officially freaked him out. "I'm not exactly sure why you want someone like me to be your, uh, master, but I'm going to tell you right now that I don't want a slave."

"I see." Though her facial expression didn't change, he had the distinct impression that she was annoyed. "It seems you need some convincing. Very well, I shall not allow you to leave until you agree to become my master."

259

A Fox's Revenge

Kevin twitched. "If I was your master, then shouldn't you be listening to me?"

"You have not accepted the terms of the contract yet. Until you do, then you shall not be my master."

"Terms of the—all right, listen here, Saber—I-I mean, Jasmine. I don't know who you think you are, but I am not going to accept any contract. I don't want a slave!" Kevin held a hand to his face. "And what's up with me today? Who the hell is Saber?"

While her expression remained dispassionate and colder than a block of ice, Jasmine's carmine eyes held a gleam within them that Kevin did not like one bit.

"It seems I have underestimated you, Master."

"W-what? Why the heck are you calling me 'Master'?! I haven't even accepted your contract!"

"I have decided that we can discuss the terms of our contract later. For now, we should begin discussing the terms of our relationship."

"What relationship?!"

"If there is one thing that you must know about me, Master, it is that I am a very traditional vixen. While I do not mind missionary position, I would much prefer to be bent over the table and taken from behind."

"Urk!"

Kevin didn't know what was worse: That he was listening to someone with the appearance of a thirteen-year-old girl talk like this, or that someone who looked like a thirteen-year-old girl was talking like this in the first place. It might have even been because he was somehow not surprised to find himself being confronted by someone who looked like a thirteen-year-old girl talking about being taken from behind.

I hate my life.

"Also, while I do not know if this will please you, Master, I feel that it is my duty to inform you that I am not afraid to swallow."

"Gurk!"

Within his mind, Kevin felt that little piece of sanity, which he'd managed to retain since Lilian came into his life, wither and die. What's worse was that he didn't even care anymore.

My life is so screwed up.

***

Kevin released a loud yawn as he and Lilian walked through the main building of the Pnévma Clan ancestral home. The *pitter patter* of

260

A Fox's Revenge

their shoes echoed along the hall of marble. Several intricate carvings reminiscent of Greek tributes to the gods were embedded into the walls. Like all decorations in this grand and extravagant place, these murals depicted the Kyūbi, the legendary nine-tailed fox from Japanese mythology—and Lilian's grandmother, hard as that was to believe.

"Are you tired, Beloved?" Lilian asked in concern. "You didn't come back to bed for a long time after your mom called."

He still didn't know how Lilian knew the exact moment he'd hopped into bed with her despite having been asleep. It was like some kind of sixth sense that the girl had. She'd once jokingly referred to it as her "Kevin Senses," though he had a feeling that she'd been serious when she said that.

"I'm fine," Kevin assured her, unwilling to mention his, um, meeting with Jasmine. "I'll just need to go to sleep a little earlier today."

Lilian studied him for a moment. Then she shrugged. "That's fine. It's not like there's much to do around here anyway, and I don't mind sleeping with you."

Kevin's smile contained amusement. "I didn't think you would."

After breakfast that morning, he had asked Lilian to take him on a tour of the grounds. This place was much larger than he'd initially been led to believe, and he wanted to know his way around. He also didn't want an incident like the one yesterday with Holly and Ivy—or the two incidents with Jasmine—to happen again.

"You've already seen the reception hall," Lilian said, humming thoughtfully. "I guess that means I'll be showing you the dining hall and the formalized training hall. Maybe I can also show you Granny's bathhouse."

Kevin didn't know if he was interested in seeing "Granny's Bathhouse." Maybe it was just because of the words she used, but he had no intention of seeing anything that was synonymous with the word "granny." Just no.

"Are those the only rooms in this place?" he asked.

"More or less," Lilian answered as she led him by the hand. "There are only two other rooms aside from those three I just mentioned: Granny's bedroom and the room that contains the Shrine Gate."

He definitely didn't want to see "Granny's Bedroom," but the Shrine Gate sounded interesting.

The training hall wasn't much to look at. It really just looked like a large room that was a combination of library and training room. There weren't any decorations, but he did see a sitting area over by the bookshelves, which were several times larger than him. They went all the way to the ceiling that he judged to be at least two stories in height.

"Most of these books are just boring history books," Lilian told Kevin as he pulled one from a shelf. It was titled *Delia Pnéyma*. "A lot of them tell about the history of our clan, which spans back several thousand years or so—about three thousand, I think."

"You think?" Kevin put the book back and raised an eyebrow at his mate.

Lilian blushed. "I never really listened to Daphne when she was trying to teach me," she admitted. "Anyway, there are a few that talk about spirit techniques and how they're used, and I think there are a few on humans and other yōkai, but that's about it."

They soon left the training room and headed for the dining hall. Unlike the previous room, this one appeared every bit as ostentatious and pomp as the rest of the estate. The dark marble floor presented a stark contrast to the white walls. The ceiling was painted with intricate artwork that made Kevin think of the Sistine Chapel, only with a kitsune theme. Even the table was a study in posh and circumstance, with intricate designs that sparkled in the light as if freshly polished.

"You know, I've noticed that it's really empty around here," Kevin said as they left the dining room. "I kind of expected there to be more people, but aside from your sisters and one or two male kitsune, I haven't seen anyone else."

"We're not a very large clan," Lilian told him. "Just the most powerful. The Pnéyma Clan was a minor clan before Lord Inari granted Granny the ninth tail. After that, she usurped the previous Great Spirit Clan's position, and we became the most powerful spirit clan in the world." She paused and tilted her head. "I can't remember who the last Great Spirit Clan was, though."

"Didn't pay much attention to that lecture either, huh?" Kevin asked in a teasing tone.

"I've never cared about the Pnéyma Clan's history," Lilian confessed. "Humans were always more interesting to me."

Kevin nodded. Where yōkai could be considered traditionalists who remained stubbornly set in their ways, humanity always sought to progress beyond their station, constantly improving upon ideas and seeking to better their lives. Progress for progress's sake. Lilian loved the free-thinking ideas that humanity possessed.

"Oh, my," a voice said from behind them. Lilian stiffened. "If it isn't Lilian and young Kevin. I hope you two are doing well this morning."

"Granny—urk!"

"Now, now, Lilian." Delphine's smile was pleasant—in the same way a viper was pleasant. "I thought I told you not to call me Granny. If you must call me something, then please call me Big Sis."

"Ugh…"

"Now then," Delphine walked up to them, "I was hoping that I might take a moment of your mate's time. It has been many years since I last spoke with a human."

Kevin stiffened when she touched his arm. An overwhelming feeling of *something* washed over him. He felt cold, like someone had stuck his arm in a freezer. The chill seeped into his veins, spread along his body, and sought entrance into his heart.

Lilian seemed to sense his discomfort, or maybe she was just feeling territorial. She wrapped her arms around his other arm.

"I'm sorry, Gran—I mean, Big Sis," Lilian almost gagged, "but I was showing Beloved around."

"There is no need to be so protective." Delphine's gentle smile looked disarming, but Kevin could sense some underlying danger lurking beneath it. "I simply wish to take but a moment of his time—and speaking of taking of time, I believe Daphne wished to take a moment of yours."

"What?" Lilian blinked.

As if Delphine's words held prophetic powers, a loud, rumbling roar caused the hallway they stood in to reverberate.

"LILIAN! GET OVER HERE, YOU BRAT! IT'S TIME FOR YOUR LESSON!"

"HIIII!"

It was almost amusing to watch Lilian. Her eyes widened, and her ears and tails stood on end, bristling in horror. Her entire body became stiffer than morning wood before a visible shiver ran from the toes of her feet up to the crown of her head.

Several seconds later, Lilian was running down the hall at near supersonic speed. Seconds after that, Daphne raced down from the other end of the hall, running straight past him and Delphine without a second glance.

"DON'T THINK I'LL LET YOU GET AWAY FROM ME THIS

TIME, BRAT! IT'S TIME FOR YOUR LESSON!"

"NO! I DON'T WANNA LEARN FROM AN OLD HAG LIKE YOU!"

"THAT'S TOO BAD! YOU'RE GOING TO LEARN AND YOU'RE GOING TO LIKE IT! AND DON'T CALL ME AN OLD HAG!"

Soon enough, the two kitsune disappeared around a corner. Kevin stared at the place they had vanished from for a second before shaking his head.

"That was odd." Despite saying this, Kevin didn't feel the least bit surprised. It must have been because the last bit of his sanity had died last night during his conversation with Jasmine.

"Indeed." Delphine's grip on his arm tightened. "Now then, let us speak, you and I."

Kevin gulped, but he allowed the woman to pull him along. It wasn't like he could do anything else.

They ended up outside. A marble walkway led to a circular gazebo with a dome-shaped roof. She led him up the walkway and to the gazebo. They passed by two columns shaped like a pair of nine-tailed foxes sitting on their hind legs. A circular table with stone benches awaited them, and Delphine bade him to sit down on one side while she sat on the opposite side.

"Hayate."

Kevin nearly jumped out of his seat when a man appeared before them. Unlike most of the kitsune he'd seen, the one Delphine called Hayate wore all-black clothing in traditional shinobi garb. It looked a little odd because he wore a full-facial mask and his triangle-shaped ears poked against the fabric as a result, but other than that, Kevin thought he actually looked kind of cool. He had three tails.

"Yes, My Lady?"

"Please have the servants create some tea for my guest and I."

Kevin thought he saw irritation flash in the kitsune's eyes, but it was gone quicker than it appeared. He wondered if he'd imagined it.

"At once."

The man bowed. Kevin blinked. In the second that it had taken him to do so, the man disappeared.

"What the heck?"

"Hayate is one of my many sons," Delphine explained to him. "I have over two dozen sons. Most go out into the world and handle the day-to-day operations of various Pnéyma Clan holdings and business investments in the human world. However, Hayate is currently serving as my bodyguard. I had him specifically trained in the shinobi arts so that he could become my shadow."

"So he's like Ayane, then?"

"Oh." Delphine appeared mildly surprised. "I had not realized that you have already met Ayane."

"I haven't seen her, if that's what you mean," Kevin hedged. "But I've heard her talking."

"That is to be expected. Most kunoichi do not allow themselves to be seen unless they are seducing you for information or assassination."

"Um, right."

Delphine studied him, and Kevin tried not to squirm. He felt like a frog on a dissection table. The look in the nine-tailed kitsune's eyes bothered him greatly, though he couldn't figure out why.

Suddenly, Delphine smiled, and it was both one of the most beautiful and terrifying things he'd ever seen.

"I make you uncomfortable, don't I?" Kevin said nothing, causing the woman to nod several times. "That is understandable. Most cannot stand to be in my presence for very long—even my own daughters. I can only imagine how a human must feel around me."

Like I'm having a conversation with the Grim Reaper.

"Why is that?" he asked out loud.

"Are you asking why my presence causes discomfort?" Delphine asked for clarification.

"Um." Kevin nodded.

"It is the result of gaining the ninth tail, I'm afraid. You see, all creatures have the ability to tell when something is a threat to their well-being, a threat detector, if you will. Even humans, who have done their best to dissociate themselves from nature have this ability to some degree."

The woman paused as their tea arrived via a maid. A steaming cup of regal china was set in front of them. Kevin took a sniff, the scent of black tea with a hint of cinnamon wafting into his olfactory senses.

Delphine sighed in pleasure as she took a sip. "Kyūbi like myself are among some of the most powerful yōkai in existence. Our power is considered to be on par with those of the gods. The only reason we are not gods ourselves is because we cannot perceive the world beyond three dimensions. In other words, our ability to perceive what's around us is still within the parameters of a mortal, whereas even the weakest of gods can perceive the world by at least six dimensions."

Kevin had no clue what she was talking about. He'd watched many anime that spoke of multiple worlds and parallel universes, but even with all the anime and manga references locked inside of his head, her words were something that he simply couldn't fathom.

Delphine either didn't realize this or, more likely, she just didn't care. "That being said, it does not change that our power is considered godlike. Humans and yōkai recognize this power. You can feel it, and it is that feeling you get when you are around me that causes you to feel such great unease. Even though I am consciously concealing my powers from you, it still leaks out, and your mind automatically categorizes that power as a threat to your well-being."

"I-I… I see," Kevin said. "So, your power is simply so overwhelming that my mind automatically assumes you're a threat."

"Oh, no. I most certainly am a threat." Delphine smiled. Kevin felt a thrill run down his spine. "If I so desired, I could crush you before the thought even crossed your mind. I was simply educating you on why you feel so uncomfortable around me."

Kevin tried to keep his breathing even and controlled. Delphine noticed this and presented him with a disarming smile that did nothing to disarm him.

"However, you need not worry about that. I might be a threat to your continued existence, but that doesn't mean I will actually treat you with hostility." Delphine took another sip of tea, her disposition calm and unharried, as if she hadn't just told him that she could snuff out his existence quicker than he could say kitsune. "If anything, I wanted to thank you."

Kevin's rapid blinking was the only sign of his confusion. "Thank me? What for?"

"For taking care of my daughter and granddaughters, of course," she answered as if it was obvious. "Especially my granddaughter. Lilian is a very unusual kitsune, as I am sure you've already realized. She is simply too pure and honest, which makes it very easy for people to take advantage of her. That is why I am grateful that you two met when you did."

Kevin needed a moment to process her words and realize what they meant. "Were you the one who let me pass the barrier nine years ago?"

"I was not," Delphine stated. "However, I will not deny that your meeting with her was most fortuitous. Had you not done so, I may have very well been forced to arrange a mating contract between her and a member of the Shénshèng Clan."

"Are you saying that you did not want to… mate her off?" He frowned at the odd wording. It seemed he was still trying to apply human concepts to kitsune culture.

"That is, indeed, what I am saying." Delphine hummed. "Do not get me wrong. An alliance with the Shénshèng Clan would be a boon, but it could also be taken as a threat by other yōkai."

Kevin knew a little bit about this subject. Kotohime had lectured him on it, though they'd never been able to go into detail.

Delphine set her cup down and idly traced the lip with a perfectly manicured finger. "Our world's power is precariously balanced. Any change within the balance of power between one race could adversely affect the yōkai world as a whole. While allying myself with the Shénshèng Clan might have proven beneficial in the short term, it could cause the already unstable power balance among yōkai to shift radically and restart hostilities between races."

Kevin took in her words, and then frowned when he realized something. "You speak of how grateful you are to me because I prevented you from allying yourself with the Shénshèng Clan. However, not once in that little speech of yours did I hear anything about Lilian or her happiness."

"Oh?" Delphine's eyes gleamed with a look that he couldn't place. "I'm surprised you're able to speak back to me like that. How interesting, huhuhu."

Kevin tightly gripped his shorts. His hands were shaking.

Delphine pretended not to notice. "While it may not seem like it, I do care for Lilian's happiness. She is a wonderful girl, and she doesn't deserve to be treated as a tool." Delphine's smile gained a quality, a softness to it that he hadn't seen yet. It put him at ease, if only slightly. "That being said, I am also the matriarch. It is my solemn duty to look after the clan as a whole. That is the burden of being the matriarch."

Her words had a ring of truth to them, but Kevin still didn't know if he could trust her. Although she sounded sincere, he knew that she could easily be masking malevolent intentions behind her charming smile. Even so, he couldn't detect a lie, and so decided to give her the benefit of the doubt.

"Now then," Delphine stood up, "I believe we have spoken long enough. Your mate has likely escaped from my daughter's clutches by now and is looking for you. I know that I am asking for much, but please, look after my granddaughter for a little while longer."

"That's not something you need to be asking me," Kevin said with quiet confidence. "Lilian is my mate. She means a lot to me. Even if you didn't ask me to look after her, I would do just that anyway."

"You do not know how pleased I am to hear that." Delphine's grateful smile was a wondrous sight to behold, and yet, for all its beauty, Kevin still could not find any solace in it.

***

The Shénshèng Clan library was not very large. As the long-lived supernal beings that they were, kitsune did not generally care to relate information through books. Why bother when they were going to live for so long that they could pass along everything someone needed to know verbally? That was the thought of most yōkai. It didn't help that books were a human creation and therefore generally seen as beneath them.

Fan was beginning to regret the size of their library. She'd never really cared for reading before, but now that she was trying to find a way to heal her beloved younger brother, she wished they had placed more importance on the written word.

"There's nothing in here," Fan growled in anger. "Nothing at all! I don't even know why I bothered coming down here in the first place!"

She glanced around their library, which probably couldn't be considered a real library since there couldn't have been more than maybe fifty books at most. What she called a library was actually just a small room with a single book shelf and some very select reading materials. Most of them were on psychology. Despite this, none of them told her what she wanted to know. If anything, everything within those books validated her father's plan.

"I believe you came down here to try and discover a way to help Lord Jiāoào recover," Li said from where he stood behind her, arms crossed over his chest and features bland. "I take it from your anger that you have not found anything worthwhile."

"No," Fan muttered bitterly. "I have not."

"Hn."

The doors to the room were suddenly opened, and Fan looked up as one of her brothers walked in.

Zhìlì was the second eldest of Father's sons. He possessed seven golden tails that matched his long hair, which had been tied into a ponytail. Unlike her eldest brother, Chao, Zhìlì wore clothing reminiscent of warriors from the Three Kingdoms Era. His silver breastplate and shoulder pads gleamed as light reflected off their surface, allowing all to see the golden nine-tailed fox emblazoned upon it. His greaves, also silver with golden trim, clanked as he walked. Underneath his armor was a plain black unitard, which made the armor stand out all the more.

"Fan, Li," he greeted with a grin that was boyish and so unlike her eldest brother. "Father has returned and called for a gathering."

Fan wasn't pleased by this. She would have liked a little more time, but time was no longer on her side, it seemed.

"Very well. Please lead the way, Honorable Brother."

"Ma, ma." Zhìlì waved her formal manner of speech off rather easily. "There is no need for you to be so formal, Sis. You know I dislike formality these days."

"That is because you have been spending too much time around humans," Fan scolded.

Zhìlì winced. "Ouch, so harsh."

"Whatever. Just lead the way."

"All right. Sa, sa, this way."

Fan sighed as she followed Zhìlì through several elegant halls. While Chao was always too harsh and snide for her tastes, Zhìlì wasn't much better. He was simply too relaxed and easygoing, never taking anything seriously, always foisting work off on others. Unreliable. That was what Zhìlì was.

Why can't I have a brother who's somewhere in the middle? Ah, if only my beloved younger brother were awake. Everything would be so much better.

"You're drooling, Lady Fan."

"Geh!"

Their father was already seated when they reached the throne room. Chao was also present. As they stepped before the raised dais, all of them knelt before their father and the most powerful Celestial Kitsune on the planet, their heads bowed.

"You may raise your heads," Father said. "I have summoned you three because I have a task that requires your aid."

"Permission to speak, Father," Fan said.

"Permission granted."

"This task that you speak of, is it the one you mentioned before?"

"Indeed it is," her father answered. "I have spoken with my contacts, and they have agreed to my proposal. You, Zhìlì, and Li shall travel to the Pnéyma Clan's ancestral home and ensure that the mission is carried out successfully."

Her father stared at them, and Fan felt a thrill travel through her at the look in his eyes. He rarely ever displayed emotion, so seeing it caused her to feel a combination of excitement and fear. She almost pitied the Pnéyma Clan.

"My allies should be making contact with the Pnéyma Clan later today. In two days' time, Lilian Pnéyma shall find herself within our grasp."

Chapter 9

Strange Happenstances

I'm dining with an entire family of kitsune.

Kevin had grown used to finding himself in odd, unusual, and downright zany situations. After ten months of knowing Lilian, strange happenstances were pretty much par for the course. Despite this simple fact, he could still find himself surprised. He had never once imagined that he would be having breakfast with an entire clan of kitsune.

His eyes swept across the large group of fox-women around him. Aster and Azalea, who'd only been briefly introduced to him that morning, sat together, feeding each other. Kevin was, well, he wanted to say that he was surprised to find a pair of lesbian twins, but he couldn't. Iris had destroyed the idea that kitsune understood what a normal relationship was supposed to be like. Lilian sat on his left, and on her left was Camellia. Meanwhile, immediately across from him sat Violet and Jasmine. Violet was annoying her sister, while Jasmine tried to ignore her in favor of staring impassively at him.

"Ne, ne, Jasmine, why are you staring at the brat so much? Do you want his weinerschnitzel?"

"Yes."

Violet must not have been expecting that answer because she sprayed food all over the table—and Ivy, who sat on her other side.

"Was that really necessary?" Ivy asked, wiping her glasses and face. Kevin didn't like the way those glasses gleamed as she readjusted them. It was just so ominous.

The Villain with Glasses has nothing on this chick.

"Of course it was necessary," Violet spat. "Didn't you hear what she just said?"

"I did." Ivy nodded, looking at Jasmine from across Violet. "Jasmine, when you and the human have raunchy, passionate sex, would you mind if Mother and I observed?" She adjusted her glasses again. They flashed... again. Kevin shuddered. "It's for science."

"I see no problem with that," Jasmine said. "Provided Master does not mind us partaking in exhibitionism."

"I do mind," Kevin informed her dryly. "I so mind." He paused. "And we are not having sex!"

"Beloved." Lilian frowned at him. "Did something happen between you and Jasmine that you wish to tell me about?"

Kevin sighed and rubbed his face. "Your youngest aunt kidnapped me last night and said some really weird crap that I would rather erase from my memory."

Standing behind him and Lilian, Kotohime chuckled. "Ufufufu, if you'd like, I can help you with that, Kevin-sama."

"Quiet, you!"

"What sort of things did she talk about?" Lilian pressed. "And why is she calling you 'Master'?"

Before Kevin could tell her to just forget about it, Jasmine spoke up in her bland, emotionless voice. "I have decided that Kevin Swift is my master, and I, his most devoted slave."

"Gu!"

"I shall devote my entire self to him, allowing him to use me as he pleases, in any way he desires."

"Urk!"

"Any hole that he wishes to fill with his hot, sticky spunk, I shall allow him to fill."

"Gurk!"

Several arrows appeared out of nowhere to violently spear him in the back. He felt them piercing his metaphorical flesh, penetrating the thick skin that he had developed from overexposure to unusual situations like it was made of melted chocolate.

"Whoa." Violet blushed. "I had no idea you were such a kinky freak, Sis." She shook her head. "It's always the quiet ones."

"Huh." Aster—or was it Azalea? Kevin couldn't tell because they looked the same—studied him with a strangely approving glance. "You've only been here for three days and have already begun working on your harem dynamics. Good job."

"There is no harem!" Kevin snapped. "I don't want a harem! I don't need a harem! And you!" He pointed at the ever-impassive Jasmine. "Stop calling yourself my slave! I don't have slaves! I don't want slaves!"

The other lesbo twin gave him a thumbs up. "Nice tsukkomi act."

Kevin slammed his face against the table. After ensuring that the table properly cracked underneath his face, he glared at the various vixens sitting across from him.

"... All my hate."

"There, there, Beloved." Lilian rubbed his back in a soothing manner. "I know that you have no desire for a harem. Don't worry, I will make sure to keep everyone but Iris and Christine from getting into your pants."

"What?"

"I said I'll keep all of these vixens away from you."

"Thank you, Lilian." Kevin sniffled as he looked at her. "You're the only person I can count on these days."

Lilian's eyes glistened with unshed, happy tears. "Of course you can count on me, Beloved. I'm your mate. You know that I would do anything for you."

"And I would do anything for you."

"Oh, Kevin."

"Lilian."

"Kevin!"

"Lilian!"

The two suddenly embraced, and everyone present witnessed something unusual—even for a group of kitsune. The dining hall that they were eating in vanished. The walls disappeared to be replaced by an alpine prairie, greenery as far as the eye could see, a true paradise of grass. The ceiling disappeared to reveal a clear blue sky and several mountains in the distance. In the center of this strange world that couldn't possibly have been real, Kevin and Lilian continued hugging each other.

"Huh." Violet stared at the scene, her face an amalgam of "*What the fuck?"* and *"I don't care. I'm eating."* "Now I've seen everything."

"What the hell is this?" asked Daphne, who gawked as several leaves blew past her face.

"Mother," Ivy said, gathering her mother's attention. "This grass is real."

"Really?" Holly bent down in her seat and plucked several blades of grass from underneath the table. She held each blade to her eyes and studied them. "Hmm, it seems you are correct. This grass is, indeed, real grass. This bears further investigation. For science."

"For science," Ivy agreed. As one, mother and daughter adjusted their glasses, which flashed in a dastardly sort of way.

Aster and Azalea also pulled out some grass and proceeded to make facial hair with them. Aster went with a handlebar mustache, while Azalea decided to create a fu manchu.

"You have now learned everything that you need to know, young grasshopper," Azalea said in a faux Chinese accent, while Aster twirled her handlebar with a thoughtful mien.

"I wonder… is it odd that I suddenly feel like riding a bicycle while singing Bohemian Rhapsody?"

"Hmm, yeah, probably, especially because neither of us have ever heard Bohemian Rhapsody."

"What a lovely scene," Marigold murmured to herself. She seemed to adore the alpine greenery surrounding her.

Standing behind her mistress like the ever-faithful maid that she was, Kirihime watched as Camellia grabbed several strands of grass, set them on the table, and began twisting them with surprisingly dexterous fingers.

"My Lady, what are you doing?"

"Um." Camellia gave Kirihime a bright smile. "I'm making a get well soon band for Iris."

"My Lady, that's so sweet." Kirihime's eyes glistened with unshed tears.

At the mention of Iris, Kevin and Lilian stopped hugging, causing the world to revert back to its normal paradigm as the tapestry of reality was restored. Oddly enough, to Kevin at least, the grass that Camellia had didn't disappear like it did for everyone else.

As breakfast resumed, Kevin's eyes strayed toward the head of the table. Delphine Pnéyma sat there, quietly eating her meal as she watched her family. Her placid smile seeped with amusement, and the way her eyes shone bothered him for reasons he still didn't understand.

Kevin couldn't place what it was about this woman that bothered him so much. Delphine had mentioned how his human mind inherently registered her power as a threat and dubbed it unsafe, but he didn't think that was the real reason he felt so uncomfortable around her. No, there had to be something else, something more than just her power, that bothered him so much.

"Oh, my." And she had noticed him looking at her. Just great. "If you keep staring at me like that, I might get pregnant."

"You can't get pregnant from someone staring at you," he grumbled irritably. He picked up a melitini from his plate and took a bite, savoring the sweet flavor. It wasn't exactly healthy for him, and Coach Deretaine would throw a fit if the man found out he'd eaten something like this. Kevin took another bite.

Just then, the dining hall doors opened and one of Delphine's sons strode into the room, his four fox tails swaying behind him.

"Ah! You're that bishy who treated Lilian like crap the other day!" Kevin pointed at the bishy in question, who glared at him in return.

"Shut up, brat! My name isn't bishy! It's Palladius!"

"Ugh, what an awful name." Kevin grimaced. "Your mother must hate you."

Delphine placed her hands on her cheeks. "Do you really think it's that awful of a name?"

"Yes." Kevin nodded. "Yes, it is. It's terrible. You should be ashamed of yourself."

"Oh, dear me, and I thought it was such a good name, too," she said, and then paused. "Then again, I was really drunk when I came up with that name…"

"… I hate you so much right now," Palladius growled.

"Is there something you needed to speak with me about, Palladius?" Delphine got back on track.

Palladius walked up to the matriarch and whispered in her ear. Kevin didn't know what was said, but whatever the bishy said to her, it must have been important, for the woman suddenly stood up, directing all attention to her.

She peered at her family, her nine silvery fox tails covering her body like a second toga. She glanced at Kevin, who clenched his fist— until Lilian's hand sought out his.

"Do forgive me, but it appears I must cut our breakfast short. It seems one of our clan's allies has become embroiled in some trouble, and they have requested my personal assistance. Daphne," she turned to her daughter, "until I return, you are in charge."

"Of course, Mother." Daphne seemed honestly astonished, but she accepted her mother's order with grace.

As the woman with nine tails left, a smattering of conversation broke out.

"That was weird," Aster mumbled before eating the grilled sausage in her sister's hand. Kevin wondered if the way she moaned around the long, cylindrical object was just how she naturally ate sausages—or if she was doing it to annoy Violet.

Probably the latter. Doesn't she go for tacos?

"Hm, hm." Marigold nodded at her younger sister's words. "It does seem odd that someone would request personal assistance from the matriarch, mukyu."

"What's so odd about that?" asked Kevin. When everyone turned to give him blank stares, he felt both embarrassed and annoyed. "What? I'm a human, remember? I don't know how your clan works."

"If you would allow me, I would be honored to explain, Kevin-sama," Kotohime said.

"Ah, go ahead, Kotohime."

"One thing that you must understand about kitsune is that our entire society has its own hierarchy. The lowest within this hierarchy are independent kitsune, those who do not belong to any clan. Following this are the members of smaller clans, then the heads of those small clans. Next in line are members of larger clans that are not one of the Thirteen Great Clans and their leaders. Then there are the Thirteen Great Clans themselves, followed by their heads. And at the top of this hierarchy are the Kyūbi, the three nine-tailed kitsune who rule over all."

"Granny's really important," Lilian added helpfully. Violet snorted into her drink.

"Pnéyma-denka is a Kyūbi," Kotohime continued. "As one of only three Kyūbi in the entire world, she stands at the top. They listen to no one's counsel but their own, and they do not take kindly to people who try to make personal requests of them. For someone to actually have the gall to personally request a Kyūbi's presence is not only unheard of, but downright foolish."

Kevin slowly nodded. "I guess that makes sense."

"Whoever asked for Mom must have balls of steel," Violet

commented, causing everyone else to nod.

***

Delphine followed Palladius through marble hallways and down a flight of stone steps. A massive room spread out before her. It appeared similar to a dome. The walls of the circular interior curved upwards into a spherical ceiling. Several gas-powered lamps lit her surroundings. In the center of this room stood a gate.

It was not an ordinary gate, like the kind found in front of a house, made from iron or steel or even wood. This gate was simply a large stone archway of intricate design. The columns holding up the triangular roof were not the standard Corinthian columns seen in other places of her estate, but were instead composed of Kyūbi statues. Each Kyūbi sat on its haunches, their nine tails arrayed behind them, twisting and curving in convoluted designs. Their eyes, two rubies, glimmered as light refracted off them.

Delphine stepped up to the Shrine Gate, her nine tails activating it. The eyes became alight with a vibrant glow. Arcs of arcane energy, youki both ancient and powerful, lanced out. The energy coalesced in the center, gathering into a ball, which soon expanded to encompass the entire space within the gate. Like a reflection on the water's surface, an image appeared within of a small garden overlooking a hamlet.

She didn't spare her son a second glance as she stepped through the portal, which rippled as she passed…

… and then she was standing on the other side, on the edge of a small cliff, the tiny hamlet she'd seen in the gate's surface expanding before her.

There was no one there.

Delphine frowned as no one greeted her, not a single living soul.

"How odd," she murmured to herself. She turned toward the path that led to the village. Deciding to continue on, she followed the path as it meandered down the cliff and soon entered the village proper.

The village before her was small, tiny, even when compared to Psyxế. She passed by small huts made of stone and wood. A few kitsune wandered the dirt road. They stopped when they saw her, and she frowned upon noticing the shocked looks etched upon their faces. She had to give them credit, though. Despite their surprise, they still stumbled into the semblance of a bow when she passed them, their bodies trembling.

A Fox's Revenge

She ignored the kitsune of the village and strode toward the small castle where the leader of this clan resided.

They appeared before her like fingers jutting up from the earth, a series of tall spires connected by a stone wall. Their design was stereotypical of castles found on the British Isles built during the Medieval Period. They were large, but she'd seen larger.

A guard stood by the portcullis. Upon seeing her stride toward him, his tails stiffened, his eyes bulged, and his mouth dropped. The expression amused her.

"L-Lady Kyūbi?!" he squeaked, then hurried to bow. "I-i-it is an honor to be in your presence, Your Grace!"

"Indeed," Delphine said. "I am here to speak with your leader. Would you please raise the gate for me?"

"O-of course!"

One of the lad's two tails extended and latched onto a lever, which it pulled. *Crank!* Delphine listened to the cranking and turning of an ancient pulley. The gate lifted slowly, a ponderous movement, like the turning of a clock whose gears had rusted over from centuries of disuse. Soon, however, the large gateway that blocked her from entering fully opened, revealing the courtyard within, and beyond that, the small castle where this clan's matriarch resided.

"Thank you. Now, if you'd please take me to your leader, I would be most appreciative." She smiled at the lad, whose face turned a bright red. Oh, my. How adorable.

"A-at once, Your Grace."

As the young kitsune lead her into the castle, Delphine hoped that this clan's leader had a good explanation for the discourteous treatment. It was an insult to not be greeted when first arriving. If she didn't find the excuse satisfactory, then family or no, there would be punishment.

No one insulted a Kyūbi.

***

Kevin sat on one of the many benches interspersed throughout the garden. He was bored. It was odd. Here he was, experiencing a world beyond anything he'd imagined, living among a group of kitsune, surrounded by more than half a dozen beautiful women, and he was bored.

Eric would be most disappointed in me.

Lilian was busy running from Daphne, who was attempting to teach

278

her something. Again. He didn't know where Kotohime was, though he imagined she was sparring with Ayane. He'd discovered this morning that those two had some kind of rivalry, which he guessed made sense. Ninja and Samurai never really got along in anime and manga. Their philosophies were too different. Something like that.

What should I do now?

He supposed he could clean his guns, but he'd already done that this morning after his and Lilian's spar with Kotohime. He could also do some exercise, but considering Kotohime had kicked the crap out of him for at least an hour before lunch, exercise wasn't something he felt keen on doing. Really, there wasn't much he could do.

Man, Lilian was right. Once the novelty of this place wears off, it's actually really boring.

His thoughts were knocked out of focus when footsteps sounded out behind him. He turned his head just in time to see four bushy fox tails rushing toward him.

He saw nothing after that.

***

Calenthia Vættir was the head of the Vættir Clan, a minor spirit clan that lived in Britain. She was actually the younger sister of Camellia, who'd originally been next in line to become clan head.

She looked almost exactly like her older sister. Long black hair reminiscent of a wave flowed down a face that looked nearly identical to Camellia's but younger. Adorning her body was a simple dress made of black satin. Despite its simplicity, it fit her well, emphasizing her womanly curves while maintaining a sense of modesty. The slit that ran up the side revealed a good amount of leg, showing off milky white thighs and calves. Further covering her body were four tails, which gently caressed her figure like velvety serpents.

"Matriarch Pnéyma," the woman greeted with a pleasant smile. Delphine withheld her frown. "It's a pleasure to see you again. I hope my sister is doing well."

"Camellia is doing fine," Delphine answered with her own composed smile. "She is happy as always."

"I am pleased to hear that." Calenthia shifted. "You know, it's very rare for you to visit another clan. May I inquire as to what brought you here?"

Now *that* made Delphine frown. "Did you not ask for my

279

presence?"

Calenthia blinked. "No, of course not. I know better than to personally ask the Silver Queen of the Netherworld for assistance when I have nothing to offer her."

Delphine closed her eyes. "I see." A mirthful smile crossed her face. "It seems I have been hoodwinked into coming here."

"Matriarch Pnéyma?"

"It is nothing," Delphine said, turning her smile on Calenthia. "Since it seems you did not call me here, and if my assumption is correct, I will not be able to return home for a while, why don't you and I have a cup of tea?"

"Ah, um, very well." Calenthia appeared confused, but fortunately for her, she decided not to argue and merely had her servants bring them a cup of tea.

***

Lilian was worried.

Kevin had gone missing. She wasn't sure how long it had been since he disappeared—mainly because she'd been getting chased by Daphne, who seemed intent on teaching her what it took to be a *proper Pnéyma female*. However, after knocking the vixen out with a stink bomb to the face, she'd managed to escape her evil aunt's clutches and went in search of her mate.

Only he wasn't anywhere to be found. She had searched the entire Pnéyma grounds, including Holly's and Ivy's dwelling, to see if they were experimenting on him, and Jasmine's abode, to make sure she wasn't trying to convince her beloved to commit acts of eroticism on her.

He hadn't been in either of those places. No one knew where he was, it seemed. Not Violet, not Kotohime or her sister, not her mother. It was like he'd disappeared. That was when she'd begun to panic.

After informing Kotohime that Kevin was missing, she and her maid convinced the other members of her family to help her search. They'd scoured the entire Pnéyma grounds, but no one could find hide nor hair of him. It truly was as if he had vanished into thin air.

Which was why Lilian had decided to search Psyxé.

The sun had begun to set. She looked up at the sky, which held the appearance of having been lit on fire. She must have been searching for at least six hours now. Her gaze came back down, and she walked up to the first person she saw. Perhaps it was fate that this person just

280

A Fox's Revenge

happened to be Berenise.

"Your mate?" Berenise blinked when Lilian asked if the woman had seen Kevin. "Yes, I saw him a while back. It must have been an hour ago. He seemed to be deep in thought. The boy barely even noticed when I greeted him."

"Which way did he go?" Lilian asked.

"That way." Berenise pointed toward the south. Lilian frowned. That was near the resort.

"Thank you." Lilian nodded at the woman before running in the direction indicated.

"You're welcome!" She heard Berenise call out to her.

Cobblestone soon became dirt. The path she'd been following disappeared. That meant the barrier was still active. It was a good thing the barrier didn't affect her. Reinforcing her legs, Lilian pushed herself toward the famous Pnévma Resort.

In many ways, the Pnévma Resort could be likened to a miniature city. It wasn't large, but it possessed a large number of amenities, such as shops, restaurants, and other attractions, just like one might expect of a city. All the buildings were connected via a series of paved walkways interspersed with plants found in tropical Mediterranean areas. She bypassed all the buildings, eventually reaching the beach.

Kevin was there.

"Beloved, there you are." Lilian walked over to the young man. He stood with his back to her, staring out at the ocean. "You really shouldn't wander off like that. I doubt anyone from the Shénshèng Clan can get here, but it's not a good idea to pass through the barrier. You wouldn't be able to get back through without one of us escorting you."

Kevin said nothing. He didn't even turn around. Lilian frowned as she stopped behind him and placed a hand on his shoulder.

"Kevin, are you—"

Lilian didn't know what happened. One second she was about to say something, and the next she was nearly swallowing her tongue as her back slammed against the sandy beach. Kevin stared down at her, and for the first time since she'd found him, Lilian saw the look in his eyes.

They were blank. Dead. The lights were on but no one was home. She recognized that look.

That's—

"A-ah—guagh!"

Lilian gasped in pain as something powerful slammed into her

281

torso, a foot, she belatedly realized. Her world spun. Sand was kicked up all around her as she tumbled for several feet before landing on her stomach.

"K-Kevin," she gasped out as tears sprung to her eyes. "W-why?"

"It isn't right to blame him," a familiar voice said. Lilian gritted her teeth as someone appeared next to Kevin, their form shimmering into existence, wavering like a ghost before solidifying. "After all, he's not really in control of himself. I'd much rather take the blame for what's happening here."

Lilian rose to her feet, wincing. Kevin's legs were damnably strong. She knew that from watching him run track, but she hadn't realized just how strong until he'd kicked her. That blow had rattled her ribs. She held a hand to her bruised torso and glared at her uncle.

"P-Palladius, why are you doing this?"

"Are you really asking me that? Can you not guess?" Palladius spread his arms wide. "I wish to see the Pnévma Clan destroyed."

"W-what?" Lilian wondered if she sounded as dumbfounded as she felt. "D-destroyed? But why? Why would you want to destroy our clan? They're family!"

Sure, she had never gotten along with any of her family members outside of her mom and Iris, but that didn't mean she wanted them dead. They were still family.

Palladius spat as if he'd just had something foul shoved into his mouth.

"Those damn vixens are no family of mine!" The anger in his voice took Lilian aback. "Ever since I gained my second tail, they've treated me like I was their slave! Three centuries of servitude and what have I gotten out of it? Nothing! The Pnévma Clan doesn't care for me! Why should they? I'm just a male, right? The Pnévma Clan is a matriarchal clan by nature. They don't care about their male members beyond what we can do for them. We're just pawns and slaves for Delphine and her ilk to use and abuse! People like that don't deserve to live!"

Lilian's heart pounded in her chest like *Mjölnir* was hitting her ribs. The look Palladius gave her was full of hatred and malice. She felt like he was cutting her skin with nothing but a glance.

"You know, I really hate you," Palladius told her, and his words hurt more than she thought they would. "For a time, I thought you and I shared a common bond. Both of us were just pawns to be used and tossed away by the matriarch when it was convenient. I used to think

282

that maybe you would be able to understand me, but I was wrong."

Palladius clenched his hands into fists. Blood leaked from between his fingers, dripping onto the sand.

"When the matriarch began setting up mating arrangements for you, you became defiant. You pranked every kitsune the matriarch sent, putting them through hell. Rather than punish you for your disobedience, Delphine became amused and allowed you to continue, until Jiāoào came along. Then the matriarch had you sent away in order to protect you."

"Protect me?" Lilian gawked.

Had the matriarch truly sent her out of Greece for her own safety? She had always thought that her grandmother had sent her away because she kept causing problems, but what if that wasn't true? What if her grandmother really had been looking to protect her from Jiāoào?

"After that, I realized how different you and I are," Palladius, unaware of her thoughts, continued. "The matriarch would have never done that for me. I would have been mated off to the first person she chose, and if I defied her, she would have banished me from the clan—a fate worse than death, as you well know."

Lilian did know. She knew quite a bit about banishing people. After all, her father had been banished from the clan before she'd even gained her second tail, and Daphne had made sure to rub that in at least once or twice a day before she'd been sent to live in the United States.

"Now then, I believe we have spoken long enough," Palladius determined. "I merely wanted you to know who to blame for your soon-to-be unfortunate fate." Palladius turned to Kevin. "Capture your mate for me—oh! And do be sure to roughen her up a bit, if you would."

Lilian had scarcely any time to comprehend Palladius's order before Kevin burst forward. Out of shock, she stumbled back, but that didn't do much. Her mate was incredibly fleet-footed. He was inside her guard within seconds.

An asphyxiating pain shot through her chest as an open palm struck her. Her head snapped back when an elbow smacked against her chin. She tumbled, almost falling backwards, before a hand latched around her wrist in an iron grip and pulled her into a powerful knee that caused all the oxygen to leave her lungs.

With her arms around her waist, Lilian slumped to her knees, trying to suck in that which would not come. The attack combination that Kevin hit her with had been specifically designed to incapacitate. She

A Fox's Revenge

knew that because it was one of the combinations they had worked on together. Her job would normally be to cast an illusion over Kevin to displace his body, making it seem like he was farther away than he really was. She never expected this combination to be used on her.

"B-Beloved," she rasped. "You have to snap out of it. Please, don't let him use you. You're stronger than that."

Kevin merely blinked. Palladius laughed.

"Oh, this is such a riot! You really think a lowly human could escape my enchantment? I'm a four-tailed kitsune, girl! My power is beyond the comprehension of some lowly ape. There's no way someone like him can escape my enchantment. Humans are weak, powerless creatures. They can only rely on technology and are unable to do anything for themselves. That's why it's so easy to manipulate and bend them to our will."

Lilian ignored Palladius. She ignored everything except Kevin, whom she stared at, pleading with him to come to his senses.

"Don't let that man control you, Beloved! You're stronger than that! I know you are!"

Kevin still did not say anything. However, while he said nothing, his lips did move. They formed a single word.

… *Run.*

Lilian's eyes widened seconds before her mate kicked her. She managed to raise her arms, blocking the kick, and she even managed to reinforce her limbs, but she was still sent sprawling backwards.

"Gya!"

She landed on her back, and looked up just in time to see Kevin's foot flying at her. Lilian rolled. The attack stomped on the ground where she'd been lying on previously. She scrambled to her feet just as Kevin came in to attack again.

Time seemed to slow down. Lilian saw Kevin moving as if he was wading through molasses. The world around her seemed distorted, like those life-changing moments before death where one's life flashed before their eyes.

Only this was different. Rather than seeing her life flashing before her, she saw choices. There were any number of choices that she could make in this moment, any number of infinite possibilities. She could run. She could fight. She could attack Kevin. She could attack Palladius. She could use illusions. A limitless number of possible options were presented to her.

A Fox's Revenge

She chose one of those options.

Kevin rushed toward her. His lips continued moving, telling her to run. Even now, with his body being controlled, he fought against the enchantment. He fought for her. She would not abandon him.

He raised a fist, prepared to hit her. Rather than run away or even defend herself, Lilian rushed forward with reinforced speed. She stumbled into him and wrapped her arms around his waist, hugging him before he could attack.

"You don't have to let this man control you, Kevin," Lilian said to the stock-still Kevin. "You're stronger than this. I know you're stronger than he is. Your will is stronger, your determination is stronger. You are my mate, and I wouldn't pick a mate whose will is weaker than someone like that."

"Li... Li..."

"I love you, Kevin. I need you, so you have to come back to me. Please, come back."

All at once, the fight went out of Kevin. He collapsed against her like a *Z Fighter* who'd run out of ki. They both went down. Lilian sat on the ground as Kevin fell against her. She held him to her chest as his breathing, hot and heavy like he'd just run a marathon, hit the bare skin of her bosoms.

"Lilian..."

"Shh." Lilian stroked his hair. "Don't talk. You're exhausted from having fought off Palladius's enchantment."

"M'sorry," Kevin mumbled tiredly. "I let him... use me to... t-to hurt you."

"Don't apologize. There's no need to. You did nothing wrong."

"But I—"

"I'm so proud of you," Lilian's words, whispered against his hair, made Kevin stop talking. "You fought off a four-tailed kitsune's enchantment. There are many yōkai who can't accomplish such a feat, yet you did. You were incredible."

"Was I Simon the Digger incredible?"

"Mm... maybe... Shinji Ikari incredible."

"That's a harsh thing to say to your mate."

"Haha, okay, how about, um, D incredible?"

Lilian felt Kevin's lips curving into a smile against her chest.

"I suppose that's fine. There are worse characters to be compared to than a ten thousand- year-old immortal vampire hunter."

"W-what is going on here?!"

It wasn't until Palladius's enraged shout sounded across the beach that Lilian remembered there was someone else with them. Lilian's attention turned from her mate to the fox who had manipulated him. The four-tail's enraged face had turned a deep red, but she could also sense his bafflement. He clearly couldn't figure out how Kevin managed to break free of his enchantment.

I'm certainly not going to tell him.

"Why aren't you doing what you're told?!" Palladius barked at Kevin, who stiffened in her arms. His hands groped against the sand, grabbing onto something and gripping it tightly. "Attack her! Attack her, attack her, attack her, att—bugufu!"

"Shut up!" Kevin shouted, whirling in Lilian's arms and throwing a seashell that beamed Palladius upside the head. "You think I'm going to listen to you anymore! Think again, Sparkles!"

"S-sparkles?!" Palladius growled, his face turning redder than Lilian's fur. "That does it! I was hoping to amuse myself by watching you beat up Lilian, but since you're not going to listen, I'll have to content myself by killing you in front of your mate!"

***

"Tch."

Kevin clicked his tongue as he tried to stand up. His legs gave out. He stumbled into Lilian, who helped him rise.

"You shouldn't move so quickly," Lilian whispered. "You're still experiencing the aftereffects of having been enchanted."

"You're probably right," Kevin agreed, forcing himself to stand in spite of his own words. "However, I don't think your uncle's going to let me just sit around, and I'm not gonna let you fight on your own."

He pulled himself from Lilian's grasp and turned to face Palladius, the man who'd manipulated him, who'd controlled him as though he were a puppet, who'd ordered him to attack his mate. Kevin always considered himself a kind person. He rarely ever allowed himself to hate someone. Over the course of his life, there were only three people that he truly hated: Jiāoào, Seth, and Luna. Now he could add a fourth to that list.

No one makes me hurt one of my loved ones and gets away with it.

"You ready?" Kevin asked, not turning to face Lilian. He didn't need to. He could sense her nodding behind him.

"Of course I am, Beloved."

"I don't have my guns on me, so we'll have to use one of the melee formations that we've devised."

"Right."

"Then let's go. I don't wanna give this guy an opportunity to attack us."

Lilian said nothing. She and Kevin rushed toward Palladius, who seemed surprised by their sudden straightforward assault. He sneered a second later, however, as though their actions amused him instead of baffled him.

"You think an ape and a two-tails are going to be a match for me? **Kitsune Art—**"

"Gomu Gomu no Extension!"

Palladius was forced to cancel his technique when Lilian's tails, twisted to look like a pair of drills, shot forward. He jumped back as one of them slammed against the ground he'd been standing on. The other struck the ground several feet away. The dust it kicked up created a smokescreen that kept Palladius from attacking them.

Lilian hung back and wove her illusion. Kevin used the smokescreen to close the gap between him and their foe. He rushed in, primed and ready to take his enemy down with a strong left hook. Palladius growled and used extension to pierce Kevin through the stomach before he could close the distance—or so Palladius thought.

"What the—?" Palladius's eyes widened as his tail went right through Kevin, who dispersed into thousands of light particles. "It was an—"

He didn't get to finish his sentence. In that single second, Kevin—the real Kevin—plowed his right fist into Palladius's face. As he drove his fist forward, Kevin felt the kitsune's nose break under the brutal attack.

Behind Kevin, Lilian wrapped her tails around a pair of metal poles meant for volleyball. She pulled herself back, the tails stretching like rubber bands. Then, all at once, she let herself go. Like a paper football, she was launched high above the heads of Kevin and Palladius.

Knowing that he couldn't give his enemy time to recover, Kevin grabbed Palladius by his ears, then yanked him down into a brutal knee before the kitsune could think of using reinforcement to weather the assault.

The four-tails stumbled back. Blood welled up in his nose. He blinked several times as though doing so might help.

Kevin smiled. It wouldn't help.

Barely a second passed before Lilian fell back to the ground, right on top of Palladius.

"Lilian Kick!"

Kevin deadpanned as Lilian's left foot slammed into Palladius like an entire pantheon of angry gods. He could swear he actually saw the four-tail's face cave in from the attack, almost like he was watching the action in slow motion. Then life sped back up and all he saw was a large cloud of sand spraying everywhere as Palladius's body was driven into the ground like a meteor striking the earth. Kevin had to raise his arms to his eyes in order to protect his vision.

"How do you like that, jerk?" The kicked-up sand cleared to reveal Lilian gloating down at her opponent, hands on her hips, and a smug look on her face. "Next time you mess with my mate, I won't go so easy on you."

"Lilian."

"Beloved!" Her smiling face lighting up like a beacon at night, Lilian ran up to him. "Did you see that? So what do you think? My attacks were really cool, right?"

"They were pretty cool," Kevin admitted slowly. "However, you really should change the name of that first move you did. Seriously, Lilian, didn't I tell you that we could be sued for copyright if you used that name?"

"But I like that attack name." Lilian crossed her arms and huffed. "I got it from the Straw Hat Pirate."

"And that is exactly why you should change it," Kevin told her. "Besides, you never used Japanese words in your technique names before. Why start now?"

Lilian pouted. "Muu, fine."

"Good girl." Kevin gave Lilian a quick peck before looking at the laid out Palladius. "Hey, Lilian, is it just me, or was that battle really easy?"

"It's not just you." Lilian shook her head. "Don't you remember? Most kitsune don't like battles. Kotohime and I weren't lying when we said that. Only a few kitsune clans actually train their members in combat. The women of our clan all receive some basic training, but none of them are what you would call fighters. Only the more martial clans like the Shénshèng Clan of Bodhisattva, the Great Void Clan of Gitsune,

A Fox's Revenge

and the Great Earth Clan of Zamlya have combat-oriented kitsune. The rest of us usually have vassals like Kotohime, Kirihime, and Ayane to protect us."

"I know that much," Kevin said. "I just, well, I guess I was expecting him to be a little more powerful."

"That's because you're so used to sparring against people like Kiara, or fighting against monsters like Seth and that Fan lady," Lilian informed him. "Of course you're going to expect yōkai to be more powerful when you use someone like Kiara and Kotohime as examples of how strong yōkai should be. And Palladius is powerful. He has four tails. He's just not a very good fighter."

"I guess…"

"It looks like Palladius lost," a voice that didn't belong to either him or Lilian said. "What an utter disappointment. Then again, what else could I have expected from a member of the Pnéyma Clan?"

Kevin and Lilian whirled around to face the source of this new voice. Three people were standing on the beach with them. Two were unfamiliar males, but the last member they both knew quite well. After all, she had attempted to kill them a little less than two weeks ago.

"It's you!" Kevin pointed.

"Hello, Lilian Pnéyma, Kevin Swift." Fan greeted them with a cruel smile. "I hope you don't mind dying for me today."

Chapter 10

Pnéyma Versus Shénshèng

Kevin knew that he and Lilian were in a bind. He stared at the trio of kitsune across from them. They stood closer to the shore, the waves nipping at their heels. He recognized Fan, of course, and she still wore her white lolita outfit. The other two were unfamiliar.

He studied the two men standing on either side of Fan. One of them was a giant of a man. He stood several heads and shoulders above Kevin. His body was like a wall of muscle. He had a buzzed head, and wore the garb of a Shaolin monk. Five tails waved behind him.

The other looked even weirder. He had blond hair like Fan and the tall bishounen looks that Kevin had come to expect from male kitsune. What really got to Kevin was his armor. It was the kind of armor expected of a Chinese warlord, shining silver with gold trimmings and a golden Kyūbi motif on the breastplate. That outfit looked like something straight out of *Dynasty Warriors*. His eyes were bright blue. He had seven tails.

"Man, that was really something to watch," the armored one said, scratching the nape of his neck. "To think a human and a two-tails were able to beat up a four-tails."

Fan scoffed. "Don't make it sound like they performed some incredible feat, Zhìlì. That kitsune was a pathetic waste of space with no

291

martial talent. He was just like every other kitsune. I could have beaten him easily."

"Heh, true enough."

The tall one crossed his arms. "Lady Fan, Honorable Father, I understand your desire for banter, and I may be out of place saying this, but perhaps we should grab the girl now before her family has time to realize she's missing?"

"Hm." The one called Zhìlì cupped his chin and hummed in thought. "Yeah, I guess you have a point. While I doubt any of those women are a match for us, it would be a pain if we had to fight them, especially since they outnumber us. All right, Li, you retrieve the girl. Oh, and kill the human while you're at it."

"You know that I abhor violence." Li stepped forward. Kevin stiffened and moved to stand in front of Lilian. "I admire your courage, young human. However, that courage is currently misplaced. Please, stand aside and allow me to take Lilian Pnéyma. There is no need for you to die this day."

"Screw that," Kevin snapped at the audacity of this man. "Who the hell do you think I am?! You think I'm just going to leave my mate to your tender mercies? That I'd let people like you take her from me? That's not the kind of person I am!"

"Kevin." Lilian's soft mutter made Kevin move further in front of her, blocking his mate from the group.

"Hmm?" Zhìlì murmured with the thoughtful air of a sage. "This boy, he's very shōnen, isn't he?"

"Be serious for once, Zhìlì," Fan chided her older brother. "We have a job to do."

He sighed. "Right. Right."

"I understand," Li said. "If that is how you feel, then I shall make your death quick and painless."

Kevin felt a chill of fear rush down his spine. The absolute certainty with which the towering mass of muscle spoke, that quiet confidence, it scared Kevin more than he was willing to admit. The way Li talked about killing him as if he was already dead truly frightened him.

But that didn't mean he could give up. No, he couldn't give up. These people were trying to take Lilian. They wanted his mate, and he would not let them take her.

"Lilian," he whispered out of the corner of his mouth.

"Yes?"

"I hope you have a plan for dealing with them because I'm stumped."

"I'm afraid I don't know what to do either," Lilian admitted. "I could cast an illusion on Fan, maybe, but I don't have enough power to pull the wool over all three of them. Those two men are beyond my power."

"I thought you'd say that." Kevin's mind ran a thousand miles a minute. "Do you have anything that can create a smokescreen?"

"Um, I do have some smoke bombs that I made to help me escape from Daphne."

"Those will work. On my mark, I want you to toss all of them on the ground."

"Okay."

"I hope you two have finished saying your goodbyes." Li sounded surprisingly sincere for someone who was about to kill a person. "While I do not like tearing two people apart, nor do I enjoy violence, I can guarantee that this will be the last time you two will ever see each other again."

Kevin didn't listen. He counted to three.

"Now, Lilian!"

Lilian reached into her Extra Dimensional Storage Space and pulled out sixteen smoke bombs, all of which she threw on the ground around them. A large cloud of acrid black smoke billowed out, covering the area. Kevin nearly gagged as the thick fumes threatened to burn his lungs. Had Lilian added pepper to these things? He covered his mouth and nose with his shirt, grabbed Lilian's hand, and took off in the direction of the resort.

***

"What do you think we should do?" asked Lilian.

Kevin looked at his mate. He and Lilian were hiding out in one of the many shops in the Pnévma Resort. All around them were various types of paraphernalia: shirts and shorts, necklaces and earrings, wakeboards and surfboards. The clothing hung in racks and the items sat on shelves. He and his mate were hiding behind the register booth.

"We need to get back to your family's home," Kevin said. "We can't take on a five-tails, much less a seven-tails. Fan we might be able to beat now that we've come up with a plan to deal with someone like her, but not those other two."

"Yeah." Lilian grimaced. "There's no way we'll be able to defeat them."

Kevin noticed the way Lilian's hands were shaking.

She must be afraid. We've been in our fair share of fights, but we've never faced off against such powerful enemies, especially not all at once.

"We'll get out of this." Kevin placed his hands over Lilian's. "Try not to worry too much. These kitsune may be powerful, but they're not infallible. Everyone has a weakness that can be exploited. We just need to find theirs."

"Paraphrasing Kotohime?" Lilian smiled.

Kevin returned it. "She knows what she's talking about. Now, let's get out of here before they discover we're hiding here."

He and Lilian moved to the front of the store. They hid underneath a large glass window, which Kevin peered through to see if their enemies were anywhere near them. It didn't look like anybody was there.

The biggest issue I can see is leaving the resort itself. There's no cover between the resort and the forest. However, once we make it into the forest surrounding the village, we should be safe. We can lose them within the foliage and pass through the barrier.

"Come on." Kevin grabbed Lilian's hand and the two of them left the store. They moved quickly down the various walkways, using trees and buildings as cover. No one seemed to be around, which meant they had a chance to escape. They just needed to reach the trees. Then they would be—

"It looks like I found you," a voice said.

Kevin moved on instinct. He spun around and put himself in front of Lilian, his body growing tense as he prepared for an attack that didn't come. Zhìlì stood before them, his armor gleaming in the moonlight.

"You didn't really think you could escape from us, did you?"

Kevin bit his lip as he shoved his fear to the side. He couldn't afford to let fear rule him.

"I was kinda hoping we could, yeah," he said.

"Hm, well, it was a good plan. On any other kitsune, it may have worked, but I've lived among humans for at least one hundred years now. I know quite a bit more about your species than most."

Kevin nearly swore. It sounded like they never really had a chance of escaping to begin with.

"Well, I guess I should end this." Three of Zhìlì's seven tails came

294

to the fore, light gathering at their tips. "I'll make it quick. **Celestial Art: Triple Helix.**"

The name resounded ominously loud. From within the light created by the three tails, a beam emerged—no, not a beam. A spiral. Three three-dimensional cylinders that spiraled around each other in the form of a helix shot at him and Lilian.

Not knowing what else to do, Kevin shoved Lilian out of the way before the beams could reach them. However, this left him defenseless and unable to save himself from the spiraling energy attack. He could do nothing but watch as his vision was filled with golden youki.

"KEVIN!"

"AEGIS!"

Kevin stared. Lilian stared. Even Zhìlì stared. A glowing sphere of unholy silver light had appeared between them. Strange figures, disturbingly anthropomorphic, danced over the sphere's surface, howling and moaning and cursing their dark fate. They gobbled up the helix attack, eating as though it were a feast, even though doing so caused them to scream even more.

Zhìlì's eyes widened. "This is…!"

"**Aegis of the Soul,**" a familiar voice said in a surprisingly solemn tone. "It is a technique that I created myself, many years ago, back before I became a mother."

Everyone turned to watch as a woman strode calmly up the walkway, her expression unbothered, her pace neither hurried nor rushed. She seemed calm, composed. She walked with a grace that Kevin had never seen before, and it disturbed him greatly, especially because he knew this woman shouldn't possess such a graceful bearing.

"M-Mom?" Lilian muttered in shock, staring at the woman with wide, unblinking eyes.

Camellia smiled at her daughter. It was not a smile of childish delight, but the kind someone gave when they felt relief at seeing a loved one safe. It was the smile of a mother.

"Lilian, my beautiful daughter."

"What… what…"

"Please, there will be time for us to talk later. For now, you and your mate must leave this place. It is about to become a battleground, and I would rather you two not see any more bloodshed than you already have."

"Battleground," Kevin muttered before noticing the other presences.

Daphne and Kirihime stood on either side of Zhìlì, both appearing more than ready to take the seven-tailed kitsune's head should he make a single wrong move.

"It was foolish of you and your clansmen to come here." Daphne's voice had never sounded so serious to Kevin's ears. Then again, she was usually shrieking at Lilian, so maybe that was why.

"Hm, I do seem to be in some trouble." Zhìlì eyed the glowing silver blade in Daphne's hand, which caressed his throat as if longing to slice it open. "**Soul Forging,** huh. I'll admit that weapon is scary, being composed of damned souls cursed to wander the earth and all, but you don't honestly think something like that is going to be a match for me, do you?"

Light erupted from Zhìlì's body like geysers of white fire bursting from the ground. The blade that Daphne held shattered as she and Kirihime were launched away from the seven-tailed kitsune. Kirihime flipped around so she landed on her feet, but Daphne proved herself to be a bit less graceful. She landed on her butt.

"Celestial Art: Quadruple Helix."

Instead of three cylinders forming a helix, four shot at Kevin and Lilian. It seemed they were still his targets.

"Aegis!"

The quadruple helix beams met the Aegis. The silvery shield howled, the unholy screams of the damned making themselves known. The helix pushed against the shield, light exploding everywhere in its attempt to pierce the defensive technique. It struggled and shoved, yet the shield held strong. The helix attack weakened, its power lessening, before it sputtered and died.

"Tch, that's an awfully powerful shield," Zhìlì admitted with a frown.

"Of course. It is a shield that uses the power of five hundred souls," Camellia said. "Even a seven-tails such as yourself would have trouble destroying it."

Camellia turned to Kevin and held out her hands. He looked down. Within her grip were his two guns.

"Uh, thank you," he mumbled as he took the weapons. The magazine clips were already inside and fully charged.

"You are welcome." Camellia's grin showed off her sharp canines. "I figured you might want them. While I don't necessarily approve of someone so young fighting, I realize there isn't much choice. Please make good use of these, and also, try not to forget them from now on, okay?"

"O-okay."

After handing Kevin his guns, Camellia walked over to Lilian, who gaped at her mother's calm demeanor. The beautiful five-tailed kitsune knelt and smiled at her daughter.

"Lilian." A hand reached up and caressed her daughter's cheek. "I want you and your mate to get out of here. I cannot fight and protect you two at the same time."

"Uh, um…"

Lilian was at a loss for words. Kevin understood. This woman who stood before them, speaking in such a calm manner, was not the same woman they had come to know. Her eyes were sharper, she spoke more clearly and, perhaps the biggest change of all, her childish demeanor had disappeared entirely. This was not the Camellia that Lilian had known all her life. This was the Camellia who'd existed before she became pregnant.

Already sensing Lilian's incertitude, Kevin spoke for them both. "We'll leave things to you, then."

Camellia directed her smile to him. "Thank you. I couldn't have asked my daughter to find a better mate."

Kevin blushed, but that was all he did in response to her words. He helped Lilian to her feet, grabbed her hand, and began pulling her along as he ran from what would soon become the place of a battle that he didn't want to get caught up in.

"Kevin… that… Mom was…"

"I know." Kevin gave the uncertain Lilian a smile. "Perhaps the damage to her mind is finally beginning to heal somehow, but we don't really have time to think about that right now. Let's focus on getting back to your family's home in one piece. Then, when all this is over, you can sit down with your mother and talk."

"I… Yes, you're right."

Kevin glanced over his shoulder, back at the spot where they'd left Camellia, Daphne, and Kirihime. He hoped they would be able to defeat that Zhìlì guy. He didn't want his mate to feel the heartache of losing her mother a second time.

***

Camellia watched her daughter and Kevin leave. It relieved her to

298

know that Lilian had chosen such a strong mate. He might have only been human, but he was clearly dedicated toward doing everything he could to stand beside Lilian as her equal. Perhaps, in time, he could even find a way to match a yōkai's strength on his own.

She shifted her attention back to Zhìlì. The fingers of her left hand began drumming against her thigh for reasons only she could understand. He had not moved since she, Kirihime, and Daphne had appeared. He stood in the same place, unbothered by how his quarry had escaped.

"I am surprised that you did not try to go after them," Camellia said as Daphne and Kirihime stood silently at her side.

Zhìlì shrugged. "There is still Fan and Li. I'm sure they will be enough to capture the girl."

Camellia wasn't too concerned by his words. While she didn't know where this Fan was, she knew that Li was already being engaged by a very eager swordswoman who wanted a rematch.

"Despite this armor that I wear, I don't really like fighting, you know," Zhìlì continued. "I only do so when Father commands me to. I would much rather go to the human world and find a nice woman to bed. That being said, Father has commanded me to capture the Pnévma girl, so here I am, despite my wish to the contrary."

"That's of little concern to me."

Camellia felt her body become primed and ready for combat. It had been many years since she last experienced a battle, and she would not deny that she was worried, but so long as Zhìlì did not discover the secret to her techniques, she was confident in their victory.

"Daphne," she said. "You are the best illusionist within the clan. I need you to distract him by engaging in a battle of illusions."

Daphne frowned at being ordered around, but she also understood that combat was not her field of expertise. Before giving birth to Lilian and Iris, Camellia had never lost in their spars despite having less tails.

"Very well."

"Kirihime, Daphne and I will create an opening for you to strike. Can I count on you?"

"Of course, My Lady. I'll be sure to rend this man's flesh from his bones." Grinning from ear to ear, Kirihime licked her daggers. "I wonder if I'll be able to make something nice once I skin him."

Camellia felt a small trail of sweat trickle down the left side of her head. "Um, right. I'm counting on you."

A Fox's Revenge

***

She stood on the beach, katana in hand. Her wakizashi was still hidden beneath her obi. She would only use it after confirming her opponent's abilities.

"I'm surprised to see you again. I guess you're eager to once more find yourself embracing defeat."

Kotohime stood across from Li, the kitsune who had beaten her the last time they fought. She slid her feet wide and bent her knees. She stared at her adversary with the look of a hardened veteran, someone who had faced countless battles and come out victorious.

"The last time you and I fought, I was at a disadvantage," Kotohime declared with quiet confidence. "You knew who I was, yet I knew nothing about you. Things will be different this time."

"Do you truly believe that?" Li asked. Kotohime didn't answer. It was a rhetorical question. "While I admire your courage in facing me again, you must realize that the power difference between us is too vast for you to overcome. I have more than five times more youki at my disposal than you."

A kitsune's power, or rather, the amount of youki they had, increased by a factor of the number of tails they had. Kitsune with three tails had two times more than they did at two. Consequently, a kitsune with five tails had five times more youki than a kitsune with four. While some four-tailed youki were born with more power than most, it was true that a five-tailed kitsune almost always possessed more youki. That was just the natural order of this world.

"Power is not everything," Kotohime said softly. *Click!* Her thumb flicked her katana out of its sheath as she settled into battoujutsu stance. "Allow me to show you right now why I was once feared as the Blood Moon Princess."

"I see there is no stopping you." Li did not change his stance, merely stood there. "If you will not desist in this course of action, then I will show you the error of your ways through force. Know that I do not fight with you because I want to. I only do so because I must."

Kotohime would have snorted at his words. If he did not enjoy battle, then he should not have come here in the first place. She said nothing, however, merely prepared herself for the second round of her battle against Li.

The two stood there on opposite ends, staring each other down. The waves washing against the beach created a gentle melody that contrasted starkly with the heavy atmosphere. This sand would soon become painted in blood.

"**Ikken Hissatsu.**"

Kotohime rushed forward in a burst of speed. She swerved around Li's body, coming at him from behind.

"**Eien Ni.**"

Her blade flashed out quicker than most beings in this world were capable of following. An indeterminate number of sword slices struck at Li. None of them hit.

Kotohime narrowed her eyes as she saw each and every one of her attacks phase right through him. Her sword would move, vanish into his skin, then emerge from the other side without a single drop of blood on it. The only thing to signify what happened were the lines of light that her blade drew across his body.

Realizing that her attacks were doing nothing, Kotohime leapt back. Li still hadn't moved.

"It seems my estimation of your ability was correct." Kotohime nodded to herself. "You are not dodging my attacks at all, nor is this some kind of illusion, or even a power like the Ghost Step. You have simply turned your body into light."

Li's frown was the only indicator that let Kotohime know she had surprised him.

"You are correct. I am most impressed that you were able to figure out my ability after only one fight. You truly are a fierce warrior. However, knowing how my power works and finding a way around it are two different things. In the end, knowing will not matter. I will defeat you regardless. You might be fast and strong, but nothing is faster than the speed of light."

Kotohime reached behind her and unsheathed her wakizashi. A strong feeling of bloodlust engulfed her. She did not fight it, but she also refused to let it consume her. She took those feelings, that desire to kill, and let her consciousness run alongside it, separate but together.

"We shall see," she said, her eyes flashing as she and her opponent were bathed in moonlight.

***

Kevin and Lilian left the resort behind.

While he was worried about Camellia and the others, he knew

neither of them would be able to help. In a battle such as that, he and Lilian would only be a hindrance.

They were nearly at the edge of the forest. He could see the thick line of trees and foliage, barely lit by the moon and stars. They appeared as little more than shadows of dark and darker.

Someone was already there waiting for them.

"You two didn't honestly think I would let you escape back to your clan's home, did you?" Fan gave them an ugly sneer. "I knew from the moment you started running that this is where you would be heading. This is the closest entry point into the forest. All I had to do was wait here."

"Well, dang," Kevin said. "And we were so close, too."

"I knew I shouldn't have used all those smoke bombs," Lilian muttered to herself. "And I'm all out of stink bombs, too. What rotten luck."

"Don't start quoting Touma Kamijou," Kevin muttered, his glare never leaving Fan.

"That's an awfully scary look you have there, human," Fan taunted, her face twisting into something so malicious, it didn't look human. "But don't think you're going to be cowing me with a look. You may have gotten the best of me last time because I underestimated you, but I won't fall for the same trick twice. I'm going to make you regret ever laying a hand on my beloved younger brother."

***

"Spirit Art: Damned Souls, Colossal Thunder."

The sky above Zhìlì became ominous. Dark shapes reminiscent of clouds but that were definitely not clouds appeared above him. Thunder that was not thunder crackled. Lightning that was not lightning flashed across the sky. Shapes appeared from within the cloud, a sea of tormented bodies, faces screaming in agony and hatred at the fate thrust upon them. The massive cloud of ectoplasmic bodies coalesced into a single point, and then a single bolt of white lightning struck the earth where he stood.

"Celestial Art: Celestial Dragon."

The attack did not hit. Appearing from within the ether was a long, oriental dragon several yards in length. Its glowing white body crackled with repressed energy. It coiled around Zhìlì, protecting him from the attack.

"Celestial Art: Celestial Breath."

The dragon opened its mouth and out spewed a bright torrent of flames. They consumed the spot Camellia stood on, spreading outward for several dozen yards to consume even more. Oddly enough, the attack did not burn anything that was living. The plants, grass, and trees caught within the conflagration remained unharmed. The same could not be said for the walkway.

Camellia was not there.

"Tch, an illusion," Zhìlì mumbled.

"Spirit Art: Pandemic of a Soulless Night."

The world shifted, morphing and twisting. It vanished, becoming nothing. Darkness consumed everything—until *they* appeared. Souls. The souls of those who had long since died. The souls of those who were doomed to never cross over. They sprung out of the nothingness and latched onto him—tried to latch onto him.

His youki flared. Its golden iridescence caused the souls in his vicinity to shy away. Damned spirits like these could not come near one representing divinity. They feared the light and all that it embodied. They would not touch him.

"Celestial Art: Divine Dispel."

A wave of golden energy emitted from his tails. It expanded in all directions. Souls cried out, screaming in agony as they were burned by his divine power. He watched them writhe and moan, their terror-filled screams of pain like banshees wailing directly into his ear.

And then it was over. He once again stood in the Pnéyma Resort. Light returned to the world. All was as it should be.

Except for the several icicles that were racing toward him. Behind the icicles stood a woman, the one in the French maid outfit.

"River Art: Glacial Crystals."

Zhìlì held up a hand.

"Celestial Art: Aegis of Divinity."

Appearing in front of him was a spherical shield. Bright gold and glowing with power, it blocked the icicles set to impale him. They shattered upon his shield like glass being dropped from a fifty-story building.

"Celestial Art: Divine Serpent."

The Aegis shrank until it was a tiny sphere the size of a baseball. He struck it with his fist, and suddenly, the sphere transformed into a serpent, which flew at Kirihime standing several yards away.

"Aegis."

The serpent splashed against a barrier that appeared before Kirihime. The souls within the shield bit into the celestial attack. Even though it burned them with its divinity, even as they moaned and screamed, they still consumed it.

That woman must be around here somewhere. Where is she hiding?

"Spirit Art: Ghostly Tendrils."

Six tentacle-like tendrils shot out from within the Aegis. They flew toward Zhìlì, who decided not to let those things touch him. He flashed away from the spot where he'd been standing—and appeared directly in front of the tendrils.

"What?!" he shouted.

The tendrils engulfed him.

"Celestial Art: Zhao Yun's Determination."

An explosion of energy erupted from within the tendrils. Rays of light shot out. The tendrils expanded as if they were swelling to incredible size. Then they exploded, bursting into particles of light and ectoplasm. Zhìlì stood in the center, still unharmed.

Kirihime appeared behind him, her twin daggers aiming right for his neck. Rather than slice him open in a spray of gore, they passed right through him.

She stumbled forward, the image of Zhìlì disappearing. Particles of light soon gathered around her. Within seconds, a dome of light surrounded her.

"Celestial Art: Sun Tsu's Trap."

Spikes emerged from the light too swiftly for Kirihime to follow. Within seconds, several spikes had impaled her from all sides. Her screams resounded throughout the resort.

***

"Kirihime!"

Camellia watched in horror as her maid and friend screamed from within what was essentially an iron maiden composed of celestial youki. She could do nothing to stop the technique, as any attack she had that could destroy one of that caliber would also harm her friend. All she could do was grit her teeth and wait it out.

A little ways to her left, Daphne and Zhìlì became locked within a battle of illusions. She could see them standing there, neither moving as they attempted to outmaneuver the other with their minds alone.

Illusionary battles were, by their very nature, not physical. They were a battle that took the concept of mind over matter to the next level. It was literally two people engaged in a fight that pitted minds together. Camellia knew that Daphne had directly engaged Zhìlì to give her time, and she would not waste that time.

When Zhìlì's iron maiden technique finally cleared, it revealed a horrid sight to her. Kirihime was still standing, but her eyes were blank. She breathed, but it was clearly labored. Several holes had been burned into her body. They didn't look as bad as they should have been—Kirihime's regenerative abilities were stronger than even her sister's—but the amount of blood pouring from her body was still cause for alarm.

"Extension."

One of Camellia's tails shot out and wrapped around Kirihime before the woman's body could fall to the ground. She pulled her maid over to her, then set her gently down on her back.

"M... My..."

"Don't try to speak," Camellia said as she checked over her maid's wounds. "You are incredibly injured right now. Any attempts at speaking could worsen your condition."

Despite her words, Kirihime still tried to speak. "I... I..."

"Do you want me to make that an order," Camellia snapped harshly, though the worry and tears in her eyes took out any sting they may have had. "Be quiet and let me look at you."

Kirihime fell silent, though Camellia attributed that to her maid losing consciousness. The three-tail's French maid outfit was covered in blood stains, which expanded the longer the wounds were left unattended. Kirihime must not have had enough youki to use her regeneration technique. She needed to act fast.

"Spirit Art: Soul Forging."

Camellia didn't know any healing techniques. Spirit Kitsune manipulated souls, not flesh. She could not heal these wounds, but she could plug them up.

Soul Forging was a simple technique that could be learned after a Spirit Kitsune gained their fourth tail. It took souls and turned them into something else. It was a surprisingly useful technique. Souls could be used to make just about anything—provided the person using **Soul Forging** had a mind keen enough and a will strong enough to create it.

Camellia, in that moment, created a needle and thread, which she used to deftly sew Kirihime's wounds shut. It would not last for long.

Souls only lasted for as long as their energy survived. Once they ran out of energy, any technique created by souls would dispel, but it should be enough to keep Kirihime from bleeding to death until they could get her to safety.

"Spirit Art: Soul Camouflage."

White mist surrounded Kirihime. Hollow screams and quiet groans reverberated across the resort. The souls that Camellia called upon combined and then stretched out, as if someone was pulling on them. The white spirit matter soon became all but invisible, or rather, it took on the same properties as the ground. It was then laid over Kirihime's prone body, which appeared to vanish before her eyes.

Camellia stood up. While she wanted to remain with Kirihime, there was still a battle being fought. They couldn't get Kirihime to safety until Zhìlì was taken care of.

She turned to look at how the fight had progressed. At first glance, Daphne and Zhìlì seemed to be evenly matched. However, it was clear to Camellia that Zhìlì had an advantage. Where he remained upright and unharried, her sister-in-law was gasping for breath, sweat dripping down her body in large rivulets as her eyes fluttered rapidly.

Daphne had talent, just like any other seven-tails, but she wasn't anything special. Her illusions were straightforward and simple. They might have been powerful, but they were easy to see through and thus overpower if the one she was fighting had more youki than her.

Zhìlì had more power. That's all there was to it. What's more, Shinkuro had clearly not let Zhìlì slack off on his training, just as Camellia would have expected from a martial-oriented family like the Shénshèng Clan.

Now, if only she could find the proper time to insert herself into this illusionary clash.

***

"Ikken Hissatsu. Ougi."

Kotohime's countless blade thrusts pierced nothing but light as Li stood there. When her attacks ended, he lashed out with a swift punch, but Kotohime had already anticipated this and moved around him.

"Ikken Hissatsu. Bunkatsu."

Appearing above him, Kotohime's blade went through Li's head and out his crotch, splitting him in half——or it would have, if he was not currently composed of light. Instead of cutting him straight through the middle like it would have with a normal yōkai, all her attack did was phase through him.

Li turned to attack her again. His fist came at her straight and true, but all his attack did was pass through an afterimage. Kotohime had moved the moment her attack failed.

"Ikken Hissatsu."

She once again appeared behind him, her body already spinning. With her wakizashi held within her left hand in a reverse grip, and her katana in her right, she became a tornado of razor death. This attack also phased through her opponent. A small line of light along Li's body marked her sword's passing.

Kotohime reinforced her body further, pumping even more youki into her muscles.

"Ichi no Ougi."

Her body became all but invisible as her speed surpassed the boundary that everybody except the fastest yōkai could perceive. Her blade flashed out, phasing through Li's celestial body. However, she could now see her attacks doing something. For every fifteen slashes of her blade, the light line from one of her attacks took .3 seconds longer to disappear.

So there is a limit to what he can do. Time to up the ante further.

"Ikken Hissatsu. Nii no Ougi."

Her speed increased further, as did the number of strikes she attacked with. Li could no longer follow her with his eyes. Several wounds opened up on his body. Small slits from which light emerged. One. Two. Three. For every thirty of her strikes, three wounds took .5 seconds longer to heal.

Faster. I need to go faster.

"Ikken Hissatsu. San no Ougi."

Over and over again she appeared and disappeared at the same time. To the unknowing eye, her body would have looked like it was multiplying, with dozens of afterimages appearing all around Li, attacking him with dozens of sword swings that were launched within hundredths of a second of each other. Within one second, Kotohime had inflicted 2,436 cuts on her opponent. Her attack lasted for ten seconds.

Li stumbled. Dozens of cuts were now refusing to close. It was time for the finisher.

"Ikken Hissatsu. Yon no Ougi."

She finally saw the damage she did stay. Her blade flashed out again and again and again, a never-ending stream that seemed to almost blur together into a single form of cohesive silver light. Wounds began appearing, and they did not go away.

Li tried to fight back. He turned and spun at the speed of light. He tried to pound away at the countless afterimages that she left in her wake, but none of his attacks landed. Every time he threw a punch, he would hit nothing but an afterimage. He could do nothing against an onslaught like this.

Finally, he fell to his knees. His body, no longer composed of light, leaked blood from several dozen wounds.

"I... I lost?" He stared at his cut up body with bulging eyes.

"It is just as I expected." Kotohime stood several feet away, gazing at her defeated opponent. "If I am not mistaken, that technique you are using is **Zhuangzi Harmonious Pacifism**. It is a technique that allows you to change your body into that of celestial youki by becoming one with the divine. It comes at the cost of limiting yourself to becoming completely defensive. That is why your attacks are so slow, and why you can't counter my attacks very well. In order to attack me, you must revert your body back to its original state, which is when you become vulnerable."

She had noticed it. Whenever she attacked, he didn't move. He only moved after her attacks were finished.

"What's more, that technique can be disrupted when someone else's youki is injected directly into your body. Camellia-sama was able to bypass this by attacking your soul, which also disrupted your technique. However, someone like myself, whose elemental nature comprises of water, would need to inject my youki directly into you."

Li's eyes widened in realization. "Then those attacks... they were..."

"Indeed, I wasn't just randomly attacking you from all sides. Every attack contained a small portion of my youki. I could only use a little bit because I knew you would feel what was happening if I used to much, but when you're being attacked from six dozen separate directions and cut open by six hundred simultaneous attacks, it doesn't really matter how little youki I use. Your youki will eventually be disrupted."

Kotohime observed her foe. Blood leaked from the uncountable number of cuts that had bypassed his technique. It ran down his arms and legs, dripping off his torso. The sand was becoming a carmine stain underneath him.

A Fox's Revenge

"I-I... see..." Li grimaced as his hand reached out toward one particularly nasty wound that ran across his stomach. "It seems a four-tails truly can defeat a kitsune of greater power."

"Power is not everything," Kotohime declared confidently. "You are more powerful than I: there is no denying that. However, what you have in power, I have in skill. I also have more experience than you. Where you were trained in the art of combat by instructors and tutors hired by Shinkuro-dono, I learned to fight through countless life-and-death struggles. You learn more when your life is on the line than you do in a dojo."

"I think I understand... heh, to think I lost because of something as simple as lacking experience... Lady Fan, I am sorry..."

As Li fell face first onto the ground, Kotohime turned around and walked away. She needed to find Kevin and Lilian. For her own peace of mine, she needed to confirm that they were safe.

***

The battle intensified. Illusions clashed with illusions and techniques collided in an orgy of destruction.

Camellia and Daphne double-teamed Zhìlì, doing everything they could to keep him on the defensive. Daphne's illusions messed with his senses, disrupting his hearing, inverting his vision. She used every ability she had to keep him on guard. Meanwhile, Camellia used her spirit techniques.

"Spirit Art: Gates of Hades."

An iron wrought gate rose from the earth, rusted with age, smeared with blood. Murals engraved along its surface showed a scene that made the blood run cold. Death. A young man being impaled by several stakes. A young woman being dragged into the ground by a dozen corpses. A middle-aged man, his skin torn from his body, consumed by the jealous dead who hoped to gain a life of their own by eating the flesh of the living. Skeletons and spikes adorned the top of the monolithic structure, and chains wrapped around it, keeping whatever lay inside from being released.

The chains snapped, breaking. There was a groan. The gates slowly opened, their loud creaking an ominous symphony.

From within that gate, they marched, a horde of skeletal warriors dressed in Spartan armor. They bore swords and shields, bows and arrows, marching onto the plane of the living.

"Well now, this looks problematic." Despite his words, Zhìlì did not appear all that worried. He raised his hand and pointed at the undead skeletons set on slaying him. **"Celestial Art: Celestial Dragon."**

The dragon appeared again. Particles of light gathered and gave it form. A large muzzle emerged from the darkness, followed by sloping twin horns that curved back. Two short arms emerged on its underside and wings formed along its back. Its long, serpentine body ended in a sharp tail.

"Attack."

That single command caused the dragon to roar and launch itself at the incoming horde. It tore through their ranks, burning the undead zombies, severing the souls bound to this plane before destroying the skeletal corpses, reducing them to ashes.

However, the dragon was one against many. The undead horde was like a wave; it surged and swelled and buried the dragon in a mass of bodies. Light burst from between the undead. Many of the horde was burned, vanishing as they exploded into dust, but it didn't matter. The dragon was gone.

Zhìlì frowned. "Tch. Then let's try this."

"Celestial Art: Twin Heavenly Dragons!"

Two dragons appeared this time. The first ploughed into the bodies of undead, tearing them apart and creating a path for the second, which continued onward, slamming into the **Gates of Hades**, which buckled and broke underneath the powerful onslaught.

Seeing this, Camellia danced away on reinforced legs. Daphne tried to backpedal, but the dragon that remained, the one which didn't get buried under undead, raced after her. She used reinforcement, but like most of her kind, she had never focused very much on reinforcement, beyond learning the basics. She was an illusionist, not a close-combat specialist.

The dragon opened its maw to take a bite out of her—

——when Camellia appeared right in front of her and smashed a fist into the dragon's snout. The dragon exploded. Celestial youki scattered to the four winds, the light dispersing like rain clouds driven away by an explosion.

"Are you all right, Daphne?"

"Yes," Daphne muttered, her breathing heavy. "I am fine. I appreciate the timely intervention."

"No problem. Now get ready. He's coming."

A Fox's Revenge

There was no more time to talk as Zhìlì appeared before them. Camellia soon realized that it was an illusion when she tried to attack it using **Soul Binding**, which created a dozen chains meant to bind a soul to a specific location on Earth.

"Celestial Art: Tsun Su's Paradox."

The world attempted to invert itself, with left becoming right and right becoming left, with up becoming down and down becoming up. Camellia dispelled the technique by dancing. Her youki rose to the surface as she danced, rejecting the false reality presented to her.

"Spirit Art: Soul Forging."

Daphne used **Soul Forging** to create several spears, which she launched at Zhìlì, who dodged the many attacks before sending a **Celestial Cannon** at his fellow seven-tailed kitsune. The attack was destroyed when Camellia moved into its path and slammed a fist against it.

"You know, that **Dancing** of yours is really annoying," Zhìlì said with a sigh. "The stronger my attacks are, the stronger it seems to make you."

"That is not my problem," Camellia's reply was short and to the point, "especially since you are now within my grasp."

Zhìlì blinked. "What do you—"

Before he could finish, Camellia disappeared and something struck his back with incredible force. The attack drove him forward, into the ground. What's more, there was a knife jutting between his shoulder blades. It was small, intangible, composed of ectoplasm. There was no blood, but this wasn't a wound of the body. It was a spiritual wound.

As Camellia leapt away, having come up behind him by using an illusion, Daphne used that moment to launch her own attack.

"Spirit Art: Damned Souls, Colossal Thunder."

Once again, darkness gathered overhead. Lightning forged from thousands of souls struck the ground where Zhìlì had stumbled. A large dome the size of a building, composed of white ghostly matter, formed around Zhìlì.

For a moment, Camellia dared to hope that they'd landed the finishing blow. Zhìlì was a powerful kitsune, but not even he could survive a direct hit from a technique designed to attack the soul. The dome soon vanished as the souls expended their energy, revealing a perfectly unharmed ground—minus the fact that all the grass, plants, and trees caught within the technique had withered and died.

There was no body.

"Celestial Art: The Sleeping Dragon," a loud voice echoed.

A loud roar rent the earth. Camellia looked up to see something horrifying.

Zhìlì stood on a building, one that sold paraphernalia to tourists. That was not what had grabbed her attention.

A large shape had formed behind him. A beast of massive proportions. It had to be at least thirty feet long. Clawed feet ended in curved talons sharper than any blade, grasping at nothing as though they were imagining the flesh of its foes being torn apart. Its wings, pinions of golden light, flapped back and forth, creating large gusts that tore at the ground and kicked up dust. Every inch of its golden body was covered in scales and muscle. It moved and, just like a real beast of legend, the muscle flexed, strong and durable. Golden fire jettisoned from its snout as it snorted. When its lips peeled back, it revealed rows of large, sharp teeth.

It was a dragon of western origins, and despite being an imitation composed of youki, it was still impressive—not to mention intimidating.

"I was really hoping I wouldn't have to use this technique," Zhìlì said out loud. "It takes so much youki, and it's very hard to use. It's also not very discriminate in what it destroys." As if the words were prophetic, the dragon landed on top of a small building, which was smashed flat, as if the creature composed solely of energy had actual mass. "You see? Indiscriminate destruction. It just leaves too much evidence, but you two really aren't leaving me with much choice. Fighting against another seven-tails is difficult enough. Fighting against a seven-tails and a five-tails who actually knows how to fight—well, that's a problem."

Zhìlì stared at them with a curious tilt of his head.

"Now then, let us see what you can do after awakening a sleeping dragon."

***

"Celestial Art: Taoist Point!"

"Celestial Art: Light Sphere!"

The qiāng launched at Kevin and Lilian was destroyed by a sphere of light launched from one of Lilian's tails, which struck the leaf-shaped blade on the side and caused it to disperse.

Kevin ran left, his guns already pointed at Fan. He pulled the

313

triggers, firing off several rounds. The woman was hit, then disappeared in a burst of light, which turned into several dozen spears that were launched at him.

"Lilian!"

"Extension!"

One of Lilian's tails extended to far beyond its normal length and tapped him on the forehead. A jolt traveled through his brain. The one dozen spears disappeared, revealing them to be an illusion. Kevin frowned as he looked around. Where had Fan run off to?

"Celestial Art: Loazi's Chains."

Chains burst from the ground and tried to pin Kevin down, but he'd already predicted that they would come and threw himself backwards, rolling along the ground and coming to his feet in a backpedaling run. He swerved his arms, aimed at a tree with a head of blonde hair poking out, and fired several red bolts of youki bullets.

Fan leapt out from behind the tree, which exploded as the red youki struck it. Kevin had already predicted the way she would move. He aimed slightly ahead of her and fired again.

"Celestial Art: Tsun Su's Shield."

The bullets struck a yin-yang shield that appeared in front of Fan. Cracks spread along the surface. Kevin continued firing, watching in satisfaction as the shield shattered into celestial fragments.

"W-what the heck?!" Fan shouted.

"Celestial Art: Orbs of an Evanescent Realm!"

The nine orbs attacked their prey. Fan, for her part, moved to dodge. She wove through the spheres of energy, proving that she also had martial arts training. While the nine orbs kept Fan distracted, Kevin fired several more times.

"Celestial Art: Taoist Point."

A qiāng formed before Fan. Rather than throwing it at them, this one she grasped with her hands. She spun it around with expert precision, slicing the orbs in half as they came her way, while simultaneously avoiding Kevin's gunfire.

Kevin frowned. While youki energy packed a lot more punch, they didn't seem to travel as fast as regular bullets. It made dodging a little easier. That could be a problem when dealing with someone who had this sort of fleet-footed dexterity. He was fortunate to have already thought up a way to defeat her.

He began firing again. Fan turned to face him, her blade spinning so fast it was nothing but a blur. Red energy lanced from his guns and was blocked. The bolts glanced off the youki qiāng, striking the ground and leaving a small crater. Cracks appeared in the qiāng as he kept up the pressure. The blade shattered, but another appeared to take its place. Despite this, Kevin didn't let up. He needed Fan to keep her attention on him and not on Lilian.

"Celestial Art: Underground Chambers Prison."

Two golden chains shot from the ground and latched around Fan's arms. They coiled around her, tightening to the point where she cried out in pain. The chains retracted back into the ground, pinning her there, leaving her vulnerable.

Kevin unloaded another barrage of bullets. Fan's body jerked back and forth. Each shot pummeled her like an old-fashioned shell. The force would have blown Fan backwards, but she was still pinned to the ground, so instead, her body became akin to a training dummy being mercilessly battered by an inu's insanely strong fists.

I don't get it. Kevin narrowed his eyes as he continued firing. *These bullets can crack boulders. A kitsune's body couldn't possibly—*

His eyes widened with sudden realization. "Lilian!"

"I know, we're in another illusion!"

Kevin bit his tongue. He tasted blood. The sharp pain disrupted the foreign energy inside of him and caused the world to revert—not back to normal.

The world before him looked nothing like the Mediterranean paradise he had come to know. A landscape barren of life greeted him. The ground, cracked and scarred, as if the earth's skin had been cooked by intense heat, surrounded him. In the center of this world sat a man, a monk, Kevin guessed, judging from his clothes. He was meditating, or so it seemed.

"Celestial Art: Buddha's Paradox."

The monk opened his eyes, and Kevin realized several seconds too late that Fan had layered two more illusions over the first.

From that moment on, Kevin's life became one of pain as brutal blades of wind ripped apart his body.

***

The key to fighting two opponents at once wasn't to take them on at the same time, but to find some way of taking them out one at a time.

Fan wasn't stupid. Arrogant maybe, but not stupid. She learned

315

from her mistakes. After their last battle, she had looked back on all the things she'd done, and she had come to the realization that she had let her arrogance cause her to underestimate her opponents.

She had played with Lilian and the girl's friends for too long.

She hadn't believed Kevin to be a serious threat until it was too late.

She should have realized the threat he represented after he dispelled her first illusion.

She had misjudged Kevin because he was human.

There was a long list of things that she could have done better. She had become determined not to make the same mistakes when they fought again. Thus, when Kevin and Lilian sought to battle her, Fan had immediately trapped Kevin within a triple-layered illusion. He somehow managed to dispel the first and second ones, but the third one would be impossible for him to break without outside help.

He lay several feet away, writhing on the ground, crying and screaming in pain. From previous experience, she'd learned that humans could dispel her illusion by experiencing pain. Pain disrupted their neural pathways. It forcibly broke whatever illusion someone was placed in.

However, that only applied to standard illusions. There was no way for a human to break an illusion where they already felt excruciating pain. After all, how could pain help a person break free of something when they already believed that they were experiencing pain? The answer was they couldn't.

"Beloved! Beloved!"

Lilian was frantic. She kept trying to reach her mate's side, but Fan wasn't letting her. She constantly attacked the two-tails with her qiāng, thrusting and stabbing, twirling and slashing. The girl was forced to continue moving away from her beloved mate. She forced the redhead back with a continuous stream of attacks, never letting up for even a second.

She had to admit, the girl could dodge. None of her attacks hit. Lilian wove through her hailstorm of fast thrusts and slashes with a speed and grace that she wouldn't have believed possible. Fan hadn't realized the girl was so good at fighting. However, she also knew this wouldn't last long. Lilian would tire out eventually.

She pressed her attack. Moving forward two steps, she thrust the leaf-shaped blade of her qiāng forward. Lilian sidestepped it.

Fan didn't let this deter her and spun around a full 360 degrees. She attacked with the blunt end of her qiāng from above, but Lilian moved back. The strike barely missed the redhead's face. Fan followed through with a thrust as she came out of her rotation, but Lilian twisted her body around the strike, avoiding it by the narrowest of margins.

She wasn't this good before. Fan frowned. *Has she been training since our battle? No, she couldn't have known about my skill at wielding a qiāng. Was she just hiding this talent like I was? No. That's improbable. She wouldn't have hidden something like this when I clearly had her and her friends beat. So then, why is she so good at evading my attacks?*

Keeping up the pressure, Fan continued to attack Lilian, who no longer shouted for her "Beloved." The girl's expression had become inscrutable. If Fan didn't know any better, she would have said that Lilian's face was almost… uncaring, as if it no longer bothered her whether Kevin lived or died.

That's not right. What happened? This girl shouldn't be this uncaring. All my observations from the past few months show that she's obsessed with her mate. Why isn't she trying to reach him now.

As if she could sense Fan's thoughts, Lilian smiled. Fan only had a second to realize what that smile meant.

Bang!

Fan's eyes widened when a bolt of red youki whizzed past her head. It struck the ground in an explosion that scorched the earth and created a miniature crater. She blinked. Then blinked again when she realized that something was missing.

Lilian was gone.

It can't be!

"Celestial Art: Divine Thrust!"

Fan whirled around to see a spear traveling toward her. With no time to counter, she threw herself to the ground, allowing it to travel over her head.

Gunshots rang out like thunder. Fan rolled along the ground. The earth she left behind was scorched as bolts of red youki struck it.

"Celestial Art: Orbs of an Evanescent Realm!"

She tried to scramble to her feet, but nine orbs whizzed around her on all sides. Fan ducked to avoid the spheres. More gunshots rang out. Panicking, she rolled backwards, just barely avoiding several youki bullets that would have put a hole through her head.

An orb struck the ground as she rolled to the left. It exploded,

317

sending chunks of rock and gravel in all directions, showering her. Fan had no time to curse as three more orbs descended from the sky like shooting stars crashing to Earth. She normally would have blocked the attacks with her shield technique, but gunfire kept her from being able to channel her youki. Instead, when she stood up, she reinforced her body and threw herself to the left.

The orbs struck the ground. There was no explosion this time. An illusion? She didn't have time to figure out the answer to her own question. Two more orbs came in, and several more bullets were fired. She gritted her teeth. Dammit! She couldn't even conjure her qiāng!

She moved again, running toward the tree line. Several bullets of red energy flew past her head. The boy's aim was off for some reason. She knew he was actually a good shot. She remembered how he'd struck the gas line that caused the junior high building to explode. She also remembered when he shot her in the kneecap. Did that mean the pain he felt from her illusion was causing his aim to be askew? She didn't know, but she was thankful nonetheless.

"Celestial Art: Shaolin Brilliance."

Youki flowed through her tails and exploded in a brilliant blaze of light. The orbs stopped coming. The gunfire ceased. Knowing that she couldn't fight them out in the open, that she needed time to rest and recuperate, Fan ran into the foliage.

It did not escape her notice that this time, she was the one who'd been forced to retreat.

***

Lilian looked at her mate in worry.

Thanks to some quick thinking, Lilian had managed to create a very convincing illusion of herself to fight Fan. She'd watched Kevin's style enough to create a mock style similar to his that relied entirely upon dodging instead of counterattacking. When their enemy was properly engaged, she'd released Kevin from the illusion that had held him, but the damage was already done.

Even though his body did not look injured, she could tell that he was in pain. His limbs shook. The guns twitched in his grasp. His fingers were shaky and weak. He'd barely been able to pull the triggers; she was actually surprised he'd managed to pull them at all. Labored breathing, the rasps of a man who'd just undergone excruciating torture, filled the night air with each breath Kevin took. She was sure he would collapse

318

soon.

She did what she could to help him, infusing him with her youki, but that did very little. Kevin was not injured. The damage done was all in his mind. The illusion made his brain think he was being injured when he really wasn't. She could mend bones, close holes, heal cuts, and repair organs. She couldn't heal damage caused by mental trauma.

"Beloved, are you okay?"

"I'll manage," he grunted. "We need to defeat that woman."

Lilian wanted to disagree. She wanted to tell Kevin that he should stop fighting and rest up, but she didn't do that. She knew that Kevin wouldn't stop. As long as she was in danger, until Fan stopped being a threat to her well-being, her mate would not stop. He was stubborn like that. She both loved and hated that part about him. She also accepted that part about him.

"Then should we go after her?"

Kevin nodded. "We'll need to be careful, though. She's probably planning to ambush us. How well would you say you know these forests?"

"Better than Fan, that's for sure."

Kevin smiled at her. It was shaky, showing clear signs of the agony he felt, but it was still a smile. "Then what do you say we show her how foolish it is to fight on your home turf? It's time for round three."

A Fox's Revenge

Chapter 11

In Victory Lies Defeat

The battles on the beach were not the only battles taking place.

Violet also found herself locked in combat. She had been searching for the brat when it happened, traveling through the part of the forest that was thick with life. The brat liked nature, she knew, though she didn't know why. Either way, she had figured he would be in a place where there was a lot of nature.

That had probably been a mistake, she conceded, if only to herself. She'd gone so far outside of her home that when someone attacked her, there was no one around who she could call for help. The person who was trying to kill her—with several dozen kunai to the head, no less—was one of her half-brothers, and the person who'd been trained in the shinobi arts to protect the matriarch.

Violet growled as she cracked her knuckles. "I don't know why you're doing this, and I don't really care. I'm gonna kick your ass for daring to attack the Great Lady Violet!"

Hayate clicked his tongue as Violet charged at him. "Out of all the matriarch's daughters, you're the one I hate the most."

"Shut up!"

Violet threw a punch right at Hayate's face. Unfortunately, Hayate was just an illusion. Her punch went straight through him like he wasn't even there, and instead her fist smashed into a large boulder behind him.

"Gah! My hand! Ouch, ouch, ouch!"

Hayate appeared several feet away and gave her a disgusted look. "This is why I hate you. You're a useless failure of a kitsune. You have no talent for our arts. You're short. You lack sex appeal. You have nothing going for you aside from that brutish strength. And yet, despite all that, the matriarch favors you over me. For no other reason than because you are female and I am not. You don't know how galling that is."

"Grr! Shut up! Shut up, shut up, shut up!" Violet ignored the pain in her hand and rushed at Hayate with every intention of pounding his ass into grass. "I'll show you talent when I rearrange your face!"

Once again, Violet did not hit Hayate. Instead she hit a tree, which snapped under the power of her fist and fell to the ground with a loud crash.

A sigh came from behind her. "You say that you're going to rearrange my face, but how can you do that when you can't even tell the real thing from an illusion?"

Violet gritted her teeth. He was looking down on her! It pissed her off so much!

"Extension!"

Her three tails tried to impale Hayate, who merely burst into a series of glowing silver butterflies. The butterflies gathered, tracing an ample ring around her, increasing in number until they had her completely surrounded. She eyed the fluttering, ephemeral creatures warily. Was this some kind of illusion? A specialty technique? She didn't know, so she guessed it would be best to just be ready for anything.

The butterflies enclosed the ring like a tightening noose.

Violet tried to punch them away.

That turned out to be a mistake.

One of the butterflies touched the skin of her arm, glowing briefly before sinking into her skin like her body was absorbing it.

"G-ga-ah!"

Violet fell to her knees. That seemed to be the cue that the other butterflies were waiting for. They swarmed her en mass, latching onto her skin, glowing, and then being absorbed into her body. Violet shrieked as she fell onto her stomach. She squirmed and kicked, flopped and trembled and clawed at her skin as though trying to pull out the butterflies that had already sank into her body.

"Spirit Art: Butterflies Fluttering Within the Netherworld."

Hayate's voice came from somewhere in front of her. Violet saw bare feet and the bottom of a toga appear in her field of vision.

"You can feel it, can't you? Every single butterfly that touches your skin pulls your soul closer to the Netherworld. You see that? Your body is already shutting down."

"W-what a pathetic technique," Violet choked out. "Butterflies? W-what k-kind of man uses butterflies... in his technique?"

An exasperated sigh came from above. "I see that even at the end of your life, you still remain obstinately stubborn. Where has that stubbornness gotten you? Dead at my feet. This is what happens to kitsune who don't know their place."

Violet gritted her teeth as her vision became blurry and indistinct.

"Now then, goodbye, my dear sister."

***

Camellia kept her breathing even as she ran up the wall of the main resort building, the hotel which served to house the many humans who paid exorbitant amounts of money to spend a few days there. It was empty now, just a large structure that no longer served any purpose. The once grand construct seemed hollow. Its rooms were empty. The many lights that often shone on it from below, lighting up the magnificent columns and showing off the structure's grandeur, had been turned off.

The wall below her exploded as something smashed into it. A giant, golden hand with massive and deadly claws. Camellia winced as the several-story building shook. She almost slipped off, but she applied youki to her feet and kept running.

She'd managed to draw the dragon's attention. Zhìlì had sent it after her while he dealt with Daphne and Kotohime, who had run into their battle while searching for Lilian and Kevin. She didn't know whether to be honored or worried.

Reaching the top of the building, Camellia spun around. The dragon soared overhead, letting out a terrifying roar that sounded almost real. She knew that it was just an illusion, a way of shaking her up. It didn't work because she knew that, but it was still a terrible thing to hear.

The dragon's glowing red eyes swiveled within their sockets. It suddenly locked onto her. With another roar, it unleashed a breath of golden fire.

Camellia started to dance. Graceful yet formless. Choreographed yet free. Her body moved almost without conscious thought. She

323

surrendered herself to the dance, becoming one with it, allowing it to consume her.

The fire reached her, threatening to engulf her in its shimmering conflagration and burn her in holy energy.

She reared her fist back and, with a resounding *boom!* like a nuclear detonation going off, Camellia punched a hole straight through the flames. They spewed around her on all sides, surrounding her, yet not engulfing her, almost like the flames refused to go near her.

The dance continued. The dragon, unable to comprehend what had happened because of its limited sentience, could do nothing but attack again. The fiery breath that it spewed met the same fate as its first attack.

Smoke rose from Camellia's hands as she continued to dance. She hoped Daphne and Kotohime could defeat Zhìlì soon. She didn't know how much youki this thing had, but if it was already damaging her despite her dance, then it wouldn't be long before even her enhanced strength would stop protecting her.

***

Kotohime considered herself to be quite lucky. During her search for Lilian and Kevin, she had stumbled upon her injured sister. Kirihime had been on the verge of death, but she'd been able to heal the younger kitsune.

After healing her sister, Kotohime had come across Daphne's battle with Zhìlì. The battlefield around the two was surprisingly clean for such a high-level fight. Kotohime figured it was because of their styles. Zhìlì used hand-to-hand combat and techniques that didn't damage the surroundings. Daphne relied mostly on illusions to fight. There were only a few craters on the sandy beach to mark where a destructive technique had been used.

She had joined the battle not long after coming across it. Zhìlì was a dangerous foe and Daphne looked like she was having trouble. Even if it was just a bit, even if she could only provide a distraction, Kotohime wanted to help.

"River Art: The Moon Goddess's Surging Waterfall."

"Celestial Art: Aegis of Divinity."

Kotohime watched as the giant tide of water she created crashed against a shield composed of light. Her attack did nothing, but then, it wasn't meant to harm, but to distract.

"Spirit Art: Damned Souls, Colossal Thunder."

Darkness gathered overhead and a bolt of white lightning struck Zhìlì, who raised another Aegis to stop it. The bolt hit the shield, then disappeared like a ghost wavering in the wind.

An illusion.

"Ikken Hissatsu. Ougi!"

Like jets had been placed under her feet, Kotohime shot forward. Her katana slid from its sheath and she swung it in a horizontal slash to cut her foe. Zhìlì blocked her attack by creating a Chinese falchion with his youki. Her blade hissed as it met Zhìlì's weapon, but it held together. It would take more than a celestial attack of that caliber to destroy her katana.

"Spirit Art: Soul Ravager."

Seven tails composed of icy spirit energy converged on their location. Kotohime created a water clone and used one of Ayane's ninja arts to replace herself with it. The tails converged, cutting through the clone and forcing Zhìlì to jump high above the ground to avoid the attack.

Kotohime was there to meet him.

"Ikken Hisatsu. Ichi."

Her blade sprung from its sheath as she rotated her body like a hacksaw. Her wakizashi also came out, increasing the appearance of the saw's spinning blade. It struck Zhìlì full on. A loud screech of metal issued forth. Sparks flew as her blade scratched against armored plating. Then Zhìlì plummeted back down to earth at rocket speed.

Then he disappeared.

An illusion.

She landed on the ground. An explosion several yards away alerted her to combat happening between Daphne and Zhìlì. The illusion must have been a distraction to get her out of the way. She rushed over just in time to see the two trading attacks.

"Celestial Art: Celestial Dragon."

"Spirit Art: Poseidon's Spear."

Two attacks met in the center of the battlefield. A white-hot spear forged from the souls of damned men, women, and children taken from the Sanzu River, and an eastern dragon composed of golden energy. They slammed into each other with a thunderous roar, the backlash of which caused Kotohime to slide several feet back, her feet digging small trenches within the ground.

Fierce winds whipped by her. Kotohime raised an arm to shield her

325

eyes from dust and gravel. She could feel abrasions appearing on her skin as the sand slamming into her tore a layer or two off. When the winds died down, she lowered her hand to see Daphne staring blankly at the sky. What was she doing?

"That was an impressive attack," a voice said behind her.

Kotohime's eyes widened. She tried to turn, but her right arm suddenly snapped as someone grabbed and twisted it in a way that it was not meant to go. Her katana clattered uselessly to the ground. Her knees shook, but she didn't fall—not until the person behind her broke her other arm, too. Only then, with pain and shock filling her, did she fall to her knees.

"You know, it's a shame we're enemies," the voice spoke some more. "You really are an amazing woman. Granted, I like my women a little more weak-willed than you, but for someone of your superior beauty, I might have made an exception."

A figure emerged out of her peripheral vision. Looking down as she was, Kotohime only saw his grieves, which clanked and clinked as he walked, sparkling in the faint traces of moonlight. Those grieves stopped directly in front of her. She finally looked up. His armor plate gleaming as if freshly polished, without a single scratch on it, Zhìlì looked down at her with an expression that somehow combined easygoing and harsh.

Kotohime gritted her teeth as she sent youki into her arms. She could feel the wounds slowly healing, her youki's regenerative properties causing them to snap back into place. Just a little bit more and —

"A-ah…"

A gasp escaped her lips as an overwhelming pain erupted from her chest. She looked down to see a golden falchion impaled between her breasts.

"A-ah…"

She tried to speak, but the pain overwhelmed her. Having lived as a mercenary for a good portion of her life, Kotohime had been in many battles. She'd experienced pain before. She thought she knew pain, how it felt, what it was like. She thought she understood pain.

She was wrong.

The sword piercing her chest felt like it was burning her from the inside out. Every muscle in her body clenched up, stiffening as if they were undergoing rigor mortis. She couldn't move. She could barely breathe. Her lungs felt like someone had dunked them in acid.

"I do apologize for doing this." Zhìlì still sounded easygoing, as if he hadn't just stabbed her in the chest. "However, right now I really do need you to stop fighting me. That Daphne chick is going to break through the layered illusion I cast over her. I have to admit, she's awfully good at recognizing illusions and breaking through them. I suppose that's her specialty. Fighting certainly isn't."

"A-ah..."

Kotohime didn't know when she fell onto her back. She couldn't even feel the ground underneath her. Everything had gone numb. She wondered if that meant her nerves had been burnt out.

"By the way," Zhìlì continued. "I should probably tell you that this is also an illusion. That sword in your chest, that strange feeling of numbness seeping through your body, even your inability to wield youki is all part of the illusion. **Celestial Art: Zhuge Liang's Hidden Fang** is an illusion that requires seven tails to cast. It's not really something a four-tails like yourself can break out of."

Which explains why he's telling me this. It was a bitter thought, to know that she didn't even register as a threat to him.

Standing above her, Zhìlì stretched his arms above his head, his armor clinking. "Welp, it looks like I need to go defeat that hot silver-haired chick. What was her name again? Ah, well, I suppose it doesn't matter. See you later, busty swordswoman."

As Zhìlì left her lying there, Kotohime cursed herself. She cursed her foolishness for picking a fight with someone much stronger than her. She cursed her inability to properly counter this man like she had done to Li. Most of all, she cursed her powerlessness. Her charge was in danger, the people who'd taken her in were fighting, and all she could do was lay there, her body numb to everything around it.

Just when had she become so weak?

***

The dragon had grown impatient, it seemed.

Camellia knew that was an euphemism. This dragon was composed of youki and granted only the barest of intelligence. She likened it to those computers that humanity was so proud of, filled with nothing but programs that told it what to do. It had no will of its own.

That still didn't change her feelings on the matter. The dragon had clearly decided to stop trying to burn her with its breath and attack her directly.

It roared as it swooped down to attack her with its claws. Camellia danced away as a large set of talons, each one taller than she, crushed the roof she'd been standing on. The tail came in when she dodged the claws. It descended from above like a kraken's giant tentacle when it was attacking a ship.

She dodged that, too.

The tail smashed the roof with earth-shattering force. Concrete exploded, not with gouts of fire and plumes of smoke, but with a concussive wave that sent chunks of stone everywhere.

Several of those stones flew at her, but she was still dancing and thus, when the stones tried to slam into her body with unrelenting force, she pummeled them with her fists. A shockwave was unleashed with each impact. The stones shattered. The dance continued.

The building rumbled as the tail continued tearing through it. Camellia could hear a loud series of crashes and bangs beneath her, the sound of objects in the floors below being smashed and slammed into other objects. She didn't know how much this kind of property damage would cost, but she imagined that Mama would not be pleased when she returned.

Camellia nearly lost her footing when the building began to tilt as the dragon tried using this opportunity to smack her off the roof with its tail. She hopped over it and slammed her fist into the tail. Her dance ensured that her power was maximized. Her youki, enhanced by the dance, disrupted the youki that the dragon was composed of.

The tail exploded in a violent surge of energy. The dragon jerked what remained of the tail back. Camellia noticed that the tail did not regenerate.

It seems this creature cannot regenerate lost parts on its own. Does that mean it lacks the youki necessary to do so?

That was one possibility. There were others, though, and she could not discount them. Perhaps the technique's limited abilities did not extend to regeneration?

She didn't have time to think on this. The dragon turned to her, its baleful eyes seeming to glow with rage. Clawed feet dug into the building, which continued to tilt, crumbling around her. This roof had no longer become a suitable battleground.

Camellia didn't wait for the dragon to attack her. She leapt off the roof and dove headfirst to the ground. The dragon roared and blasted off with a mighty flap of its wings.

That flapping must have caused more property damage because chunks of stone fell all around her. Camellia was forced out of her fall when several nearly hit her. She twisted her body, feet rebounding off one of the stones and allowing her to bounce to another.

Another earth-shattering roar from above alerted her to the dragon's presence bearing down on her. A deluge golden fire descended toward her, prepared to swallow her up. Her dance had stopped, so she couldn't break the attack. Instead, she speared her tails into a large block of stone and flipped it around, using it as cover.

There was no heat as the flames washed over the stone. Celestial attacks were not like fire, even if some of them looked and acted as such. The attacks were meant to burn living matter, not the inanimate.

As the flames licked at the edges of her stone, Camellia pushed off and bounced to a large block several feet below her. She flipped around and landed on her feet, then used that last stone to land on the ground.

Her feet hit gravel and she took off running. A roar from overhead alerted her to the dragon giving chase, and she realized that running wasn't an option. If she wanted to save her family, she would have to find some way to beat this technique.

She spun around to face the dragon as it swooped down on her like, well, like a giant ass reptile with wings. This was one battle she wouldn't be able to just walk away from, it seemed.

"All right," Camellia muttered to herself as her dance began anew. "I've never faced a technique of this caliber before now, but let's see if I can't bust you up."

***

Daphne was beginning to curse her luck.

Like most kitsune, she was not a fighter. Combat was abhorrent to her. It was inelegant and barbaric.

Of course, she still knew how to fight—well, she knew how to defend herself. All women of the Pnévma Clan were taught basic self-defense, but that didn't mean she was good at it. She could defend herself, and she excelled at using illusions. However, that was the extent of her skill.

"Spirit Art: Spartan Cannon."

Her tails curved around her body. Youki gathered along the tips of her seven tails and formed a giant sphere in front of her. The **Spartan Cannon** was one of her less powerful seven-tailed techniques. She would have preferred using **Damned Souls, Colossal Thunder**, as it packed more of a punch, but that took time to prepare, and time was something she no longer had.

Like igniting gunpowder, the cannon blasted off with a shock wave and a *bang*!

"Celestial Art: Celestial Dragon."

Her canon met a giant golden dragon. The two attacks clashed, exploding with energy. Fierce winds whipped her hair about her face as a large dome of clashing silver and gold youki erupted from where the two techniques made contact. Daphne had to close her eyes to avoid having her retinas damaged. When she opened them again, it was to see…

… Her dwelling? Yes, it was indeed her dwelling, the house she lived in inside of the Pnévma Clan ancestral home. She recognized the room easily. It was the one where she taught—tried to teach—Lilian about kitsune politics and, as of recently, human culture and history.

What am I doing here? I could've sworn I was somewhere else…

"Daphne-sensei," a familiar voice called out.

She blinked. Though the voice was familiar, it sounded way too cheerful. That girl would never speak to her with such a cheerful mien. And why was she calling her sensei?

Lilian walked into the room. Her red ears twitched on her head, and her two tails waved back and forth, reflections of joy. Daphne was graced with a bright smile from the girl who had never once smiled at her.

"Lilian?" Daphne felt nothing but confusion. "What are you doing here?"

"I'm here because we're having lessons today." Lilian's tone suggested her reason for being there should have been obvious. "Weren't you going to start teaching me about how the former matriarch, Delia Pnévma, made a peace treaty between the Pnévma Clan and the Shionzaki Clan of the Singing Hills?"

More blinking occurred.

"I was?"

"Yes." Lilian's concerned look bothered Daphne. "Are you feeling all right, Daphne-sensei? You're not sick or something, are you?"

"Um, no?"

Okay, something strange was going on here. Lilian never spoke to her with such enthusiasm, nor had she displayed such concern. She never called her sensei either.

A Fox's Revenge

Daphne tried to recall what she had been doing before Lilian walked in, but her mind seemed fuzzy, almost as if something was hampering her ability to concentrate. Every time she reached out for her most recent memories, they slipped away like slimy eels bathed in oil. It was almost like...

Of course!

"Spirit Art: Spiritual Dispersal."

The world around her crumbled; Lilian disappeared, the walls disappeared, her ceiling disappeared. She was back in the real world. The night sky greeted her, a cool breeze chilled her skin, and the sound of waves crashing against the ocean met her ears.

Zhìlì stood several yards away.

"Now I see." He looked at her with an easygoing expression that saw far too much. "So that's how you dispel all of my illusions, regardless of how many illusions I layer on top of each other. That technique of yours shatters any and all illusions that use less power than your dispelling technique. Very impressive. Did you come up with that yourself?"

"You can't honestly think I'll answer you." Daphne frowned at her fellow seven-tailed kitsune. She spotted Kotohime lying on the ground several feet behind her opponent and grimaced.

Zhìlì's carefree shrug answered her. "I was kinda hoping you would, yeah. Isn't that how these things work? You and I exchange blows; then we tell each other how our attacks work and why the other person fell for it. I'm pretty sure that's how all battles go in shōnen manga."

"Please do not say things like that while in the middle of a battle," Daphne muttered.

"I suppose you have a point," Zhìlì stroked his chin. "It's not really proper battle etiquette, is it? Then again, I have never really been one for proper battle etiquette, or battle at all, really. It's just not my thing."

Daphne frowned. This kitsune was way too relaxed for someone who was in the middle of a battle. It was like he wasn't even taking her seriously. She felt insulted.

Kitsune are proud creatures. This is a fact. It does not matter if they found themselves being forced to perform an unenviable task. For someone to act so dismissive of her prowess as a warrior was insulting, regardless of how much she detested battle.

"You have a lot of gall to treat me like this," Daphne seethed. "I do not know if you are simply an insulting person by nature, or if you are stupid, but I will not stand for your dismissive attitude."

Zhìlì scratched the side of his head. "Eh? Dismissive? I'm not being dismissive. I was complimenting you!"

"A compliment given during a battle because you do not feel threatened by my presence isn't a compliment at all," Daphne snapped as her tails became a rictus of activity. "Now prepare yourself. I will not allow you to mock me any further!"

"N-now just hold on a second here! I wasn't—"

"Spirit Art: Soul Ravager!"

"Don't interrupt me when I'm talking, dammit!"

***

Camellia's problem began with a headache.

She had known ever since her mind came back that it would not last. That was why, for the past month, she had pretended that nothing had changed. She didn't want to get her daughters' hopes up when she knew it would only end tragically.

It seems my time is almost up.

It was a sad thing, the realization that her mind's returned mental stability would not last. Even though she had known it, even though she had prepared for it, that didn't make the knowledge easier to bear.

Still, she wouldn't deny that the limited time she'd been able to spend with her family had been pleasant. Camellia had watched Lilian snuggling with her mate, had seen her two daughters bicker after Iris tried seducing either Lilian, Kevin, or both of them at the same time. Watching her family with a mind that hadn't degraded to that of a child had been a blessing and a joy, one for which she would always be grateful, even if the her that emerged once her sanity left did not remember.

The dragon did not care about her degrading mentality. It roared and tried to squash her flat. Despite her growing headache, she proved deft at dodging the large clawed feet that slammed into the ground with enough force to cause a miniature earthquake.

I need to beat this thing before my mind is gone.

That much was obvious. She'd long since given up hope on backup coming to help her. This battle would have to be won on her own, without aid from anyone else.

I need to find this technique's weakness.

332

Every technique had a weakness, cracks within the technique itself that, when struck, would cause the entire technique to collapse in on itself. Some techniques had more obvious cracks, such as that golden breath the dragon launched at her. However, the dragon, the being created by Zhìlì, didn't have any obvious weaknesses. She could damage it, as shown by when she struck its tail, but that was a far cry from defeating it.

The dragon lumbered after her. Its clawed front foot swiped at her, but she avoided being hit by jumping and twisting her body so that she passed through the gap between its talons. Even so, the wind whished by her, and Camellia could almost feel the claws as they rent the air.

She landed on the ground and ran behind it.

Come on, Camellia, think! This thing has to have some kind of weakness!

Camellia called up all the information she had on dragons. As the rarest of yōkai species, she didn't know much. Dragons were considered among some of the most powerful yōkai in the world. Each one had at least the strength of a seven-tailed kitsune, and their king, *Ryūjin*, was said to possess power greater than even a Kyūbi.

Their hardened leathery skin made all but the most powerful of attacks useless. This dragon was comprised of energy, and it wasn't as strong as a true dragon, but it was still powerful enough to withstand most head-on attacks. Its tail seemed to be an exception, probably because the youki was less dense there.

What about the eyes?

Dragons had one known weakness. Their eyes. It was the only unprotected region on their bodies. It stood to reason that this technique would have the same weakness... but, no, getting to those eyes would be a problem. Still, maybe she could attack its underside? A dragon's belly was oftentimes another vulnerable point. The belly was never covered in scales like the rest of it.

Her decision made, Camellia prepared herself for one final clash.

The dragon loomed before her. Its massive body rippled as it stalked toward her, no longer flying in the air. Camellia wondered if that meant it was running out of youki, but she didn't ponder the thought for long. It didn't matter anyway. Hopefully, this would all be over with one final technique.

"Extension."

Four of Camellia's long tails shot out and latched onto a pair of trees that jutted from the ground behind the dragon. She did not bother testing their elasticity, as she did not really care. Shōnen plot armor would ensure her success.

She moved back and the trees moved with her, bending like they were made of rubber. The dragon now towered over her, its red eyes glaring down at her balefully. She knew that, too, was an illusion. Zhìlì had done all he could to make this dragon seem as lifelike as possible, and she had to admit he'd done a marvelous job. Minus the fact that it was made entirely of golden energy, it really did look just like a real dragon.

The dragon raised a clawed foot, intent on smashing her flat.

Camellia released a breath, and then let herself go.

The dragon's claw didn't even have time to smash the ground where she'd been standing. Camellia, using her tails-turned-slingshot, was launched off the ground and flown head first straight through the belly of the beast. She punched a hole through the creature's stomach and burst out the other side. The dragon, unable to maintain cohesion after having a hole ripped through it, exploded into particles of light.

Camellia kept soaring forward until she inevitably struck the ground. The world around her spun as she tumbled. Her body was battered and beaten by the mercilessly hard earth. Her bones were jarred and her skin was scraped as she rolled along the ground like a doll thrown by an angry child.

And then she stopped, lying on her back, staring at the starry sky. She sat up, blinking several times, and then proceeded to look around. She blinked again.

"Hawa?"

***

It had become a battle of illusions.

Deaf to everything around them, blind to all but each other, the two seven-tailed kitsune continued to battle.

Illusions were a very peculiar branch of yōkai technique. They were not flashy nor were they destructive. Illusions could not cause massive explosions, create dragons made from youki, or summon the dead to do battle. All they could do was trick the mind into believing that something was happening when it really wasn't.

Illusions required a very unique mindset. It required a mental state that most beings, be they yōkai or human, found hard to attain. Most kitsune—as in, kitsune that were not Violet—had a mindset that was naturally predisposed toward illusions.

Unparalleled spatial awareness was key to crafting a believable illusion. A glamour woven on top of the surrounding environment had to blend seamlessly and without any obvious distortions that would suggest the world the target was looking at was not the real world. Any obvious signs of change from the norm would tip off the target, making them realize they were seeing a false world, and thus allow them to break free —provided they had the ability to break out of an illusion.

There were illusions that did not follow this particular mindset. Illusions that were so obvious anyone could tell they were not real. However, these illusions were often designed to cause pain or confusion. Most illusions tricked people into believing that what was happening around them was what was really happening, fooling the mind into believing that the falsehoods presented were real.

Daphne's body unraveled into countless white flower blossoms. Zhìlì looked around as the amount of blossoms surrounding him increased. They circled around him, encasing him in a dome of pure white that blocked out everything else, completely isolating him from the world outside. He could see nothing but this incredible whiteness.

Calmly, without showing any signs of nervousness, he took a single step forward.

He blinked when he bumped into something soft and warm. A wall of white flower blossoms stood in front of him. That was when he realized the whiteness had messed with his depth perception. Things that seemed far away were actually much closer than they appeared.

Zhìlì shattered the illusion with youki. The dome of flower blossoms disappeared to reveal reality—or what looked like reality.

Daphne stood in front of him, her right hand almost gently touching his chest. Then several dozen ghostly white spikes erupted from Zhìlì's body.

A body which dispersed into a flock of golden rabbits.

The rabbits bounced away, then gathered in front of her, merging and taking on an anthropomorphic shape. The rabbits soon melted away to reveal an unharmed Zhìlì. Daphne frowned, then a stake erupted from the ground underneath Zhìlì, who dispersed into particles of light, which took on the forms of spears that soon impaled her body at every unimaginable angle.

Except that wasn't Daphne.

The real Daphne seemingly emerged from the ground some distance away—or at least, what seemed like the real Daphne. When several golden spears struck her, Daphne's body split and formed several silvery foxes that ran toward a specific point and bit down on something invisible.

Zhìlì reappeared in a shimmer of light. The foxes bit down harder, but despite their teeth sinking into his skin, no blood came out. That was when several dozen dragon heads erupted from his body and bit down on the foxes, which burst into mist.

Daphne and Zhìlì reappeared, standing in the same place they had been at the start of this battle.

Zhìlì blinked several times and shook his head as if a slight dizziness had come over it.

"It seems my technique is finally beginning to affect you," Daphne declared.

"Spirit Art: Central Half Vision."

Just as the name suggested, Zhìlì's vision had narrowed significantly. He could see absolutely nothing in front of him, yet he still possessed a peripheral view on both sides. There was a medical name for this condition: binasal hemianopsia.

Zhìlì's frown was that of someone faced with a minor annoyance. With the front of his vision completely gone, that meant he would have to turn his head like a parrot to see what was in front of him. The moment he did that, however, Daphne attacked. This did not bother him as it might have bothered others. Having his vision limited like this did not hamper him. He could predict where Daphne would attack with some degree of accuracy; after all, logic dictated that she would always attack from his blind spot.

He turned around and several beams of light erupted from his tails, forcing Daphne to move back. In return, he was forced to dodge seven glowing silver fox tails that extended toward him. He couldn't see them, but he could feel the youki from them.

When he leapt back a safe distance, one of his tails launched a spear that it conjured at the place where Daphne had been standing. The sound of his spear sinking into sand told him that Daphne was no longer there.

His head swiveled before he eventually spotted Daphne coming in from his left. He turned and several golden discs flew from his tails. They struck Daphne and tore through her like she was made of paper—or an illusion.

336

Zhìlì jumped back just as Daphne descended to the ground with a mighty heel drop. If the sudden physical attack surprised him, he did not show it. His seven tails curled around him and shot beams of energy that forced her to backpedal. The beams then curved around in mid-flight and struck Daphne from behind. When Daphne burst into ghostly white mist, he knew that he had been tricked.

His seven tails spun around and created an impenetrable barrier of golden light. Something struck the barrier and shattered like glass. The youki emitted from the tails were released in a wave that caused several other illusions, which he had not been aware of, to shatter.

"Damn." Zhìlì whistled. "This woman really is impressive."

Despite facing off against a talented illusionist, Zhìlì did not appear the least bit concerned.

"Seriously, I never imagined I would be facing someone with this much talent. I guess that's what happens when we've got so little intel to go off."

Just then, several ghostly white spikes erupted from the ground and impaled Zhìlì with ease. Daphne appeared before him, then, her form emerging from within a ghostly pale mist that formed from nothingness.

"This battle is over," she declared.

Zhìlì's nod surprised Daphne. "You're right. This battle is over."

Before Daphne understood what was happening, her mind erupted in pain as something impaled her through the back. The world around her shattered to reveal her standing in the same place she had been at the start of their illusionary battle. Zhìlì was nowhere to be seen. She looked down and saw the end of a golden sword poking out of her belly.

"What... what..."

"You're good," Zhìlì's voice said from behind her. "Honestly, you're probably even better at illusions than I am. But however enviable your skill is, none of that matters if you lack the experience to properly use that talent. This battle was over the minute you were caught within my illusion."

Daphne turned her head to look Zhìlì in the eye. "Are you so sure about that?"

Zhìlì opened his mouth to respond, but he couldn't. His mouth refused to open. In fact, his body seemed incapable of moving at all, like his muscles refused to respond to his brain's commands.

"You might have more experience in combat, and you might have been extensively trained to fight other yōkai, but you forgot something very fundamental when battling me." Blood leaked from Daphne's mouth as she spoke, dribbling out of the corners and dripping down her chin. "I am a Spirit Kitsune. My specialty lies in manipulating souls."

Zhìlì noticed the problem only after she spoke. Her tails. All seven of her tails had pierced his body. They had not torn flesh or penetrated skin. They did not damage muscles and break his bones. If he looked closely enough, he could see how the tails turned ethereal centimeters before entering his skin.

Her tails were grabbing his soul.

Zhìlì would have spoken. This would have been the perfect time for a witty one-liner about her tails and how she'd captured his heart. He couldn't speak, however, as the tails did not let him.

"Spirit Art: Persephone's Prison," Daphne declared the name of her technique. "This is the pinnacle of Pnéyma Clan illusions, one of only five seven-tailed illusionary techniques that are unbreakable by anyone who does not possess at least eight tails of power. Right now, your soul believes it is outside of your physical body. It believes that you are dead."

Ah, so that was how it was. Zhìlì would admit to being impressed. He hadn't known there were illusions like that. While he might have been a talented illusionist, his specialty lay in the celestial-specialized techniques of his clan and hand-to-hand combat, which he had only used a little bit of during this battle.

The tails were pulled from his body, and Zhìlì, no longer held up by something, collapsed like a marionette with its strings cut.

***

Daphne stared impassively at the motionless form of her opponent.

"You are very lucky that I do not have the youki necessary to pull your soul from its body," she declared seconds before collapsing onto her stomach. Inexperienced as she was with combat, she'd ended up wasting a lot of youki. What's more, she still had a sword piercing her back.

Speaking of that sword…

With the last of her strength, Daphne used one of her tails to pull the sword from her back. Seconds after that, the sword dispersed as the youki holding it together ran out. She blinked several times as she stared at the spot where the sword had been lying.

"Tch." She clicked her tongue. Daphne couldn't believe she'd just wasted so much effort on a useless gesture.

***

Violet woke up when ice-cold water drenched her face.

"Buagh!"

Shooting into a sitting position, her eyes widened as she searched the area for the soon-to-be-dead kitsune who'd done it.

"I am glad to see you're awake, Violet."

Emotionless eyes stared down at her. Violet noticed the bucket in Jasmine's hand.

"Did you have to dump a bucket of water on me?"

"Yes."

"Tch."

Violet gazed around the field, her eyes eventually landing on the motionless form of Hayate. He lay on his back, sightless eyes staring at nothing. She could tell that he was still alive because his chest rose and fell, but his mind was clearly not there anymore.

She turned back to Jasmine. "Did you do that?"

"I had help." Jasmine felt no shame in admitting this. "Ayane held him down while I used **Soul Ravager**. I lack the power necessary to pull a soul from a body, but it was more than sufficient to temporarily shut down his mind."

"Oh." Violet grasped at the ground beneath her as her hands clenched into fists.

"Is there a problem, Violet?"

"No." Violet shook her head. "I was just thinking about Hayate. I was just trying to figure out why he attacked me."

"I do not know," Jasmine admitted. "However, I do know that this was not an isolated incident."

"Really?"

"Indeed." Jasmine nodded. "Cadmus tried sneaking into my dwelling to kill me. Were it not for Ayane being constantly on guard for such things, he may have succeeded."

Cadmus was another of their half-brothers. He, Palladius, Hayate, and Caleb were the only male kitsune currently allowed inside of the Pnévma Clan ancestral home.

"I see. So Hayate isn't the only one who's betrayed us. What about Palladius and Caleb? Did they also try to kill anyone?"

Jasmine's shrug was that of someone who lacked answers. "I don't know. It doesn't look like anyone else was attacked. I went to check on Holly and Ivy, and the twins. Holly and Ivy were conducting experiments, as usual."

"And the twins?"

"They were eating each other out."

Violet twitched. "Same as usual, then."

Jasmine didn't really need to nod, but she did anyway. "Indeed."

***

Fan ran through the forest. She wasn't sure how long she'd been running, though it must have been for a while. Sweat had broken out on her brow and skin. The cold air hit her glistening wet body and chilled it, making goosebumps break out.

The canopy above her blotted out the stars. She could barely see more than five feet in front of her. Everything around her was cast in shadows so dark it was like staring into a black hole.

Her mind jumped at shadows. Everything around her seemed as if it was trying to grab her. A vine latched onto her wrist. Roots rose from the ground to trip her up. The entire forest was out to get her!

She rushed past a tree. That was when she ran into someone. He appeared before her like an apparition, standing naught but a few yards away. It was the human boy she'd been fighting. His smirking face inflamed the hatred within her soul like gasoline on a fire.

"DIE!"

A qiāng flew from one of her tails and went straight through the human, who vanished into particles of light. He reappeared again, several yards from where he'd been standing. He was still smirking, as if saying, *"You are inferior to me."*

"Damn you!!"

She launched two more qiāngs. They, too, went straight through Kevin's body like he wasn't there. The boy vanished.

Was that an illusion? It has to be an illusion!

"Come out!" she yelled at the darkness of the forest. Her eyes darted back and forth frantically. They were hiding somewhere in here! They had to be! "Come out now! Come out and face me!"

Bang! A gunshot went off somewhere to her right. It flashed red, striking a tree, bark exploding and bouncing off her skin. Fan screamed as she used her arms to shield her eyes and ran in the opposite direction.

Several more shots followed her. All of them missed, but a few

340

came close enough to make her scream.

"Extension!"

Something long appeared in front of her. Because she'd been running full tilt, she couldn't stop in time, and thus she ended up crashing straight into it. She gasped in asphyxiated agony as she ran neck first into the thing, a tail. Her feet flew off the ground, carried by momentum. They swung like a gymnast swinging around a high bar. The tail retracted, then, and Fan flipped end over end before landing flat on her stomach.

"G-gu..."

The crunching of footsteps appeared in front of her. She looked up to see glowing blue eyes staring down at her. She recognized those eyes and the face they were attached to.

"Y-you," she tried to growl, but it was hard to speak. She could hardly breath. "Y-you damn human!"

Fueled by hate, she surged to her feet and charged at Kevin with a defiant roar.

Her fist was dodged. The boy seemed to flow around her attack. Her head then snapped back as his right fist smashed into her face.

She stumbled backwards, shaking her head, and then charged back in.

"Damn you—gu!"

All the air was expelled from her lungs when a fist was embedded into her gut. She spit out bile and saliva, hacking and coughing. That punch, it hurt so much, like her insides were being turned into pulp. How could a human hit so hard?

When the fist was removed, she fell to her knees, arms curling around her abused stomach. She looked up to snarl at the human boy, but she was unable to turn her malicious intent on him when a tail wrapped around her throat. She grabbed at the object as she was lifted into the air. Her feet kicked out uselessly as the tail rose higher and higher. Then she screamed as the tail slammed her face first into the ground.

After that, Fan saw nothing.

***

Kevin stared at the unconscious kitsune.

Once she'd entered the forest, defeating her had been surprisingly easy. With her mind already in a panic from their previous bout, it had been simple for Lilian to ensnare her with a basic illusion. Fan hadn't

341

even realized that she'd been trapped by the time he appeared before her.

"It looks like we won," Lilian said as she walked out from behind a tree.

"Yeah." Kevin ignored the discomfort that speaking caused to his ribs. "It certainly seems that way, doesn't it?"

"How are you feeling?" Lilian asked as she gazed at him with the concerned eyes of a lover.

Kevin wanted to lie. He wanted to tell her that everything was okay, that he felt fine, but he couldn't. Lilian was his mate. She didn't lie to him. He would not do the injustice of lying to her.

"I think… I'll be a lot better once we get some sleep."

Lilian accepted his answer with a slow nod. "Then let's go back home."

"Right." He looked down at the unconscious Fan. "What should we do with her?"

Lilian opened her mouth to speak.

Someone else spoke first.

"You shall do nothing with Lady Fan," a male voice came from behind him.

Kevin felt one moment of intense, white-hot pain the likes of which he'd never felt before. His body then went through a moment of weightlessness. The world around him seemed to spin. Then he crashed into something hard and unyielding.

"BELOVED!"

The last thing Kevin heard was Lilian screaming out to him.

A Fox's Revenge

Chapter 12

The Choices We Make

Delphine Pnéyma sat on her throne-like chair in the reception hall. Because Daphne was still injured, Marigold was the one kneeling before her and giving a verbal report on the events that had transpired while she was gone. This would have actually been Holly's job, seeing how she was the second eldest, but Delphine couldn't count on that one to do this. She supposed that was the price one paid for having a scientist for a daughter.

"This is quite the mess," Delphine said with a sigh. "My own sons have betrayed us for the Shénshèng Clan; my eldest daughter, two of our faithful vassals, and Violet were injured in battle, and Lilian has gone missing, presumably kidnapped by the Shénshèng Clan. Problematic does not really do this situation justice, does it?"

Marigold did nothing more than shift uncomfortably. Delphine waved the girl's concerned gaze off.

"Do not worry, dear daughter. I am not blaming you for what happened. This isn't really anyone's fault. No one could have foreseen my sons betraying our family."

She frowned at the disquieting thoughts this knowledge caused. In all her years as matriarch, Delphine had never expected to be betrayed to a rival clan by her own kin. Why had they betrayed her? How many more traitors were in her midst? How long would it take to root them out and dispose of them? She could already see a long and troubling road ahead of her.

"What happened to the Shénshèng Clan members who attacked us?" she asked, returning to the matter at hand.

"They disappeared, Momma," Marigold told her. "Kotohime and Kirihime have checked the entire island and haven't found a trace of them. We can only assume they left shortly after acquiring Lilian."

That was troubling. Lilian was a very special kitsune, along with her sister. Delphine couldn't allow anyone else to have her. That was the whole reason she had allowed the girl to become Kevin's mate.

Speaking of the boy...

"And how is young Kevin Swift doing?" she asked, resting her right cheek on her hand.

"Mukyu, we've healed all of his injuries, but he hasn't spoken since waking up." Marigold wilted as though she understood Kevin's pain first hand. "I believe he is feeling a combination of heartbreak and guilt, though without actually speaking to him, I cannot be sure. But, mukyu, knowing what I do know about Kevin's nature, it is likely that his inability to protect his mate is eating away at him. Kotohime is currently staying by his side."

"Hmm…"

Knowing of the katana-wielding maid's past, she was not surprised by the dedication and loyalty Kotohime showed the boy. It was good that he had someone by his side right now. She couldn't afford to let him lose himself to despair.

"Very well." She stood up from her throne.

Marigold's startled eyes rose to look at her. "Momma?"

"Let us go see how young Kevin is doing." A placid smile graced her face. "I believe our human friend could do with a pep talk."

***

Kevin felt horrible.

In the past ten months, he had gone through a lot, more than most, he would say. He'd learned about things most humans would never have believed existed, fought against creatures whose existence surpassed him, and learned hard lessons that no teenager should have been forced to learn. The accumulation of life experiences had forged a once shy and insecure boy into someone Kevin could feel proud of.

None of that mattered now.

A Fox's Revenge

He stared out the window of his bedroom, the bedroom he had shared with Lilian, the bedroom that Lilian *should* have been residing in as well. She wasn't there now. The grounds outside looked the same as always, green and lush and full of vibrant colors. The flowers and trees swayed with life in the gentle breeze that blew across the grounds.

They looked lifeless and dull to him. Monochrome.

A hand came to rest on his shoulder. It was soft and delicate, feminine, despite the katana it wielded with deadly grace. It belonged to Kotohime, the woman who'd not left his side since he woke up.

"It is not your fault, you know." Kotohime's lilting, gentle voice would have normally soothed him. Not today. "If anyone is to blame for Lilian-sama being kidnapped, then it is me for not killing Li before running off to battle a kitsune with more power than myself. Had I done that, Lilian-sama would still be here."

Kevin said nothing. He merely shook his head. It was not her fault that Lilian had been kidnapped. Had he been more attentive, that man would have never snuck up on him. Had he been more prepared, then maybe he could have reacted in time. Had he not been so stupid, he would have never dropped his guard after defeating Fan. The blame laid solely with him.

He didn't know if Kotohime felt his emotions, or if she wanted the same comfort that he did, but she pulled him back until the back of his head rested against her chest. The two soft mountains that made up her breasts were more comfortable than any pillow. As Kotohime's slender arms engulfed him, Kevin allowed himself the luxury of being comforted by her, even though doing so made him feel guilty.

Footsteps alerted him to a presence approaching before the door opened. Kotohime released him from her hug and stepped away, though one hand remained on his shoulder.

"I am pleased to see that you are finally awake," a voice said.

He turned around alongside Kotohime. The matriarch stood in the doorway. She looked immaculate, as always. Even her expression appeared untroubled, more amused than anything.

That expression really pissed him off. Her granddaughter had been kidnapped, and she didn't even seem to care.

"You took quite the beating, you know," Delphine continued when it became obvious that he would not answer her. "According to Jasmine, who discovered you, someone had punched you straight through a tree. Your spine was all but broken. Had it not been for Kotohime here, I dare say you would have been crippled for life."

Kevin's hand went up to grasp the one on his shoulder. In response, Kotohime tightened her grip in warm reassurance.

"I know how you are feeling right now." Delphine's suddenly compassionate gaze made Kevin almost forget that he felt wary of this woman. "It is difficult to lose someone you love. However, are you sure you should be giving in to despair right now? Can you afford to do that when there is still a chance to save Lilian?"

Kevin frowned. A chance to save Lilian?

"Pnévma-denka—"

Kotohime was silenced by a sharp glance from the matriarch.

"What do you mean?" Kevin asked, the first words he'd spoken since waking up.

The smile Delphine gave him was that of someone relinquishing a secret.

"The answer is simple; Lilian isn't dead." Kevin's eyes widened. "So long as someone is alive, they can be rescued—provided you are willing to brave the dangers such an undertaking entails."

Kevin felt like smacking himself. If Lilian was alive, then she could be rescued. If she was out there, then he could find her. He'd been so caught up in feeling sorry for himself and guilty over not protecting Lilian that he'd forgotten this simple fact.

"I believe I shall leave you alone for now." Delphine's voice snapped him out of his thoughts. "I merely came to check up on you. While Lilian's currently away, you are still her mate, and I would hate it if something happened to you. What you do with the information that I have given is up to you. Should you require any assistance, whether that is in going home or information on where Lilian is likely being held captive, then please do not hesitate to ask."

Delphine left, the door closing behind her.

Kevin turned back to look out the window, his thoughts solidifying into a single point.

"I'm going after her," he told Kotohime.

"I suspected as much." Kotohime's warm hand on his shoulder comforted him. "I shall help you in whatever I can, Kevin-sama."

Kevin knew that Kotohime was doing this more for Lilian than him, but he was grateful all the same. No, perhaps he was grateful because he knew she was supporting him for Lilian.

"I know. Thank you, Kotohime."

The smile that Kotohime graced him with was not her usual placid and calm smile, but one filled with warmth and assurances. He imagined an older sister might smile at her younger brother like that.

"Of course. You should know that this Kotohime will do everything she can to help Kevin-sama and Lilian-sama have their happily ever after."

The two shared a smile. Kevin wondered just when he and Kotohime had created this bond of theirs. He supposed it had happened the moment he chose to become Lilian's mate.

The door opened just then. Kevin at first thought Delphine had returned, or perhaps she had never left and merely waited outside for him to make his decision. That seemed like something she would do.

It was not Delphine who appeared.

The person who stood in the doorway was Iris.

She was awake.

And she was giving Kevin a look of pure, unbridled determination. It was an expression that he had never seen on her before.

"Hey, Stud." Her voice was raspy from disuse. "What's this I hear about my sister being kidnapped?"

Afterword

Here are we at the end of A Fox's Revenge. This particular story was probably the most difficult one for me to write—for a number of reasons. However, I believe the biggest reason would definitely have to be the cultural shock.

Let me discuss kitsune in this afterword.

Kitsune are, to put it bluntly, immoral creatures who are so different from humans that a lot of what they do seems morally corrupt to us. Things that we as humans find abhorrent, kitsune find perfectly acceptable. In fact, there is very little that kitsune do not find acceptable from a moral standpoint. Individual morals aside, you would be hard-pressed to find a kitsune who has an issue with many of the moral quandaries that we have. Even mild-mannered and kind kitsune like Kotohime, Lilian, and Kirihime do not have a problem with moral dilemmas that a human would be up in arms over.

That is what I wanted to show in this volume. The difference in morality between kitsune and humans.

Thus far, I have only ever shown kitsune when they are living in the human world. In the human world, kitsune have to conform, at least to a certain degree, to the laws and ideals that humans set, lest they run the risk of alerting humans to their existence. To that end, they are forced to "behave themselves" in a way that many kitsune find restricting.

You've seen a little of how kitsune act with Iris. Kotohime and Kirihime have experience with living in the human world, so they conformed more easily. While Lilian had some issues at first, she's very straightforward and accommodating for Kevin's sake. Camellia might have had troubles if she wasn't such a cinnamon roll, but she is, so there. Iris is the only kitsune who doesn't have experience with humans and wasn't willing to conform for the longest time. Even at the beginning of A Fox's Revenge, you can see that she hasn't completely conformed to human society.

A Fox's Revenge shows how kitsune act in their natural habitat, when they don't have to worry about humans and their silly morals, when they are free to do whatever they want.

Of course, it's not as if kitsune act completely different from us. Kitsune mimic humans to an astounding degree. They look like humans, act similar to humans, but they are not human. I struggled a great deal when trying to figure out how I could show the difference between humans and kitsune when they act so similar.

One of the greatest examples that I used to display the difference between humans and kitsune is sex, and I used sex because the US is very prude about it. It's something that the United States both shuns and glorifies in equal measure.

In kitsune culture, sex is just sex. You can use it to reproduce, or you can use it for pleasure. While this is somewhat similar to humanity, the amount of acceptance toward various sexual acts is far greater in kitsune culture than it is in human culture. A lot of the things that a kitsune would find acceptable about sexual relationships are things that I personally cannot accept as right. A lot of the stuff that happened in this volume is stuff that I believe is morally corrupt and appalling: Ivy and her mother when they were trying to, uh, practice reproduction with an unwilling Kevin, Jasmine and her slave fetish, Delphine and the harems she's formed, and the incestuous relationship between Aster and Azalea. Roleplay aside, while none of this is considered wrong in the kitsune world, quite a bit of it is something that I believe most humans would find morally reprehensible.

Displaying these sort of differences are difficult, especially because I have no real reference outside of anime, and while anime can be downright freaky at times, especially in the ecchi/hentai department, it does not contain enough depth that I can create an entirely new culture out of it. I felt like I was writing blind most of the time when I wrote this volume!

Anyway, I feel like I have lectured you all enough. I hope this little afterward was informative. I would like to thank all of you for reading this story. I hope you had as much fun reading it as I had writing it, and I further hope that you will all read the next book in the American Kitsune series when it comes out.

Until next time!

Don't forget these other awsome light novels!

American Kitsune
Volumes 1-7

The Executioner Series
Volumes 1-2

 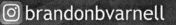

CPSIA information can be obtained
at www.ICGtesting.com
Printed in the USA
LVOW10s0244230418
574496LV00010B/160/P